6-9-04 arp

A MÍRACLE IN PARADÍSE

Lupe Solano Mysteries
by Carolina Garcia-Aguilera

Bloody Waters
Bloody Shame
Bloody Secrets

A Miracle in Paradise

a Lupe Solano Mystery

Carolina García-Aguilera

AVON BOOKS, INC.
1350 Avenue of the Americas
New York, New York 10019

Copyright © 1999 by Carolina Garcia-Aguilera
Interior design by Kellan Peck
ISBN: 0-380-97779-6

Library of Congress Cataloging in Publication Data:
Garcia-Aguilera, Carolina.
A miracle in paradise : a Lupe Solano mystery /
Carolina Garcia-Aguilera.—1st ed.
p.   cm.
I. Title.
PS3557.A71124M57   1999   99-32209
813'.54—dc21   CIP

First Avon Twilight Printing: October 1999

AVON TWILIGHT TRADEMARK REG. U.S. PAT. OFF. AND IN OTHER COUNTRIES, MARCA REGISTRADA, HECHO EN U.S.A.

Printed in the U.S.A.

FIRST EDITION

QPM   10   9   8   7   6   5   4   3   2   1

www.avonbooks.com/twilight

This book is dedicated to my three daughters,
Sarah, Antonia and Gabriella,
the loves and passions of my life

and, as always, to my beloved Cuba,
PLEASE, VIRGENCITA,
LET A MIRACLE HAPPEN THERE SOON!

acknowledgments

AS always, I would like to thank my agent, Elizabeth Ziemska, for all she has accomplished on my behalf. It is because of her that I have been able to write secure in the knowledge that I am in very capable hands. Elizabeth's faith in my talent has never wavered nor has mine in her abilities. I would also like to thank my editor at Avon Books, Jennifer Sawyer Fisher, for her vision and her understanding and acceptance of Lupe's world. Quinton Skinner, as usual, deserves my gratitude for the unique way in which he molds and massages the manuscript.

I could not have written a book such as this one without conducting an enormous amount of research. There were many individuals who helped me in this process, sharing their knowledge and expertise willingly, and to them I would like to express my gratitude. In particular, I would like to thank Sister Marie Angela of the School Sisters of Notre Dame for all the time she spent with me explaining the sometimes confusing workings of the Catholic Church. I am indebted to Jasper Hupert for his candor in relating his experiences of growing up in a family with three older sisters who were nuns. Dr. Max Castro patiently and laboriously guided me through the labyrinth of Cuban politics, both on the island and in exile, and for that I am most grateful.

Of course, my family deserves special mention. I would like to thank my husband, Robert Hamshaw, for his confidence and encouragement. It has meant a great deal to me throughout the years. I want to thank my mother, Lourdes Aguilera de Garcia, for her pride in me and for the displays of my books in the living room of her house. My sister, Sara O'Connell, and my brother, Carlos Antonio Garcia, have always been very supportive of me, and for that I am most grateful. I am very thankful for the enthusiasm my nephew, Richard O'Connell, has always shown for my books.

To my daughters, Sarita, Antonia, and Gabby, gracias for allowing me the freedom to be the kind of writer I am. Thank you for the times when I was on deadline, conducting research, or away on book tour, and thus not available to you, yet you did not make me feel guilty, instead reassuring me that writing the books was important. Muchas gracias for the pride you have in my accomplishments, although I don't consider them mine alone. They belong to all of us because without the three of you, none of them could have happened.

Les doy las gracias con todo mi corazon.

A MÍRACLE IN PARADÍSE

prologue

IT was unusual to see a visitor to the shrine this late after midnight, though his demeanor indicated he felt nothing was out of the ordinary. He stood before the altar as though he owned the place. The moonlight shining on his face outlined the furrows on his forehead where the wind and salty air had buffeted his skin for years. His hair was cropped close to his head, military-style.

A slight trace of incense hung in the air, a reminder of devotions that had been conducted there hours earlier, when the faithful had filled the place with their prayers. Now their voices were silenced, and the man's shoe squeaking on the floor pierced the stillness, then was swallowed in quiet.

He stood there for almost an hour, immobile, his arms hanging down at his sides. He stared at the small statue of the *Virgen de la Caridad del Cobre* resplendent in her pearly raiment; the glow from votive candles all around lent her a pallid, almost supernatural sheen.

He looked up. The wall behind the altar was painted from floor to ceiling with a mural depicting the heroes and heroines of Cuba. There in Miami, their faces looked out over the more than one million exiles who had fled their home country. It looked almost as though they were trying to speak to him, to tell him the story of their island nation, of their wishes and dreams.

He looked down again, not interested in those faces from the past. His total attention was directed toward the small statue in front of him, the tiny representation of the Cuban Virgin.

He was waiting for her to speak. He strained to hear the low-pitched, melodious voice that was somewhere hidden in the silence all around him. When he heard that voice, he knew, it would tell him how much she approved of what he planned. Though the world was full of darkness and ignorance, she would understand.

"The miracle will happen," he whispered, looking into her eyes. "One way or another. It will happen."

1

"LUPE, are you almost finished? You've been in there for half an hour already. We can't keep Mother Superior waiting!"

Even though I had the shower on full-blast, I could hear my sister Lourdes pounding on the bathroom door and screaming at me. I had to smile at what she had said. Half an hour—a perfect Cuban exaggeration. I had been in there for fifteen minutes at the most. It's a well-known fact that Cubans have no real sense of time. Whenever a Cuban relates a particular time, it's normally wise to add or subtract thirty percent one way or the other.

Still, fifteen minutes had been ample time to clean up. I had soaped myself so many times that my skin had actually taken on a slight pinkish tinge—no mean feat for a Cuban. I had washed my hair twice, and now I was considering a third conditioning treatment. I hadn't spent fifteen minutes in the shower because I was so filthy; the truth was that I wanted to delay my morning meeting as long as I possibly could.

Lourdes stopped knocking for the moment. I knew she was almost as apprehensive as me about our appointment with her mother superior. My sister had never before found herself arranging a tête-à-tête between the head of her order and a private investigator. I was almost positive Lourdes knew what the meeting was about, but she wasn't talking.

Every Catholic, no matter how holy and devout, or how worldly and fallen, still gets a case of knocking knees at the very notion of meeting with a mother superior. We all suspect that such a high-level nun can look into our eyes and somehow see all the sins we never admitted at confession. And the Catholic Church is pretty strict about human behavior—a sin contemplated is a sin committed, as a general rule. It's a miracle anyone ever gets to Heaven.

The pounding started again. Lourdes had been working out lately, and it was starting to pay off. She was able to simulate the sound of a lumberjack beating on the door, trying to get in.

I turned off the water. I couldn't claim to be clean of mind, but I could be clean of body. I would have to be content with a fifty-percent success rate.

"Lupe! One more minute and I'm coming in! I swear it!"

I started to towel off. It was a little disconcerting to have a nun make that kind of oath, especially in the morning. I knew I had better hurry, or else soon I would have company in the shower stall.

"Ten minutes," I called out.

I could almost hear a sigh of relief through the two-inch-thick wooden door. Lourdes had known she would have to drag me to the convent, but she probably hadn't counted on nearly having to break down a door first.

"It's exactly eight forty-five," she announced. I could picture her looking at her wristwatch, tracking the course of the second hand.

"Ten minutes," I repeated, louder. "I promise."

"We have to be in the car with the motor running at nine," she said. "I'll go tell Osvaldo to get ready."

I listened to her footsteps receding down the hall. Then I sighed in resignation. She had set the schedule, I would have to follow it. It wasn't easy being the younger sister of a nun, even one as progressive and cool as Lourdes.

So I had ten minutes to make myself presentable for Mother Superior. I wasn't sure what would be considered acceptable attire as I flipped through the racks of clothes in my closet. I had to chuckle at the sight of three pairs of black patent-leather shoes at the front of the closet—those would never do for this morning's meeting. I would never forget Sister Mary Magdalene's tone of voice in parochial school, when she said that no good Catholic girl should ever wear patent-leather shoes—because, she had said, a girl's underpants could be spotted in the shoes' shiny reflection. When I thought about it, it was amazing that Lourdes and I grew up to be reasonably well-adjusted adults.

I started to rummage around. Something demure—a high-necked, long-sleeve, floor-skimming outfit? No, it might make me come off as a wannabe nun. Anyway, I didn't think I could carry it off. A mother superior would have the ability to spot me as the sinner I was, even if I dressed in a habit and wimple. Both of which, incidentally, I had packed away in a box in the back of the closet—souvenirs from a particularly memorable Halloween party.

Armani? No, too expensive. Everyone knew what that designer's clothes cost. Another universal attribute of the Catholic clergy is their ability to assess a person's bank account in a single glance. If I wore one of my Armani suits, even the linen ones, Mother Superior would expect me to donate my services instead of paying me. She would figure that I was making too much money already from my other cases, and could forfeit my fee without much hardship. I don't work for free; it's a principle as far as I'm concerned.

But the truth was, no matter whether I appeared pious or profane, prosperous or poor, I wouldn't be able to bill the Order of the Holy Rosary my usual fee of a hundred dollars per hour plus expenses. I had already decided that I would cut it in half—but that was as low as I would go. I'd give the mother superior her due, but I was no Mother Teresa, and Solano Investigations was no charity.

I fished out a khaki-colored two-piece suit, put it on over a white cotton T-shirt, and examined myself in the mirror. Just right. Had Mother Superior been a monsignor I might have dispensed with the T-shirt and showed a touch of cleavage. Every good investigator knows that part of the job is understanding people, whether they be clients or marks.

Just a couple of minutes left before I would really be risking the wrath of Lourdes. I jogged back into the bathroom and twisted my long dark brown hair into a braid, hoping that this would keep Mother Superior from noticing that it was still dripping wet. I didn't want to arrive at the meeting looking like a loose, painted woman, but I knew that I would feel naked and defenseless without wearing some kind of cosmetics. So I lightly applied a little blush and rouge to my face. I considered mascara indispensable, no matter who the client was, so I brushed some around my lashes until it made my caramel-colored eyes stand out. Then I sprayed myself with a little Chanel No. 5—since smelling good never offended anyone's sensibilities, unless you count some hysterical fragrance-free fanatic.

After one last critical look in the mirror I was ready—and, amazingly enough, with two full minutes to spare. Just before I went downstairs I checked my purse to make sure the Beretta was safely tucked away inside. I almost never took it out, but reassuring myself that it was available was a habit I'd never been able to shake in my seven years as an investigator. You could never be too cautious in Miami, as I had learned the hard way more than once.

I had a shelf full of purses and handbags, but my big black Chanel shoulder bag was my favorite. That purse was like an old friend to me since the time it had saved my life. I stopped in the hall and lovingly ran my finger along a patch of barely discernible stitching: a perfect little circle near the bottom, one inch in circumference.

That hole had been another of life's little souvenirs. A couple of years back I had been forced to use my Beretta to shoot a man—with the gun still inside my purse. I had since come to terms with that horrible event; I knew it was a clear-cut instance of self-defense but I also knew I never wanted to go through anything like that again. The purse served as a daily reminder to be careful, and to look out for trouble before it found me first.

I often found myself lingering over that little stitched-up hole. Someday I would be able to pick up the purse without thinking about it, but the shooting was still too fresh in my heart. (At one point I considered sending off a letter to Chanel, telling them the story of how one of their bags saved my life, but I never did. The French were the French—practical to the core. I worried they might have accused me of Chanel-bag abuse, saying that I didn't know how to appreciate their fine product. They might have tried to extradite the purse back to France, where it could live free of such callow mutilation at the hands of vulgar Americans.)

"Well, good morning," Lourdes said when I found her at the foot of the stairs. I could see she was trying not to look at her watch, not wanting to give me the satisfaction of admitting that I wasn't going to be late after all.

I hadn't seen her yet that morning, and I wasn't prepared for the sight of her in her nun's regulation outfit. My sister seldom wore the navy blue, mid-calf serge dress the members of her order considered their formal attire. It wasn't a bad look—as far as nun's garb goes—but Lourdes's chief complaint was that it wasn't possible to conceal her cellular phone in its folds without being spotted. She was resourceful, though, and she'd taken the dress to a seamstress in Little Havana who had made clever changes in the basic design.

As a result, Lourdes had a secret compartment around her waist, and she could carry her phone without receiving any withering comments from her mother superior or, Heaven forbid, looking wide-hipped. Our *mami* didn't raise fools for daughters.

"Good morning yourself," I replied. "Where're Fatima and the twins? Are we the only ones up?" It was a well-known fact in our household that I was drastically allergic to the early-morning hours. To me, nine o'clock felt like dawn. It was inconceivable that people could regularly get up and function at such an hour.

I have another older sister, Fatima—Mami named each of us after sites of genuine Catholic miracles. Lourdes, being a nun, should have been temperamentally the most distant from me in the family, but somehow we've always been the closest.

"The twins are at school," Lourdes said. "Papi's at the office already. Fatima's out shopping, hunting for specials at Costco. You were the last one out of bed this morning."

My sister made it seem as though it were mid-afternoon. I was and, I supposed, would always be a sinner. But I was a cheerful one, with a good heart. Lourdes had pretty much given up trying to reform me, limiting herself to praying for me instead. That had been a turning point in our relationship that improved it dramatically. That's not to say she gave up on everything: she still made me pin three medals (one gold, one silver, one mother-of-pearl) to my brassiere. Each represented the Cuban Virgin—*la Virgen de la Caridad del Cobre*—and ostensibly were supposed to keep the Virgin close to my heart at all times. I think Lourdes wanted them to serve as a passion-killer to any man who might find himself in the privileged position of seeing them. In fact the medals seemed to have the opposite effect, but I never told Lourdes that. Who knew what she might come up with then. At least she gave up on making me wrap rosary beads around the muzzle of my Beretta—even she had to admit that was ridiculous. Thank God she didn't make me hang them from the rearview mirror of my car, alongside the little plastic bottles of holy water Mami had brought back from a pilgrimage to Lourdes. There were limits to how much protection from above I was willing to have pressed on me.

"And you look tired," she said, lightly touching my chin and looking into my eyes.

"Oh, come on," I said, instantly a little girl in the light of her scrutiny. "I'm fine. I just need to get going."

It had been a very late night. I had been with my friend and lover, criminal-defense attorney Tommy McDonald, and we had celebrated on South Beach until morning. A client we shared—Tommy had defended him, I had conducted the investigation—had been freed from jail yesterday afternoon. It was so late by the time I had gotten home that I considered dropping by the seven-o'clock service at St. Hugh's in the Grove, just so I could tell Mother Superior that I had recently attended Mass.

But there was no way I could take Communion during the early-morning Mass. I would have needed to schedule an hour-long appointment with the priest to run through my confession before receiving the holiest of Sacraments. Besides, confessing my sins would not only reflect badly on me, it would also blot my family's good name. There were few secrets in our parish. Since attending the service without receiving Communion would have only gotten me halfway to a state of grace, I figured there was no point. By then I had been bleary-eyed and dreaming of bed; I had opted for an hour of sleep and headed back to Cocoplum.

So, as usual, Lourdes was right. I was tired, maybe a little hungover. My mouth was dry and my temples throbbed. I wasn't in the best state of mind to confront Mother Superior.

"Well, I suppose that's true," Lourdes agreed. "You always bounce back quickly."

I kissed her cheek. *"Buenos días,"* I said. "I'm here. I'm ready. Everything will be great."

"Osvaldo has the car ready," Lourdes said. She chewed on her lip, an uncharacteristic slip showing her nervousness. She took a step toward the door. "It's time to go."

"Let me grab an orange juice," I said. My mouth was a desert, and orange juice was just about the only thing I could inflict on my stomach that morning. Well, other than the four Advils that were already in there, hard at work even if I wasn't.

Lourdes shrugged and stepped outside into the hot morning. I looked out the open front door from the kitchen and saw that I'd better hurry. Osvaldo was already there, holding the car door open for Lourdes. That gave me a couple of minutes. Lourdes was Osvaldo's favorite of the three daughters and he would want to chat for a couple of minutes before sending her on her way.

Osvaldo had been with our family for more than a half a century, along with his wife, Aida. When Fidel Castro came to power in 1959, the situation in Cuba became intolerable for them and our family. They went into exile with my maternal grandparents and their children, the only members of our household staff to do so. Upon my grandparents' deaths, Mami had taken responsibility for employing them.

Aida and Osvaldo were now both in their eighties, a fact that could easily slip past the undiscriminating eye. They were still nearly as active as when they first worked for our family in Havana—the day that they returned to the city after their honeymoon. Aida was crotchety and cross, but without a doubt the best cook in Miami. Osvaldo, butler and gardener, was as sweet-natured as his wife was crabby. Together they had kept our household functioning when Mami died eight years before. They had suffered during that sad time as much as anyone in the family because they had known and loved my mother since she was a little girl.

I came out of the house clutching a carton of orange juice (somehow it just didn't seen right to call it OJ anymore) in one hand and a chunk of Aida's homemade bread in the other. Sure enough, Lourdes and Osvaldo were laughing at some joke together.

The laughter stopped when they saw me. "Hey," I said. "I don't look that bad."

"It's a good thing your sainted mother is not alive to see your manners, Lupe," Osvaldo said, pointing at the carton of orange juice and the bread, which had left a trail of crumbs all the way back to the kitchen.

The old man stepped back from the car and, with a practiced theatrical flourish, crossed himself and rolled his eyes to Heaven. He then actually held his arms upward, as though shielding Mami from such a horrific sight.

"We're late, Osvaldo, and I'm hungry!" I protested. It didn't help; the old man shuffled back toward the house, shaking his head, each step heavy with dejection.

Lourdes gave me an accusing look. "If you'd gotten home before the rooster crowed, you might have had time to dry your hair and eat a proper breakfast!"

Nothing got past my sister the nun, no slip, transgression, or little white lie. When you had God, the Virgin, and all the Saints in your corner, you presented a tough team to go up against. There was no point telling Lourdes that her knowledge of barnyard animal habits was limited to the wildlife found around the multimillion-dollar homes in Cocoplum—and that those, knowing the relentlessly rigid laws in Coral Gables, were bound to be tagged and licensed.

Instead I meekly got behind the wheel. When Lourdes had buckled her belt in the passenger seat, I eased the car out of the driveway. It was nice and cool inside the car, since Osvaldo had turned on the air-conditioning when he had started it a few minutes before.

I munched on the Cuban bread and drove slowly. Then I glanced at Lourdes. She seemed to have forgotten she was mad at me, because she looked out at the road with a placid expression, her hands folded in her lap.

"So, anyway," I said between bites of bread. "What's this meeting going to be about? Come on, we'll be there in a few minutes. At least give me a little hint."

I hated—no, detested—going into a meeting unprepared. It was my habit to, at the very least, have an idea what the problem was, why my client might possibly need a private investigator.

Lourdes shook her head. She had the same look as I'd imagined on her face when she called me the day before at my office, informing me that her mother superior needed to see me as soon as possible.

"I can't," she said in a flat voice. "Mother Superior asked me to wait until our meeting. I gave her my word."

I drove on, the wheels of the Mercedes spinning. Then I thought of something.

"Hey, she isn't going to ambush me, is she?" I asked. "Do you need recruits so badly that you're going to try to draft someone like me?"

Lourdes looked over, frowning. "Women entering holy orders are not recruits. They have a calling. Lupe, do you have any respect at all for the Catholic Church?" She bit her lip again, seeming disgusted, then raised her hand to silence me before I could tell her I had been joking. "No, don't answer. Please, just drive."

Wow. Lourdes rarely lost her sense of humor. I knew then that this had to be serious. I slowed down as we reached the security checkpoint for the enclosed development where we lived.

"Come on, it's me," I cajoled. "You can give me a little hint."

Lourdes smiled sweetly at the guard, who tipped his hat in a courtly, old-fashioned way. Lourdes could always bring out the gentility in people. Except for me. I somehow always managed to worry and infuriate her. Just as I had apparently done again. As soon as we pulled away from the guard station her smile disappeared and I saw a familiar tightening in her jaw.

"Lupe, you have to promise me you'll behave," she said. "And don't—I repeat, don't you dare—get into an argument with Mother Superior about your favorite issues within the church."

I tried to give her an innocent look as I said, "Who? Me?"

"You know what I'm talking about," she said. "Women priests. Birth control. Excommunication for divorced people who remarry. Homosexuality. All of it. Promise me. Please."

She had enumerated each issue on her fingers, finally making a tense fist. She didn't seem to realize she had done this.

"Don't worry, don't worry." I washed down the last of the bread with a mouthful of orange juice, feeling a little better. "I won't embarrass you, I promise."

I drove on Douglas Avenue toward the Grove, where the convent was located.

"Tell you what," I added. "I'll just limit my editorializing to same-sex marriages performed by divorcée woman priests. Is that OK?"

2

LOURDES and I sat in aggressively uncomfortable, straight-backed red-velvet chairs in Mother Superior's waiting room, struggling not to look at each other or at our watches. Morning light filtered into the room through thick drapes, making the place seem somber and timeless.

Unlike the other nuns, Lourdes didn't live at the Order of the Holy Rosary. Supposedly she shared a small house with two other sisters in Miami's Little Havana, but the reality was that she lived in our family home in Cocoplum. Papi had made an unorthodox arrangement with the order's administration in order to bring this about. And it's well known that whenever the Catholic Church grants special permission for no apparent compelling reason, some exchange of funds is involved. It's a practical issue, not a moral one. Our family wanted Lourdes to live with us full-time, and simultaneously the order needed an infusion of cash for a series of charitable projects it wished to get off the ground. It was a perfect match. The arrangement had started after Mami died, when both Lourdes and I moved back home for family warmth, comfort, and companionship. It had been a hard time, and we had all felt a deep need to be together. My sister Fatima had lived at home for a while already, along with her twin daughters.

So all three Solano daughters were brought back together again as a result of a tragedy—Mami's illness and subsequent death. The situation had worked out so well that it seemed natural we all stay in a semipermanent arrangement. Papi liked to complain about how he was surrounded by women—three daughters and two grand-daughters—who dominated and ruled his life, but we all knew he loved it. After all, he hadn't built a ten-thousand-square-foot, ten-bedroom house so that he could live alone. It's not as though he had intended to take on boarders to help pay the mortgage.

Papi still showed no signs of looking for female companionship, a woman his age to grow old with. Anyway, if that had happened, I don't know what any of us would have done. It seemed unimaginable that any woman could take our sainted mother's place. And how could Papi possibly go out on a date? He had three daughters aged thirty-two (Fatima), thirty (Lourdes), and twenty-eight (me)—the youngest a private investigator, no less. He had twelve-year-old twin granddaughters and an elderly couple in their eighties in his full-time, live-in employ. All of us would scrutinize his every move. It was like living with the CIA and KGB all wrapped into one. It would have taken a brave woman to even begin to deal with that crowd.

I straightened my skirt and took a deep breath. My head was still throbbing but the bread on the way to the convent had helped, along with the painkillers. I closed my eyes while we waited, and tried not to notice Lourdes fidgeting next to me.

Papi's main interest—besides the fortunes of Solano Construction—was Fidel Castro's overthrow. Papi and the dictator were thirteen years apart, fifty-nine and seventy-two years old, respectively. One of Papi's greatest causes for melancholy was that Mami died before he could take her back to Cuba, something he had always promised her. Now he planned to keep his word, though not in the way that she might have envisioned. Mami's ashes were housed in a silver urn on the main cabin of the *Concepción*, the fifty-two-foot Hatteras docked behind our house. She awaited internment in Havana's Colon cemetery upon our return to our native country. Part of Osvaldo's daily duties was to make sure the urn was polished and positioned so that it faced Havana Harbor.

Papi refused to even think of removing Mami's ashes from the boat until they returned to Cuba, even when we all pointed out that she used to get seasick every time she went out on the water with him. It was impossible for Papi to accept this, even though it was true. He loved the boat with all the force of his heart, so much so that he had named it after Mami.

While he waited to return to Cuba, Papi followed every bit of information, innuendo, and rumor concerning Fidel's health. When

Castro gave up cigars, so did Papi. When Castro was reported to have started taking ginseng pills, Papi went to the health-food store and bought a carton of them. Papi was determined that the old bastard wouldn't outlive him, the way he had Mami. All my sisters and I could do was to monitor Papi's obsession, taking small measures from time to time when it looked as though it was getting out of hand.

Miami was the worst place to try to persuade someone to give up an addiction to following Castro's every move. It was like an alcoholic living in a distillery. Fidel had been in power for forty years and, as far as I could see, had no intention of giving up. There should have been a support group for people like Papi: Fidel Anonymous. It would teach exiles to manage their obsession and channel it into something constructive—like organizing a death squad— rather than simply fixating upon it. This group could adopt and rewrite all the Twelve Steps. The first step would require people to admit that they were powerless over Fidel Castro, that their lives had become unmanageable. Maybe it would help some people come to grips with reality. Or maybe they would just decide to hire the Mossad—the secret security of Israel—to get rid of the tyrant. That would be just right, since they were known to be brave, ruthless, and frighteningly efficient.

I opened my eyes. These were definitely unchristian thoughts. The receptionist—a nun, naturally—sat behind a massive old-fashioned dark-wood desk; she pretended to straighten papers, trying not to stare at me with curiosity. It wasn't that I was such an expert on the decor of Catholic convents, but it seemed to me that they were all the same—done in a Hollywood-movie-set motif of heavy dark wood and red velvet, with matching tones on the drapes. All of this was true even in the tropics. The atmosphere was oppressive, with heat seeming to emanate from all corners. Even though an air conditioner hummed away in the hall, a thin sheen of sweat had sprouted on my forehead.

There was a big white-faced clock on the wall next to the door leading into Mother Superior's office. One minute to go. I noticed that Lourdes and I had completely regressed to our Catholic-school-girl days: our feet were crossed at the ankles, hands folded on our laps, skirts pulled down to cover our knees. The latter was easy in Lourdes's case, since her dress was calf-length to begin with. The skirt of my cotton suit was more problematic. I had pulled it down so many times that I was starting to stretch the fabric.

Nine o'clock, precisely. The door opened, the receptionist ushered us silently into the inner sanctum. Lourdes and I smiled our thanks and went inside. Mother Superior was waiting for us behind yet another massive wooden desk. She was dressed in the same habit as Lourdes; presumably, hers didn't have a secret compartment for a cellular phone.

"Please," Mother Superior said.

She motioned toward two straight-backed chairs—red velvet, of course—arranged directly in front of her desk. No introductions, no handshakes, no small talk. So much for the new warm-and-friendly face of the Catholic Church.

Mother Superior sat with her hands clasped in front of her. Her light blue eyes focused on me like twin cold lasers. Her eyes missed nothing. Her face was rounded, almost thick, but her features seemed somehow as sharp and acute as her presence. The room was cool, better than the outer room, but I started to feel uncomfortably warm. I heard the soft ticking of the wall clock.

All I knew about this mother superior was that she was the only Cuban American to hold such a high office in the United States Catholic Church. She had been appointed head of the Order of the Holy Rosary ten years before, predating the time when Lourdes took her vows. She was respected but not universally liked—not surprising, since popularity wasn't a prerequisite for her position.

I found myself fumbling in my mind for protocol. She was saying nothing, just looking at me. Should I begin the conversation, or should I wait for her? Anyway, what was I going to say? *So, what am I here for at this ungodly hour? What's the big secret that even my own sister couldn't share with me?*

It was Lourdes who broke the silence. "Mother Superior, this is my sister, Lupe," she said. "I did as you requested and brought her here this morning. And, as per your order, I have told her nothing about why you wish to see her."

Mother Superior nodded curtly. It was obvious that she expected nothing less than complete obedience from both Lourdes and me.

"I trust that everything said here today will be kept in total confidence," she began.

That was fine with me. All my clients said that at the beginning of our first meeting. It's not as though I wanted to leave the room and make a phone call to the *Miami Herald* city desk.

"Of course," I assured her. It surprised me, the way my voice was so calm and even. Inside I felt as though punishment was coming, at the very least a stern lecture. "I'd be honored to do anything to help," I added.

Mother Superior nodded at Lourdes, as if in approval. I felt my sister relax a little next to me.

"There is another order of nuns in Dade County, you probably have not heard of them," she said. "The Order of the Illumination of the Sacred Virgin."

Mother Superior waited for my reaction. "I agree," she said, "it seems a peculiar name. But they are relatively new to the United States. They were established in Yugoslavia in the mid-fifteenth century. Only in the past ten years have they come to America. They moved to Dade County six months ago, and have kept a low profile until now."

I played this back in my mind. Where was this headed? Was this going to be about investigating a bunch of nuns? In my most rebellious teenage days I had questioned and even doubted God's existence. When Mami's suffering was at its worst I had even been angry with God for permitting her sickness to happen. But even then I never would have sunk so low as to consider investigating an order of nuns. I sat up straighter in my chair. I knew I had better not miss a word.

"I'm—" I began, "I'm not familiar with that order."

"Not many were." Mother Superior nodded in agreement. "Until now. And soon, everyone will know about them."

That sounded ominous. I fought off the impulse to run out of the room. My hands were still folded, my feet crossed at the ankles. I had given up pulling down at my skirt.

"Most of the nuns in the Dade County chapter came from Yugoslavia," Mother Superior continued. "There are fifteen of those. But lately they have been adding to their ranks."

Mother Superior was now speaking through clenched teeth. Perhaps it wasn't ice water in her veins after all.

"My latest information is that their ranks have doubled," she said. "Imagine! Just imagine! That means they have had fifteen young women sign up to begin as postulants."

I wasn't sure how I was expected to respond to this. Obviously, as far as Mother Superior was concerned, this was bad news.

"That seems like a lot," I said. "Does the order recruit heavily, or are all these young women determined to join only this particular order?"

I simply couldn't find a frame of reference for what Mother Superior was talking about. Lourdes had come to the family dinner table one night and announced that she wanted to become a nun; a few days later she had entered the convent. Maybe we should have seen the signs before then, but no one in our family had ever entered into a religious order before. It's not like other huge life changes. There weren't empty bottles hidden in dressers, used needles in the trash, or receipts from hot-sheets motels on Eighth Street.

"There's an attraction to joining this particular order," Mother Superior said, sighing. "The order is known . . . for having members who can produce miracles. Real, verifiable miracles. The sort that have attracted the attention of the Vatican."

"You mean they're performing miracles in Dade County?" I asked, stunned. "Real ones? Right here and now? That's why they're having such success recruiting new members?"

Mother Superior gave a small smile that softened her features, just a little. "Your sister said you had an astute mind," she said. "There have been two in the past century. There is an exhaustive formal investigative process involved within the Vatican, but it is a known fact that what they claim happened did, in fact, occur. The two miracles involved healing the sick—both as a result of the Virgin's direct intervention. They were both verified within twelve months of each other, two years ago."

Mother Superior looked at me meaningfully, as though to make sure I was following her.

"Since they were both verified, and within recent memory, whatever announcement the order makes in the present day will be taken seriously. What is worrisome is that they've become so daring that they are predicting the next one before it happens. Their mother superior has announced the time, place, and date of the next miracle."

"And what sort of miracle might that be?" I asked. "Another healing?"

Mother Superior's lips tightened, all warmth disappeared. She shook her head slightly.

"On October tenth the Virgin at the *Ermita de la Caridad* will cry," she whispered. "There will apparently be real tears."

Lourdes and I took a sharp breath in unison. No Cuban could fail to understand the significance of that statement: October 10, Cuban Independence Day. It was the day the War of Independence against Spain was launched, the equivalent of the Fourth of July for Cubans. And the Virgin—the Virgin of Our Lady of Charity was the patron saint of Cuba. What Mother Superior had just shared with us was nothing short of astounding.

No wonder she seemed beside herself. If this new order could deliver on the promise of this miracle, it would place it at the forefront of all religious orders. Every Cuban woman in Dade County, in the entire United States, would want to be a part of it. The full consequences were hard to imagine.

"Mother Superior, that date is—" I made a quick mental calculation. "Twenty-five days away."

She didn't reply, just stared at me, waiting.

"What is it, exactly," I began, "that you would like me to do?"

Mother Superior spread her hands out on the desk. They were big, with thick knuckles.

"I want you to investigate them," she said. Her hands formed into loose fists. "Find out exactly what's going to happen on October tenth, and how it's going to be done. Find out what's behind the other two reported miracles!"

With this, she laid both fists on her desk with a thud. "I want you to tell me who is masterminding this!" she demanded, louder now. She was almost losing it. Each statement was more insistent, to the point that I feared she would really start pounding on that desk and hurt her hands.

I had no idea how to investigate a bunch of transplanted Yugoslavian nuns—to say nothing of their supposed miracles. But I nodded, as though her commands were routine and presented no problem to me at all. I simply didn't know how to say no to a nun, especially not a mother superior. If nothing else, I figured, I would earn a few points toward admission into Heaven. Mother Superior stared at me and took a series of deep breaths, trying to bring herself back from the brink of the rage that had threatened to possess her.

I looked over at Lourdes, who seemed alarmed at her mother superior's behavior. She jerked her head toward the door, a not-so-subtle gesture that we should go. We stood up in unison and waited for Mother Superior to acknowledge that we wished to leave.

Lourdes, again, broke the silence. "Lupe will be in touch with you, Mother Superior," she said.

Mother Superior didn't even reply. She sat at her desk fingering her rosary beads, staring at a huge painting of the Virgin on the opposite wall that I hadn't noticed until then. Obviously this was a major calamity for her.

Miracles are very serious in the Catholic world, and a predicted miracle on Cuban Independence Day would be off the charts of importance in Miami. I could imagine the predicament in which Mother Superior found herself. If the miracle did occur, then prospective candidates for the novitiate might flock to the competing order. It was a harsh reality, but all orders competed for the small group of women who wished to take vows. Yet, in the long term, if the miracle fizzled out, it would undermine the legitimacy of Catholic orders and even of the church itself.

There was no way for Mother Superior to win. Unless she was successful in debunking the claims that this was a real, genuine miracle. And if she exposed the nuns of the Illumination of the Sacred Virgin to be a bunch of fakes, Mother Superior would be a heroine, and young women would hear of her and come to her order. It was a gamble for her, I could see that now, but it was one that she had to take.

Lourdes touched my elbow to lead me out. She didn't have to do much more. I was ready to sprint out of the place. I took one last look over my shoulder and saw Mother Superior staring down at her desk, her husky shoulders slumped.

Lourdes and I didn't exchange a word until we were strapped into the Mercedes and the engine was running.

Then Lourdes turned to face me and hissed, "You'd better not screw this up, Lupe. I don't want to have to move back into the convent if you screw everything up."

I felt my face fall with shock. Lourdes never talked like that, not since we were teenagers. The skin of her face seemed tight with tension, her hands were clenched in her lap.

So she felt strongly about it. Well, so did I. For me, the downside of the investigation was a potential trip to hell. Well, maybe not, but at least a very long stint in purgatory.

I pulled out of the parking lot and accelerated into traffic. The sun shone in my eyes, and I had forgotten my sunglasses. Lourdes wasn't speaking to me, she was just watching the traffic and letting herself become lost in the world of her own thoughts.

Then I realized something. I had forgotten to bring up the subject of my fees and expenses. Did that mean they expected me to do this for free?

Mierda!

3

"OUR new client is *who?"*

Leonardo's eyes bugged out in a familiar expression of surprise. He was my cousin, my office manager, my administrative assistant, my accountant. Last and most importantly—in his opinion, at least— he was the self-appointed supervisor of any and all matters per- taining to physical, emotional, and spiritual health at Solano Investigations.

I had just returned to the office a few minutes before and broken the news to Leonardo about Mother Superior's request. Then I asked him to open a file for Mother Superior—our custom upon taking on a new client. Leonardo was no fool. He immediately recognized that if our new client had anything to do with the Catholic Church, it was extremely unlikely that we would make any money. In fact, the opposite was bound to be true—we would probably lose money.

The timing for a pro bono case was terrible. Leonardo wanted to buy a new piece of gym equipment, a contraption that he had de- scribed to me in detail just the day before. Apparently this miracu- lous device could eliminate what is commonly known as the "Cuban ass." I couldn't remember precisely how it worked, something about contorting the body into unnatural positions while drinking prune juice laced with rum. It had taken as much self-control as I possessed to keep a straight face while Leonardo described this ninth wonder of the world; he was so sensitive, I knew he would be insulted if I laughed.

Leonardo's "Cuban ass" had become the center of his existence. His primary goal in life seemed to be to eliminate it or, in lieu of that, to reduce it to the point at which he could pass himself off as a citizen of the world and not of his native island. Unfortunately, this exercise machine was quite pricey. When I thought about it, though, we would have to purchase it. Eliminating Cuban derrieres was a notoriously difficult challenge—as anyone who had tried could tell you.

Leonardo had started in on me almost immediately after his testimonial, trying to get me to break down and take on a couple of domestic cases that would raise quick cash for the purchase. Two quick hits, he had said—two cheating husbands or wives—and the equipment could be installed in the room of our office that doubled as his personal gym. The timing was perfect, he said. The machine could be delivered soon enough that its results could be displayed during the Thanksgiving holidays.

So far, I had resisted. I hated domestics with a passion—most investigators did. I would only take them if I was in serious financial trouble. I didn't consider Leonardo's Cuban-ass-eliminating equipment to be sufficient incentive for me to go out and chase a couple of philandering husbands acting out on their midlife crises.

"You heard me," I said to him. "Our new client is the Order of the Holy Rosary. The mother superior, to be precise."

"That's Lourdes's order," Leonardo moaned. His face dropped. "Now we'll never get paid. Oh, Lupe. How could you?"

Leonardo rested his face in his hands. I knew he could feel his ass spreading by the second. I could almost feel his pain. Never would it be nice and tight.

"Listen, just start the file. Please." Maybe I sounded a little too harsh, but I was getting sick of his histrionics. And maybe in my heart I knew that he was right. I turned on my heel and went back to my own office before I said something I didn't mean.

I loved Leonardo dearly. But sometimes he crossed all the boundaries that were supposed to be in place between an employee and employer. In all fairness, though, I supposed those boundaries had never been too clear. Our dress code was admittedly lax, subject to our moods, the weather, and our physical condition at any given time. In how many offices could the receptionist wear bicycle shorts, tank tops, and Tevas to work—and still be taken seriously?

The world of private investigators was unorthodox, but we were maybe a little unusual even in that context. Our office was housed in a little three-bedroom cottage in Coconut Grove and hidden from the street by thick tropical foliage. From outside there was no indication as to what sort of business we were, so people only stopped in for specific reasons. We weren't on the normal routes taken by messengers delivering flyers for takeout Chinese restaurants, or erotic massages from transsexual ambidextrous Scientologist albinos.

Another factor that set us apart was our smallness. Our entire organization consisted of me and my twenty-four-year-old cousin Leonardo. Giving Leonardo a job had been the only condition Papi had attached to loaning me enough money to get Solano Investigations started. I had been so desperate at the time that employing my cousin hadn't seemed like much of a burden.

Perhaps I would have reconsidered, had I known that Leonardo would start converting the place into a gym within weeks of setting up the office and starting his job. First came the treadmill. Then the StairMaster, followed closely by the recumbent bicycle.

That had just been the beginning. Then Leonardo got serious, installing a terrifying machine called "the Gauntlet" that was just as horrible as its name implied. Others followed, too weird and scary for me to even figure out—I only knew they worked because I could hear Leonardo's screams through my closed office door when I was trying to talk on the phone. In fairness to my cousin, he did ask in the beginning whether he could move some of his personal equipment into the spare room in the back. I had agreed, unable to imagine what it would all lead to.

Our arrangement worked quite well, though from time to time I had to rein him in a little. I had to absolutely forbid the nude yoga sessions—not to mention the "hashish for health" symposium he tried to organize one weekend. And one inviolable rule was that his clothing had to weigh more than eight ounces—verifiable at any time with a postal scale I kept on a shelf. This was in response to the day he showed up for work in a tanga.

One subject the family knew not to bring up with me was speculation regarding Leonardo's sexuality. There was a lot of conjecture about his possible choices for preferred companionship. I considered it none of my business and would never comment on it. But my secret opinion was that Leonardo was sexually confused; however, it didn't matter to me because, for the most part, he seemed happy.

I opened the blinds in my office and checked the pile of phone messages Leonardo had arranged in a fan-like pattern on my desk.

Most of them were from contract investigators calling to see if I had work for them. In my years in the business I had set up a network of investigators I could call for particular cases. None of them were on Solano's payroll; they all worked on a case-by-case basis. Each individual specialized in a particular aspect of the business: video surveillance, personal surveillance, financial expertise. I had made a lot of friends that way, and I thought I had some of the best talent in Miami at my disposal.

I sat down in my chair and stared out the window at the avocado tree outside. In the back of my mind I was waiting for Leonardo to bring me the file marked "Mother Superior." I would start working the case then, I figured. Until then I had a reprieve.

I flipped through the phone messages again. I needed to call a couple of investigators, get this case going. It was the last thing I wanted to do. How was I supposed to investigate a bunch of nuns making miracles?

Just then Leonardo walked into the office and dropped the new file on my desk. He left without a word, probably still mourning the perfect ass that he would never have.

The file read: "Mother Superior—Order of the Holy Rosary."

I sighed. It was time to start filling it.

4

MARISOL sat up straight on the sofa in my office and shook her head.

"No way," she said. "I'm sorry. I can't do it. Checking out nuns, investigating miracles—"

"We've worked a lot of weird cases together," I pointed out.

Marisol looked at me with disbelief, as though I had sunk to a new low in her estimation.

"But Lupe," she said, "your sister is a nun. How can you even think about doing this?"

I thought about pointing out that a nun had hired us for this case—and a mother superior, no less. But Marisol seemed adamant. My heart sinking, I looked over at Nestor, who was slouched back in the chair in the corner.

I had just finished explaining to the two investigators the substance of my new case. It was apparent from both their reactions that it wouldn't have mattered if the pope was our client—nothing changed the fact that I was talking about investigating an order of nuns. I would have wagered that neither of them had set foot inside a church in years, but Catholicism ran deep in both of them.

"How about it, Nestor?" I asked hopefully. I needed him for background work, and he had no peers when it came to digging up information.

Nestor's gaze was fixed on the family of parrots building yet another nest in the avocado tree outside my office window. If the birds kept reproducing at the rate they were, I was going to have to slip some kind of aviary sex-suppressant into their food—some kind of anti-Viagra for birds. As it was their population was in the dozens, mostly young, rowdy, and oversexed. The backyard was starting to look like a branch of Parrot Jungle.

Nestor shrugged. "I never turned you down on a case," he said. "But investigating nuns? Debunking miracles?"

He frowned at me, looking scandalized. I tried not to show my frustration. Nestor was dressed all in black, his trademark raccoon circles heavy under his eyes. He didn't exactly look like an altar boy.

"I explained this once before," I said to them, standing up and walking around the desk. "Our client is a mother superior. I am not picking on the church. I *like* the church. But she came to me for help."

Marisol and Nestor were seasoned, jaded investigators who had seen the worst of Miami without flinching. If I couldn't get them to work with me, it would be hopeless trying to find someone else.

Marisol suddenly decided that her fuschia-painted fingernails required great scrutiny. She sat quietly, her long bottle-blonde hair spilling over the ample cleavage of her low-cut white lace blouse. Her jeans were so tight I could see the outline of her underwear through them. From her feet dangled a pair of three-inch platform heels. My thirty-something Venezuelan video-whiz investigator Marisol would never pass for a convent girl. Though apparently she thought like one.

Without looking up from her nails, she whispered, "What if we find out that something really bad is going on? We could get excommunicated. Think about it."

"*Coño*, Marisol!" I said, trying to downplay her concerns. "How are you going to get excommunicated for conducting a video surveillance? Listen, both of you. You won't go to hell for working this case. I guarantee it. We were hired by a mother superior. Surely the church knows what we're doing and approves—otherwise we never would have been called in the first place."

It was incredible. The power of the Catholic Church never ceased to amaze me. Its tendrils of fear traveled easily through the decades of people's lives. Marisol definitely had a point when she wondered what might be the implications of unearthing fraud perpetrated by nuns—which was what Mother Superior had hired me to do, even if she hadn't really come out and said it.

I didn't want Marisol to worry because it would affect her work. I would do all the worrying for everyone, I'd decided. I certainly didn't take this investigation lightly, but it would serve no purpose to let Nestor and Marisol see me fretting. Anyway, we all grew up in the all-knowing, always-correct Catholic Church. We knew in our hearts that there was a friction here between the church as dispenser of truth and the possibility that a group of nuns was cooking up a hoax.

"Nuns are holy women," Marisol said, still averting her eyes. My mollification hadn't been entirely successful. "This is a sin. I know it is."

Mortal or venal? I considered asking her, but I restrained myself. The two of them were convinced I was on the road to damnation as it was. Pretty soon they would be blaming El Niño on my lapse of judgment.

"Nestor," I said, ready to start begging. "Come on, Nestor."

I knew he needed the money. He was still bringing his relatives over from the Dominican Republic one by one, and as far as I knew he had a brother and baby sister left to go. He had managed to bring over ten siblings already and, incredibly, had placed them all in productive, self-supporting jobs. I knew I had a chance with Nestor as long as he still had siblings in the D.R., though I feared what might happen when they were all in Miami. It was horrible to think he might start turning me down. I hoped Mrs. Gomez, his mother in Puerto Plata, would be like my parrots—producing offspring at a rapid clip—though it was a little troubling to know that she'd slowed down of late, producing her last daughter a full five years before.

"Maybe Lupe's right," he said slowly. "A mother superior did initiate the investigation. I mean, we will be working for the church. Won't the church ultimately be responsible for what we discover? Mother Superior hired us, so it's on her back whatever happens."

"My point exactly," I said. Maybe this was going to work out after all.

"What about purgatory?" Marisol asked, chewing her lower lip like a Latin Lolita. "We might not go to hell, but we could get sent there."

Every Catholic worries about purgatory, Heaven's waiting room. It's not a place of angels playing harps on clouds; instead it is the place Catholics go to atone for their sins before they can reach Heaven. On one hand, purgatory is good because someone there will definitely go to Heaven one day. But at the same time it's a place of suffering—with the prayers of those on Earth speeding up the passage.

"Face it, Marisol," Nestor said. "You're going to purgatory whether you work this case or not. There's no changing the past."

Marisol blushed; they had been friends for years, and there were no secrets between them.

"Purgatory's not so bad," I offered.

"You're no angel," Nestor added. "You'll have sins to atone for. You might as well have done something for the church if you're going to sweat down there for a few hundred years. And remember, Marisol, the mother superior approached us to conduct the investigation. That's all we need to know: this was her idea."

"Nestor's making sense," I said. "Anyway, I know you have your eye on that newest model BMW convertible. The baby-blue one with the white leather interior to replace the one you have now."

"The church understands temptation," Nestor said.

The tide had turned.

"Lupe, I know it's none of my business," Marisol said, apparently unfazed by the fact that her time in Heaven would be delayed for centuries. "But how are you charging on this case?"

"What do you mean?"

"The money you're getting paid, it's not coming out of funds for the poor, is it?"

Marisol still looked nervous. I had never known her to get stuck in ethical dilemmas before. First she was worried about sullying the church, next she was worried about being paid from the poor box. I wondered what attack of conscience was going to strike her next.

"I'm not sure," I told her. "But don't worry. I'm certain it's not coming straight from the collection plate at Sunday Mass."

Marisol nodded, apparently satisfied. I should have known I would eventually be able to break them down, get them to work the case. Nestor and Marisol both loved their work, and would always find a way to justify to themselves taking a questionable case with a potentially problematic outcome.

"I'll get each of your files ready," I said, not allowing them any more time to question what I was getting them into. "Come by for them tomorrow morning and we'll get started."

They nodded their still-lukewarm agreement and left. I sat down at my desk and started sketching out how I wanted to begin the investigation. I had been working for no more than five minutes when I looked up and saw Leonardo standing in my doorway, glaring at me. There was no health-food shake in his hand, or any magic vitamins. This wasn't a good sign.

"I understand Marisol and Nestor are now officially on the Holy Rosary case," he said in an acid tone.

That afternoon he had really outdone himself sartorially; he wore a particularly stylish body-hugging unitard in deep violet.

"Unless I'm totally out of the loop regarding the finances of this business," he continued, "I'm guessing you still haven't nailed down how we're getting paid on this case."

"Leo—"

"Are you counting on manna from Heaven to pay our bills?" he asked.

I could have done without the sarcasm, but he was right. Mother Superior and I hadn't talked money, and expenses mounted quickly at the beginning of any investigation. And I had gone ahead and hired Nestor and Marisol without establishing a budget for the case.

But I had no choice. The miracle of the *Virgen de la Caridad del Cobre* was going to take place on October 10. The calendar on my desk told me that today was September 15. I had twenty-five days.

"So what's it going to be?" Leonardo pressed. "We work for free now? Or are we going to stop by all the Miami Catholic churches and empty out the poor boxes?"

I smiled at my cousin, tried to pretend that either option was ridiculous. But the money problem had to be solved fast, or else I would be praying to the Order of the Illumination of the Sacred Virgin for my own, custom-made miracle.

5

WHEN I called Mother Superior I had written out on a yellow legal pad in front of me my script for how I wanted the conversation to go. As I waited on hold for her, I started to think more about the political dimensions of the case. I hadn't talked about it to Nestor and Marisol—not wanting to scare them off—but we were wading deep into the pressure-cooker world of Cuban exile politics. Cuban issues were volatile enough, but this case wrapped them in a blanket of religion. Cuban independence. The Virgin. The miraculous. I felt that pretty soon I was going to be nostalgic for waiting outside hotel rooms to photograph cheating husbands.

"This is Mother Superior," a voice said suddenly on the line.

"I—" I paused, shocked out of my reverie. I looked down at the notes I had written out, not sure where to start.

"I assume you are calling about your payment," she said, brisk and businesslike. "What is your fee?"

I quoted her half my usual rate of a hundred dollars an hour.

"That will be fine," she said.

I felt like kicking myself. I had lowballed Solano Investigations. But how could I gouge the church?

"Come by the convent at your convenience," she said. "There will be an envelope waiting for you at the reception area."

"Thank you," I said.

"Have you made any progress on the case?"

My notes were useless. Mother Superior was accustomed to setting the tone for dozens of young women in her charge. I was out of my league.

"I've hired two junior investigators," I told her. "I've begun putting together a plan for how to proceed."

A beat of silence. I didn't know whether this news pleased her or not. To my surprise I found myself worried it might not.

"The so-called miracle is scheduled for October tenth," she said, as if I needed reminding. "I hope you work quickly. And I need you to understand something else. This case is very delicate. I will not be in a position to help you in any way. I trust in your professionalism and that the good Lord will guide you. Good day, Guadalupe."

She hung up before I could stutter a reply. I didn't know how Lourdes could take it. Fine, she had a calling. But I could never bear being bossed around all the time by such an intimidating woman. I had had clients leave me on my own before, but never so imperiously. Another investigator would have dropped the case right then. But only a non-Catholic investigator.

I wondered about Mother Superior's emphasis on the need for secrecy on the case. I had understood it during our first meeting, given the sensitive nature of the investigation. But now she was cutting off communication with me. In the past, my clients had wanted—no, demanded—they be continually informed of my progress on their cases. Why was Mother Superior, in effect, hiding from her own investigator? It would, after all, have been possible to communicate in secret.

There was no point being paranoid, I tried to tell myself. This was a very sensitive case. Surely Mother Superior had her reasons. For one, she was almost certainly unfamiliar with dealing with a private investigator. Perhaps I made her just as uncomfortable as she made me. I let this argument rattle in my head until it fell away, left me unconvinced. No, there was such a thing as too much secrecy.

I didn't want Mother Superior to think I was desperate for the money, so I refrained from hopping into my car the moment I had replaced the phone in its cradle. I got my files organized for an hour, then drove to the Cubanteria—my favorite restaurant—to have lunch while I waited a little more.

I sat at the counter eating a *medianoche* sandwich: ham, turkey, pork, melted cheese, pickles. The sandwich was called "midnight" because Cubans considered it the perfect meal after a night of drinking and carousing. I washed it down with a mango shake as Gregorio, the cook, watched me with a sly grin on his face.

"What's up?" I finally asked him. "What's with the smile?"

Gregorio was in his eighties, and he was really more than just the Cubanteria cook. He was also the waiter, the greeter, the purveyor of all things Cuban. As he grinned, the topography of lines on his deeply tanned face shifted and rearranged themselves.

"I was just thinking," he said. "How many years have you come in here?"

"I don't know, Gregorio," I said, wiping my hands on a paper napkin. "Eight years? Ten? Since I was in college."

"All that time, and a beautiful girl like you hasn't found a man to marry," he replied.

I put a ten-dollar bill on the counter. Latino chivalry. Of course it had never occurred to Gregorio that a young woman might not want to get married.

"Do you have someone in mind?" I asked him playfully.

Gregorio shrugged. "I am too old. But my grandson, he owns two gas stations. And he is single."

I got up from the stool. "Well, if he's anything like you, Gregorio, I'm sure he doesn't need any help meeting women."

Gregorio smiled deeper as he wiped off the countertop. "This is true," he said. "But I'll tell him about you. You need a good man."

"You do that," I called out as I opened the door to the midday heat. I didn't give Gregorio a chance to add anything. The last thing I needed was a blind date with a guy who probably smelled like petroleum. I wasn't a snob, but I couldn't see myself getting old while punching an adding machine in the back room of a Little Havana gas station. Somehow it just didn't fit with my self-image.

When I reached the convent I found that Mother Superior was a woman of her word. But instead of the thin envelope containing a check that I had been expecting, I found waiting for me a bulky manila envelope. Curiosity was killing me, but I didn't want to open it in front of the inquisitive-looking sister at the front desk. So I thanked her and tucked it into my bag.

Out in the parking lot, comfortably ensconced in my Mercedes with the air-conditioning blasting away, I opened the envelope. Inside was cash. Lots of it. Five neatly tied stacks of ten hundred-dollar bills held together with rubber bands. I upended the envelope, hoping to find a note inside from Mother Superior. Nothing.

I took out a couple of the stacks and fingered the bills. My suspicions went into overdrive. First Mother Superior wanted to cut off all contact with me, then I was given five thousand dollars without any acknowledgment. Apart from our meeting in her office, with my sister Lourdes present, there was probably no evidence that she had ever hired me in the first place to investigate the order of Yugoslavian nuns. There was next to no physical paper trail connecting Solano Investigations with Mother Superior, just my own notes.

My instinct was to write up a receipt. But, following orders, I didn't. Taking this much cash from a client without paperwork made me extremely uneasy. Maybe the church conducted its business based on trust, but it wasn't likely. I had to trust Mother Superior personally, assume that she was aboveboard. I had to hope my trust wouldn't prove to be gullibility.

I replaced the bills in the envelope and resealed it. No doubt about it, this was a lot of cash to hand over, especially without even demanding a signed receipt. But money was money. I put the car in gear and drove toward the Grove, dreading the confrontation with Leonardo that I knew would take place.

"I knew you wouldn't have the guts to charge our usual rate!" Leonardo fumed.

He filled out the deposit slip at his desk, shaking his head and muttering to himself, then wrapped it around the Holy Rosary cash. I noticed he had only filled out the slip for four thousand dollars, then slipped one of the bundles of cash into his desk drawer. I knew better than to ask questions about our accounting practices, and shuddered with fear at the very idea of ever having to undergo an audit.

I stood by his desk without commenting as he put the four grand into the dark blue zippered bag the bank had given us for deposits. I could tell my cousin wanted to give me the silent treatment, but he finally relented and looked up at me.

"*Mierda*, Lupe," he said. "If you're going to take a case from the church, leave your Catholic guilt about money at the door. We're not running a charity here. If you keep this up we're going to have to start a 1-800 charity line, taking donations."

He slapped the desk, on a roll now; part of him probably wanted to show me that the money he spent on acting classes hadn't been wasted.

"I can just see it!" he said. "We'll put you in a room, with Marisol and Nestor. You can all wear trenchcoats, fedoras pulled down over your faces, dark glasses. We'll set up a table with a bunch of investigator's gear on it: video cameras open to show they don't have film, your Beretta open with no bullets in the magazine, computers without disks, printers without paper, tape recorders without cassettes. Then I'll do the voiceover: 'Once these people ran one of the most successful investigative firms in Miami. Now look at them. They cut their prices to work with the church, and now they need your help. They were good, they caved in to their guilt, and now they are steps away from destitution. Please send your referrals. Help them help themselves!' "

Leonardo was hamming it up at my expense, getting down on his knees and pretending to cry. Despite myself, I started laughing.

"Please have mercy, Leo," I said. "I am but a lowly sinner."

But he wasn't going to let me off the hook that easily. It wasn't often that I allowed him such a perfect opportunity to give me a hard time—even if the price exacted was that he wasn't going to get his Cuban-ass contraption anytime in the near future.

"You know, you really won't make a good charity case," he said. "Not with that closet full of Armani and Versace."

"Give me a break," I pled. "I'm sorry I cut our fee in half, I really am. But what could I do? They're nuns."

"Lupe, *querida*," Leonardo said condescendingly, "I'll let it drop because there's nothing we can do now. But remember—they may be nuns, but they've hired us to check out other nuns."

"I know," I said, contrite.

"Well then, I'm heading to the kitchen," Leonardo said, shifting gears. "Want anything? I just whipped up a batch of spiny eel drink. It's supposed to prevent osteoporosis in postmenopausal women. If it works for them, just think what it can do for us."

I knew the FDA had nothing to do with this. "I didn't know eels had spines," I said. "Don't they just slither around?"

"Oh, they have spines," Leonardo said, a dreamy expression on his face. He went to the kitchen and returned with two juice glasses full of green gunk the color and consistency of Flubber.

"No thanks, I already ate," I said, putting mine down on his desk. I thought I could almost see things slithering around in the glass. "Doesn't it strike you as odd that the Holy Rosary paid us in cash?" I asked, motioning toward the deposit bag. "I can't remember ever getting paid that much in cash—by a respectable client, that is."

As soon as I spoke I recalled an old client, the Happy Times-Sweet Dreams Adult Motel in Little Havana. Mercifully, Leonardo chose not to bring up our brief stint working for the goodwill ambassadoresses of the night.

"It occurred to me," he said between sips of his green potion. "But I didn't think about it too much because it was such a small retainer. I mean, it's good for about two days of investigating, isn't it?"

I gave him as dirty a look as I could muster and stalked off to my office. Leonardo called out to me that he was leaving for the bank; I could tell from his tone that he was pleased with himself for making a gratuitous dig at me for having taken a lowered fee for the case. I said nothing in return. It was my turn to sulk.

Early the next morning I spotted my father having breakfast on the terrace, sitting in his favorite cane chair facing Biscayne Bay. I watched him reading the paper for a full minute, sipping his mug of *café con leche*. It wasn't often that I could watch Papi unnoticed. He was dressed for the day in blue linen slacks and a perfectly starched white linen *guayabera*, the creases expertly ironed by Aida. With a smile I saw on his sockless feet his favorite pair of scuffed brown leather boat shoes—something unthinkable when Mami was alive. Two oversized Cohibas stuck out of the pocket of his *guayabera* for smoking later in the day, completely against his doctor's orders, of course.

Papi's reading glasses kept sliding down his nose, and every so often he pushed them up in a distracted manner. It seemed as though his abundant dark hair wasn't as thick as usual. I did a quick calculation. Papi was almost sixty years old! It seemed impossible. But he had been in his late twenties when Fatima was born. That meant Papi had been a widower at fifty-two. He was too young to spend the rest of his life alone, but I don't think that ever occurred to any of us. Papi was still good-looking, and he could attract any number of eligible women. I really didn't want to think to what extent my sisters and I kept him single.

"Papi, *buenos días.*" I kissed his cheek, surprising him so much he spilled coffee on his *Miami Herald*. I felt bad for an instant, until I looked down and saw that I had ruined the editorial page—a section of the paper that consistently elevated his blood pressure to dangerous levels. Papi felt the *Herald* was too liberal. Of course his benchmark for forming this opinion was its treatment of Fidel Castro. Papi, like a lot of other exiles, believed philosophically in freedom of the press. But this largesse didn't extend to reports about Castro. Any news about the dictator had to be not just negative, but downright derogatory.

Papi tossed the newspaper aside and squeezed my hand. The delight in his eyes was so transparent that I felt a pang of guilt at the realization of how seldom I joined him for breakfast.

"How wonderful to see you so early," he said. Then his happiness turned to concern. "Is something wrong? You're never down here at this hour."

Now I really felt badly. It was eight o'clock—not exactly sunrise, but definitely early for me.

"Nothing's the matter," I assured him, helping him clean up the mess. "I'm just up a little early."

Relief spread over his face, combined with a hint of concerned suspicion. I think he was waiting for me to spring some bad news on him.

Osvaldo came out to the terrace with a silver tray bearing my breakfast, which he sat down carefully in front of me. Osvaldo frowned when he saw Papi's soaked newspaper, then glared at me accusingly. Maybe getting up early wasn't such a good idea. Apparently things were a lot more peaceful when I wasn't around.

"So, Lupe, how is your work?" Papi asked as he accepted a fresh cup of coffee from Osvaldo. "Any interesting cases?"

I had to give Papi credit for trying. He had long ago despaired of trying to pressure me into taking up a more socially acceptable career, something more in line with what he saw as my social standing. And although he promised Mami before she died that he would get me married to a nice young Cuban man, he was realistic enough to know that the chances of that happening, at least for the foreseeable future, were slim to none.

"I'm helping the mother superior at the Holy Rosary with a situation," I replied carefully.

"That seems interesting," Papi said. "Anything you can talk about?"

Papi knew about the confidentiality requirements of my work, so he was treading delicately. It wasn't often that I could discuss my work with my family. But it suddenly occurred to me that Papi could help me somewhat—and that I could make him feel more involved with my life.

"There is something," I told him. "The case involves Cuban history."

"Cuban history?" he asked, his eyes lighting up. "What part of our history do you need to know about?"

Papi was the historian of our family. He had books on Cuban history in his study that he had read two or three times.

"Tell me about October the tenth," I said.

"*El Grito de Yara*," Papi replied immediately. He gave me a complicated look. For a second he seemed to wonder whether I was serious, that I needed information on the holiday of our country's independence. Then he seemed slightly disappointed. What could I say? I was a patriot, but I wasn't a fanatic.

"Well, you must know that October tenth was the date the war for Cuban independence started," he said. I nodded. "Carlos Manuel de Céspedes—*el padre de la patria*—he led the uprising against the Spanish. He freed his thirty slaves and incorporated them into his army to fight for independence against Spain."

Papi's voice was rising; this impromptu lecture was filling him with a spirit of *patriotismo*.

"De Cespedes was a farmer, but he became the commander of the entire area of Bayamo," Papi said. "Think of it, Lupe. What a glorious time that was! All Cubans united—whites, blacks, mulattos, all fighting as equals, side-by-side, for their freedom."

I watched Papi transform into someone else, someone dreamy and idealistic instead of my practical, hard-nosed father.

"They had few weapons," Papi said. "The patriots fought with the machetes they used to cut cane." His expression turned somber. "But of course you must know that we lost that first war," he continued. "Those ten years took a tremendous toll on all of Cuba. It would be forty more before we would win our independence from Spain."

"Do all Cubans think the same way about this history as you, Papi?" I asked him. He looked at me strangely. "I mean, is there a difference between the Cubans in exile and the Cubans living on the island? Do they remember this as the time when we were all united for a common cause?"

"*Ay*, Lupe, I understand now," Papi replied. "Are we so divided now by politics that we can agree on nothing? Can we not even agree on the beginnings of our republic and the time when we were one? Is that what you mean?"

"*Sí*, Papi." I smiled wistfully at my father. Although I grew up and lived in America, it felt like an accident to me. I was Cuban. When asked where I was from I would say Miami, but in truth my soul was in Cuba. I had lived a full and rich life in Miami, like many other exiles, but I had always felt as though I was in a state of suspended animation—my "real" life would begin as soon as Castro fell from power and I was able to return to the island. But part of me also knew it might not be that simple. Cubans were a people divided and fractured by political acrimony. The days of *el Grito de Yara*, when we were united, were in a distant and almost unimaginable past.

"Cubans seldom agree on anything—it's our nature," Papi mused. "It is a matter of pride."

He looked off over the water toward the southeast, in the direction of Cuba. I saw lines around his eyes that frightened me. I had always thought of Papi as ageless, immune to the effects of time.

"But we all agree on the Virgin, I suppose," he added. "Perhaps the church and the Virgin are our unifying factors."

I almost made him repeat what he had said. I hadn't mentioned anything about the Virgin.

"Lupe, do you remember the rafts Cubans used to escape in August of 1994?" he asked.

"Of course I do," I replied. I might have been ignorant, but all Cubans remembered the great exodus when more than forty thousand of our countrymen fled the island by any means possible. Almost any craft that could float—and, tragically, some that couldn't—were used to cross the Florida Straits. It was a frightening and exhilarating time. Hundreds of Cubans arrived daily on American shores, greeted as heroes for having the courage to make the deadly crossing. The sighting of each raft had brought cheers, offers to help, and instant hospitality extended to the newcomers. It had been a miracle so many survived the treacherous winds and shark-infested seas.

Papi had used the word "rafts"—a term that described what many of these crafts were. Some were little more than gasoline drums tied together with rope. Others were made of planks of rotten wood. One man even set sail on an ice chest—incredibly, he was rescued on the high seas by the British royal yacht, the *Britannia*. Many people weren't as fortunate. I remembered crying at the thought of the rafts found floating empty, with no clues to learn who had perished save for a woman's hair clip or a child's toy. People were tossed from their rafts into the sea, and the sharks had developed a taste for human flesh.

So I did know something. Papi nodded with satisfaction. I might have been a party girl in college, but I had learned to pay attention to at least Cuba's contemporary history.

"Here's something you might not know," Papi said. "A great many of those rafts had a statue of the *Virgen de la Caridad del Cobre* somewhere inside—even if they had little else. That should tell you something. People risked their lives setting out to sea with the belief that she would look out for them. After all, she had saved those three fishermen off the Cuban coast, four hundred years ago, and brought them to safety in a terrible storm. She would do the same now—steering them to safety."

Papi reached into his pocket for a handkerchief and started to wipe his glasses. I looked away, pretending not to notice when he dried his eyes with the clean white cloth. He was a Cuban man. He wouldn't want his daughter to see him shed tears.

I poured fresh *café con leche* from a pot that Osvaldo had left on my tray. I watched the pelicans who seemed to have set up permanent residence on a channel marker in the bay in front of our house. What could be more Cuban, I asked myself, than drinking copious amounts of heart-stopping coffee while listening to my papi talk about our *patria*?

6

THE nest the parrots were building in the avocado tree outside my office window was now so intricate that I had to fight off the urge to photograph it and send it into *Architectural Digest*. I did some of my best thinking watching those birds. Maybe it was their industriousness that rubbed off on me, inspiring creative thoughts.

There was one fact I couldn't get away from. I had to get someone inside the convent of the Order of the Illumination of the Sacred Virgin—and fast. Just then it was out of the question for me to become a postulant, or pose as one. However, I might be forced to if I could not come up with a plan. No order worth their rosaries would ever have me, once they looked into my background. I could feel the outline of a solution forming in my mind, but I couldn't bring it to the surface. I watched the parrots work for a while, carrying branches in their beaks like the long arms of construction cranes. Then I picked up the phone and punched number three on the speed dial. Within a few seconds I heard the ringing of Lourdes's cell phone.

"Lourdes, I'm working on the case," I said by way of introduction. "And I need your help."

"Can't talk now. Let me call you back." Then she hung up.

Mierda. I needed her right away. But she didn't make me wait long; within five minutes my phone rang.

"Sorry, Lupe," Lourdes said. "I didn't mean to be rude, but I'm in deep shit as it is for having the cell phone. I'm not supposed to use it anymore."

"I caught you at a bad time?"

"You might say that," Lourdes sighed. "During morning prayers. I'm calling you now from the ladies' room."

That explained the echo in her voice. "So you've lied to the nuns and kept the phone?" It was somewhat comforting to know that I wasn't the only sinner among the Solano girls.

"Well, this is Catholic business," Lourdes said. "I think in this instance the end justifies the means."

If there was an Olympic competition for rationalization, my sisters and I would have been perennial medal contenders.

"I won't keep you long," I told her. "I would hate to see you have to flagellate yourself with a dried-out palm branch."

"Lupe! Show some respect!"

I smiled. I was still capable of shocking my jaded nun sister.

"Sorry, sorry," I said. "Look, does your order still have that Jamaican gardener, Theofilus? The one who takes care of the grounds?"

"Theofilus? Yes, he still works here." A pause. "Why, do you want some of that Jamaican gold you used to buy from him? Because I hardly think that qualifies as church business."

"No, no, it's not that. Not right now anyway." I didn't want to burn my bridges. His stuff was excellent. "I remember you said that Theofilus worked under a contract with the Catholic archdiocese of Dade County, that he worked on the grounds of a bunch of convents. Do you know if that's still true?"

"I think so," Lourdes said. "I don't know about the other convents, but if he's still here at the Holy Rosary I suppose he does the other ones as well. I could find out, if you want."

"Yes, please," I said. "Find out specifically if he works the Illumination of the Sacred Virgin—also when and what day."

"Lupe, does this mean you want to get Theofilus to spy on those nuns?" Lourdes asked.

"Look, don't worry about it," I said. So many cases were like this. The clients wanted the case solved, but they would always start balking when they found out how I was going to approach it. "Just find out for me, and fast. Call me as soon as you know."

It was my turn to hang up. It wouldn't help the case if Lourdes were excommunicated for possessing secular technology.

Now I felt my mind working. I started to write. This case had four distinct aspects that I was going to have to tackle. First I would have to get a list of all the nuns who belonged to the Illumination of the Sacred Virgin. I would need to conduct background checks on them if I could—including the mother superior. That would be Nestor's responsibility.

Then I would have to check out the order itself. How legitimate were they—and what was their reputation in Yugoslavia? Why had they suddenly felt the need to come to Dade County, a place that wasn't exactly known for its Yugoslavian community? Marisol would have to set up a surveillance on the convent. Maybe she would learn something from watching who came in and who left. I didn't know what I might gain from that. I knew quite a few local drug dealers, prostitutes, extortionists, and other leading community lights, but spotting fake miracle workers might well prove to be outside the range of my abilities.

The third question was the miracles themselves. Mother Superior at the Holy Rosary hadn't really given me much information about the October 10 miracle. Who was supposed to be responsible for the miracle, for what purpose was it going to occur? I remembered my CCD classes from seventh grade in parochial school; miracles were seldom announced in advance. I would have to look into the nature of miracles and apparitions, see what the church itself had to say.

The fourth aspect, which I left as a huge blank space on my legal pad, involved open-ended, general aspects of the case that I couldn't readily explain. Why in the world, for instance, should an Eastern European order claim a miracle directly relating to Cuba? The announced miracle involved such a detailed knowledge of Cuban history and imagery that it couldn't possibly be an accident.

I had almost finished writing all this down when the phone rang at my elbow. I tore my sheet of paper in surprise, pressing down hard with the ink pen.

"Lupe, Theofilus works at the Illumination convent," Lourdes panted into the phone. "He goes there every Wednesday."

"Great," I said. Today was Tuesday. "And when does he work at yours?"

"Today," Lourdes said, a little triumphantly. "I went out and saw him unloading his truck in our driveway. That's how I got the information, I just walked right up and asked him. He also wanted to know if I wanted some more Jamaican gold for my little sister."

Great. The guy must think I'm a total pothead and that my sister the nun is my connection. It didn't exactly paint a picture of me as the consummate professional. But I knew I was lucky—Theofilus had figuratively fallen right into my lap. The question was whether I could get him to agree to spy on a convent full of nuns. I had to hope Theofilus was willing, or that at least he was open to debate on matters of morality and ethics. After all, I was becoming an expert on rationalizing spying on nuns.

7

FINDING Theofilus on the grounds of the Order of the Holy Rosary wasn't difficult—all I had to do was follow the strains of Bob Marley and the Wailers coming from his Walkman. He had it turned up so loud his headphones were acting more like stereo speakers. If that hadn't been enough, I was also able to follow the scent of Jamaican gold smoke from the ficus bushes he was trimming on the north end of the grounds, far enough from the convent that no one could tell what he was doing—if they'd recognized the sweet aroma in the first place.

Theofilus wore bright gold coveralls without a shirt underneath, and high-top red canvas sneakers on his feet. He was so engrossed in his work and music that he didn't see me coming. I took advantage of the opportunity and moved slightly downwind of him, breathing in a deep lungful of his smoke. I closed my eyes and inhaled deeply just as Marley's "No Woman, No Cry" started to play. It brought back memories of my crazy youth. The sun shone down, the breeze played in the lush grounds, and I swayed to the music until it stopped abruptly.

"Hey. Detective lady."

I must have been drifting off. I opened up my eyes and saw Theofilus standing right in front of me, waving the joint under my nose. "You want to take a hit?"

It was tempting. But it didn't really seem appropriate to be getting high in a convent garden in the middle of the day. Never mind that I was already halfway there.

"No thanks," I said. Theofilus nodded, sending his long dreadlocks swaying. He was a handsome man, with sharp features and big brown eyes—albeit a bit bloodshot at the moment.

"Your sister said you might be coming by to talk to me," he said. "About the other convent. The one with the foreign nuns."

Theofilus took a big puff of his joint, the end of it glowing red. I sort of hoped he would exhale in my direction. It might lessen my irritation at Lourdes for having told the gardener what I wanted before I had the chance to speak with him myself.

"It's true," I said as he coughed away the last of his hit.

"OK, cool," he said. "What do you want to know?"

Theofilus reached into his back pocket and brought out a small, colorful knit bag. He unzipped it and rummaged around a bunch of smaller bags inside until he found what he was looking for. He put the end of the still-smoking joint into the roach clip, then blew on his thumb and index finger to cool off his skin.

"I've heard rumors that the Order of the Illumination of the Sacred Virgin says they're going to make a miracle happen soon," I told him as he smoked the joint into nothingness.

Instead of replying, Theofilus walked over to the ficus hedge and started to inspect his handiwork. He might have been stoned out of his mind, but he had done outstanding work. All the leaves were trimmed to a uniform height, and they glittered a healthy dark green in the sunshine. The entire grounds were, in fact, beautifully kept.

"Maybe I know about that," he said. "Or I *could* know. You know?"

"Would you tell me about it?"

"Look, detective lady," Theofilus said in a deceptively mellow voice while moving his hand over the hedge. "I'm not going to spy on nuns for you, if that's what you want. I know your sister is a nun, and I can tell you're not a bad person, but this is serious shit. These are holy women. I'm not Catholic, but still I'm not going to mess with it. It's not right."

I wanted to tell Theofilus that the head of an order of nuns had initiated all this, but of course I couldn't.

"I'm really not asking you to spy on anyone," I said. "I'm just interested in learning more about their miracle."

Theofilus shook his head, dreads flying. I felt like ducking to avoid getting hit.

"Then ask them," he said. "Or is this miracle a secret?"

"I'm not sure how well known it is, outside the religious community," I said, avoiding a direct answer. I wasn't sure myself just how secret the miracle was. "I just . . . I just want to find out more about it."

Theofilus's face twisted into an expression of sincere confusion. I couldn't blame him, given my wimpy explanation.

"I've been working for the archdiocese for years," he said slowly. "I know all the important shit goes through the bishop. So call him up and ask." He pretended to punch numbers into an imaginary phone. "Hello? Is this Archbishop John Clement Favalora's office? Yes? Well, is it true there's going to be a miracle in Miami soon? Yes or no."

"Now you're being silly," I said, even though his proposal had a certain irrefutable logic about it.

"Am I? But that's all you have to do."

But I didn't even know whether the archbishop himself was aware that Mother Superior had hired me for the investigation. My hunch was that Mother Superior had initiated it herself, that the archbishop was out of the loop. Of course I wouldn't be able to ask her, not after her unequivocal statements of the day before. I wondered what would happen if I blew the religious/political aspect of this case. I could just see the newspaper headline: NUNGATE.

"I can't really do that, Theofilus," I said. "This isn't the kind of information the church gives out over the phone. There are processes regarding miracles—if this really is one."

Theofilus started gathering up his clippers and edgers, moving toward his truck. "I'd like to help you, lady," he said. "But I don't think I'm going to be able to."

I watched him walk away. "I'll pay you," I called out.

He stopped. "How much?"

I thought fast. "A thousand dollars."

"Not worth it," Theofilus said in a singsong voice as he kept on walking. I couldn't let him go. He was the one person I knew who regularly went into that convent. There might have been others, maybe many others—but I didn't have time to find them. I jogged ahead and joined Theofilus as he was loading his gear into his ragged old pickup truck. The convent was behind us, through a grove of trees, so I knew we could still speak freely.

"Have you ever been busted?" I asked, barely knowing what I

was saying as the words escaped my lips. But I had his attention. I was right to assume that someone who smoked ganja as copiously as Theofilus apparently did was bound to have been busted at one point or another.

"And what business is it of yours?" he asked, insulted. His easygoing friendliness disappeared in an instant.

"What happened to your case?" I asked. "Did you get off?"

Theofilus now looked completely miserable; his mouth screwed into a pout and he folded his arms. "It hasn't come to trial yet. Two years ago I got busted—they called it possession and trafficking, even though it was all for my personal use. It's been hell, the waiting. I already feel like a prisoner in a Babylon cell!"

Theofilus had started to raise his voice and sound like a Rastafari prophet. But he had every right to be upset, federal drug sentencing guidelines being as draconian as they were.

"I'm innocent," Theofilus said. "But I have such a shitty lawyer. I make too much money to get a public defender, and the only lawyer I can afford is a fuckup and a moron. I give this guy money and he doesn't even make court deadlines. All he has are excuses. And if I get convicted I can lose my green card and get sent back to Jamaica. Then I won't be able to support my family back home in Jamaica! All for a crime I didn't commit—I tell you, lady, I am not a drug dealer."

In all my years of investigations I had yet to meet a guilty person. But the Constitution said everyone was to be assumed innocent. I was there to do my job, not to judge Theofilus.

I took a deep breath. "Have you ever heard of a criminal-defense attorney named Tommy McDonald?" I said low, almost whispering.

Who hadn't heard of Tommy? Anyone who read the *Herald* or watched the TV news would have seen him coming out of a courthouse, his arm around his latest client who had beaten a rap, yelling about entrapment and civil liberties. The press loved to cover Tommy's exploits.

Theofilus's eyes lit up. He knew where we were going with this. The nuns' miracle would hopefully not be a secret much longer. Of course, I would soon need to have a very interesting conversation with the aforementioned Mr. McDonald.

8

"YOU did what?"

Tommy sat up in bed; the warm affectionate feeling of the evening evaporated in an instant. He yelled at me so loudly I seriously worried that he was going to have a stroke. I watched the red vein in his neck pulsating and cursed myself for having misjudged his reaction so badly. I had thought that a night of passion followed by watching the sunrise—Tommy's favorite time of day—would have made him receptive to hearing about my tricky situation with Theofilus. So much for the strategy of using sex to soften him up.

"Tommy, *querido*," I purred. I had just told him my story, beginning with my meeting with Mother Superior. He had heard me out in silence until I reached the part about my agreement with Theofilus—then he exploded. And with justification. It had been out of line for me to offer Tommy's services without consulting him first. I must have thought my relationship with Tommy was secure enough that he would fall into line with my needs without argument.

Tommy went quiet and turned away, which frightened me more than if he had kept on yelling. I didn't know how much longer he would let me reach him, so I adopted my most persuasive tone of voice.

"Tommy, please try to understand my position. I needed the information so badly, and Theofilus wasn't going to take cash for helping me. His eyes lit up when I mentioned your name. Tommy, you have to believe me, my back was against the wall."

Tommy turned around and looked at me sternly, his mouth a tight straight line. It sent shivers down my spine, made me frightened. In all our years of knowing each other I had taken plenty of liberties with Tommy—more often than not, he had offered to bail me out without even being asked. But this time I had crossed an invisible boundary.

"Lupe," he said sadly. "How could you? How could you promise this man that I would represent him with his case?"

Tommy wore an expression that looked as though he was seeing me for the first time. I felt my stomach sink inside.

"You don't know anything about his situation—only what he told you," Tommy said. "How could you do this to me?"

Tommy was right. I was wrong. But I was desperate, and offering Tommy's services was the only carrot that Theofilus was going to bite.

"I'm sorry. I didn't think it through. I screwed up, Tommy." My eyes grew moist, and I started to blink rapidly. It felt as if my relationship with Tommy was about to end, all because of this stupid action on my part. I couldn't imagine life without him, either professionally or personally.

"Lupe." Tommy put his hand under my chin and lifted up my face to his. I heard him breathe in sharply. "Are you crying?"

I shook my head. I couldn't let him see that.

"You are!" He tenderly wiped my cheek with his hand. "How long have I known you? Seven years, eight?"

I shrugged.

"I've never seen you cry," he said, "not even when you shot and killed that guy."

"And you still have not seen me cry," I replied, defiant. I pulled away. Whatever happened, I wouldn't lose whatever respect Tommy still had for me.

"*Ay*, Lupe," Tommy said softly as he stroked my hair. "Tough all the way. Never let 'em see you cry, right?"

Tommy's enemies—and there were a lot of them—would have been stunned to see this gentle side. In Miami, his name was typically uttered with an adjective or adverb tacked on—usually describing a bodily function of some sort.

Appealing to his more sensitive side, I gave in and let my eyes water, stopped fighting the tears. So Tommy would have to respect me even though I was capable of crying. "I'm sorry, Tommy," I said. "I was so wrong. I can't believe what I've done. Please, you have to forgive me."

"Oh, shit," he muttered, shaking his head. "I can't stand seeing you like this. I can't stand to see a woman cry, especially you."

He got out of bed and went to the bathroom. "I'm taking a shower," he called out from the doorway, no longer sounding angry. "Get in touch with your guy and have him call Sonia first thing in the morning. Tell him to set up an appointment to come into the office as soon as he can. I might as well know what you've gotten me into."

"Oh, Tommy, I love you." I sprang out of bed and went to him, kissing him all over. My relief at not losing him—or the case—proved to be a powerful aphrodisiac. I knew it had been a close call. Tommy and I had been together off and on for years, but it was unlike me to show such gratitude. Tommy rolled his eyes at me, not fooled by my sudden amorous advances. We knew each other too well for there to be any illusions between us.

"Oh, hell," he said. He led me back to the bed, forgetting his shower for the moment. Our lovemaking that morning definitely had a new intensity. For my part, I still had Tommy and I was moving forward with the case—a perfect combination.

Tommy paused for a moment and looked at me. "You must have really been in a tight spot," he said, panting. "Because you've never told me you loved me before."

Afterward I lay motionless in bed listening to water running in the bathroom. I concentrated on deep breathing, trying to get my heart rate down. I had gotten lucky. I had escaped Tommy's wrath, made him accept what I had done even though it was wrong.

Maybe I had to admit that what surprised me the most was how much I really cared about Tommy. He had always been special to me, but my fear over losing him had been genuine, my tears real.

Perhaps I was getting soft in my old age. The implications were enough to make me shudder. I hated to think where all this might be heading, and I vowed to take all necessary measures to make sure the world didn't find out.

9

I swore under my breath as I checked out the high walls of the convent of the Order of the Illumination of the Sacred Virgin. For the past few minutes I had stood on the running board of my Mercedes facing the place, binoculars pressed to my eyes, focusing and fiddling with them as though I could somehow find camouflage among the dwellings, the trees, the desolate road. No such luck. The area surrounding the town of Homestead was open country. The convent's high stucco walls stood in lonely splendor from everything else around, as though daring me to even think of penetrating their secrets.

The prospects were even worse than Coral Gables, where surveillances were consistently a logistical nightmare. Marisol was very skilled with video, but I couldn't imagine how much she could get from taping her view of the high convent walls and the flat vacant areas all around.

From the Mercedes' running board I couldn't see the convent grounds. So I took a quick look around to make sure I wasn't being watched, then hoisted myself up onto the car roof. I stood up, wobbled, regained my balance, then pointed the binoculars back toward the convent.

No wonder Theofilus was always stoned. Tending this convent's grounds would have been like trying to tame the Everglades. Now that I could see inside, I was stunned at how extensive the convent's grounds were. With a quick mental calculation I figured that the open area inside the outer walls measured at least half an acre on each side of the convent. Theofilus must have needed to smoke an entire joint for each quarter of the grounds.

There were three buildings inside the compound. Their functions were pretty easy to guess: a main administrative building, a chapel, a larger dormitory. All were in identical tan stucco. With the high wall around and single gate at the entrance, the place was like a fortress as far as I was concerned.

I had risked discovery long enough, so I hopped down off the Mercedes, careful to make sure not to scratch the paint finish. Osvaldo would never forgive me if I did.

I looked around. The convent was smack in the middle of agricultural fields in various states of cultivation. It rose up from the center of a very flat landscape, with crops emanating in all directions. I was no farmer myself, so it took me a few minutes to realize that the little pink-and-red things growing on green shrubs planted in neat rows all around were strawberries. In my life I had only seen strawberries in green containers at Publix, wrapped in plastic and arranged in little pyramids.

It was still early in the day, and my Mercedes was the only car in sight on the two-lane road that led west to the long driveway in front of the convent. I had been there, my motor running, for fifteen minutes. There was no point in making myself conspicuous any longer, so I got back in the car, stepped on the accelerator, and made a U-turn back to the turnpike.

As soon as I had left Tommy's apartment that morning I had driven straight for Homestead, knowing I needed to check out the arrangement of the site before I could send Marisol out on surveillance. The situation was even worse than I had feared.

I drove back to the house while muttering to myself and shaking my head. I was going to have to change Marisol's usual strategies because a hidden surveillance wasn't going to work in this case. I had a meeting scheduled with her and Nestor for noon, which gave me a few hours to detail my plans and assignments for them. I looked at my watch. A little after eight. Plenty of time, I lied to myself.

I hit seventy on the turnpike, deep in thought, my eyes on the road. A moment later I heard a muffled sound coming from my purse. I swore as I fished around for my cellular phone while trying to steer with my free hand. Luckily the northbound traffic was light.

"Lupe?" There was so much static on the line that I could barely hear the voice calling my name.

"Can you speak louder?" I yelled into the phone.

"God! You don't have to shout!" Lourdes snapped into the phone. Oops. It was apparently only a one-way bad connection.

"I'm sorry, I'm sorry," I said. Now I was curious. Lourdes was seldom uptight enough to get annoyed with me about anything.

"Now, listen, Lupe, I don't want you to get mad at me," she began.

Me mad at Lourdes? That would be a change of pace.

"But I thought I might do some investigating on my own," she added in a timid voice as the connection cleared.

She paused and I felt my guts tighten.

"I thought I would call the convent—the other convent," she said, quick to clarify. I heard her breathing heavily, as though very nervous. "I thought I would tell whoever answered that I had heard a rumor about a miracle that was going to take place there."

I could taste the coffee I'd drunk at Tommy's start to come up my throat. Served me right for drinking American coffee.

"All right, what happened?" I asked. What a morning. Tommy yelling at me, then me finding out that the convent was unsurveill-able, then Lourdes trying her hand at detective work. Next I'd probably find out that Leonardo'd been spiking my office coffee with female hormones to get me in touch with my feminine side. Actually, that would explain my embarrassing conduct that morning.

"The receptionist gave me another number to call," Lourdes said, a hiss almost obscuring her voice. "It's a special line the order's set up to handle miracle-related inquiries."

I switched the receiver from my left ear to my right. "What? A hot line?" I shook my head. "Well, did you call it?"

"Well, the number I was given—" Lourdes paused. I couldn't tell whether someone had come in or whether she was fiddling with the phone to make the static go away.

"What?" I said louder, mentally cursing the taste of American coffee on my tongue.

She took a deep breath. "The number, the number . . ." She laughed harshly. "Let's just say I didn't have to write it down. The number the receptionist gave me was 1-800-MIRACLE."

I almost dropped the phone. An 800 number. The nuns had set

up a hot line, even if they hadn't made the miracle public yet. This was serious. I wondered how this was going to affect the secrecy that Mother Superior wanted to maintain, and how it would impact the investigation from my point of view.

I braked sharply to avoid rear-ending a car full of red-faced tourists driving the speed limit. In Dade County it was easy to spot the tourists—they were generally the ones driving the four-door red, blue, or white American cars with license plates from Lee, Collier, or Manatee Counties. That, and the fact that they were the only drivers who observed the traffic laws.

"It gets worse," Lourdes said.

"How can it get worse?" I asked. My mouth tasted terrible, from the coffee and the rising panic inside me. I rolled down the window and spat out, praying that Mami wasn't looking down from Heaven at that precise instant. The sight would have devastated her.

"The receptionist noticed I had a slight accent," Lourdes said.

"What the hell are you talking about?" I honked and swerved to avoid hitting a dump truck scattering pebbles in its wake. The driver gave me the finger as I passed him on the right.

"There's a second number for Spanish speakers," Lourdes said. "1-800-MILAGRO. Lupe, this is going to be serious. I have a suspicion this is going to be made public all at once. And when it is, there's not going to be any going back."

Mierda. Mierda. Mierda.

I didn't like the mutinous atmosphere developing in my office. Time for a little levity, so I told them about the 1-800 numbers the convent had set up; thankfully, they both burst out laughing. I played it up as a joke, not volunteering the foreboding the hot-line numbers had initially given me.

"Let's give them a call," I said. I took out my cellular phone, thinking I didn't want to call from the office phone in case the convent was using a caller ID function on the line. "Miracles or *Milagros?*" I asked.

"Well, this is America," Marisol said, a little more cheery. "Let's go for the English option."

I twirled the small plastic dial on the side of my cell phone until the volume was all the way up, then punched in the number. As soon as the call went through I put the phone on the corner of my desk; we all moved in close so we could hear.

"God bless you and thank you for calling the official miracle hot line at the Convent of the Order of the Illumination of the Sacred Virgin," a soft, melodious voice welcomed us in unaccented English. "You will be offered a menu of five choices.

"Press one if you wish to receive information about the miracles the Holy Mother has performed throughout the ages."

All three of us put our hands to our mouths in astonishment. We were all products of a Catholic education and a lifetime inside the church. Hearing this sort of reference to holy works coming out of AT&T's latest technology certainly stripped away the religious mystique to which we were all accustomed.

The voice was almost mesmerizing. Huddled close together, we looked like aboriginal natives who had never before heard a voice on the telephone line.

"Press two if you wish to know what constitutes a miracle within the doctrine of the Catholic Church."

There was a pause. I was surprised not to hear the "Ave Maria" hymn playing in the background.

"Press three if you wish to know about the miracles with which the Order of the Illumination of the Sacred Virgin has been associated."

The three of us were beyond reacting. There was a moment of silence provided for callers to make up their minds.

10

NESTOR, Marisol, and I were staring at each other from opposing ends of my office, forming a morose triangle. I had just finished briefing them on the difficult logistics of the investigation.

"I still don't know," Marisol said. "Doesn't this sound like a sign from above, that we shouldn't have taken this case?"

Nestor perked up at this, though I could still barely differentiate his eyes from the dark circles that ringed them. He could have used a healthy dollop of concealer—not to mention eventual plastic surgery to deal with his eye bags.

"Every investigation has some type of trouble," I said, trying to sound soothing. "Let's put aside the religious aspects of this one. Think of it as an everyday, typical case."

I felt like a hypocrite for saying this, for underplaying the religious and political aspects of what we were doing—as well as Mother Superior's insistence on secrecy and the absence of any proof that we had been retained to investigate the miracle. Marisol was Venezuelan and Nestor a Dominican. They probably wouldn't understand the depth of the miracle's symbolism for Cubans, or the metaphor of the Virgin's tears for the waters that separate exiles and island Cubans. I could have explained everything, but they probably would have walked out the door. Part of me wanted to dismiss them as superstitious; another part kicked myself for not dropping the case. I had taken it, and that was that. I had accepted payment and started work—there was no way for me to back out, as far as I was concerned.

"Sure, this is just like a domestic," Nestor said, his voice de and sarcastic. "We'll pretend these nuns are philanderers."

"Press four if you wish to hear of any known upcoming miracles or apparitions by the Virgin."

At this all three of us stiffened upright. I decided that we should hear the last option before listening to number four.

"Press five if you wish to receive a blessing from our Holy Father Pope John Paul II."

Another silence. "Thank you very much for calling. Good-bye and God bless."

And then, so help me, the strains of the "Ave Maria" could be heard for several seconds before fading into silence. At least everything about the church hadn't changed.

I flipped off the phone and slumped into my chair. Nestor headed back to his favorite spot on the sofa, while Marisol made herself comfortable on her windowsill perch.

"I don't think it's necessary to call and listen to it in Spanish, is it?" I asked.

"I'm sure it's the same," Nestor replied.

All three of us were in the throes of severe culture shock. A convent of nuns had gone into business advertising miracles via a 1-800 number and telephone tree. It was quite a shift from the days of Sister Mary Maria in her habit and wimple, her rosary beads clattering at her side as she walked down the hall of my parochial school. This was all so worldly, bringing the substance of our faith into the mundane and everyday. We were going to have to get used to the idea, in order to effectively work the case. At least I was already used to the idea that nuns didn't have to be dowdy brides of Christ, thanks to Lourdes.

"I wonder how many people are calling this number?" Nestor said.

"Not many, or else it would be on the news," Marisol said. "Wouldn't it, Lupe?"

Marisol was right. The miracle would be big news in Miami. This meant that, even though the 1-800 number was set up, it wasn't being aggressively publicized. Still, Lourdes had found out about it simply by calling the order. There might not be much time before the public caught on—certainly a big announcement would be made at least in the final days before the miracle. Once that happened I knew I could forget about putting together an effective investigation. Reporters, photographers, and thousands of the faithful would converge on the convent. It would be hard to mount a clandestine surveillance with *Miami Herald* reporters taking my picture.

"We're OK for now," I said.

Surely Mother Superior knew about the 1-800 hot line. I would have informed her myself, but that would have been breaking the rules. I considered having Lourdes tell her, but I didn't want to involve Lourdes in the case any more than she already was.

"Well, what's next?" Nestor asked. He had leaned back on the sofa, almost lying flat, his eyes closed.

"I'm going to listen to it again—and pay close attention to the information it provides about the miracle itself," I said. "We'll tape it so we call it as few times as possible. There's no need to arouse suspicion."

The door to my office opened with a whoosh and Leonardo came in bearing a tray with four oversized tumblers filled with sea-green liquid.

"Avocado shakes!" he announced triumphantly, apparently oblivious to the fact that I was having a strategy meeting with my investigators. "From our very own tree!"

He pissed me off, but I still had trouble suppressing a smile. I thought of Leonardo in his spandex outfit as the good farmer bringing in the crops. He handed each of us a drink and waited expectantly for us to taste his creation.

"It's very good for you. Lots of vitamins and minerals." Our lack of enthusiasm must have been obvious, because he added, "You know—avocados are good for smooth skin and strong bones."

I was familiar with Leonardo in his mother-hen role, so I knew he wasn't going to leave until we had all consumed at least half our shakes. I took a deep breath, put the glass to my lips, and swallowed. Marisol and Nestor followed my lead. The taste was like a blend of Hawaiian suntan oil and sambuca. Maybe not so bad, actually, but not worth getting a stomachache over. In a show of solidarity, Nestor and Marisol kept up with me and we nearly finished our tumblers. I hoped the mix wasn't a laxative—we probably wouldn't have easy access to bathroom facilities for the rest of the day.

"Tasty!" I pronounced.

Leonardo beamed with pleasure. "How's the case coming?" he asked. "Any progress?"

I knew this wasn't an idle question. Leonardo wanted to know how much of the retainer we had burned through, and what were the tangible results.

"The nuns have an 800 number," I answered. "Actually, two— one in English and one in Spanish. Looks like they want to be prepared for the rush of interest in their miracle."

This news seemed to put Leonardo in a rare thoughtful mood. He frowned as he collected our glasses. Well, this case was enough to throw any Catholic into a funk of apprehension.

Just before he left, Leonardo's eyes shone with an idea. "If these nuns are so into technology," he said, "have you checked to see if they have a Web page?"

Nestor, Marisol, and I immediately looked at each other. None of us, of course, had thought of it. We were all computer illiterate, for the most part. Unlike, I now suspected, the supposedly unworldly nuns we had been hired to investigate.

"We'll look into it," I said. "For now, I have an idea I want to discuss."

11

I waited in the reception area of the Women's Detention Center for Marisol's release. I wondered who thought that this room should be painted pink—probably they had the misguided idea it would be some sort of deference to the gender of the people spending time there as temporary guests of Dade County. Instead it was simply nauseating.

I was growing stiff from sitting in the hard-backed chair, so I got up and paced the room. I hadn't eaten lunch, and I considered getting a Coke and bag of chips from the vending machines in the corner. But I decided not to. I was trying to eat healthier, even though that avocado shake from yesterday was still turning cartwheels in my stomach. I would rather have Fritos anytime, but Leonardo possessed junk-food antennae so highly developed he could sense a HoHo from a mile away.

On a framed display just next to the door was a list of bail bondsmen available for helping damsels in distress. Out of boredom I counted the names posted: sixty-four. I wondered how many other American cities could boast such a high number. It was a testament to free enterprise. And an exploding crime rate.

I walked over to the enclosed area where three corrections officers were busy with their paperwork, hoping for an idea as to how much longer it might take before Marisol would be released. None of them looked up at me, though, and I knew better than to make a nuisance of myself by asking about my investigator's status. After all, I knew all of the officers by name, having met them many times before while visiting clients in jail. This was my first visit to the Detention Center in which I actually had to adhere to a timetable not of my own making. As investigator of record in past cases, I had had the luxury of coming and going as I pleased—and unlimited access to my clients. I had never needed to pay attention to the official visitors' hours posted on the wall.

I cleared my throat loudly. I hadn't said anything to the officers because I didn't want them to think I expected any sort of preferential treatment. But in fact I *did* want preferential treatment, and I wanted them to know I wasn't happy cooling my heels in the reception area indefinitely. They would probably figure I was working on billable hours, that I was making money by standing around waiting. That couldn't have been farther from the truth. I was there on my own account. And I was there because my colossal blunder had ended up with Marisol in jail.

I was getting jittery, so I decided to take a quick walk outside for a change of scenery. Not that there was much to see on Northwest Seventh Avenue and Fourteenth Street—it wasn't exactly a scenic part of town. Shopping carts filled with debris lined the street leading to the parking lot just west of the Detention Center. A dozen or so overpasses circled the three-story building, intriguingly designed to curve within a few feet of each other without touching.

I walked east toward the Miami River. The drawbridge there was in the raised position, and I strained to see the vessel that had necessitated lifting it. I walked past the Booker T. Washington Middle School: HOME OF THE TORNADOES. NOT THE LARGEST, BUT THE BEST. I imagined that having a jail on the next block might be a deterrent to budding young criminals. But this was Miami. Who knew what effect it might have had. I only hoped that none of the students at the school had mothers incarcerated a block away. I shook my head to get rid of the depressing thought.

I had walked another block when I found myself drenched in sweat, due in part to the late-afternoon sun beaming through the humid air. Suddenly the relatively cool reception area back at the Detention Center didn't seem bad at all. I hurried back to the jail and bounded up the five concrete steps leading inside.

As soon as I opened the door Juanita Washington, a corrections officer I'd known for years, looked up and called out to me. "Lupe, your investigator is ready to come out."

"Thanks, Juanita," I said. "Where do I go to meet her?"

"Hey, you can come inside," she said with a wink. "Professional courtesy and all that."

"Thanks," I said, walking past.

Juanita frowned. "You're not carrying, are you?"

I shrugged. Of course I was. I was also carrying a cell phone and a pager, totally in contradiction to the rules that were clearly posted in the reception area. Normally I left all this stuff in one of the lockers lining the wall by the ladies' room, but I hadn't felt like it today. I was too upset by the predicament Marisol had landed herself in, as well as my culpability for it.

"Give me your purse." Juanita grinned at me as I handed it over. "You know better than that."

She shook her finger in mock admonishment, knowing that I'd never paid too much attention to the rules. I admired her six-inch-long fingernails, painted in wild funky swirls. She was pretty cool, unlike some of the other corrections officers who thought they had to be tight-asses just because they wore a uniform to work in the morning.

"I'll put this in the drawer, next to mine," Juanita said before walking outside the guards' enclosed space and unlocking the door separating the reception area from the secure zone inside. I followed her down a corridor, waited while she stopped in front of a door.

Marisol's expression when I met her in the changing room would have had me pushing up flowers if looks were lethal. She barely acknowledged my presence otherwise, so I stood by quietly while Juanita handed her her belongings wrapped in a plastic bag.

The room was small, cramped for three people. Even though she wasn't looking at me, it was hard to avoid Marisol's look of pure fury as she took off her orange county-issued jumpsuit, pulled her T-shirt over her head, then buttoned up her jeans. While she changed from one outfit to another I couldn't help noticing that she still wore the skimpy bikini she had put on earlier in the day.

I had already paid Marisol's bail, so we were free to go. I stopped quickly on the way out and retrieved my purse. Marisol didn't say a word to me as I held the door open for her on the way out, nor did she speak while we walked across the parking lot to the Mercedes. I was pleasantly surprised to see the car was still there, undamaged, considering that this wasn't an enclosed parking lot. The concertina wire on top of the chain-link fence was there to keep inmates inside, not to protect visitors' vehicles, but it had done the job that day.

We sat in the car, waiting for the air conditioner to cool off the interior. Marisol folded her arms and scowled out the window.

"I'm double-billing on this one, Lupe," she said, her tone of voice leaving no room for argument. "Double my fee."

I nodded, relieved that she had at least said something to me, even if it was decidedly unpleasant. This wasn't the best time to inform Marisol of the ramifications of her arrest. As soon as I had received her phone call from jail I had checked out the extent of her legal troubles. Things weren't settled simply because I had gotten her out on bond. But I would deal with that later; or, rather, Tommy would. I was more and more indebted to him as the case progressed, and I was really pushing my luck with him.

"We'll go to Homestead to pick up your car," I said, trying to make conversation.

Marisol stared straight ahead, silent. Her anger was palpable. It permeated every centimeter of the car, clung to the leather upholstery like the humidity beaded on the windows. She was furious with me. I had pressured her into doing something she didn't want to do, and she subsequently was carted off and thrown in jail. I had screwed up again. I had apologized to her profusely over the phone, but she wasn't hearing it. I figured apologizing again would probably just make her even more angry.

I had been eager to set up surveillance outside the convent. Too eager. I had come up with a spur-of-the-moment plan that had sounded brilliant to me, but I had failed to do the legwork to make sure that everything went smoothly. It was a rookie mistake, not doing my homework, and Marisol had paid the price for my stupidity.

It had sounded so good at the time. I had thought: who could legitimately stand by a highway in Homestead for several hours without arousing the Order of the Illumination's suspicion? The answer had been so simple that I had laughed out loud when I thought of it: a hot-dog cart, Miami-style. I had seen them everywhere, invariably run by scantily clad young girls who sold hot dogs to motorists and passersby in all sorts of South Florida locations. They were part of the landscape, one of Miami's many idiosyncrasies.

So I had rented a hot-dog cart for the day, along with hot dogs and buns. Then I had dressed—or, more accurately, undressed—Marisol in a string bikini and set her up near the turnoff for the convent, where she could observe the goings-on there. She had protested about the bikini, but this was what the hot-dog girls wore. Fortunately for her, topless hot-dog trucks had been banned a few years before. No one, I figured, would see anything out of the ordinary in a half-naked (actually, much more than half) girl serving hot dogs out of a cart on a South Florida roadside.

Marisol had fought me, and I had suggested she think of a better idea. She had been unable to counter with another plan, but she added a provision. At the first sign of trouble—if, for instance, a customer gave her a hard time—she was going to quit.

As it turned out, no customers gave her trouble. Except for a Dade County occupational license official, who fined her for selling hot dogs without proper documentation.

In the arrest complaint the official said that as soon as he asked Marisol for her permit, she had assaulted him and that he had feared for his life. Never mind that he was a foot taller and a hundred pounds heavier than her. Her "violent" reaction had necessitated him using his arrest powers and bringing her to the Detention Center, where she was thrown in a cell until I bailed her out.

Marisol had told me all this, and more, during our brief conversation when she called me from jail. There was no doubt that her arrest had more to do with her decision to have "told that asshole to fuck off" when he commented on how she looked in her bikini. According to Marisol the official had originally approached her for a hot dog and soft drink, then became belligerent when she didn't respond to his advances. That's when he identified himself as a county official and asked to see her license to sell hot dogs. That's when she really lost her temper, and things got out of control.

I was concerned for Marisol, but my first worry was that all this commotion might have been noticed by someone at the convent. I hadn't had the chance to ask her about this, and right now certainly wasn't the most diplomatic time.

I swung the car around and merged into one of the dozen overpasses which led onto the southbound lane of I-95, the interstate highway that crossed Miami, toward Homestead. Marisol let out a breath.

"Men are so low and despicable," she said, more to herself than to me. "I swear to God I'm going to become celibate. Or gay."

She ranted on, teaching me in the process a few Spanish swear words that even I didn't know. This wasn't too much of a surprise: Marisol, being Venezuelan, spoke a different sort of Spanish than that of the Caribbean countries. Central Americans spoke yet another brand. Sometimes Latinos from various countries could barely understand each other, even though ostensibly we were speaking the same language.

Listening to Marisol vent like this was better than enduring the silent treatment. I didn't take much of what she said seriously, knowing that she wasn't about to swear off men because of one idiot. She never had before, and she had met her fair share of them—starting with her former husband.

I waited for a break in her diatribe. "How long were you there before that bastard had you arrested?" I asked.

She shifted to business mode and brought out her log. She flipped through a few creased pages. "I arrived at eleven o'clock and made my last sale at three-oh-three P.M. Just a little more than four hours."

She flipped through a few more sheets. "I wrote down the license tags of all the vehicles that entered or exited the convent," she added. "I'll give them to Leo as soon as I get back to the office, so he can run them."

"What kind of activity did you observe?"

"There were . . ." I saw her lips moving as she counted. "Four delivery trucks. UPS, FedEx, Crystal Springs Water, and a fishmonger. Oh, and Theofilus, your gardener. I got tags on all of them, of course."

I nodded. I had known in advance that Theofilus was scheduled to work there that day. I hoped to get a follow-up call from him soon.

"What about private vehicles?"

Marisol looked at her pad again. "Eleven."

"Anything catch your attention?" I asked hopefully.

Marisol chewed on her lip and searched her memory. "Nothing that stands out," she said. "But when we get to the hot-dog cart I'll show you something I rigged up."

"What do you mean?" I asked.

"The day wasn't totally lost," she said mysteriously.

Traffic was light on the turnpike and we were able to make good time on our drive south. Marisol didn't speak again until we reached the Homestead exit which led to the convent. I held my breath until I saw Marisol's car was still where we left it, discreetly parked under a tree a few feet past the hot-dog cart.

Marisol must have been thinking along the same lines; she sighed with relief when she saw her dark blue Taurus, her working car, backed up to a hedge so its plates couldn't be easily read from the road. Marisol usually drove a light blue BMW, her pleasure car, but for work she preferred the Taurus—steady, dependable, and easily forgettable. In other words, an investigator's dream car.

Neither of us wanted to spend more time there than we had to, so we quickly hitched the cart to the back of the Taurus. After agreeing to meet later at the office Marisol drove off to Little Havana, to return the ill-fated cart to the company from which we had rented it. Using it the next day was obviously not an option.

I watched the hot-dog cart's taillights disappear into the distance as she drove away. I felt shitty about what I had put her through, and I knew her legal troubles weren't over. Tommy could probably do a lot in court with the county official's conduct on the job, but I wondered what price would be exacted on our relationship. Once I had felt I had an unlimited line of credit with Tommy; now, somehow, that had changed.

As I drove off I remembered: Marisol had something to show me. I considered calling her on her cell phone but thought better of it. At least she was still speaking to me. No sense pushing my luck.

12

I had played the tape recording of 1-800-MILAGRO's option four so many times that I had made the tip of my index finger sore. The female voice on the tape was so melodious, so seductive, that I was tempted over and over to forget that I was investigating the claims she was making.

After the fiasco with Marisol I drove back to my office disgusted and depressed. Even though we had agreed to meet Marisol hadn't showed up, nor had she called, so after waiting an extra hour for her I went home.

As soon as I entered the house in Cocoplum I discovered that I was the only family member home—a very unusual occurrence. Osvaldo gave me a detailed account of everyone's whereabouts. I was very conscious of not seeing my family much recently, and it was disappointing to find none of them around. I could have used a double dose of family bonding, even though in my state of mind I knew I wouldn't be very good company.

I took a long bath and had dinner outside on the terrace alone, watched the sun go down over Key Biscayne, admired the pelicans skirting down low over the water, soaking their bellies searching for the perfect fish for dinner. I drank a *mojito* with my dinner after making sure none of my family was coming home anytime soon, then washed down two Tylenol PMs with the second. Otherwise I would have been awake the rest of the night, flagellating myself mentally for screwing up the investigation and my relationships.

It simply hadn't occurred to me that Marisol would need all sorts of permits—including an occupational one, for God's sake—to operate a hot-dog cart in the open air on a back road in Homestead. I figured the surveillance would last a week at the most, and so I had bypassed looking into the rules and regulations required by the county. I had been sloppy, and got busted. Of course the company I rented the truck from had neglected to tell me anything, but I suppose I should have asked.

Now Marisol was going to pay the price. Fortunately I didn't dream that night. I could live without seeing an image of Marisol in prison, selling hot dogs in a bikini until she was seventy years old.

In the morning I felt better. When I set out for the office I felt almost optimistic. There was nothing like ten hours of uninterrupted sleep to heal the psyche, followed by a slice of Cuban bread buttered with an obscene amount of dripping yellow butter dipped into a steaming mug of Aida's turbocharged *café con leche*.

I arrived at the office before Leonardo so I turned off the alarm and set about starting his usual chores. I finished listening to all the messages on the answering machine—including Marisol's plaintive voice apologizing for not stopping by yesterday afternoon. She said she wanted to be alone after her lousy day, a feeling with which I was certainly in no position to argue.

As soon as the office was awakened and everything was humming along nicely, I sat down at my desk and played my 1-800-MILA-GRO tape again. I listened to option four a few more times, the branch of the phone tree which explained the nature of the upcoming miracle.

There was no ambiguity at all on the message. At 5:30 A.M. on October 10, 1999, the statue of the *Virgen de la Caridad*, at the shrine erected in her honor in the *Ermita de la Caridad* in Coconut Grove, would shed real tears. She would cry for a full minute to demonstrate her deep sadness over the split between her flock in Cuba and the exile community in Miami. I couldn't help but conclude that the Virgin wanted the new millennium to begin with the Cuban people united.

I couldn't believe the message was so specific. Again I had to shudder at the thought of what would happen as soon as the news media got hold of the story. It had religion, politics, and a millennial angle. Already the news was full of stories pertaining to the passage into the twenty-first century: the Y2K computer problem, the uncertainty and fear among religious and secular people alike. This story would take off and probably catch on on an international scale.

I realized with a sinking feeling in my stomach that if the miracle was exposed as a fraud, the news would be broadcast to the four corners of the Earth—not an encouraging prospect. The Catholic Church would be ridiculed. Then there could be a backlash against the Virgin's supposed message. Some might take the hoax as proof that Cubans would never be reunified, that all hope was lost. I could feel the pressure mounting on my shoulders as I listened again to the familiar voice on the recording. I could feel the stakes getting higher with every hour that passed.

This forty-second recording had touched on just about every single issue near and dear to Cuban islanders and exiles alike: the Virgin, the shrine of the *Ermita de la Caridad*, the separation of our people, and our shared history. It was all wrapped in tears which, I thought, neatly symbolized the water that pervades our consciousness. Whoever conceived of the miracle—whether it was the Virgin or an earthly trickster—knew how to get the attention of every living Cuban.

But why now? I was Catholic enough to still feel strange about questioning an ostensible miracle, but I was still an investigator who had been hired to do so. Why a miracle directed at the Cuban population forty years after the revolution? Perhaps it had to do with the pope's visit to the island in January of 1998; maybe some forces had been unleashed by that historic event that only now were coming to fruition.

I also knew there was another basic question that needed to be answered in every investigation. Who stood to profit?

I sat back and let my attention wander to the parrots outside my window. They were building so many new chambers onto their giant nests that it looked like they were planning to start renting space to other birds, tenement-style.

I closed my eyes and let my mind work on its own. The Virgin of Our Lady of Charity was the patron saint of Cuba. Every Cuban schoolchild learned of how the statue of the Virgin floated toward the three fishermen in the early 1600s after a roaring storm off the coast of the island. It had been miraculously dry, and a small tablet had been attached to her proclaiming her to be Our Lady of Charity. No one knew the origin of the statue, but everyone agreed her appearance to the storm-wracked fishermen was miraculous.

There had to be more, but I couldn't remember it. I should have paid more attention in school. Mami, of course, would have been able to tell me the story in great detail, as she had always been intensely interested in religious matters. All I knew was that the symbolism associated with the diminutive statue was overwhelming to Cubans. Representing Cuba itself, she was full of power and magic.

I heard noises from the outer office so I got up, happy that Leonardo had finally arrived. I certainly could use his company, not to mention an injection of the industrial-strength coffee I could hear him preparing in the kitchen. For all his health-food fanaticism Leonardo couldn't live without Cuban coffee—like the rest of us, he had started drinking it soon after being weaned from his mother's milk.

I found Leonardo in the kitchen, totally engrossed in measuring out the perfect portion of coffee to put in the basket of our espresso maker. Today's outfit was a pair of paisley bicycle shorts in varying shades of green topped by an emerald Lurex muscle shirt. He must have felt particularly close to nature that morning, because he also wore green Converse All-Star high-tops on his sockless feet. I hated to think what kind of outfit Leonardo might choose if he adopted an office policy of dress-down Fridays.

"Buenos días!" I called out as soon as I was sure Leonardo had got the coffee going.

"Oh my God, Lupe!" Leonardo said, grabbing his chest. "Don't ever sneak up on me like that again. You almost gave me a stroke."

He started fanning himself with that morning's *Herald* to demonstrate the extent of his distress. I apologized and kissed him on the cheek, then walked over to the stove and breathed deep the aroma of brewing coffee.

Leonardo crossed his arms and leaned against the wall. "So, is Marisol speaking to you yet?"

I had hoped to forget the previous day's fiasco. "I haven't seen her since we split up in Homestead, after I took her there to pick up her car."

"You really fucked that one up," Leonardo said.

I stared at him. He seemed to want to gloat over my mistake—I certainly had given him a hard time in the past about his—but my withering stare notified him that I wasn't in the mood for games that morning. Leo shrugged and continued fanning himself.

"Tell me what you know about Our Lady of Charity," I said to change the subject. "What does she mean to you?"

Leonardo went to the counter and started whipping the milk into a froth for our coffees. "The Virgin?" he asked. "Well, I don't know. She's a symbol of everything Cuban."

"But what about for you?" I asked.

He looked up from the mugs of milk. "There's no way to describe what the Virgin means to me," he said, very serious. "She's been a part of my life since I was a child. You know, Lupe, it's the same for all us Cubans, isn't it?"

I nodded in agreement. Listening to New Age Leonardo speak this way only reinforced what I had already figured out—that whoever engineered the upcoming miracle knew Cubans very well.

Leonardo and I settled down onto the couch in the reception area with our mugs of coffee. Neither of us spoke. It was a little unusual for Leonardo not to ramble on about the miracle, I realized; he typically loved to provide a commentary on all matters spiritual and metaphysical. Probably, I thought, he felt the same as I did about this one: it was too heavy, too rich with meaning.

A fleeting thought crossed my mind. What if it were real?

An instant later we both heard a strange grunting noise coming from the driveway outside the cottage. Leonardo and I looked at each other with alarm. Whatever had made that noise sounded like it was in trouble. Although our office had been incident-free since we moved into the Grove, there was no point being naive. There were a lot of weirdos out there.

I ran into my office and took the Beretta out of my purse, checked to make sure it was loaded. I came back into the reception area and found Leonardo looking scared to death on the sofa. We could still hear the groaning outside, coming closer to our door, followed by a scraping sound. Leonardo's face was turning a shade of green suitable for matching his outfit.

I clicked the safety off the gun and walked quietly to the front door. My heart beat so loudly I feared that whoever was outside would be able to hear it. I felt a little foolish to be taking a gun to the door like that, but a strong feeling of paranoia had gripped me. Leonardo looked as if he was about to pass out when we heard the groaning again, guttural and loud, right outside the cottage.

Holding my breath, I gritted my teeth and, on the count of three, flung the door open. I pointed the gun out, my finger on the trigger, the weapon chest-high.

On the driveway, cool as a cucumber, crouched a familiar figure. There was a white fiberglass cooler at her feet, trailed by skid marks all along the driveway left from her dragging it.

"Oh, put that thing down," Marisol said. "Come out here and get yourself a hot dog. They're great for breakfast."

"Are you crazy?" I shouted, starting to laugh from relief. "I could have shot you!"

Marisol, seeming totally unimpressed, continued pushing the cooler toward the cottage. She grunted as she did so, making a sound that I couldn't believe had come from her svelte frame. I had to fight off the urge to open fire on the cooler. I was pumped and ready to shoot *something*—why not a cooler full of wieners?

Marisol flipped open the lid and proudly displayed rows and rows of neatly stacked hot dogs. There must have been a hundred of them.

"I went back yesterday to return the cart," she explained. "The guy said these were already paid for, and he wasn't going to take them back. So I thought I might as well keep them."

I had almost shot my friend and investigator over a cooler full of hot dogs. Maybe this was what I got for meddling in church business.

Marisol looked up, as though reading my mind. "Well, they're paid for," she said. "Didn't they teach us in Catholic school that it's wrong to waste food?"

I could only nod. Leonardo brushed past me, clumsily staggering out onto the porch and down the stairs. He looked at Marisol as though trying to comprehend what had just happened. His hands shook, and his face had gone from green to pasty white.

"Hey, Leo, are you all right?"

His foot bumped into the cooler and he looked down.

"You don't look so good," Marisol said, alarmed. "Maybe you should go sit down on the grass or something."

The sight of so many hot dogs was too much for his delicate sensibilities. Leonardo grabbed his stomach and, with a loud retch, threw up all over the wieners.

Just another sign from above, I thought, telling us not to mess with the order of the universe.

13

MARISOL had just made herself comfortable on the sofa in my office with a mug of *café con leche* when Leonardo came on the intercom to tell me I had a phone call.

"It's a man," my cousin said. "But he won't identify himself."

Leonardo still sounded embarrassed and sheepish; he had been mortified over having thrown up on a case of hot dogs. Marisol and I had, of course, reassured him and told him we still loved and respected him even though he had totally humiliated himself right in front of us.

I picked up the phone. "Detective lady," declared a soft voice with a Jamaican accent.

"Theofilus," I said. "It's good to hear from you."

I felt my heart quicken. The gardener and I had made an agreement that our contact should be kept to a minimum, that he should call me only when he had something to report. He claimed not to have a phone, so I was at his mercy whenever he decided to reach me. He had already been to see Tommy, who was looking into his case.

"Something unusual happened yesterday at the convent," Theofilus said. "I don't know if this helps you. But you said to call if I heard or saw anything out of the ordinary."

I suppressed a smile at Theofilus's delicate use of the word "unusual." It reminded me of a case I had worked a few years before with Tommy. Our client had been accused of killing three men with an Uzi in a late-night shoot-out inside a bar in a seedy part of Miami. The bar had been the sight of many violent confrontations over the years, and more than a few deaths. I remembered the prosecutor in court asking the bouncer if he remembered anything unusual happening in the bar that night. The bouncer—huge, tattooed, his head shaved—had shook his head: no, nothing unusual had happened that night.

The prosecutor had been clearly frustrated. His main witness wasn't testifying the way he'd expected. So he asked the question a couple of different ways, careful not to lead the bouncer's testimony. Finally the prosecutor lost it. Just out of law school, he probably saw his failure to get a conviction on this triple homicide following him around throughout the rest of his legal career.

The prosecutor bellowed out, "Do you mean to tell me that you saw nothing unusual in the murder of three men taking place right before your eyes?"

"Yes, I saw three men murdered that night," the bouncer had replied. "But there's really nothing unusual about that. Give me a break. You saw where I work."

After that case, I had revised my definition of the word "unusual." As an investigator, I always had to keep in mind the weird environment in which strange things tended to happen.

"What's up, Theofilus?" I asked. I pressed the button for the speakerphone so that Marisol could listen in.

"It was yesterday afternoon," Theofilus began in a slow, dreamy voice. I hoped that the Jamaican gold wasn't clouding his recollection. "One of the nuns here got in a big fight with the sister superior. A big fight, lady! Loud screaming, yelling. Then the nun left the place with a suitcase. I think she got kicked out."

Well, this did qualify as unusual. "Which nun was it?"

"How would I know?" Theofilus asked with a stoned chuckle. "I'm not supposed to get close to any of them, I can't tell them apart. They all look the same to me."

"What was the fight about?" I wasn't very well versed in religious protocol, but I didn't imagine that screaming fights and evictions were everyday occurrences.

"I don't know, man." Theofilus was speaking so softly that I had to turn up the volume on the phone. "I just heard the voices. Screaming women. Yelling in Spanish."

Spanish? I thought they were Yugoslavian nuns.

"How did the nun leave the convent?" I asked. "Did she walk out? Did someone call a taxi for her?"

A moment of silence. "No, she left in a car. Someone came and picked her up."

"Who was it?" I asked, holding my breath.

"Some man," Theofilus replied. "Driving a silver car, a big American car. I don't know much more. I'm not a detective."

I told myself to be careful. A sullen, resentful tone was creeping into the edge of Theofilus's voice. I couldn't afford to alienate him.

"Do you remember what time it was?" I asked gently.

"I leave at four o'clock," he said. "She left before me. Not too much before." A sigh. "Sorry, lady, I can't help you more than that."

"Don't be sorry, this is helping me," I told him. I wanted to make sure he understood his call hadn't been wasted; otherwise he might never call me again. "Thank you for telling me this. You did exactly the right thing."

"Mr. McDonald, the lawyer, he's helping me with my case," Theofilus added. "I think I'm going to be all right now. I thank you."

With that, the gardener hung up. I switched off the phone and looked up at Marisol.

"What do you think?" I asked.

"I can't imagine nuns fighting unless it was really serious," she replied. "Nuns don't get into screaming hissy fits over religious dogma, do they?"

"I can't imagine."

"Do you think the debate over Adam and Eve would cause that kind of reaction?" she asked with a wicked gleam. "Maybe we should ask Lourdes. She'd know what nuns fight about."

I could see that Marisol would be a Catholic schoolgirl inside until the day she died. The thrill of her little half-assed joke at the expense of nuns had made her face light up with mischievous pleasure.

"Theofilus said something important," I told her. "That the nun left before he quit working at four."

I took out my logbook for the case and flipped it to yesterday's entries. "Four o'clock," I read aloud. "Marisol called from jail. What time exactly did you leave your post?"

Marisol took out her own logbook. "By my 'post' I assume you mean my hot-dog stand," she said dryly. "And I didn't 'leave' it, I was dragged away from it kicking and screaming."

"Sorry."

"Well, all right," she said, looking in her log. "Three-oh-eight
P.M. Arrested. Off to jail. Closing time."

"*Mierda*." I pounded softly on my desk. "That means you
wouldn't have been able to get the tag number for the car that
came to pick up the nun."

"Hey, Lupe, *calmate*. Remember I told you I rigged something
up?"

I knew that if Marisol was being this mellow, she must have
something good to show me. She sipped at her coffee, savoring the
moment. In another minute I was going to pour it down her throat
if it made her reveal her secret any faster.

Marisol reached into her bag and took out a videocassette. She
tossed it onto my desk, where it slid across the slick wood surface.
I barely caught it in my hands before it shot into my lap.

"What's this?" I asked.

Marisol smiled demurely as she wiped her blood-red lips with a
napkin Leonardo had provided.

"Picture this," she said. "Yesterday I was standing practically
naked on that highway in west Bumfuck. I had a lot of time on my
hands. So I had an idea. I took out my video camera and rigged it
under the umbrella of the hot-dog cart—aiming it toward the convent, so it would film any vehicle entering or leaving the convent.
In case I might find myself busy attending to customers when I
needed to be taking down a tag number."

She smiled like a cat.

"So you're sure you have the car that picked up the nun on this
tape?" I asked. I could have kissed her. No wonder I was always
willing to overpay for her services. She was worth it—even if I had
to put up with her infuriating ways.

Marisol shrugged. "Beats me," she said. "Should be there."

Leonardo burst into the office clutching a few papers. "The tag
numbers you asked me to run just came back," he said. "I had
them expedited."

Thank God Leonardo was already bouncing back and becoming
his old self. Between him and Marisol, my faith in humanity was
returning. I decided to give him a break and wait until later to tell
him to hose out the cooler that was still sitting in our driveway.

14

"IS that a six or an eight?" I asked Marisol, squinting to read the tag number on the light gray Buick in the center of the television screen.

Marisol froze the frame and rewound it to the point at which the car was turning into the driveway leading to the convent. She took out the magnifying glass in my desk drawer and put her face with it up to the screen.

"Six," she said.

I jotted down the number. "Ready for the next one," I said.

We were well into our second hour of examining the surveillance-camera videotape, and it showed. Our eyes were red and bleary from focusing on the TV screen. So far we had gotten eight tag numbers, but it had been meticulous, painstaking work.

Marisol had rigged the camera from the aluminum bars that anchored the red-striped umbrella to the hot-dog cart, trying to capture as wide a view of the convent entrance as possible. We had hoped the tape would show the faces of people going in and out of the convent, but we had had to settle for the number of passengers in the vehicles and, in a few cases, their gender. But the tag numbers had come through perfectly, and we would be able to trace the automobiles' owners. I cursed the fact that there had been so many visitors to the convent; perhaps there was a lot of work to be done inside because the order was new to the area. My attention was focused on the silver Buick, the one Theofilus said had taken away the screaming nun.

The tape quality was pretty good, and we had been able to write down the tag numbers with reasonable accuracy. A few times, though, circumstances had arisen that were out of our control—

specifically, vapor from the hot dogs had covered the lens with a sporadic film. But it had been so hot out there that the vapor disappeared within a few seconds.

As soon as we were finished we rewound the tape and went through the whole, tedious exercise again from scratch. We treated the second viewing as though it were the first, writing down the numbers without referring to our first set of notes. There had been a total of sixteen visitors to the convent during the time Marisol had been able to conduct her surveillance.

We might have been tempted to take shortcuts, but that would have amounted to professional malpractice. It was too easy to screw up, and investigations stood up or fell on the amount of attention paid to little details. Invariably it was the sum total of all the little nuggets of seemingly innocuous information that would eventually allow the investigator to see the bigger picture. Identifying which ones might lead somewhere was simply a matter of experience and patience.

Soon after we opened Solano Investigations, years ago, Leonardo had been frustrated with my lack of patience. He decided that he would be the one to do something about it, so he recommended a yoga class taught in the Grove. He was convinced it would teach me patience, how to be calm, how to let events develop in their own time. And the class he selected for me was taught by one of the most respected local teachers of that form of physical and mental discipline. In other words, I was all set.

Leonardo never said so, but I knew that he'd had to pull some strings to get me admitted into the class. I heard via the touchy-feely underground that I had jumped from number three-hundred-and-something on the waiting list to being accepted in a matter of days. As a result, expectations were high.

It scarcely needs to be said that I was a complete failure. I remember my shock when I walked in the first night and got a look at my fellow pupils. Never had I seen a room full of such serenity and calm. It made me jumpy. I started to wonder what kind of drugs they were on. They looked like they had never even heard of Cuban coffee—and I had consumed my customary seven or eight cups of it already that day.

Cool, smooth, calming thoughts were supposed to begin washing over me. Instead, I kept wishing the teacher would get to the point of the class and start the aerobics. I thought I was going to get to sweat, to burn calories, to get my heart rate going.

I didn't say anything during class, and I tried to follow everything the teacher was saying and doing. But word was discreetly passed on to Leonardo that I wasn't invited to return the following week. I had been on my best behavior, but my teacher had obviously picked up on the fact that I generally worked on one gear only: overdrive. Maybe he didn't want me contaminating the rest of the class with my fast-forward vibes.

So I had failed at yoga.

But in my professional life I had trained myself to be patient when I needed to be. It was essential for succeeding in my field. After all, a hyper, jumpy person couldn't possibly sit in a car on surveillance for hours and hours. I could. Maybe it drove me half-crazy, but I was able to do it.

When we had finished going through the tape a second time Marisol and I compared our notes. They were identical. This convinced us that there was no need to watch it a third time.

Our job was finished for the moment because of the relative paucity of our information. All that was left was to give the tag numbers to Leonardo and wait for the list of the registered owners of the various vehicles. I knew that we finally had some solid information—and from this, other facts would follow. As soon as we had names and addresses, then Nestor could start running background checks. I just hoped we could do all this before Ted Koppel showed up at the convent with his crew to film a special millennial edition of *Nightline*.

15

I had put in a long enough day, and I decided to drive home to see the family. I missed them. If I was lucky, Fatima's twins would be home from school and their after-school activities. I would probably be able to talk them into getting into the pool with me. I had neglected the girls recently, not spending enough time with them. To be honest, they weren't the only ones I'd neglected. I really hadn't spent much time at all with my family lately.

I started the Mercedes and headed south, pleased with myself for hitting the road before the afternoon traffic got heavy. Instead of playing a CD I turned on the radio to *Radio Romántico*, one of the many Spanish-language FM stations on the air in Miami. It was one of my favorites, specializing in the sappiest, cheesiest songs ever recorded. The year before, after listening to *Radio Romántico* non-stop for a few days, I discerned that Mexican songs beat out all others in the realm of sappiness. The best example was a tune in which a young woman addressed her former lover: *I wore pure white at my wedding, even though I had been your mistress since I was fifteen years old. And now I'm thirty, and although you possessed my body you never possessed my soul.*

But my all-time favorite was by a group from Belize that, for some unfathomable reason, was played repeatedly every Valentine's Day: *I will love you forever, even though you had an intimate relationship with my brother, brother-in-law, stepbrother, and my cousin.*

I tuned in for the lyrics, but also to keep up with different nationalities' idioms and slang expressions. Today the station was starting a half-hour set of songs without commercials. I was able to relax and think about the case without distraction as I drove. I sang softly to a familiar song as I focused my mind.

I had checked into the religious aspects of the case, the nature of the Order of the Illumination, and the background of its nuns. But the political aspect of the case still nagged at me. Mother Superior had presented the case as strictly religious, a struggle between orders within the church, but there was more. Everything that related to Cuba had a volatile political aspect. And whoever designed the upcoming miracle knew a lot about Cuba—whether they were atheists or devout believers. This was more than a simple miracle—if there had ever even been such a thing.

What I was dealing with here, under the surface, was the concept of Cuban reunification, the bringing together of those on the island and the exiles. Part of me regarded this idea as a great and wondrous thing. But I also knew that reality might be something different.

The reason for the Virgin's tears was her unhappiness over the divide between two parts of her Cuban flock. If the Virgin was sad, it was our job to make her happy. It followed that we Cubans were supposed to find a way to come together, to set aside our political and social differences. When the *Virgen de la Caridad del Cobre* cried, Cubans took notice.

But reunification was no simple thing. We weren't necessarily separated by choice. Many, many Cubans had fled the island because of Castro's repression, even though they would have given anything in order to stay. Of those who remained in Cuba, some wished to leave. Others supported Castro, for their own reasons. This divide would be hard to repair. There had been too much history for everyone to shake hands and come together.

On the one hand, Fidel Castro still stood in our way. But while he was loathed in Miami and feared in Cuba itself, there again were those who supported him. Perhaps not many, but they existed. That was a reality. And this line of thinking led me to other important questions for which I had no answers: what happens after Fidel? What sort of country will Cuba become? There was a lot of speculation and few definite facts. I prayed that Cuba would become truly reunified then. But it wasn't a given.

For a moment I considered whether the miracle of the Virgin might be directly aimed at Fidel. Was she saying, *I cry for Cubans, because they have suffered under Castro for so long?* It was part of it, surely, but I doubted that it was the only point. After all, wouldn't the miracle then take place in Havana, right in front of the tyrant himself? No, this was a Miami miracle, it was taking place in the heart of the exile community. This was a message to us, not to Castro.

Mother Superior didn't seem interested in these realities. And I had been expressly told not to contact her, so I couldn't talk these ideas over with her. It was frustrating. I had been hired to investigate, not to solve my country's political problems. And from Mother Superior's point of view, I was becoming increasingly convinced, my job was to debunk the miracle taking place under the hand of a convent that competed with her own. I was sure that if I exposed the miracle as a scam, Mother Superior would be able to step forward and take the credit. I was simply the agent through which her demands were met.

I turned up the radio and hummed along. I hadn't really been following politics much the past few years. Hell, I never really had. I opposed Castro like every other exile, and my every waking thought somehow always related back to Cuba, but the truth was that I had partied my way through college and had been pretty apolitical ever since. It was just my nature. I didn't like to fret too much over things I couldn't change.

Most of my knowledge came from listening to Papi and his cronies sitting together and bemoaning what had become of Cuba. I knew they represented the right-wing segment of Cuban-exile politics, beliefs that were becoming more and more outdated as time passed. Papi knew a lot of people who had stayed on the island, determined to live in their homeland even if it meant enduring Castro's regime. Every so often one of Papi's old friends would arrive from the island, finally acknowledging that life was unsustainable there. Papi would go to greet him, make the visitor feel welcome—and get the most current, up-to-date, firsthand information on what was going on in Cuba.

The worst days were when one of Papi's friends would die here in Miami. Papi would go to the funeral home, offer his condolences to the widow. He would become depressed that his friend had died without seeing his beloved Cuba one final time. The widow would inevitably reply that her husband was being buried in Miami only temporarily, that as soon as possible the bones would be disinterred and taken back to Havana for a proper burial in the family crypt in the *Cementerio Colon.*

Sometimes Papi would receive word that one of his friends who had stayed behind had died in Cuba. It would take time for the news to reach Miami, sometimes weeks or months after the death. Papi would mope around, shaking his head at the unfairness of fate that had denied him the opportunity to say good-bye to an old friend. As time passed, these things were happening with more and more frequency. Papi's generation was getting old. The Cuban people had been divided for a long forty years, separated by ninety miles of water but a million miles emotionally.

I remembered a few roller-coaster rides in my own time. Such as the collapse of the Soviet Union and the liberation of the Iron Curtain countries, the fall of the Sandinistas in Nicaragua. Everyone assumed that Cuba would be the next to usher in democracy. No one believed that Castro could hold out forever against the sweeping changes that were altering the political landscape of the rest of the world. But hold out he did.

Papi and I had sat together in front of the television the day the Berlin Wall came down, laughing like children. FOR SALE signs appeared all over Miami, homeowners preparing for their long-awaited return home. At our house, Papi sent Osvaldo out to stock the *Concepción* for our triumphant entry into Havana Harbor as soon as Castro fell—or, better still, was killed like the corrupt leadership of Romania.

We prayed. We knelt. But the situation in Cuba did not change. Freedom did not come to Cuba. Our country continued to be enslaved by a megalomaniac dictator determined to keep his power even if it meant running the country into the ground. It had been heartbreaking, like lying in the desert dying of thirst, watching clouds rain down water everywhere except where we were. Castro survived one prediction of doom after another, becoming weakened each time but still holding onto power.

Finally the harsh realization had sunk in, that Cuba wasn't going the way of other countries. The yoke of Communism wasn't going to be lifted. Papi gave in to Osvaldo's entreaties that he cease running the *Concepción*'s engines hourly, and that he allow Mami's ashes to be brought back into the house for a brief visit to reinforce the fact that she wasn't returning to her homeland. It had been a sad day in the Solano household, the sky dark and cloudy, our wishes postponed again.

When I pulled up to the house that most Cuban of songs, "Guantanamera," was playing on the radio. I tried not to take it as some kind of omen. I drove past Osvaldo watering the impatiens by the front gate. He approached me as I got out of the car, then took the keys and slid into the driver's seat with the agility of a man forty years younger.

"*Ay*, Lupe. Please don't park under the poinciana tree in your office driveway," he said, shaking his head. "You're ruining the paint."

We had this conversation weekly, whether or not the poinciana was even in bloom. "Sorry, Osvaldo," I said.

"You don't take care of this beautiful car," he scolded. "It's a disgrace, Lupe."

"I'm so sorry, Osvaldo," I recited. "I promise I won't do it again."

I had made the same pledge for the past seven years. There was no other place for me to park at the office, and we both knew it. Just before he closed the car door I impulsively leaned over and kissed his cheek. I didn't care if he nagged me like a mother hen. He blushed with pleasure, and I immediately felt guilty that I didn't spend more time with him and Aida. They were like a second set of parents to me, and they loved my sisters and me like the children they never had.

I stuck my head into the kitchen, intending to pour myself a soda and get the family news from Aida. I found her listening intently to the radio—a Cuban station, of course, but not *Radio Romántico*. Aida preferred Cuban talk radio, the infamous AM station that analyzed the happenings on the island and in Miami in the same fashion that scientists looked at bacteria under a microscope. Aida was tuned into the most right-wing program, one that, in my opinion, professed politics just to the right of Attila the Hun.

I had only listened to that station—*la Cubaninity*—on a few occasions, and I had generally been appalled by what I had heard. All they did, in my opinion, was agitate the exile community and foster divisions among us. Anyone willing to even entertain a different point of view than that of the talk-show host was quickly pilloried as a Castro-lover and a Communist. The hosts talked a lot, and they were known to actively encourage listeners to take matters into their own hands. I had heard rumors that they were associated with violence—such as bombing local Cuban establishments that didn't agree with their politics. Nothing had been proven, but the finger of suspicion had been pointed at them.

"Lupe! *Hola!*" Aida saw me standing in the doorway, listening to what was being said on the radio. "Can I get you something? I just made *merengues*, your mami's favorite, you remember. I'm going to serve them for dessert tonight, with mango ice cream. But you can have some if you want."

"You're sure?"

Aida put a finger to her lips. "Don't say anything to the twins. I told them the *merengues* had to cool yet."

"Maybe one," I said, unable to resist a special treat. I picked up one of the beautiful, fluffy sweets made of sugar and egg whites, popped it in my mouth.

Aida knew me well. If she said Mami had liked something, I would always fall for it. She watched me chew the treat, her light brown face lined with old age and beaming with pride.

"Your friend Alvarito, he's in big trouble," she said then, pointing to the radio. "I'm listening to *la Cubaninity*. They're saying some really bad things about him. He'd better watch himself."

"What are you talking about?" I asked, trying not to spew out bits of flaky pastry.

"Your friend, Alvarito Mendoza," Aida explained. "You remember. He was your boyfriend for about fifteen minutes. Until you dropped him."

Aida had noted the relish with which I had inhaled the first *merengue;* she started scraping another from the baking dish to give to me.

"Oh, right," I said. Now I remembered Alvaro Mendoza. I had accepted an invitation years ago to go to his cousin's *quince* party, thinking that a guy I had a crush on might be there. I had planned to go with Alvaro until the real object of my affection called up and asked me to go with him instead—naturally, I accepted and planned to break the date with Alvaro. It had not been one of my finest and most uplifting hours, especially when Fatima told Mami what I had done. My despicable behavior had landed me a grounding for the night.

My subsequent reputation was naturally mud in the Mendoza

household, although I wondered what would have happened between me and my crush had I been allowed to go to the party. As for Alvaro Mendoza, I had never given him much thought. I doubted he thought of me much either, though for a little while he had written me poetry and slipped it under the front door in the morning before school.

"You haven't been in touch with Alvaro, have you?" Aida asked, handing me my second *merengue*.

"Not really," I said. "I heard he became a lawyer. But he practices immigration law, so I've never worked with him. Most of the lawyers I deal with are criminal attorneys."

I stuffed the pastry into my mouth. It was so sweet it made my teeth sting, reminding me that I was overdue for a checkup. I worried that I had Grand Canyon–sized craters in my mouth. I knew I should take better care of myself, but I had developed a laissez-faire attitude since the time I was shot at. Why, I thought, should I waste time and energy, inflicting pain on myself to be good, when I could be wiped out with a single squeeze of a trigger? It was a rationalization, perhaps, and a grim one, but I stuck to it.

Aida walked toward the windowsill and turned up the radio. "Listen," she said.

". . . that worm, that good-for-nothing lawyer Alvaro Mendoza. That traitor to the Cuban exile movement, how can he walk the streets of Miami knowing what he has done? Where is this man's conscience? Is it lying at the bottom of the Florida Straits, along with all the Cuban babies he's helped murder? Is it in the stomach of the sharks that ate his countrymen when they tried to escape the tyrant Castro?"

The woman talk-show host's voice turned even more shrill.

"He should not be allowed to live in Miami! He should be sent back to Cuba! Now! So he can be with his best friend Fidel Castro, his soul mate for all time!"

I couldn't believe what I was hearing. "Aida, what did Alvaro do? Did he kill someone?"

"He might as well have," Aida replied somberly. She put down her pastry cutter and looked at me. "Your old friend Alvaro Mendoza has agreed to represent *el Chacal Rojo* in his application for political exile in the United States."

El Chacal Rojo. Of course I knew who that was—the Red Jackal,

Castro's enforcer. He was infamous in Miami, a known murderer and torturer. No wonder the talk-show host was so agitated. Representing him was like defending Mengele.

"I can't believe it," I said. "Alvaro is representing that scum?"

Aida leaned over conspiratorially. "I heard Alvaro speak on the radio a few minutes ago," she explained. "He said that the Constitution of the United States entitles everyone to a legal defense. People are presumed innocent until proven guilty. That's what Alvarito said before they cut him off."

"Well, Aida, he's right," I said. "Those are the things that separate us from the regime in Cuba."

Aida shook her head, looking up to the heavens. I wanted to convince her of this basic point.

"We came to this country for freedom," I said. "Alvaro is free in America to represent *el Chacal Rojo*. Everyone, no matter how despicable, is entitled to a fair chance in court."

Aida waved her hands at me. I knew it was hopeless, so I opened the refrigerator and poured myself a glass of freshly squeezed lemonade from the pitcher I saw on the top shelf.

"Who's home?" I asked, knowing she would want to change the subject.

"Fatima and the twins," Aida said. "They are supposed to be doing their homework, but your sister is upstairs taking a nap and I heard the sound of those computer games."

"*Gracias,*" I said. I turned to leave. "And thank you for the *merengues*. They were delicious."

"Listen, Lupe. That friend of yours, Alvaro. If you see him, you tell him he's going to get in trouble if he keeps mixing with Cubans from the island." Aida focused her piercing black eyes on mine.

"You know, it's not for me to—"

"On the radio they said that nothing goes on in Cuba that Alvaro Mendoza does not know about!" Aida said, exhaling loudly. "They say he has his finger on the pulse of Cuba. He lives here, a fancy lawyer in a big house. But his heart and soul are really in his native home. And something bad is going to happen to him if he keeps mixing with the wrong Cubans!"

Satisfied that she'd made her point, Aida turned up the volume on the radio. The host was railing on another subject, having forgotten Alvaro for the moment. Aida's tone sent shivers down my spine.

I didn't know why she was so adamant with me about Alvaro. I hadn't seen the man since high school, and I'd essentially forgotten that he existed.

As I walked upstairs to see the girls, I tried to remember what Alvaro was like. I stopped in my room, placed my lemonade glass on my bedside table, and pulled out my old high-school yearbook from the bookshelf. I looked up Alvaro's senior class picture. Why, I thought, hadn't I noticed the intelligent expression in his eyes when I was in school with him?

I lay back on the bed and thought about my conversation with Aida. What had she said about Alvaro, that nothing happened in Cuba without his knowing about it? Interesting, especially in terms of the case I was working. If I wanted to find out more about the miracle and about Cuban life, it seemed that I had found someone new to speak with. For starters, I could find out if word of the miracle had filtered to the island. The only problem was whether Alvaro would agree to speak with me. Some men have long memories, and I had behaved terribly toward him.

I took out a telephone directory from the drawer of my nightstand and flipped through the yellow pages to the "Attorneys" section. He was listed right there: Alvaro B. Mendoza. His office was on Twenty-Seventh Avenue in the Grove, not far from my office.

I punched in the number and listened to the ringing line. Alvaro, after all these years, had fallen right back into my lap. I had to wonder whether it was an omen.

"Alvaro Mendoza, please," I said to the receptionist. "Tell him it's an old friend calling."

16

NOW this was something new. Lupe Solano having butterflies in her stomach at the prospect of meeting with a man. Normally I was a poster child for control, especially where men were concerned. Yet I felt anxious and apprehensive seated at one of the tables by the back wall at the News Cafe in Coconut Grove, waiting for Alvaro Mendoza to join me.

I looked over the wine list, wondering whether I should order a bottle. I was the hostess, after all; I could order early without seeming like a freeloader.

Yesterday when I'd phoned Alvaro's office, I thought that someone of his notoriety might be hard to reach. But after I gave my name to his receptionist, he got on the line in a matter of seconds.

"Lupe!" he said in a deep, resonant voice. "Imagine hearing from you after all these years!"

This clearly was not a man who harbored grudges. He asked about my family, expressed his sadness over hearing about Mami's death. I warmed to him instantly, and we exchanged pleasantries for a few minutes longer. Alvaro, to his credit, was savvy enough not to ask the real reason why I'd called him. After a while I figured I'd better initiate things.

"Alvaro, listen," I said. "Would you be free for lunch sometime this week?" I thought about asking him to dinner, but that might seem too compromising. I knew nothing at all about his personal life. "I could use your expertise on a case I'm working, if you don't mind."

"Would I mind meeting to help you with a case?" Alvaro asked, as though such a question were completely absurd. I heard him rustling around, probably looking through his daily planner. "How about tomorrow? Will you be free then?"

"Perfect!" I said. "What time and where? Whatever you say is fine."

Alvaro chuckled. "Well, I hope you don't have your heart set on Cuban food. I would hate to disappoint you, Lupe."

"No, not really," I replied. "Why, don't you like Cuban food?"

"It's not that," Alvaro said quickly. "I love Cuban food. It's just that it's not safe right now for me to go into Little Havana."

I thought about Aida and her radio show. It was no surprise that Alvaro feared for his safety, after the inflammatory rhetoric of the radio host. I suggested the News Cafe.

"That's far enough from Little Havana," Alvaro said, laughing softly again in a way that seemed both warm and self-deprecating.

I looked at my watch and forced myself to snap back to the present. Alvaro would be here in five minutes or so. I thought about going to the ladies' room to apply more concealer under my eyes. I guess I had to admit to myself that I wanted to look my best for my old teenage admirer.

I signaled the waiter and ordered a bottle of Cabernet Sauvignon, something not too cheap and not too expensive. I didn't know if Alvaro drank at lunchtime, but I figured a man with a price on his head would want to take advantage of his every moment. A glass of wine with his meal, after all, could turn out to be his last.

I had just finished approving the wine and watching the waiter fill my glass when a tall, dark man entered the restaurant. He was silhouetted against the light outside, so I couldn't see his features, but I was sure he was Alvaro. I sat quietly, waiting for him to recognize me first.

He walked through the place. The fifteen years since I had seen Alvaro had been very kind to him. More than kind. Actually, he was breathtaking. He reminded me of the old Cuban saying, that he was good-looking enough to take away my hiccups.

"Lupe!" Alvaro called out. He rushed over and kissed me on both cheeks, European-style, and hugged me. I got a whiff of his woodsy cologne, wished he'd pull me even closer.

"You are even more beautiful than I remembered," Alvaro said in Spanish, holding me at arm's length and looking at me.

I couldn't believe I'd treated him in such a shitty manner in high school. No doubt about it, the frogs of yesterday sometimes turned into the princes of tomorrow. Alvaro's big brown eyes locked on mine with an expression of pleasure. I fidgeted slightly at the intensity of his gaze, realizing that I wouldn't have known him if I'd seen him on the street. The gawky teenage boy I remembered had turned into a hunk. He had grown a full foot, now standing at least six-three. His hair was longish, spilling in waves over his shirt collar. He was dressed in Miami's unofficial version of business wear for self-employed professionals—a dark sports coat, khakis, a light blue shirt, no tie, and leather boat shoes.

Alvaro smiled at me then looked around the room. "Do you mind if we move to that corner?" He indicated a table where we could sit side-by-side looking out over the room. Not waiting for an answer, he motioned to the waiter that we were moving. Alvaro whisked the wine and glasses to the other table, leaving the waiter to bring the rest.

"It's really nice to see you after all this time," I said to Alvaro when we were settled in. Since he had spoken in Spanish, I continued the conversation in that language. My Spanish was fluent but rusty. I hoped I could keep up with him.

"It is, isn't it?" Alvaro looked all around the restaurant, as though expecting someone. He caught himself, and focused his attention on me. "Sorry I made us move. It's just that I've gotten under the skin of some people who feel I don't deserve to breathe the same air as them. I'm not paranoid, at least I don't think so. Just careful."

Alvaro examined the wine-bottle label with approval and poured some into both our glasses. We toasted.

"You know who Doc Holliday was, with the Earp brothers in the Old West—Wyatt, Virgil, and Morgan?" he asked. I must have looked blank. "He was a doctor friend of the Earp brothers when they were lawmen. He was a gambler, and he said never to sit with your back to the door if you want to enjoy a long life."

"How old was Doc Holliday when he died?" I asked.

"Young." Alvaro's expression darkened, then he laughed. "But he didn't get shot. He died in bed of TB."

It was surreal. Alvaro Mendoza, a classmate of mine from fifteen years ago, was sitting here sipping wine and comparing himself to a gambler from the Old West.

"You must be wondering why I called you out of the blue," I

said, a little tentative. "It has to do with a case, like I explained. I'd like to tell you a bit about it, if I can be assured of your total discretion."

He was cool, I had to give him that. He gave no sign that he might have expected a more personal reason for our meeting. He raised his right hand as though taking an oath.

"I swear that nothing I learn from Guadalupe Solano's lips will ever come out of my own." He tipped his wineglass to me and took a long drink.

God. I wished Alvaro hadn't mentioned my lips like that. Putting his lips and mine in the same sentence sent a rush of erotic thoughts to my brain—not exactly fostering the professional attitude I wished to convey. Our waiter must have picked up on something between us, because he moved away, apparently giving up on taking our orders anytime soon.

I thanked Alvaro and told him the history of the case—including my suspicions and foreboding about my responsibility for its out-come. I stopped only to give my lunch order—a mushroom omelet, runny. Alvaro ordered a rare cheeseburger. We also asked for an-other bottle of wine, because ours was running low.

I kept talking, going through my thoughts on the case. The food came and we both devoured our meals. I wasn't finished talking until the espressos arrived, and Alvaro had still offered no comment. Finally I was done, and I put my hands on the table.

"Well?" I said.

"It looks like you have your work cut out for you," he replied. "The fate of Cuba and the Catholic Church have been dropped in your lap. One question. Where do I fit in?"

"How do you think this apparition would impact Cuban politics—both on the island and among the exiles?" I shot back.

Alvaro looked down at the table. I noticed for the first time that he wasn't wearing a wedding band.

"That's a big question," he said quietly.

"You have a unique point of view," I said.

"You mean because I'm about as liberal as a Cuban can be in Miami without getting killed?" he asked, laughing. He pushed the espresso away and poured another glass of wine.

"I guess so," I said.

Alvaro frowned. "Lupe, how many true liberal exiles do you know in Miami?" he asked. "I mean real liberals—people who speak out about their views in public and take the heat for it? Not just registered Democrats who pull the Republican lever in the privacy of the voting booth because the candidate supports the Helms-Burton Act. I'm talking about people who get death threats, whose offices get picketed, who get tagged friends of Fidel Castro."

I listened to him, heard the depth of his feeling. "I guess I don't really know anyone like that," I admitted. For an instant, hearing Alvaro speak of the right-wing tone of Miami politics, I felt embarrassed about the fervor of my own family's beliefs.

"Do you know why people like me get ostracized?" he asked. "We are hated because we don't agree with the American hard-line policy on Cuba. It's as simple as that. Among the exiles there's no room for disagreement, no room for debate. Not only that, but we believe our fate should be in our own hands and not in the Americans'. They've meddled too long in exile politics as it is."

I knew he was right. Cuban history had been deeply affected by the Americans' belief that they had the right to determine Cuba's fate—from the Platt Amendment to the embargo.

Somehow over the decades a segment of Cuban exile community had become the mirror image of the Castro regime. Neither side allowed free thinking, free discourse. Both sides punished those who stepped out of line, both through social ostracism and physical violence.

"The policy hasn't worked, and it's been forty years," Alvaro added. Again I caught the smell of his cologne. "It's morally wrong. Starving a population through an embargo isn't going to get rid of Castro. All it's done is give Castro an enemy to focus on. And the United States has alienated the rest of the world in the process—all the other countries are trading with Cuba. The U.S. is the only one who insists on this ridiculous hard line. They continue to act as though they have a God-given right to determine Cuba's fate."

I had heard these arguments before, so nothing Alvaro was saying really surprised me. But I was excited by the passion of his thinking, even if I didn't entirely agree.

"So, you're considered a *dialoguero?*" I asked, referring to those exiles who favored dialogue with Castro rather than taking the hard line, who believed that a peaceful transition to democracy in Cuba could be achieved by working with the regime rather than overthrowing the Castro government through threats, sanctions, and violence.

"I don't really care for labels," Alvaro replied with a tight smile. "But yes, I guess I'm more in that camp than in a lot of others. But imagine, the fact that I favor talking over bombs has made me a pariah in my hometown, among my own people. That, and the fact that I advocate Cuba being the master of its own destiny, without continuing to rely on America."

"I'm sorry," I said quietly. And I was. It made me ashamed, when I remembered hearing Papi, Osvaldo, and Aida express their contempt for those who thought as Alvaro did. Alvaro's point of view sounded rational and sensible, now that I was removed from the inflamed passion of Little Havana. Who knew how I might have thought, if I had grown up in that hotbed of exile politics rather than the affluent seclusion of Cocoplum. Maybe I would have been among those calling for Alvaro's head.

But what if I had had family members who died under Castro's regime? I had no friends or relatives who had perished on a raft crossing the Florida Straits. I hadn't lost years of my life in a Havana jail for expressing my political beliefs.

Castro's coming into power had displaced my family, sending us into exile and causing us to lose everything we'd owned on the island. But none of us had died or been thrown in jail as a result. And all my family members were out of Cuba, we had no relatives who still lived on the island and suffered daily under repressive Communist rule. We didn't have to pack boxes of food and medicine to send back to Cuba so our loved ones could survive. My family enjoyed privileges few exiles could claim. Maybe this was why I had the luxury of entertaining the politics of a *dialoguero*.

I could understand the powerful emotions that compelled exiled Cubans to take their extreme positions, attacking those who were even suspected of dealing with the Castro government. But I had also always believed in the First Amendment of the U.S. Constitution, that people were guaranteed the freedom to speak their minds. That was the law in America, and that freedom made this society different from that on the island. I also knew, though, that those who opposed Castro most violently were of Papi's generation, those who had suffered directly under Castro. Time was passing, and they were starting to seem more and more as though they came from a different era.

I knew the depth of Papi's feelings, his total hatred for Castro. Perhaps his generation felt that, if they didn't oppose Castro to the death, then who would? Who would remind the world of the atrocities committed by the bearded man in green fatigues and his regime? Papi had said more than once, when talking to his friends, that it was up to them to keep the issue of Cuba alive. My generation, on the other hand, wasn't as closely tied to Cuba. A lot of us were marrying non-Cubans. Very, very few of us had ever been there at all—I had, once, albeit illegally and for a brief time in a rural area. Cuba might have been in our veins, but we had no reality on which to hang our convictions. The Cuba of old was seen through rose-colored lenses, creating the memory of a romantic, idealized existence.

"So what does a liberal like me think about your apparition?" Alvaro said, stroking his chin. "Well, according to what you're saying, the Virgin is going to cry because she's sad about the rift among her people. That seems pretty clear. She wants her Cuban flock to be reunited, right?"

"That's what I think," I said. "Although no one has come out and said it."

"This is going to be big when it's made public," Alvaro said, letting out a soft whistle as he thought about the ramifications. "And with this telephone hot line established, things are going to go down very soon for sure."

"Tell me about it," I replied. "Please explain further."

Alvaro sat in silence, thinking to himself. I had seen this before, with Tommy. I knew I was asking Alvaro to go against his legal training and offer an opinion without many facts.

"Is it good or bad for the Virgin to cry?" I asked. "Who would benefit and who would lose if the Cuban people were reunited as a result of this message?"

"Let me understand this," Alvaro said. "You want to know who would win and who would lose, if the two Cubas were brought together again?"

I nodded. "I guess that's the question."

"Well, as I see it, it all depends on the conditions of the reunification." Alvaro took a sip of wine. "Under whose mandate would it take place, and who would rule the new Cuba? It might be the exiles, with their money and their demands to take back the property that was confiscated from them. Or it could be the current regime, which would want to basically hold onto power and maintain some form of the status quo. And there's the issue of the regular people who have remained in Cuba, what their reaction would be to the returning exiles. After all, a lot of the people in Cuba are living in homes that were expropriated from the exiles. A lot of contention would spring up."

Alvaro sighed with weariness, as though he had thought through this scenario countless times.

"And we just don't know whether these different groups could get along," he added. "The Sacred Virgin might wish to see us together again, but could she make it go smoothly? There's a lot of hate and resentment between the two factions, the ones who stayed and the ones who got out."

The truth of what he was saying was deep and depressing to contemplate. I had always believed that, eventually, Castro would fall and our people would be reunited somehow. But listening to Alvaro, I realized how naive my viewpoint had been. There was so much anger, intolerance, and inflexibility—both on the part of the Communists and the exiles.

We had been at our table so long we were among the few customers left from lunch. I had drunk so much wine I needed to go to the ladies' room, but I didn't want to interrupt the mood.

"Think about this reunification under the current political climate—say, if it happened next month." Alvaro scooted his chair a little closer to mine and lowered his voice. "Think of what each group of Cubans would have to face. The Cubans who remained behind on the island might have to think about their lives under Castro and admit that he basically ruined their country. Then all their sacrifices and suffering would have been for nothing. Forty years down the drain. As for the exiles, they would have to admit that they abandoned their country. That they were returning to a country they were no longer a part of, a homeland that they surrendered to the enemy." Alvaro shook his head. "It's a tragedy from both sides," he whispered. "Wasted lives. Wasted time."

Alvaro had such a grasp of politics, such a humane point of view. He would have made a good politician, one of the few decent ones.

"Why are you so hated here?" I asked, hoping I wouldn't offend him. "I heard them talking about you on the radio, and it shocked me. Our own housekeeper was talking about you like you were a criminal."

Alvaro smiled. "Believe it or not, not all the exile groups hate my guts. Only the rabid right-wing ones. There are actually moderate-thinking exiles who listen to different points of view, and even a sprinkling or two of liberals. They just have a hard time being heard over the yelling and screaming of the fanatics."

I laughed softly. "I'm pleased to hear it," I said.

"I oppose many of the policies of Castro's government, too. They probably didn't mention that on the radio. But the minute you ask questions you're branded a Communist. That's when a few lunatics decide that shooting you would be the cure for all of our country's problems."

We had finished the wine, and another bottle wasn't in the plan. I sipped water instead.

"See, you can't be in the middle of the road in Miami," Alvaro continued. "Nothing is acceptable short of Castro's slow painful death. And if someone knocks me off, then they'll be a hero in some exile circles."

I started to speak, but could think of nothing to say. I couldn't imagine the stress Alvaro lived under every day.

"I can just hear the talk shows announcing my death," he said with a perverse laugh. "No one's going to fly their flags at half-staff in Dade County that day."

I almost told him to stop it, but I could see that saying these sorts of things was a way for him to vent steam.

"You know, the sad thing is," he added, "that no one will come forward to take credit for killing me. For all their rhetoric, they are cowards. They live under the protection of the First Amendment but I don't get the same rights. They can insult me, threaten me, but I'm not allowed to state my view or represent those who try."

"It's ironic," I said.

Alvaro slapped himself on the forehead. "Listen to me," he said. "I take a beautiful woman to lunch and all I can talk about are these depressing things. I hope you can forgive me."

"No, no, it's all right," I said. "I'm glad I had the chance to hear what you have to say."

Alvaro smiled at me, and I could see the implacable calm beneath his frustrations. At the core, I thought, he was someone who believed in what he was saying and derived strength from it.

A moment later my cellular phone rang. I jumped, knocking my knee on the underside of the table. I arched an eyebrow at Alvaro to ask him if he minded if I answered. He shrugged.

I looked at the caller-ID screen and saw that it was Leonardo phoning from the office.

"We just got faxed the vehicle-registration information from Marisol's surveillance tape," he said. "You told me to call as soon as it came in."

"Good work," I said. My heart started to beat harder. "Just give me the name and address for the silver Buick, would you?"

I fished in my purse for my small spiral notebook, then wrote down the information Leonardo recited from the report. I cursed under my breath when I realized how far away was the address from the News Cafe.

I glanced up; Alvaro was watching me with a bemused expression. I smiled back, trying to look apologetic for conducting business at the table.

"Thanks, Leo," I said. "I'll call you later."

I hung up the phone, pushed it off to the side of the table, and drained my glass of water. I then pulled a breadstick from the basket on the table to counter the effects of all the wine I had just consumed. Fortunately I tolerated alcohol well, and the adrenaline coursing through my system made me feel wide awake.

"I'm sorry about this," I said to Alvaro as I put away the phone. "I have to go back to work. It can't wait."

Alvaro smiled and nodded. "No problem," he said.

I looked at his strong features, his kind shining eyes. It seemed incredible that he lived under constant fear of death.

"You'd better get going, then." Alvaro looked around for our waiter. As soon as he caught his eye, Alvaro mimed writing in the air, the universal signal for the bill.

Without opening the dark leather portfolio containing the check, he handed an American Express card to the waiter. He sat back, arms folded, his body language indicating that there would be no argument over who paid for lunch. He might have been a liberal, but he was still a Cuban man.

"I invited you!" I protested. "You did me a favor by coming here today."

"The pleasure was all mine," Alvaro said as the waiter returned for his signature.

I should have known he wouldn't let me pay. It was just the way both of us were brought up. I kicked myself for not having made arrangements to pick up the check before Alvaro arrived. I should have dropped off my credit card with the waiter immediately after stepping in the door, instead of allowing the bill to be presented to the table.

There was obviously no room for debate with Alvaro. "Well, thank you," I said. "It was a delicious meal."

"So, Lupe, tell me the truth," he said as we both stood up. "Was I at all helpful to you?"

"Very much so," I said. "But I might have more questions. Would it be all right if I contact you again?"

Alvaro's face lit up. "Of course," he said. "It's been a long fifteen years, hasn't it. You know, in some ways I've been waiting for the chance to invite you somewhere again."

He kissed me good-bye. I watched Alvaro cross the street, heading for the covered lot where he'd parked his car. I had walked to the restaurant, since it was only three blocks from my office. It must have taken a full minute before my goose bumps went away. It was like being in high school again, only this time I certainly wouldn't have spurned Alvaro Mendoza for anyone.

It took another minute before I realized that, as informative as my talk with Alvaro had been, I still didn't know who stood to gain or lose from the Virgin's message. All I knew was that Cuban reunification would be a complicated mess that could go in one of a number of directions. Alvaro had told me a lot of interesting things about the exile community, but he hadn't given me any definitive answers.

Part of me didn't mind, though. It meant that I would have to call him again. The next time, I thought, we should definitely meet in the evening.

17

EVEN at the early-afternoon hour, traffic was heavy on I-95. I seldom took that highway during rush hour, and it caught me unprepared. It reminded me of how painless was my morning commute from Cocoplum to the Grove. The hardest part of my typical morning drive was slowing down so I didn't spill *café con leche* from my ceramic mug as I drove—a task made more difficult by my insistence on keeping the Cuban flag on the mug facing toward me at all times. It was a compulsion I was unable to shake.

It took me almost a full hour to reach the Northwest 125th Street exit. At the bottom of the ramp I headed east, toward the ocean, then made a left and went north at Biscayne Boulevard. A mile or so later I neared the O'Donnell residence. As I drove I thought through what I was going to say to the owner of the silver Buick— if, that is, he even agreed to speak with me at all.

James J. O'Donnell lived in a modest, sand-colored, single-story house with a fenced-in yard—one of thousands that dotted the South Florida landscape. I drove by the house once without stopping, just getting a look around. My heart skipped when I saw the silver four-door Buick Regal parked in the driveway. I didn't see anyone in the yard, saw no motion through the curtained front windows.

I reached the corner, stopped, turned left. I wanted to get behind the house, see if anyone was in the backyard. I got lucky. The lot behind the house was empty. I was able to see the property fairly clearly through the small trees planted behind the house. James

O'Donnell, or whoever was in charge of the garden, had been blessed with a green thumb. The landscaping was lush and fecund.

The back curtains were closed as well. This didn't mean much. In Miami homeowners often kept their curtains closed through the morning and afternoon, in an attempt to minimize the sun damage to their possessions. I drove to the corner again and waited. I had to do something soon.

James O'Donnell's neighborhood was a modest one; my Mercedes was the only luxury car in sight. I would call attention to myself if I kept circling around. I had already seen a couple of neighborhood-watch signs posted. That meant the residents were on the lookout for unusual activity—and my activity was starting to verge on out-of-the-ordinary.

I picked up my cellular phone and dialed the office. Leonardo answered on the second ring.

"Leo, it's me."

"Lupe, where are you?" My cousin sounded somewhat other-worldly. I must have interrupted his afternoon meditation.

I read Leonardo the O'Donnell home address, the one he had given me over the phone earlier. It never hurt to be safe. "I'm going to try to speak to this guy."

"So this is not a surveillance?" Leonardo asked, sounding more focused now. I was glad to hear it, since he was the only person in the world who knew where I was. "You're going into the house to speak with the subject, right? Be careful, Lupe."

I wouldn't have admitted it, but I had misgivings about what I was about to do. And Leonardo's concerned tone did little to allay them.

"I'll call when I'm finished," I said. "Then I'll be coming in to the office. Wish me luck."

I hung up and drove around to the front of the house, slowing down as I approached the property. I had decided during my first pass where I wanted to park. It was an old investigative technique, scoping out the street and determining where to leave my car with a minimum of risk. I parked just past the house, between two royal palm trees. This gave me a little privacy without blocking me in if I needed to get away fast. I sat in the car for a few seconds, looking at the house, trying to see if anything was happening. Nothing seemed changed. I took a long, deep breath, checked for the Beretta in my purse, and opened the car door.

The front gate of the chain-link fence was closed and latched, but unlocked. I went up to the front door and rang the bell. I thought I saw the curtains move slightly, but it might have been my imagination. I rang again without an answer. The Buick was parked in the driveway, so it was safe to assume that someone was inside.

I rang the bell a couple more times. "Hello?" I called out to the glass-front door. "Is anyone home?"

Nothing. I turned around to leave but stopped myself. I had come all the way out there. The car was in the driveway. My every instinct told me that I was at the right place.

The screen door was unlocked. I called out again and rapped the horseshoe-shaped brass knocker on the wooden door. The loud noise almost made me jump back, but still no one came to answer. I felt a twinge of nervousness moving up my spine. I knocked again, gentler this time. No response.

The mid-morning sun blazed down on me. I looked up and down the street: no traffic. I suddenly decided that I wasn't leaving the O'Donnell residence without some answers. Someone was in that house, I could almost feel their presence.

But I wasn't going to get anywhere banging on the door knocker. I had succeeded only in chipping the paint where the brass met the wood of the door. This wasn't TV. I couldn't just pick the lock and go inside. Not sure precisely what I intended to happen, I stepped off the porch and walked around the side of the house.

"Hello?" I called out to the side windows. "Mr. O'Donnell?"

The shades were drawn in the windows next door; the two houses were close together, and formed a shaded corridor hard to see from the street. I put my hand inside my purse and reached for the Beretta. I switched off the safety and tightly gripped the handle. A bead of sweat trickled down the back of my neck.

"Hello?" I said, trying to sound casual. This was Miami. People sometimes got shot for trespassing.

I reached the back of the house and saw a screened-in pool, obstructed from my vision when I had driven around the back of the place. The day was getting hot, and the cool water looked inviting to me.

Then my foot hit something. The ground rushed up to meet me.

My last thought was to take my hand off the gun in case it accidentally fired. I had already shot a hole through my Chanel bag once, and I didn't want to do it again. The second time it might be beyond repair.

18

"**PRIVATE** investigator." I heard a man's raspy voice close to my ear, smelled his stale cigarette breath. "And carrying a nice, fancy gun. A Beretta, no less."

The pain in my head was so intense that I couldn't open my eyes. But I saw no reason to speed up my return to reality. All I knew was that I was lying on my side on some sort of bed or sofa. Mercifully, I was still dressed. I heard the man breathing close to me. Not exactly a comforting scenario.

"Guadalupe Solano." He enunciated every syllable, pronouncing my name "Gooadiloopy." I stayed quiet. "Well, that's a nice Catholic name if I ever heard one."

His tone of voice indicated his lack of reverence for the faith. Fear started to creep through my delirium. His tone was rough and angry. And he knew about guns, had been able to identify mine on sight.

I tried to move my head and was rewarded with icy shards of pain. I needed some Tylenol and an ice bag. I hadn't felt a headache like this since my cousin Iris's *quince* ten years before, a night still discussed with awe and amazement in my family circles. Then, like now, I had awoken in a strange room, my head pounding, a man whispering in my ear. But *he* had had sweeter breath.

I cracked open my eyes, trying not to make any movement that would agitate him. I wished I knew where my purse was, and the gun that had been inside it. My eyes focused painfully. I was lying on a sofa in a living room. The place was so dark it was impossible to see more than a few feet—at least, I hoped that was true. Otherwise I had sustained permanent damage from, I now finally realized, the head blow I'd sustained outside the house.

"Jimmy," I heard a woman's soft voice say from across the room. "What have you done?"

Jimmy. James J. O'Donnell. I turned my head so I could hear his reply. Even that small movement got his attention.

"So, Ms. Sherlock Holmes is awake," he said, a sneer in his voice. "You had a nice nap, little lady?"

It was the "little lady" comment that finally got to me. Jimmy was bent over close to me as he spoke. I pulled my legs up to my chest quickly and kicked out as hard as I could. The excruciating pain that followed this tactic was worth enduring; I heard Jimmy yell out with surprise and hit the floor.

I tried to stand up but my legs were cooked pasta. I fell back on the sofa, clutching my head. It felt as though, if I let up pressure on it, it was going to explode all over the carpet.

"Miss, are you all right?" the woman asked me, moving closer through the gloom.

She had asked about my state, rather than Jimmy's, who was still lying on the floor. I took that as a good sign. And Jimmy would think twice before intimidating a woman again because of her size.

"I'm not all right!" I tried to yell, my throat scratchy. "My head is killing me. Do you have any aspirin?"

I omitted the "please" and "thank you." Then I leaned back upright on the sofa as Jimmy got up, swearing under his breath. Still, he stayed away from me, plopping down heavily on a sofa across the room. I looked at the windows, which were covered by heavy curtains. It might as well have been midnight. I strained to see Jimmy's face in the darkness but instead saw spirals of light.

The woman returned with a bottle of Tylenol—regular, not extra-strength. I popped four in my mouth and washed them down with a glass of water she handed me. She left for a moment, and I heard banging around in the kitchen. She came back with a plastic bag filled with ice. I noticed her hands were shaking.

She went to the window and opened the curtains a few inches, allowing in a slim beam of daylight. I looked around for my purse, for my gun and phone. They weren't around.

I put the ice bag to my head and breathed deep. Neither Jimmy nor the woman said anything. I heard a car going by outside. As my eyes adjusted to the new light I felt a strange sensation of apprehension. The room around me was surreal, like a time warp of the fifties. The terrazzo floor had gaudy gold and silver flecks, the furniture was covered in orange velour.

"Jimmy," I said across the room. "I assume you were the one who hit me over the head. Why did you do it?"

I tried to keep my voice mellow, measured, nonthreatening. Jimmy replied with a growl.

"I saw your ID," he said. "You're a private eye."

"Yes, that's true," I answered him, glad he didn't mangle my name again by trying to pronounce it. It would have been too painful to listen to again in my fragile state.

Jimmy got up from his chair. "Who do you work for?" he asked.

"You assaulted me," I said. "Let's all try to keep calm."

Jimmy took a step closer. "You were trespassing on my property," he said. "I could have you arrested."

Touché. I sat still, my eyes getting better. Jimmy and the woman were older than I thought at first, in their late fifties or early sixties. And they bore a strong similarity in appearance, both with short iron-colored curly hair—Jimmy's in a military crew cut, the woman's in a sort of old-fashioned housewife style. They were almost exactly the same height. They were definitely related, I thought. Brother and sister. If not twins.

Even in the room's penumbra I could see that the woman's coloring was terrible. She was pasty white, with red blotches on her cheeks. She wore oversized plain metal-framed glasses that covered almost half her face. Her eyes, as well as Jimmy's, were blue, almost translucent, and the lashes were strangely thin. She wore a shapeless flower-print cotton dress, like a housewife in a fifties TV show. Her lips quivered with anxiety.

And Jimmy was the male version of the woman. He didn't wear glasses, but his lashes were also unnaturally thin. However, while she was pale, Jimmy's face was tanned and ruddy. He was probably the gardener of the family. He wore a worn blue work shirt and scruffy stained chinos.

"You've seen my identification," I offered, trying to smile. "I came here to speak with Mr. James J. O'Donnell. I assume that's you, Jimmy."

"We don't talk until you tell me who you work for," Jimmy said.

He folded his arms, trying to look tough. It had the opposite effect. I could see that with his face lined and his posture slightly stooped, Jimmy had lived hard.

"Listen, I came to talk, not to start trouble," I said, moving the ice bag to the other side of my head. "And you assaulted me. You hit me so hard that I passed out. That's a felony, you know."

"You were trespassing," Jimmy said. He looked around the room, unsure what to do.

"Fine. Call the cops," I said. "They'll ask if I was threatening you in any way. And what will you tell them?"

"Listen, Miss Solano," the woman interrupted. She spoke my name with a roll of the tongue, making me think she spoke Spanish. "This situation is not good for any of us. We simply want to know why you were snooping around in our backyard."

She spoke calmly, rationally, with a hint of kindness. She could have been the nun, I realized, that had been kicked out of the Order of the Illumination convent. And, at the moment, she had a good point. I had trespassed on their property, with a gun in my purse.

"I'm investigating a case," I said carefully. "It has to do with an event taking place in the near future. My job is to find out whether this event will really take place."

"It's the nuns," Jimmy hissed. "They hired you to check up on Mary, to find out what she was doing." Turning away from me he said, "Mary, I told you they wouldn't let you go! Didn't I tell you?"

This was getting interesting. It was worth the pain, and the growing bump on my head, to see that my instincts had been right. James O'Donnell and his sister were key to this case. But how?

"I think there's been a misunderstanding," I said. "No one sent me to check up on Mary."

They looked wary, skeptical. "I only came here to speak with James," I added.

"What event?" Mary asked quietly, inching closer. I wished they would both sit down instead of hovering around me. "What event have you been hired to investigate?"

Neither of them apparently wanted to know why I wanted to speak with James, which would have been the natural first question for most people in their position. All three of us almost surely knew about the "event" to which I had referred, so I decided to play it straight. It was my only way to earn their trust.

"The miracle that is scheduled to take place," I said. They both nodded slightly. "The miracle of the Virgin crying."

"Why did you want Jimmy?" Mary asked.

"Look, I know this is your house, but could you please sit down?" I asked. Having them both right in front of me, like male/female mirror images, wasn't helping me regain my wits.

Mary and Jimmy looked at each other, shrugged at the precise same instant. It was like having double vision. They sat down in two armchairs across the small room.

Jimmy leaned forward and put his elbows on his knees. "Who do you work for?" he asked impatiently.

"I'll tell you," I finally said after a moment's contemplation. "Even though I'm taking a risk here. What I'm going to say to you is confidential. If it became public it could cause a lot of trouble for a lot of people. Do you understand me?"

Two sets of icy blue eyes bore into mine. They nodded in unison. I hated to tell them anything, but I could see it was my only hope of getting information in return. As a private investigator I dealt in secrets. The biggest secret at the moment, though, was the upcoming miracle—which the siblings in front of me already knew about. And Mary was a nun. I hoped I could count on her to keep her brother in check.

I told them about Lourdes's mother superior hiring me to look into the miracle of the Order of the Illumination of the Sacred Virgin. Then I had some questions of my own.

"What was the fight about, Mary?" I asked. "The one that resulted in you leaving the convent?"

"How do you know about that?" Mary asked.

I shrugged.

"Mary, you don't have to tell her anything," Jimmy said. I could sense his sudden tension. "We don't know if this girl is on the level. She's giving us a good line, that's all. She's probably just here fishing for something to use against us."

"Guadalupe, please forgive my brother," Mary said. "He only wants to protect me."

Mary smiled at Jimmy, who stared at me with a hard, unflinching expression. As much as I disliked the man, and in spite of the fact that he was making my job more difficult, I had to admit that he was sincerely trying to guard his sister against harm. But what kind of harm?

"And I appreciate your candor," Mary added. "I can see that it was a difficult decision for you to open up to us the way you did."

I started to relax a fraction. My headache had begun to subside a little. I thought about calling Leonardo to tell him I was all right. I glanced at my watch and saw that I had been a guest of the O'Donnell household for almost an hour and a half. But I didn't want to break the aura of cooperation that Mary had started to create.

"It all started with the order of Yugoslavian nuns in Homestead," Mary said, looking into my eyes. "Would you like me to tell you how I came to be involved with them?"

Would I? Was the pope Catholic?

Mary folded her hands in her lap as though she was about to tell a story in Sunday school. I reached up and felt the egg-sized lump on top of my head, no longer caring how much it hurt.

"Do you know much about religious orders?" Mary asked me.

I didn't care to mention my sister, so I kept quiet. I gave her an ambiguous look of curiosity.

"Well, not too many people do, in this day and age," she said with a twinge of regret. "Being a nun today seems old-fashioned, like something from another time. There are only about eighty-five thousand of us in America right now."

I stole a look at Jimmy. Surprisingly, I felt a moment of sympathy for him as he listened to his sister. He looked as though he shared her melancholy and regret.

"Here's something else you wouldn't know," Mary said. "There are sixty-seven registered religious orders in Dade County alone. We may be old-fashioned, but Miami is a very Catholic city."

I had known that approximate number from conversations I'd had with Lourdes, but I didn't let on. I could see that convent life had taught Mary to think and live at a slower pace than those of us who lived in the rat race. I could sense that she was eventually going to get to the point, even though I felt like knocking her on the shoulder to prod her thoughts into higher gear.

Jimmy shifted uncomfortably. "C'mon, Mary," he said. "If you're going to talk to Miss Solano, then tell her what you have to say."

Mary seemed surprised. "Oh, I'm sorry," she said. "Guadalupe, the point is that I am persona non grata as far as the Order of the

Illumination of the Sacred Virgin is concerned. I know that for a fact. The sister superior informed me herself."

"I see," I said quietly. Mary was no doubt referring to the fight at the convent, the one overheard by Theofilus.

We were approaching midday, and Jimmy's house didn't have air-conditioning. It might have been autumn on the calendar, but in Miami there were two seasons—hot and too hot. Neither of the O'Donnells seemed to mind the stuffy atmosphere in the living room.

"Jimmy and I grew up in Altoona, Pennsylvania," Mary mused. "Doesn't that seem light-years away?"

Mary looked over at her brother, who grunted his agreement. Mary shook her head, as though her birthplace was a dream. Miami tended to have that effect. The reality of the rest of the world becomes difficult to contemplate at times.

"Jimmy and I are two of a set of triplets," Mary said with a new warmth. "We were born in 1936."

Triplets. Because of their age, I hadn't considered the possibility. I thought of multiple births as a present-day occurrence along with fertility treatments and test-tube babies. But I had sensed they were more than mere brother and sister.

"Some people in our family have always gone into religious life," Mary explained. "Our sister Rose is also a nun. She's in Massachusetts, in Springfield, with the Sisters of St. Joseph's."

"Tell her what it was like when you left home to go to the convent," Jimmy said, his voice cold.

"Well, Mother wanted us to become nuns," Mary said. "We had been in Catholic school all our lives. Did you go to Catholic school, Guadalupe?"

I nodded.

"Well, then you know how children there are taught to examine themselves to see if they have a calling," Mary said. "Mother was very happy when Rose and I decided that we did."

"Your mother encouraged both of you?" I asked. I could see a Catholic thinking it was wonderful to have one daughter serving God, but both of them? I had a hard time relating to that, but I softened my tone. "I mean, knowing that neither of you would ever marry or have children, she still wanted both of you to take Holy Orders?"

"I know it might seem strange to you," Mary said with a little sad smile. "For us it was an honor. It takes a special person to have a calling. It meant that God chose us to serve Him. In our time, no parent would resent their children having a calling."

Mary seemed slightly offended by my question. I couldn't remember any talk at home about Lourdes having a calling. As far as we were concerned, Lourdes went into the convent like another young woman might have left for college. Maybe it was because no one in our family had ever entered a religious order before. I think we saw it more as a profession than a way of life, especially because she lived at home and often wore regular clothes. For me, as her younger sister, it simply meant that Lourdes was going to miss out on one of the best parts of life: men.

"I didn't mean to offend you," I said sincerely.

The longer I sat in that living room—itself a testament to the staying power of the fifties in the O'Donnell siblings' lives—the clearer it became to me how comfortable it was for them to traipse down memory lane. And I could also see how gentle and calm was Mary's nature. Something serious must have happened for her to bolt screaming from the convent.

I was also feeling a little embarrassed. There was me, a Miamian all my life, getting drenched in my own sweat. Mary and Jimmy, Northern transplants, were looking comfortable and cool.

"Mary, I understand the impact this had on you," I said. "But could you tell me now what happened at the convent a couple of days ago?"

No sooner had I spoken than I realized my mistake. I was totally unprepared for the severity of Mary's reaction. She started to shake her head and rock back and forth, as though she was having some kind of neurological fit. It was frightening to watch. I wondered why she had not been as affected the first time I brought up the subject of the fight.

Jimmy got up and knelt down in front of her, stroked her arm and whispered to her with surprising gentleness.

"Come on, now," he said. "Take a deep breath."

It looked as though he had been through this before, that he knew what to do to calm her.

Mary started to respond to her brother. Her rocking subsided, and she breathed deeply. Her eyes cleared and she looked up at me again.

"Mary, are you all right?" I asked. She didn't answer, instead turned and looked out the window. "I'm so sorry. I really didn't mean to upset you in any way."

The warm, almost friendly mood in the room had disappeared in an instant. I could have kicked myself for blowing it, but how could I have known she would flip out over a single question?

Jimmy stood up. "Listen, I think you'd better leave."

His request—an order, really—hadn't been unexpected, but it was crushing nonetheless. Mary held the key to my case, I was sure of it now. She was at the center of everything, but I knew little more than when I had first knocked on the door. I had rushed the situation, and there was no sense beating myself up about it.

I didn't want to antagonize them any further, so I got up slowly. I looked around the room.

"Over there," Jimmy said, pointing to an end table in the corner that had been hidden from my vision by a big houseplant. On it I found my purse. I resisted checking inside for my Beretta; from the bag's weight, I could tell it was inside.

Mary stayed in her chair, staring out the window, a beam of light shining on her high forehead. The sight was enough to make my mouth drop open. Jimmy noticed my reaction and nodded, as though the sight was perfectly ordinary to him.

Jimmy followed me out to the front gate. "I had no idea how much I was going to upset your sister," I said. "Please believe me."

Jimmy looked out at the street as though transfixed by the sight of a Chevy driving past.

"How could you have known?" he asked suddenly. "You have no idea what's really going on."

We stood there for almost a minute, Jimmy seeming to wrestle with something inside.

"Were you telling the truth before, when you said you were working for another mother superior?" he asked.

I raised my right hand. "I swear it's the truth."

"I can't talk now. I have to go take care of Mary." Jimmy waved vaguely back toward his house. "But I'll try to get in touch with you. There are some things you need to know."

I dug desperately in my purse and produced several of my business cards, which I shoved into his hand.

"Call me anytime," I said. I took out a pen and wrote down my home number on two of the cards, something I seldom divulged. "Night or day, it doesn't matter when. Please give Mary one of these cards and tell her the same thing."

"I will." Jimmy nodded. "Now I'd better go back in."

I unlatched the front gate and stepped out onto the street, feeling Jimmy's eyes on my back all the while.

"Hey, Sherlock," he called out to me. "Listen. Sorry about that bump on your head."

I smiled as I turned away. We were making progress.

19

I drove back to Coconut Grove at a snail's pace, a long line of red brake lights stretching out endlessly before me.

I tried to get my mind off my headache by concentrating on the case. I had gathered a lot of background information, and considerably fewer hard facts. Of course Mother Superior could have made things easier on me by making herself more accessible. If I had been able to contact her directly, then I might have better been able to assess her own motives and goals—and perhaps that was a reason why she didn't want me contacting her. But there was no point bemoaning things I couldn't change.

I was convinced that Mary was the key to the miracle. Why would an American nun launch into a screaming fight with the sister superior of an order of nuns from Yugoslavia? It had to be no coincidence that they were both in Miami, that they had come to a passionate conflict. I still couldn't see the link between any of the participants and Cuba itself, but there had to be one. I just had to find it.

And there was also the political angle. My lunch with Alvaro had opened my eyes to a different point of view—both in regard to Cubans in exile and those on the island. My thinking on Cuban politics had been broadened, but I still had more questions than answers. I understood the liberal position, as well as the hard-liners. But I grasped for a sensible middle ground between the two. This kind of problem was known in Cuba as an *arroz con mango*—a rice with mango. The two foods, like two opposing viewpoints, could be consumed separately but never mixed.

October 10 was getting closer. I knew it was time to start moving fast, to outrun events as they happened. Whatever happened, I thought, the status quo was about to disappear. The clock was ticking, and the only certainty was that events would soon ignite. The only question was what the magnitude of the explosion would be.

As soon as I was back at the office I opened the manila envelope containing vehicle information that Leonardo had left on my desk. I looked at the second list, the one compiled from Marisol's videotape. I read through the names and compared them with Marisol's notes. I forced myself to take it slow, not to be impatient.

The tenth name on the list might as well have been written in boldface. All the information was just as Leonardo had read to me over the phone. A silver four-door 1991 Buick Regal, registered to James J. O'Donnell. An address in northeast Miami. The description of the car fit Theofilus's observations.

I attached a yellow Post-it Note to the printout, though I probably could have pointed to the name blindfolded in a dark room. I kept reading down the list until I reached the end, knowing all the while that the tenth name was what I had been looking for.

James J. O'Donnell. He had been the key. He had led me to Mary.

I stapled the printouts together and looked through them again. Then I picked up the phone and hit the fifth button on my speed dial.

"Nestor?" I said.

"*Hola*, Lupe," he replied in his room-temperature-whiskey voice. He not only always looked like an unmade bed, he sounded like the morning after the night before—no matter what the time of day.

"I got the tag searches," I said. "I need you to check them out for me, *por favor*. I need backgrounds, especially on James J. O'Donnell."

"No prob," Nestor drawled, his typical reply to a request from me. I heard rustling sounds and a quiet moan. I couldn't tell if it had come from Nestor or if he had company who was protesting his abrupt departure. "I'm on my way to pick them up."

"*Gracias*," I replied. "I'll be leaving soon, so I'll place them for you in the usual spot."

I carefully replaced the receiver in its cradle. I ran my hand over my face, trying to force myself to stop frowning. It was a bad habit. Instead of the usual anxiety tics—chewing lips, biting nails, smoking—I had always been a frowner. Mami had regularly been on my case about it, telling me I'd end up with forehead creases as deep as the Grand Canyon.

I straightened up my desk, grabbed my purse, and headed toward the door, throwing a good-night kiss toward the parrots outside. As usual, they were completely oblivious to my comings and goings.

In the reception area I heard New Age music coming from the gym, so I knew Leonardo had retired for the day. He was probably engrossed in his self-exploring, inner-child nighttime exercises. I thought about going in to tell him I was leaving, but I didn't feel like entering Twinkle Land. It was also a matter of consideration; in my current frame of mind I might have set off bad vibes that would wreck the mellow atmosphere Leonardo worked so hard to achieve.

Leonardo labored with such intensity to reach his personal state of Cuban nirvana that he had actually confessed to me that his goal was a state of psychic control in which he could eat as much fried food as he wished without it reaching his Cuban ass. Unfortunately, just a few days after he shared this intimate secret I had walked into the gym with a sufficiently bad aura that I almost cracked his crystal wind chimes. Leonardo, it seemed, would never again be able to repair the damage—or to eat fried foods again. Only a Cuban could understand what I had done to him. Every Cuban recipe starts off with "Pour a cup of oil into an iron skillet over high heat."

So I bypassed the gym and stepped outside. Before I left I slipped a manila envelope with Nestor's name on it into the mailbox by the door, where I usually left papers for after-hours pickup. It also wouldn't do to have Nestor ring the front doorbell and interrupt Leonardo. I would have faxed the papers to Nestor, but he always preferred hard copies—he claimed faxes from his machine were too hard to read, making him prone to mistakes. I thought his eyesight might have been going, having seen him bring documents closer and closer to his face the past few years. I also suspected he didn't regret charging for travel time to and from my office to pick up the original documents.

I hurried to the driveway where, always a pleasant surprise, my Mercedes was waiting for me. Another day in which it wasn't on a freighter bound for South America and a new owner. I turned off the alarm, started it up, and blasted the air conditioner. I turned onto Main Highway heading south, and decided not to punch the engine.

I was tired, and it had been a very long day, and I was eager to see my family—but not so eager that I was willing to risk another speeding ticket. I had received too many of those over the last few months, and my insurance carrier was threatening to drop me. For now they simply limited their punishment to forcing me to pay sky-high premiums. My insurance agent had the patience of a saint, but there were limits.

So I drove home at a sane, sedate speed—and still arrived home in time for dinner with my family. I considered it an auspicious sign—since by that point, I was taking good omens wherever I could find them.

20

THE telephone rang five or six times before I could coordinate myself enough to answer it. I opened one eye and looked at the lighted green dial of my bedside clock. Almost four in the morning. I felt a sensation of dread. Nothing good ever happened at four in the morning, at least not when one was alone in bed. I picked up the receiver and grunted something totally unintelligible.

"Gooadiloopy?"

"Jimmy? What's wrong?" I sat up in bed and started feeling around for the light. Only one person had ever butchered my name in that way. I knew this wasn't a social call.

"It's Mary," he replied. A pause, a labored breath. "She's missing."

I turned on the light and shook my head, trying to clear away the cobwebs. I never should have accepted that lethal third after-dinner *mojito*.

"What do you mean, missing?"

"She asked if she could borrow the car. She said she wanted to run an errand." Jimmy spoke quickly, and I strained to follow. "She said she'd be back in an hour but she didn't come back. I haven't heard anything from her and I'm worried. It's been five hours."

"Where do you think she went?" I couldn't imagine where a sixty-three-year-old nun would go at four in the morning in Miami. Not clubbing on South Beach, that was certain. I felt a familiar pang in my stomach—the precursor to bad news.

"I don't know. She said she was going to the drugstore, but she's been gone way too long for that," Jimmy said, his misery and despair palpable. He sounded like a helpless child who'd been separated

from his mother. "It's got me worried, especially with the trouble at the convent."

That perked my ears up. "Have you contacted the police to report her missing?"

"Mary wouldn't want me to go to the police, she told me not to go to them about anything." I heard a sob. "I don't know what to do. So I called you."

It figured. I was always the kind of person people in trouble called at four in the morning.

"Where are you?" I asked as I swung my legs over the bed. It was time to start the day.

"I'm at the house," Jimmy said. "I don't even know where to begin to look for her. I . . . I thought I should stay here, in case she came home or called or something."

"Jimmy, I'm going to get dressed and drive over to your house," I said. "Get a paper and a pencil. I want to give you my cellular phone number." I read it off. "Call me if you hear something. I'll be there as fast as I can."

Jimmy hung up. Ten minutes later I was in the Mercedes going north. Dawn was still a couple hours away, and traffic was light. I got to the O'Donnells' house in about twenty minutes. Jimmy must have been waiting by the window, because he came outside as soon as I slowed down and parked.

"No news," he said as I locked the car. "I haven't heard anything from Mary."

Jimmy was dressed in the same clothes he'd worn during my visit yesterday. "Let's go inside," I said. Since I had no idea what happened to Mary, or what the O'Donnells might be mixed up in, it didn't seem like a good idea to be standing outside in plain view.

Jimmy locked the door behind us and leaned against the wall in the entryway. His eyes were red, sunk deep in their sockets.

"You have to find her," he blurted out. "Isn't that what you do? Find missing persons?"

"Well—"

"Look," he said, almost accusatory. "I saw it on television."

If it had been on television, obviously, then it had to be true. I sighed.

Everyone was always trying to tell me my job description. Those private-eye movies and TV shows were the bane of those of us who

worked in the real world. If we did a fraction of what they did in those shows, we'd be nailed by the Florida Department of Professional Regulation—with fines and possible license revocation, if not jail time.

Clients in the past have actually expected me to break into homes and businesses, to tape private telephone calls, to access credit reports—all because they had seen it done on some program. Inevitably, they got annoyed when I said I wasn't going to break the law. A few offered me extra cash, as though they hadn't heard me say that I wasn't interested in committing a felony.

It reminded me of the time an eighty-something old lady came into my office and asked me to find a missing person. I immediately assumed she wanted me to find an old friend, a wayward granddaughter, maybe a former love. But then she told me, quite seriously, that she knew where *all* missing persons went, and that the only problem was the difficulty of reaching them. She went on to explain that they were all held together in a magnetic field somewhere, that she would pay me whatever I asked if I could find them. I politely responded that my investigator's license permitted me to work only in the state of Florida, not in metaphysical realms or magnetic fields.

So I snapped back into it and tried not to get annoyed with Jimmy for telling me to act like a TV cop. It was way past four in the morning, and I hadn't driven across town to get into another fight with the man. "Sometimes we do find missing persons," I said to him. "But listen, Jimmy, think. Has Mary ever disappeared like this before?"

Jimmy scrunched up his face. "No, Mary never really goes anywhere," he said. "She doesn't even know her way around Miami. She gets lost here."

Alarm bells went off in my head. "What do you mean she doesn't know her way around?" I asked. "Hasn't she been living at the convent in Homestead for a while?"

"No, no." Jimmy shook his head. "She's only been there for a week. That order of Yugoslavian nuns, that's not Mary's order. Mary is a nun in the Order of St. Joseph's back in Massachusetts, just like our sister Rose."

Mierda! I could have kicked myself. Sure, I had just been hit over the head when I spoke with Mary, but I had neglected to ask her the

right questions. I guessed I had assumed that she had come with the other nuns from Medjugorge when the other sisters established the convent in Miami a few months before. Because she was older, and seemed so stable, I hadn't thought that she would be one of the recent additions to the convent. And I knew it wasn't that unusual for American nuns to go to convents in other countries—Lourdes had once considered moving to Spain for a couple of years with a mission from her order.

But I should have thought through the fact that Mary and Rose had entered the same order at the same time. Nuns didn't transfer from one order to another, like changing jobs or transferring to another university. Mary's presence at the Order of the Illumination was a definite oddity, one that I had been too stunned to notice.

"It's not Mary's order," I repeated to Jimmy. "What exactly does that mean? Don't nuns stay with their orders and not move around?"

"Yeah, usually that's the way it is," Jimmy said dismissively. "But in Mary's case she was sent here to live with those European nuns."

"But why? Why was Mary sent here from her order?"

Jimmy's eyes narrowed. "Why are we talking about that?" he snapped. "You're here to find my sister!"

"I need to know more about her if I'm going to know where to look for her," I explained. I spoke carefully, trying not to spook Jimmy any more than he already was.

Jimmy's face moved quickly through a range of emotions—suspicion, anger, fear, frustration, then resignation.

"Come on," he said, walking into the living room. "Let's at least sit down."

I walked across the room and sat down on the same sofa on which I'd awoken less than a day before. It was a strange sensation. The room was silent, the sun still yet to come up. Apparently Jimmy's hospitality didn't extend to an offer of coffee. I could have used some, even the American kind.

"Mary didn't want to leave Rose," Jimmy said softly, staring down at his folded hands. "She was happy at St. Joseph's, but when Mother Superior tells a nun to do something, there's no room for asking questions. Do you understand that?"

I sure did, having met a mother superior not too long ago. I nodded, silently encouraging Jimmy to unburden himself.

"But at least they sent her to Miami, and since I live here, she thought it wouldn't be all bad." Jimmy looked up at me. "That's what Rose and I told her. She would be leaving her sister, but she would be staying close to me. So she wouldn't be alone."

Again I sensed the power of Jimmy's protectiveness. "Why do you live in Miami?" I asked. "Since your family's up north, in Massachusetts and Pennsylvania."

"Three years after my sisters took their vows and left home, then I left home, too," Jimmy said. He rubbed his eyes. "I joined the navy and got posted to Key West. There's a big naval station there, you know."

He seemed to be waiting for a reply. "Yeah, I know," I said.

"I stayed in for twenty years and then I retired. I went back up north for a while but I couldn't take the cold anymore." He smiled sheepishly. "I guess the blood really does thin out. I'd saved a lot of my pay, and I had a pension and benefits. I figured I'd move back to Florida. But not Key West, it's too damned expensive. I bought this place from the widow of a guy I knew in the service. It's real reasonable, low upkeep. I paid cash for it, and the taxes aren't too bad."

I had to admit that I'd wondered how Jimmy ended up here. But more than a few servicemen had retired here in Florida after their stints in the military.

"Where do you think Mary went, Jimmy?" I asked. I hit him with the question fast, hoping to catch him off guard. Jimmy merely shrugged, but I could tell he knew more than he was telling me. I tried not to let my annoyance show. Why the hell had he called me, if he wasn't going to help me find his sister?

"What was the fight about at the convent?" I asked. "The one between Mary and the sister superior. Were you and Mary frightened about that fight for some reason?"

"What do you know about that?" Jimmy yelled. He got up from his chair so quickly that I instinctively raised up my hands to defend myself.

That very same question had almost made his sister go into convulsions, and now it had made Jimmy completely lose what was left of his cool.

"Help me out, Jimmy," I said. "Whatever the fight was about, I need to know. We both have an interest in this now. I'm working a case, you want to find Mary. We have to work together."

"Mary said it was private," Jimmy whined, miserable. "She told me not to tell, and I can't. I can't betray my sister's confidence."

"Well, then I can't help you," I said. I threw up my hands and got up from the sofa. "I'm sorry."

I walked across the room. The first hint of light had begun to play low on the horizon outside.

"The more time passes, the more trouble Mary might be in," I added. "Call me if you change your mind—but only if you're willing to tell me everything. Otherwise you're wasting both our time."

I hated to walk out on him like that, but how was I supposed to locate a nun I'd met once, with no information and no idea where she might have gone? Jimmy and Mary had withheld a lot of information from me, it was obvious now, and maybe the circumstances would compel Jimmy to start talking. I could only hope. After all, I had liked Mary. I also wanted to find her safe and sound.

I left him sitting there, obviously wrestling with his conscience. I opened the door and stepped out on the porch. It would be a miracle if his sister came home, I could feel it in my bones. And my instincts had been batting a thousand so far.

21

NESTOR lay back on the sofa in my office, his eyes closed, waving a sea-green pamphlet over his head. He had been in there waiting for me when I opened the door.

"Do you know what this is?" he asked.

"No," I said tersely. "What is it?"

I wasn't in the mood for Nestor's games. My head ached; the bump Jimmy gave me had started to throb again. If it didn't get better soon I was going to have to see a doctor. I had a hard head, but this time I'd really taken a shot.

Nestor waved the book dramatically. "This is an official publication of the Miami Archdiocese," he said.

"What the hell are you talking about?" I barked. I rubbed my head. "I'm not up for this, Nestor. Whatever you have to say had better be good. I've had a really shitty day so far."

I stretched my legs and put them up on my desk. I had a jumbo bottle of extra-strength Tylenol cradled in my lap. After a few false starts I was able to open it by wrenching at it with my teeth. A good thing—if it fought me any more, I was going to have to shoot it.

I shook out three pills. The recommended dose on the label was two every four hours, but I rationalized that the ones I'd taken at the O'Donnells' were regular strength and didn't count. Besides, they no doubt were out of my system at that point.

I realized I must have hurt Nestor's feelings, because he still hadn't answered me. That was fine with me. I could use a moment of silence. I glanced outside. If the parrots kept it up, we'd have to get our backyard rezoned as a multi-dwelling residential district.

Nestor was staring into space with a downcast expression.

"Look, I'm sorry," I said. "It's been a bitch of a day."

"What happened to you?" Nestor asked. "You hit that aspirin bottle like it was a lifeline and you were on a raft in the Florida Straits."

Only in Miami would such an analogy occur to anyone. "I'm seriously sleep-deprived. Plus, someone hit me in the head and it hurts."

"Really?" Nestor asked, perking up. He shifted to a semi-sitting position.

"I got hit in the head with a—" I paused, realizing that I didn't know what Jimmy had hit me with. "Oh, never mind. What is it you were so excited about?"

Trying to think gave me a sharp pain in my head. I willed myself to focus.

"This book," Nestor declared, held it up again for me to see. "It's a listing of all the religious women in Dade County."

"So what?" I asked. "How does the archdiocese know who's religious and who isn't?"

"Jesus, Lupe. That bump must have affected your brain." Nestor shook his head. "This isn't a listing of all the women in Miami who go to Mass on Sunday and say their prayers before bed. This book lists all the nuns in the county. Each and every nun in Dade County is listed in this pamphlet."

I must not have been reacting the way Nestor thought I would. He spoke to me slowly, repeating himself as though I were mentally challenged.

"Including those in the Order of the Illumination of the Sacred Virgin," I said, catching on.

"Sí," Nestor replied, beaming.

"I'm going to refrain from asking how you got your hands on that," I told him, knowing that such a booklet wasn't something the church would distribute to the general public.

"There are sixty-seven orders of nuns in Dade County," Nestor said, paging through his pamphlet. Obviously I didn't want to know how he got it. If it hadn't been through very shady means, then he would have been bragging about his guile.

"I actually knew that," I said, recalling my conversation with Mary.

"Pretty amazing," Nestor mused. He flipped to a page and cleared his throat. "There are currently fifteen nuns listed for the Homestead convent of the Order of the Illumination. If I remember correctly, Mother Superior said that the order had only been established here in the past six months. The information I have here must be current, then."

"Right. But she also said that their numbers have been increasing since rumors of the miracle started to circulate." I thought for a moment. "That book lists only the nuns, right? Not the postulants or novices."

Nestor frowned. "Strange. Some of the convents list only the nuns, and some of them list postulants and novices as well. The order we're interested in lists only the nuns. I wonder if that means anything important."

"Probably not," I said. "Just that none of the new recruits had become full nuns when the book was printed. And now, with the hot line set up, the numbers can only increase. When the press gets hold of this story, who knows how many more people are going to want to get involved. Here, let me have a look at that thing."

Nestor got up from the sofa with a grunt and handed me the book gingerly, as though he didn't want to damage it. Nestor always acted in this proprietary manner toward information he'd uncovered on his own.

"*Gracias.*" I turned to the page that referenced the Order of the Illumination. It gave the order's origin as Medjugorge.

I looked down the list of names of nuns. All of them seemed to be Slavic. Something didn't make sense. Theofilus had said that the sister superior and another nun—Mary—had had a big screaming fight in Spanish. There wasn't a single Spanish-sounding name among the fifteen listed. This could have meant that Sister Superior was fluent in Spanish although she wasn't native-born. It might also mean that a new sister superior, a Latina, had been appointed to the job since this booklet was printed. It was strange that Mary's name wasn't listed anywhere, and also strange that Mary had fought in Spanish—I doubted there was a lot of Spanish spoken in Altoona in the fifties. One had to be fluent in a language to fight in it. I had always heard four things were always done in one's native language: counting, dreaming, swearing, and making love. Fighting should have been added to those four.

The nuns were listed alphabetically under the heading for each convent, without any indication who the mother superior was. I flipped to the entry for the Order of the Holy Rosary and saw that the format was the same as the other convents'. Mother Superior's name in Lourdes's order was the third-to-last given, right after my sister's. Very democratic, but no help for finding the name of the sister superior at the Order of the Illumination.

"What do you think?" Nestor asked. "Pretty good, finding it, no? All that information in there is confidential."

"Don't say anything more," I said, grasping my aching head. "I'm getting a migraine at the thought of what you did to get this. For all I know you seduced some young novice into giving it to you."

Nestor twitched on the sofa, knocking over his briefcase. The noise it made hitting the floor frightened the parrots outside. They began to squawk at an unbearably high pitch.

Mercifully, Nestor didn't say anything more on the subject. He held out his hand for the pamphlet.

"Lupe, those are some jumpy birds," he said. "Leo should feed them some of his New Age vitamins or something to calm them down. I know they're Cuban birds, but Jesus, you'd think they were drinking coffee all day like you. You'd better be careful, or the ASPCA will come around and ask what you've been giving them."

Nestor stuffed the pamphlet into his worn canvas briefcase and got up. "I'll get right on it," he said. "I'll call as soon as I have anything. I'm also still working on the other background checks. I should have something real soon."

He slipped out without another word. Like Marisol, Nestor might have been infuriating at times, but he had some of the best contacts in the business. I also knew he used women with no remorse at all in order to get information he needed to work a case. One time I started to lecture him about his methods, but he stopped me in mid-sentence and pointed out that I did the same thing with men— even if it tended to be with a better-educated, higher class of individuals, and in an ostensibly more subtle way. Ever since then I had kept my objections to myself.

My head was still pounding, like there was something inside my skull fighting to get out. I walked out to the reception area. Nestor was gone. Leonardo wasn't at his desk. There were only two other places where he might be: in the kitchen mixing up some concoction, or in the gym working out or meditating.

"Leo!" I called out, wincing. "Leo, where are you? I need you!"

"Lupe, what's wrong?" Leonardo came running out of the kitchen, concern written all over his face. "You look terrible!"

"My head," I said feebly. I was so miserable that I had no choice but to bite the bullet and tempt fate. "Do you think you could make me one of those natural drinks? Something that would help me?"

My whole body shuddered when I saw his face light up. Rarely in the seven years we had worked together had I asked him for help from his realm of health-food quackery.

"You want me to mix up something for you," he said slowly. Now the shine in his eyes turned to a narrow glint of suspicion. "Why? How many pills did you take before you were desperate enough to call on me?"

"Spare me the lecture," I moaned. "Please. Just do something to make me feel better."

"All right. No problem."

Leonardo marched off to the kitchen; I had no choice but to tag along, like a virgin being led to the sacrificial altar to please the gods. All this might not have been so bad, but in my case the magician who was going to deliver me from earthly pain was dressed in a gold Lurex unitard, with fluorescent-yellow high-tops on his feet. He might have been some ancient Mayan priest who took a detour and somehow ended up in present-day Miami.

"Heaven help me," I whispered, not for the first time that month.

Leonardo's remedy was double-pronged—one part topical, the other ingested. It was a no-holds-barred, take-no-prisoners assault consisting of mashed avocado applied to my temples, followed by a potion made of frozen avocado frappe mixed with Courvoisier VSOP.

"This will work extra well because the avocados came from our tree," he said reverently, going into a sort of trance. "They were all pecked at by our friends the parrots."

I endured his ministrations and tried to ignore that last piece of information. Sometimes too much knowledge is a dangerous thing. Now I knew I would always be looking out at the parrots, wondering which one used his magic beak to try to cure me. It was the investigator's curse, always wanting to know who done it.

The funny part was, I started to feel better. I could open my eyes all the way. I could swivel my head on my neck without feeling like I was passing out.

"Not bad," I said. "Really not bad."

Leonardo smiled enigmatically. "There's a lot of wisdom in the ancient healing arts—" he started to say.

I held up my hand. "I'm sure there is," I said. "However, I think I'd better leave well enough alone for now. But thanks. You really bailed me out this time."

"Suit yourself," Leonardo sniffed. "But I think you really should start to listen to—"

Just then my cell phone rang, providing us with an excuse to break off what might have turned into an unpleasant exchange. I smiled at Leonardo and motioned for him to leave the room.

A glance down at the caller ID revealed a number that I hadn't seen in a long time. My heart began to beat a little faster. I had a feeling this wasn't a social call.

"Lupe?" a familiar voice boomed on the line. "This is Charlie."

"Hello, Charlie," I replied cautiously. Assistant State Attorney Charlie Miliken. My friend and former lover.

"I think you'd better get down to my office," he said, not bothering with pleasantries. "As soon as possible."

"Is this an invitation or an order?" I asked. Although I already knew the answer.

22

WHY did I ever let Charlie Miliken go, I asked myself, as I always did the instant I laid eyes on him. Charlie had just closed the door of his office and kissed me, enveloped me in the intoxicatingly familiar nimbus of Jack Daniel's and cigarettes.

"Let me look at you," Charlie said with his big smile. "As beautiful as ever."

"*Gracias*. You don't look too shabby yourself."

He did look good, even better than usual. The relationship between me and Charlie had been officially over for a number of years, although every so often we rekindled it. Not for any significant reason, or with any intention of resuming it—it was more like preventative maintenance, to make sure things were still workable in case we decided to take it up again in the distant future.

Times like these, when I hadn't seen him for a while, tempted me to wade into the waters again—up to the waist, let's say. But now I asked myself, did I really feel that way, or was it residual romantic feelings for Charlie combined with perhaps a hidden need for some kind of closure? I couldn't honestly tell.

"Come on, sit down," Charlie guided me to one of the chairs opposite his desk. He opened the bottom drawer of his battered gray aluminum filing cabinet and took out a bottle of Jack Daniel's and two plastic glasses. I groaned inside as he poured two healthy drinks for us. I took mine, thinking that the Holy Rosary case was going to turn me into a lush if I wasn't careful.

Charlie Miliken was one of the most respected and experienced prosecutors in the Dade County state attorney's office—if not the most. He might have been state attorney by that time, but he always did things his way with a willful disregard for politics. Anyway, the cops loved him. They were overjoyed whenever he was assigned to prosecute one of their arrests. Defense attorneys hated to deal with him, knowing that he was relentless and a workaholic.

I looked around the room. Charlie had draped a T-shirt over the smoke detector on the wall, something I couldn't believe he had gotten away with. He had taken this measure a few days after the Justice Building had been declared a smoke-free zone; Charlie had tried to abide by the rule, but he found himself leaving the building about twenty times a day to go smoke outside and decided that all those trips were a waste of the taxpayers' money. He was, after all, a public employee. Then he tried to give up smoking, but that was a disaster. All the staff on his floor were probably relieved when Charlie relented and started smoking again, because two days of quitting had turned him into an irritable, paranoid, sunflower-seed-chomping mess. Charlie was careful enough that he wouldn't start a fire in his office, and he didn't smoke around most visitors. He had even chipped through the paint on the windowsill and forced the window open a foot or so. His system seemed to be working.

The office itself had never changed in all the years I'd known Charlie. Files were stacked shoulder-high. Pink telephone message slips—few of which he had probably answered—were relegated to a box on the floor by his chair. The fax machine had inches of paper stacked in the receiving box, tons of stuff Charlie had surely never looked at. The place was chaos, and it was amazing that so many successful prosecutions came out of it.

We tapped glasses and took a sip of bourbon. I knew that because we had remained in his office, Charlie definitely had some news for me that affected me professionally. I was really in no hurry to hear it.

"Nice to see you, Lupe," Charlie said, settling into his chair with a groan. "It's too bad it's because of such an unfortunate reason."

"Unfortunate reason?" I repeated, feeling the bourbon burn its way down my esophagus.

"It doesn't get any more unfortunate than homicide."

My stomach lurched. "Enough of this, Charlie," I said. "Who got killed?"

Charlie found a manila envelope on his desk and took out some glossy 8x10s. He turned them face-down on his desk and looked up at me with a weary expression.

"Mary Margaret O'Donnell. A nun from Springfield, Massachusetts. She belonged to the Order of St. Joseph's there. She was found in St. Anthony's, South Miami, on Red Road. Her purse was found stuffed behind a pew a few feet away from her body."

I didn't reply. I had expected the worst, and now it had happened. I remembered Mary's kind voice, the fear that had paralyzed her when I asked about the fight at the Order of the Illumination.

"Crime scene," Charlie said, tapping the photographs with an ink pen. "Want to see them?"

Mary, dead. My mind raced, and I struggled to hide my shock and dismay. I felt overwhelmed for a moment, wondering if I might have been somehow culpable for her death, then I willed the doubts away for the time being. Charlie had asked me to his office to tell me about the murder, and I had to deal with him.

I guess on some level I'd known this was why Charlie called me in; what other reason could there have been? Mary had been missing less than a day when Charlie summoned me. I suppose I hadn't wanted to admit it to myself. Part of me wondered if I could have done anything more to help Jimmy find her, whether I could have saved her life. But my every instinct said no, that I had nothing to go on, no idea where to start looking. I didn't want to look at the photographs, knowing how stark they would be. But I nodded and reached for them.

The flash bulb had driven away all the shadows. Mary O'Donnell was lying face-down across what I recognized as a baptismal font, her arms outstretched to the sides as though she had been crucified. She was wearing the same flowered housedress she had had on the first and last time I saw her alive. I looked over the half dozen photographs of the same scene taken at different angles. There were what looked like rope burns on her wrists.

"What's the preliminary determination of cause of death?" I asked, though it seemed pretty obvious.

"Suffocation, to be technically correct," Charlie said. "She drowned in that water."

I looked at the photos again. "She was drowned in holy water, wasn't she, Charlie?"

"Well, it's speculation for now, we don't have a formal report yet," Charlie said, taking the pictures and putting them back in the envelope. "But that's what it looks like."

It was horrible. I felt my hand shaking in my lap.

"You haven't asked me why I called you in," Charlie said in an offhand way.

"My business card," I said. I remembered passing several to Jimmy, telling him to give one to his sister. Obviously he had followed my suggestion. It was the only logical answer. I didn't want to divulge too much, but I knew Charlie would rip me apart if he felt I was holding back or somehow trying to mislead him. I finished my drink and held out my cup for a refill.

"That's right," Charlie replied. "You're here, instead of answering questions at the police station, because the homicide detective on the case is your old friend Anderson. As a professional courtesy, he told me about finding your card on the nun."

I was glad Detective Anderson had had the consideration to call Charlie before talking to me, but it wasn't a surprise. Anderson was a pro. And law-enforcement professionals in Dade County did favors such as this for each other all the time. We had to work together repeatedly over the years, in a lot of different situations. Once someone established a reputation as a stand-up person who behaved reasonably honorably, then professional courtesies were extended as a matter of course.

Charlie rocked back in his creaky wooden chair, sipping his drink. "Is there anything you want to tell me?" he asked. "Such as how a dead nun came to be carrying your business card in her brassiere, for example?"

I wished I hadn't sipped Charlie's bourbon so quickly. I needed to explain my involvement with Mary in a plausible fashion, both satisfying Charlie and maintaining the confidentiality of the case. I didn't really have to answer any of his questions—Statute 493 regulating private investigators in the state of Florida said so. Charlie knew this, but he also wanted to see how much I might reveal. We were both walking a fine line.

"I went to see her yesterday in connection with a case I'm working," I said. "That's all."

Charlie absorbed this. "Care to tell me more?"

"You know I can't," I said, trying to sound as reluctant as possible.

Charlie would know I was holding out on him, but I didn't see I had much choice.

"Well, who's the attorney you're working for on the case?" Charlie asked.

Mierda. There was no attorney on the case. And confidentiality applied only if there was an attorney of record on board. Otherwise I was just a regular citizen—open to subpoenas, discoveries, and all the recourses of the legal system. Only if I had been retained by an attorney could I claim attorney-client privilege.

"Tommy McDonald," I said, trying to sound sure of myself.

"Should have known he would be the lawyer on a case that ended up with a dead nun," Charlie said with open disgust as he reached for the bottle of Jack Daniel's. "A nun drowned in the holy water of a baptismal font—just the kind of case for McDonald."

Charlie's reaction wasn't surprising; no one in law enforcement had anything good to say about Tommy. His reputation for fighting for his clients was as fierce as was Charlie's on behalf of the state. I didn't recall them ever facing off in the courtroom, which was a little surprising considering the number of cases they'd each worked. And both men knew about my relationship with the other. Male jealousy combined with professional rivalry wasn't a recipe for creating a lot of goodwill between them.

"Can you tell me any more details?" I asked. Might as well press my luck, I figured.

"You mean, such as who killed her?" Charlie topped off his cup, cracked open the window behind his desk, and shook out a Marlboro from the pack in his pocket. He lit it with a match and took a deep sensual drag.

"I don't think you know that," I said, "or else you wouldn't have called me down here."

Who would want Mary dead, and why? Surely she hadn't been killed by her fellow nuns. All of a sudden I remembered Jimmy, wondered if he knew yet. It was a matter of time before the police learned about Mary's brother and sister. In any case, Jimmy would take it hard.

I watched Charlie take another drink. I could see that Mary's murder upset him; he always took his cases personally, it was part of the reason for his professional success. I knew I wasn't obligated to tell Charlie about Mary's brother in Miami, not if Tommy was indeed the attorney of record on the case—which he now was, although he didn't know it. I decided to let Charlie conduct his own investigation. Once I had more answers, perhaps I would share some of what I knew.

"When was she found?" I asked. "And who found her?"

"I don't have a lot of details," Charlie said. "Detective Anderson just asked me to talk to you."

I must have looked skeptical. The two of them had apparently decided they would get more out of me if Charlie spoke to me first.

"To speak with you as a friend," he added. "That's all."

"Well, I'm sorry," I said.

Charlie nodded, resigned. "Anderson did tell me something," he said. "When he went to Mary O'Donnell's order here—St. Joseph's—they didn't know her at all. Anderson said Mary might have been here on vacation or something. But the local branch of her order had no information at all. How does that strike you?"

"What do you mean?"

Charlie exhaled smoke. "Well, your sister is a nun," he said. "Is this how they operate? Not telling their own order their plans?"

"I don't know all the procedures," I said. "I don't think Lourdes has to sign out of the convent when she leaves town." I shrugged. Frankly, I didn't think Lourdes had ever bothered to find out all her order's rules, since a lot of them didn't apply to her anyway. She pretty much did what she wanted.

I tried to piece this all together. Mary had been found in the church of her order, but they hadn't known she was in Miami. Had she left Massachusetts without telling her order? I couldn't remember whether or not she had told me that during our conversation—probably the blow to my head hadn't helped my powers of recall. What had brought her to the Order of the Illumination—and made her leave so abruptly, with so much fear afterward? It all had to come back to the miracle, it was the only logical answer.

A shiver came over me when I recalled the crime-scene photos. I knew that Mary would have been incapable of harming anyone. Maybe that's why she had been killed, because she wouldn't perform some sort of bad deed. I knew I had to speak to her brother Jimmy right away.

My business card had been tucked in her brassiere. She must have meant to call me. Perhaps she had left Jimmy's house as a result of my visit. *Dios mio.* I hadn't thought of it before then, but I might have had some responsibility for her death. The thought steamrollered through my mind.

"Any chance this was a random killing?" I asked. "Wrong place, wrong time? A mugging gone bad?"

"There's always that possibility, but it's not being investigated that way," Charlie said. "As I said, her purse was found on the floor, everything intact. That's how she was identified so quickly. Otherwise you'd be down in the morgue IDing her. Anyway, Anderson knows more than me. You're welcome to talk to him, if you think you can get anything out of him."

Charlie finished his drink with a big gulp and stood up. I stood up as well, put my nearly untouched cup on his desk. I had had enough.

"Not so fast," Charlie said in a fond, soft voice. He came over to me and took me in his arms, kissed me lightly. "It's great to see you again, even if you're holding out on me."

"You know I can't talk about my cases," I said. "Nice try, though."

I laughed in spite of the seriousness of the situation. Charlie kissed my neck. It had been like this when we were together; the hardest times in our professional lives had always brought us closer.

"Tell me, Charlie, was it your idea or Anderson's to get me in here?"

"Lupe!" Charlie tried to look shocked, then kissed me again. "How could you possibly think that?"

I hummed in pleasure. It had been a long time since I smelled that combination of bourbon and cigarettes. But I started to pull away, resolute not to mix business with pleasure.

"I should go," I said, somewhat feebly. *Ay! Ay! Ay!* At this rate I would never get to Heaven, no matter how many mother superiors I worked for.

"I can lock the door," Charlie said. I didn't protest, so he did. To the naked eye his office looked institutional, cold and loveless. But it had always been an aphrodisiac for Charlie and me.

We had actually sunk down to the carpet before I came to my senses and stood up again. As tempted as I was to relive old times, this wasn't the way to conduct an investigation.

Charlie seemed disappointed by my sudden change of heart but, as I gently pushed him away, he recovered nicely. He stood up with a congenial smile on his face, his hands folded.

"All right," I said, trying to dispel the tension.

"OK," Charlie said.

We laughed nervously in unison. Charlie shook his head as though he had heard something I didn't, then went to the door. He paused in the doorway before opening it.

"Just one thing, Lupe," he said, serious now. "Watch yourself."

"Thanks." I gave him a peck on the cheek as I walked past him, feeling quite virtuous. Maybe all the religious aspects of the case were rubbing off on me; I felt I had just passed a chastity test in a fashion that Mother Teresa would have approved of.

As I waited for the elevator down, I took a deep breath. I wasn't sure what had gone on in Charlie's office. I had been tempted by him, there was no getting around it. But it had been the wrong time and place. Besides, I was still trying to pay back Tommy for all my transgressions. It wouldn't do to add more to the list—even those which he might never find out about.

As I rode downstairs I sank into a gloom thinking about Mary. I couldn't shake the feeling that I might have been somehow connected to the fate that befell her. She had disappeared one day after I visited her. It was too coincidental. I figured she had feared some sort of reprisal from the Order of the Illumination, or someone connected to the miracle, but I couldn't get rid of the worry that I had been the catalyst.

And now Jimmy might be in danger. I had to contact him—at the very least, I wanted to be the one to tell him about his sister. It was possible that Rose had spoken to him, I guessed, but I doubted that the police had found her in Massachusetts yet.

After I got back to my car I drove straight to Jimmy's house— this time not worrying about speeding tickets.

The house was empty, the silver Buick wasn't in the driveway. I drove past the little house three or four times, then parked and walked around the block twice. It was useless. There was no one in the house, no one around the house, no one who even seemed to notice the house except for me.

I decided I was wasting my time. After one last pass around the block, I drove away. I hoped the neighbors hadn't noticed me lurking around, but there wasn't anything I could do if they did. My need to see Jimmy overrode my investigator's desire for stealth.

On the way back to Cocoplum something strange happened. The road blurred, and I had to get off the highway.

I was thinking about Mary. My eyes were full of tears. There had been no reason in the world worth killing her.

"I'll find out who did it," I said quietly, speaking to her in Heaven. I owed her at least that much.

23

I kept phoning Jimmy at regular intervals throughout the night, with no success. After finally going to sleep around dawn, I awoke a few hours later feeling less than refreshed. I called Jimmy's number again, then sat and listened to it ring. Jimmy really did live in a time warp. He was probably the only person left in the civilized world who didn't have an answering machine or voice mail.

After coffee I decided that I had to get something done that morning, I couldn't just wait for Jimmy to come home. I determined that I could use the time to investigate the religious realities of the case—especially since Mary's body had been found in a church. Maybe understanding religious orders better would help me make some sense of what had happened to her.

I drove to the main branch of the Miami Public Library, parked in the public lot, then put a five-dollar bill into a homeless man's outstretched hand for good luck. I went inside and found the section devoted to Catholicism—if nothing else, I thought, I would keep my mind occupied as the time passed until I was able to reach Jimmy.

Three hours later I tried to wiggle my toes with no luck. Feeling in my lower extremities had started to desert me some time ago. I dreaded the agonizing pins-and-needles sensation that awaited me once I tried to rise. All the blood had left my legs in the hours I'd spent on the floor between the neat stacks, going through every reference book on the shelves that might contain some information about the Order of the Illumination of the Sacred Virgin. To my dismay I had found there wasn't much.

After three hours of searching, all I had to show for my labors was a half-sheet of a legal pad filled with handwritten notes—this after searching through dozens of books and religious publications. There simply wasn't much recorded information, useful or otherwise, about religious orders either in the United States or abroad.

Before I had set out I'd called the office and asked Leonardo to log onto the Internet from our office computer to see what he could find. I had faith in him—after all, many of his recent radical health-food recipes had come from nebulous Web sites set up by the granola underground. But he had come up dry. He told me, to my relief, that the Order of the Illumination didn't have its own Web page. If they had, he explained, someone might have found it by asking an Internet search program to look for keywords like "miracle," or "Virgin." If that had happened, the October 10 miracle might have gone public already.

I slowly massaged my ankles and read through my notes again. The Order of the Illumination of the Sacred Virgin was an old order, having been formed in the middle of the eighteenth century in the part of Eastern Europe that had become Yugoslavia after World War II. The town in which it had been founded—Medjugorge—seemed to have remained part of Yugoslavia, or Serbia, as it was now known to much of the world after the wars there throughout the decade of the 90s.

The order had apparently established branches in several different countries, but the United States had not been among them. Nor was Cuba. I flipped back to the reference book which had yielded that piece of information and saw that its publication date was three years ago—which didn't contradict Lourdes's mother superior's claim that the order had come to South Florida six months ago. I wondered what other information in these books might be misleading or out of date. There was no way to know, and Mother Superior had made it clear that she wasn't going to serve as a resource on the case. I would simply have to learn more about Catholicism there on the library floor.

The Order of the Illumination of the Sacred Virgin counted almost five thousand members, making it one of the largest orders in the church. And their numbers had recently swelled with Dade County recruits. How many more members would they recruit if they pulled off their miracle? I could begin to see why Mother Superior was so anxious, and that her stated reason for retaining me was quite plausible.

My reference book on religious orders said the Order of the Illumination was founded "with the intention of educating poor Catholic girls." At the time of its foundation, in that part of the world, education had been reserved for the wealthy. Poor girls weren't granted the opportunity to pursue learning. From a practical perspective, the order thought that the fabric of society would be bettered if underprivileged Catholic girls were taught to at least read and write.

I thought about this for a minute. That meant this was an activist order, firmly believing in clear and concrete action, trying to steer society toward a definite vision of improvement. It was a real hands-on approach. Perhaps making the Virgin weep fit into this viewpoint, because it could potentially change the societal and political attitudes of Cubans. But why Cubans? This was a European order. I couldn't see why they would be concerned with a speck of an island in the Caribbean at the end of the millennium.

I did the math. The order was founded in the middle of the eighteenth century, so they had been around for about two hundred and fifty years. Plenty of time to perfect their methods, to become a force to be reckoned with.

I had a small section in my notes that outlined the hierarchy of the order itself. The head of the Order of the Illumination of the Sacred Virgin was called the general superior. She lived in Medjugorge and governed over all the convents in Eastern Europe and throughout the world. The heads of the individual convents were called sister superiors. Regardless of where the convents were located, they were obliged to report directly to the general superior in Medjugorge.

This was important to me, because it spelled out the fact that the general superior in Medjugorge would be involved in all decisions concerning the Miami miracle—assuming that the sister superior here was following the rules of the order. It was difficult to imagine the local sister superior as a rogue nun going off claiming a major miracle was going to soon take place without the general superior's knowledge and approval. I didn't know much about the daily activity at convents, but I imagined that in some sense it had a bureaucratic structure like any other organization. Setting up a 1-800 number under a veil of secrecy would be improbable. Approval would have to come from above—not to mention the funds to pay for it.

There was another piece of information that I had jotted down and circled in the margin of my notes. I had known the name of Medjugorge was familiar to me somehow, although at first I had thought I probably heard it on the news reports about the war and human-rights abuses in Yugoslavia. That hadn't been it. In fact, I had learned, Medjugorge was a place where apparitions of the Virgin and various miracles had occurred for centuries. Some Catholic pilgrims, in more peaceful times, had actually booked package tours of the place so they could see the site of church-verified miracles. So the people of Medjugorge, as well as the order that called it home, were no strangers to miraculous happenings. And now they were attempting to export some of that magic to Dade County on October 10.

I didn't know much about the church from personal experience, but Mami used to be very involved with it. I remembered a thing or two from listening to her stories. Nothing in the church was ever undertaken on the spur of the moment. Mami used to describe her frustration at the amount of time it used to take to get approval for even the most modest undertaking. Everything had to be approved by the office of the archbishop, no matter how insignificant. So how, I wondered, could a foreign order of nuns announce the occurrence of this momentous miracle without consultation or approval from the top—in this case, the general superior in Medjugorge in conjunction with the archbishop of Miami?

I had no answer for this. And another question occurred to me. What about Lourdes's mother superior? Where did she fit into all this? She was, in effect, aligning herself against the miracle. At least that was the impression I'd carried since our interview: she was convinced the Yugoslavian nuns were fakers, their miracle a fraud. Was it possible that Mother Superior had set me up somehow? And what about her superiors? Were they aware that she had hired a private investigator to debunk the crying Virgin?

My instincts led me to believe that she was acting on her own. She seemed to me to be a woman of powerful ambition. She had worked hard to reach the position she held in the church hierarchy—and she wasn't going to lose any of her influence without a fight.

For a second my mind wandered, and I remembered the hard

glint in Mother Superior's eyes. I wondered how deep her ambition went. Was she hungry enough to murder? I didn't know what kind of threat, if any, Mary might have presented to Mother Superior. She certainly had been a threat to someone, enough that they had killed her to get her out of the way. Surely Mother Superior hadn't been involved in *that*.

I put down my notes and leaned back against the stacks. I had been working this case as just another investigation to be solved. I had brought Marisol, Nestor, Leonardo, and even Theofilus into the case based on my orders from Lourdes's mother superior. I had assumed, since Mother Superior was a religious official, that we weren't going against the will of the church or of God—thus avoiding subjecting us to excommunication. (Except for Theofilus, of course. As a Rasta, I couldn't imagine that he much cared.) I had been working under the assumption that the miracle was a scam, a ruse to attract attention to the Order of the Illumination, a recruiting tactic for a bunch of nuns.

The air was freezing in the library. In Miami you were always either sweating or freezing, there was no middle ground. But now I felt a bead of sweat trickle down my neck. It seemed entirely likely that the order wasn't acting on its own. The miracle had to have been, at the least, approved by the general superior in Medjugorge. And then probably by the archbishop of Dade County. Would people like this give approval to a scam? It didn't seem likely.

I started to shiver, not due to the lack of effective climate control in the library but because of a possibility that I hadn't considered in any real way. What if it were all real? What if Mother Superior was wrong? What if the miracle was going to happen? What if I was in the way of God's will? And what had Mary done that led to her death?

"Holy shit," I said aloud.

Someone in the next row of stacks shushed me.

"Sorry," I whispered.

I had to learn more about miracles, if only to better understand what I was getting myself into, then to uncover why Mary had died and eventually to find her killer. First I had to compare the information on the Order of the Illumination's phone recording with that listed in official church publications. Any sort of information could be manipulated for political ends, and the church certainly had never refrained from taking political action. The exploits of the Jesuits came to mind, as did an example closer to home—John Paul II's visit to Cuba to meet Fidel Castro.

I put the books on convents and religious orders back in place on the shelves and moved further down the row. The number of books on saints and miracles surprised me. There were rows of books that covered a wide range of perspectives on miracles, from church publications to personal testimonies to social-theory debunkers. There would obviously be no one book that would answer all my questions. Feeling overwhelmed, I pulled four or five down and sank to the floor again.

It was slow going. I couldn't understand why the Catholic Church seemed unwilling to write in plain English. I had to think through the convoluted language and logic in their writings and, when I was finished, I felt as though I barely understood the point they were trying to make. I wanted a simple statement of what the church considered a miracle. I had always considered myself a reasonably intelligent person, but reading Catholic texts made me feel as though I had sunk about thirty or forty IQ points.

But finally, a common thread started to emerge from what I was reading. A miracle is when divine power reveals itself through the existence of specific events. And they didn't occur in a vacuum— the purpose of a miracle was to let us know something about God's will through whatever event He was calling attention to. That seemed simple enough, after sifting through several arcane texts and convoluted explanations.

I leaned back against the shelf. Option number three on the 1-800 number had offered a list of miracles with which the Order of the Illumination had been closely associated. There were two major ones, and they had taken place in Medjugorge. One had taken place a hundred years ago, the other seventy-three years ago. The first had involved a nun from the order healing a young girl of blindness, the second entailed another nun saving a woman's life who had been dying from a mysterious, unexplained illness.

Basically both had been healings, and had been verified by church authorities without much recorded controversy. I digested that, and thought that there was little controversial about healing—certainly neither miracle of the past had been politically connected in any way that I could discern.

But there was something else. I ran my finger along a column of text and realized something that substantiated Mother Superior's comment during our initial interview. Both miracles *had* been verified by the Vatican recently, after a labryrinthine process, and both within the same calendar year: 1997. Perhaps this had emboldened the Order of the Illumination's sister superior to strike while the iron was hot. I knew that miracles sometimes had to wait decades for verification, so I had to take the timing of the two healings receiving approval as a coincidence.

The Order of the Illumination was claiming a very political miracle was about to occur, one that would affect millions of Cubans. But the order's roots were in educating young women, not in meddling with politics. Their miracles had been religious-oriented medical healings, not politically charged predictions of crying Virgins. Why the change? Was it sheer opportunism, a desire to be associated with a profoundly significant miracle?

I flipped through my notebook. Leonardo had transcribed the 1-800-MIRACLE tape for me, probably because he was so tired of hearing me play it in my office. Funny, I thought. The tape gave information about the upcoming miracle, but it contained nothing to explain why this particular order of nuns might receive the information that it was going to take place. I put a big question mark on the transcript.

I opened another book, a church-printed volume on miracles. The pattern, it seemed, was that word of an upcoming miracle was usually announced to an individual. In this case, it followed, the information was transmitted somehow to one of the nuns of the Order of the Illumination.

This sort of message historically was sent in one of a few ways. Sometimes an individual heard a voice speaking to them, or saw a symbolic event occur that triggered the truth in their mind. Sometimes they heard thoughts that they immediately knew weren't their own, telling them that something momentous was about to occur. But from what I was reading it seemed that the church was often skeptical of these sorts of claims. It was possible something else had happened to trigger news of future events at the

Ermita de la Caridad. A vision in a dream, I thought. Some kind of secret message.

What was I thinking? I asked myself. If one of these things had happened, then the miracle was real. And I was on the wrong side.

I needed to know how the nuns found out about the miracle, if indeed they had been sent a mystical message. It was strange they hadn't included this in their message; I would think it would have given them greater credibility. But perhaps they didn't want skeptics investigating the announcement. From what I could tell from my few hours of reasearch, what was about to happen in Miami was unique.

I stretched out my legs and surprised myself by yawning. The place was quiet. A few minutes before I had heard the person in the next stacks leave, and I was alone in my little section. In my lap was an etching of an eighteenth-century saint, his eyes cast up to Heaven, stigmata on his hands and ankles. His face looked as though he had already been transported to Heaven, to a place where worldly pain and suffering didn't exist.

I took in a sharp breath and looked to my right. Had someone been there? I thought I had sensed a presence, seen a dark shadow in the corner of my eye. I got up, leaving my books on the floor, and peered around the corner of the stacks.

No one was there.

I slapped myself on the cheek lightly. I must have gotten delirious sitting there on the floor, cutting off my circulation. If I wasn't careful this case was going to make me paranoid.

I gathered up my books and felt in my purse for change, knowing I would need it for the photocopy machines at the other end of the third floor. I needed to copy some of the material I had found, so I could examine it at my leisure once I got back to the office. For some reason, I was no longer feeling comfortable or safe at the library.

I stood in front of the photocopier, books stacked on the nearby table, and tried to find a way to detach my mounting feelings from the reality of what I'd been hired to do. I reached out and took the book I'd been copying from the glass of the machine—in the process knocking my change purse to the floor.

"Shit," I hissed as the coins went all over. A bearded man in glasses glanced up from the next copier, looking a little offended by my language.

"Excuse me," I said. It seemed as though I was always apologizing about something lately. I got down on the floor and reached for a few quarters that had rolled under the machine, producing the coins as well as a handful of dust bunnies.

The machine whirred on, and I fed it, trying to identify the feeling in my guts. I was messing with the church, with Cuba, with the Virgin. There was no way for me to guess whether I was on the right side or the wrong side.

What had they said in parochial school—that the pure of heart did God's will, sometimes without knowing it? I hoped they were right. Heaven help me if they weren't.

My cellular phone was tightly wedged between my ear and my shoulder as I fished around in my purse for the parking ticket to give the attendant. At the same time I was trying to extract a few bills from my wallet—all the while attempting to ignore the honking horns of the irritated motorists waiting behind me in line.

Mario Mencia, the Colombian attendant, couldn't have cared less how long it took me to pay. As far as he was concerned, the longer I dallied the more he could charge those waiting behind me—a fact that he had confessed to me once when I was apologizing for my slowness in getting out of his downtown parking lot. I don't think Mario ever left his post. In all the years I had parked in his lot he had been absent only once—during the World Cup finals. This afternoon he was watching a soccer match on a small portable TV in his booth, the smoke from his cigar forming a cloud that spilled out into the humid air.

Mario's calm appearance was actually deceiving. He looked as if he were surgically attached to his leather armchair, but I knew he was capable of action if necessary. After all, he worked with the public in downtown Miami. If trouble broke out, he had his Glock encased in a holster right next to the TV. A few years ago I had seen him get it out, to quiet a group of drunken lawyers who had carried on too long at happy hour—time probably spent, I thought, on some client's billable hours.

"Tommy? Hold on a second." I decided I'd better concentrate

on getting out of the parking lot in one piece before continuing my conversation.

One never knew what irritated Miami motorists might do. Road rage has a different meaning here. Instead of being shot at with a .38, which might happen in other parts of the country, in Miami someone would be more likely to come up firing an Uzi. Dade County residents take pride in being different.

"Lupe?" Tommy's voice called out. "Lupe, are you still there?"

"Sorry, Tommy. One more second." I handed Mario the ticket and a twenty-dollar bill, rolled up the window after Mario gave me a receipt. I knew there would be no change. Parking lots downtown charged so much it was a form of legalized robbery. Mario's little parking lot had put three of his children through Ivy League schools on fees alone.

The wooden barrier lifted and I was free to go, no doubt much to the pleasure of the drivers behind me. I didn't look back in my mirror, having no desire to see their red faces and bulging forehead veins.

"Sorry, Tommy," I said. "I was just paying Mario for parking."

"Are his kids in grad school yet?" Tommy asked, familiar with Mario's pricing.

"Two in med school, I think. At least one in law school."

"So what's up?" Tommy asked. "I don't mean to rush you, but I have clients waiting outside my office."

"Maybe I should take a number and get in line," I said. I groaned as I spotted a huge yellow school bus driving in the lane ahead. I would probably be stuck behind it all the way back to the office, watching it disgorging children all the way. The thought had barely crossed my mind when the red stop sign shot out from the side of the vehicle.

"*Mierda!*" I swore.

"What's the matter?" Tommy asked.

I didn't say anything. I wouldn't want him thinking I was a child-hater. I knew that Tommy had two rules in life that he never violated: he never sped in school zones, and he never kept library books past their due dates because someone else might want to read them. Of course, everything else was fair game.

"Nothing," I said. "So, are you saying I should get in line behind everyone else who's desperate to see you?"

"You? Desperate to see me?" Tommy asked, sounding pleased. "The great Miss Guadalupe Solano? This is quite a day."

"Are you free for dinner tonight?" I asked. The fact was, I did feel a little desperate. I just didn't like him knowing it, especially when the source of my anxiety was the fact that I had to tell him about something I'd done involving him. He wasn't going to be at all happy.

"For you I'm always free," Tommy replied. Ever the gentleman.

We made arrangements for when and where to meet before hanging up. I kept driving south toward my office, my head swirling with thoughts I was struggling to organize.

"Some of the preliminary backgrounds came back. Nestor had them couriered over, he said there's more coming. I put them on your desk," Leonardo said as soon as I stepped inside. He kept his gaze on me for a few seconds, as though detecting that something was wrong.

"You hungry?" he asked brightly. "I made something special for you. It's in the fridge."

Leonardo adhered to the tried and true Cuban philosophy for dealing with life's obstacles: the greater the difficulty, the more food was required to address it. His reaction to my appearance affirmed the fact that there was little I could hide from my cousin.

I groaned inside, though, knowing what was coming. Some sort of health-food monstrosity. I didn't want to insult Leonardo, but I also wasn't in the mood for some exotic confection like pickled puree of iguana nails marinated in fermented mango juice.

"Maybe later, *gracias*," I said, waving as I went toward my office. Leonardo's crestfallen look almost broke my heart; his nurturing instinct was too strong to take such a blow lightly.

"I just finished a *pastelito de guayaba*," I fibbed. If I had, I couldn't realistically be expected to eat another bite anytime soon, not after a sugar-filled, flaky, calorie-packed guava-packed pastry.

"OK. Well, let me know if you get the munchies," Leonardo called out as I closed the office door behind me.

I dropped my purse down on the sofa and found Nestor's manila envelope in the middle of my desk. A quick look out the window revealed that the parrots were still busy. They had started to erect a second edifice in the upper branches of the avocado tree, one that looked to me a lot like the Eiffel Tower.

I stared out the window as I dialed Jimmy's number again from memory. I let it ring ten times before hanging up.

From atop the credenza against the wall I took out the file marked "Mother Superior—Order of the Holy Rosary." I took a deep breath to calm myself. It would only hurt my understanding of the case to start ripping through the pages without a clear mind.

I opened the file and took out the notes Marisol and I had made from the surveillance video. Slowly and methodically I read through the list of tag numbers, matching them against Leonardo's printout. I did this one at a time, trying not to rush ahead to the silver Buick Theofilus had seen taking away the rebellious nun.

There was another set of tag printouts, the ones Leonardo had run from Marisol's pre-arrest list. I added the two lists together. In eight hours of surveillance, the convent had had a total of twenty-seven visitors arriving in private vehicles—eleven observed by Marisol, sixteen more from the videotape. There had been seven commercial vehicles—including Theofilus's truck. It wasn't an exceptionally long list, and it was one that Nestor, fortunately, had been able to check out in a short period of time.

I knew that the moment I opened the envelope, the names on the list would turn into real identities, people who nearly all would turn out to have innocent, legitimate business with the church. However, every one of them had to be considered a suspect. Normally this stage of an investigation made me excited—and I was, but my anticipation was tinged with something else. I may not have adhered to all the church's rules, but I was still a Catholic. I had no wish to see the church's reputation smeared in any way—though it certainly would be if I found the miracle to be a scam.

The press would go crazy one way or the other. *Miraclegate* came to mind or, even worse, *Virgingate*. I shuddered at the thought of the church being ridiculed, and hoped that the church administrators would be able to deal with spin control if everything became public.

I looked down at my desk. *Concentrate.* I needed to find hard facts, not speculate on how this investigation was going to end. I had learned a year ago how things could go wrong when I let my

24

I looked at my watch. It was almost seven. I was going to have to hurry to be on time for my date with Tommy, who was due to pick me up at the house in an hour. It wasn't a major problem, though. Tommy was accustomed to Cuban time, and I knew Osvaldo and Aida would take good care of him, serve him *mojitos* and conch fritters out on the terrace. I suspected that Tommy was so punctual with me because he liked spending time with the old couple, joking around while eating and drinking. This was fine with me. I certainly wanted my attorney friend to be in a pliable state of mind for our dinner conversation.

I learned from Osvaldo that Tommy had consumed three *mojitos* before I arrived at the house. Unfortunately the drinks seemed to have had little effect on him. Maybe the two platters of conch fritters he had also inhaled had countered the effect of the alcohol in his system, but I doubted it. Tommy never seemed to suffer any adverse effects from drinking. Maybe it was his Irish ancestry. When I first met him I tried to keep up drink for drink, but I quickly had to give in to his physical and genetic advantages. I was about five feet tall, if the wind was blowing the right way, and a hundred pounds soaking wet. Tommy was a little more than six feet tall, slouching, and two hundred pounds naked.

It was enough to make me jealous at times. Tommy could drink a river and eat an elephant without putting on an ounce. As far as I could tell, his only exercise was sexual activity with me. But I really shouldn't have complained. I was able to eat pretty much whatever I wanted. I put chocolate mousse cake on top of the food pyramid. I thought that ground coffee beans satisfied protein re-

personal feelings interfere with an investigation. I had to be detached to be effective, which wasn't easy when I thought about Mary.

Be detached. Be objective. I repeated this to myself several times, until it became a sort of mantra.

I was almost successful in dealing with Mary's memory when a picture of Jimmy appeared in my mind's eye. I picked up the phone again, not really expecting him to answer.

quirements in the same way as lentils and chickpeas—this was why I never, ever drank instant coffee, for nutritional reasons. When I worried that I hadn't eaten any fruit lately I uncorked a bottle of wine. As with everything else, I figured rules should fit a lifestyle and not the other way around.

A few years ago Leonardo had given me a particularly viscous bombardment about my unhealthy diet, and I had actually toyed with the idea of becoming a vegetarian. One meal at Versailles— the landmark Cuban restaurant on Eighth Street in the heart of Little Havana—took care of that. I must have reread the menu a dozen times, looking for anything that might serve as a vegetarian dish. All I could find was a side dish of avocado and onions, so I settled on two fried eggs served atop a bed of white rice—Cuban comfort food. There was no way I could be a vegetarian and still eat at Cuban restaurants—not unless I wanted to carry around little plastic containers of hummus and tofu in my purse. Any self-respecting Cuban place would have thrown me out for that kind of behavior.

I stole a sideways glance at Tommy as he drove around Cocoplum Circle before going over the Lejeune Bridge toward the business area of Coral Gables heading to Les Halles, the restaurant where Tommy had made reservations. We had been going there quite a bit lately, and we were automatically seated at our usual table with our usual waiter, Christian. He brought us a bottle of 1993 Chateau Floridene, the Graves Bordeaux wine we had ordered the last few times.

Christian, his dark curly hair combed back from his high forehead, brought no menus. Instead he asked us if we would like our usual order. This was a true sign of acceptance in a French restaurant, especially for two nonnationals like Tommy and me.

Our table was the first in a long row of banquettes alongside the mirrored wall. I sat on the inside, Tommy on the outside. We watched Christian open the bottle and place the cork in front of Tommy on the table. Tommy picked it up in a perfunctory manner and watched Christian pour a splash of dark red into his glass. One sip, a nod, and my glass was filled, followed by Tommy's.

"Give me a good toast," Tommy requested.

"To miracles," I said. "May those we wish for become reality."

"To miracles," Tommy agreed; we both took a sip.

"You look well," I said.

And he certainly did. He was dressed impeccably, as usual, in one of his tailored dark gray suits with vertical gray lines so fine that I would have missed them in the tissue-thin fabric if I hadn't known all his suits were pinstriped. He was wearing his favorite Charvet light pink shirt with French cuffs, and the gold Cartier cuff links I had given him for Christmas a few years before. Since we had made our date that day, I knew he had worn them that morning without knowing he was going to see me. His burgundy tie had an animal motif, frolicking tigers that looked as though they might have been eating their young. But that couldn't have been. That would be too much even for Tommy.

When he opened his jacket at the table I had spotted his ever-present Montecristo *Numero Uno* cigar inside his pocket for after dinner. Tommy never believed in openly breaking the law, but he made an exception for Cuban cigars. He bought them on the black market, in total violation of the U.S. embargo. One of the reasons Tommy liked Les Halles so much was that the manager let him light up his cigar at the table without giving him a hard time, a result of the French's disgust and disdain for American laws that eroded life's little pleasures.

Tommy gave me the little half-smile that always made my pulse race. It was like Pavlov's dogs hearing the dinner bell. I forced myself to concentrate on the reason I'd asked Tommy to meet me, and not to be distracted by carnal feelings.

We did indeed order our usual from Christian—steak, rare, with *frites* and salad. I looked up in wonder at the formidable art deco chandelier that hung in the center of the long dining room. Tommy and I settled into a comfortable, familiar silence.

Sometimes I wondered whether I had made a serious mistake not marrying Tommy. If I had drawn up a wish list of what I wanted from a husband, Tommy's characteristics would appear at the top of every category. We knew each other as well as a husband and wife possibly could.

"Tommy," I said, knowing I couldn't procrastinate any longer. "Don't laugh at me. I need to ask you a serious question."

Tommy's blue eyes lost their hazy, languid look and went into sharp focus. "Sure," he replied. "Anything you want. I'll answer you to the best of my ability."

I smiled at his lawyerly answer. Tommy always left himself with an out, no matter who he was talking to.

"Do you believe in miracles?" I asked. I had hoped to push the topic of the investigation back until later in the evening. There was no point ruining the meal over some unpleasantness—especially since I had created it.

"Miracles? What do you mean?" A frown crossed his forehead as he recalled my toast of a moment before. "This has to do with your case, the one you're working for Lourdes's mother superior. Right? The one that got me the Jamaican gardener as a pro bono client."

Tommy finished his wine and poured fresh glasses for each of us. The bottle was already getting low, so he motioned for Christian to bring us another.

"I get it. You wanted to see me so we could discuss the case," Tommy said. "And here I thought you just missed me."

"I did," I said, meaning it. He looked so pleased that I hated to consider my other motives.

Tommy wagged his finger. "Lupe, one of these days you're going to have to stop using me. You're going to have to decide you want me and need me for myself—not for what you can get out of me."

My heart sank, but then Tommy took a long sip of wine and laughed. "What the hell," he said. "That day hasn't come yet. So give me a minute and I'll tell you what I think."

Even though he was laughing, I could see that Tommy meant every word he had said. I remembered the fear I felt in his apartment a couple of days past, when I thought I was losing him. In his own way Tommy had put me on notice that the days of taking his help for granted were coming to an end. The very thought filled me with anxiety just as Christian arrived with the wine and our dinner.

There was nothing like a mouthwatering plate of food to chase away my worries. I started to slather ketchup all over my French fries. I knew it was disgusting and basically an insult to the chef— just like indiscriminately pouring *mojo* over Cuban food or soy sauce over Chinese—but I loved ketchup and Les Halles' French fries too much to resist. Anyway, Tommy overtipped so much that I didn't think the staff was going to comment on my abominable habits anytime soon.

"Miracles," Tommy said slowly between bites of steak. "Well, yes, I do believe in miracles. Now, I'm using a definition that means feats or events that are unexplainable by conventional scientific means."

He sipped his wine, very serious. "But to believe in miracles one first has to believe in God," he added. "The Virgin birth, Adam and Eve—all of it—if one takes that on faith, then miracles have to follow. Do you see my logic?"

"I guess I hadn't looked at it that way," I admitted. "But I suppose you're right. Belief in miracles isn't a great leap of faith if belief in God is already there."

"So how's the case going?" he asked. "You getting anywhere?" Tommy looked at the date on his watch. "Today is September twenty-fourth. Looks like you have a little more than two weeks."

"It's slow going," I said. "I mean, it's not like I have any experience in this field. Proving or disproving a miracle isn't something I learned about when I was training to be an investigator."

"It's more than a professional problem," Tommy said confidently. "I can see that. Working this case is pushing you to examine your feelings about your faith."

We sat in silence for a moment. Tommy was always right when it came to me.

"If this miracle turns out to be a scam, you don't really want to be the one who blows the whistle on the church," he said.

Tommy poured more wine. This time it reminded me of Communion wine during Mass, when Christ's blood was transubstantiated just before the priest drank it.

I shrugged in misery. I remembered why I had wanted to meet with Tommy. Because he always helped focus my thinking. But I also needed a favor, and I wasn't sure whether I could get away with asking for it.

"And if that wasn't enough, there's also the Cuban element of the case," Tommy said, wiping his mouth with his napkin. Somehow during this conversation he had wolfed his entire meal. I was only about halfway through with mine.

"I don't want to mess with Cuban politics," I said in a low voice. "And this case has politics running right through the heart of it." As well as murder, I thought to myself—a topic that I didn't want to discuss with Tommy, not just yet.

Tommy nodded. He would understand. More and more I thought about the symbolism behind the upcoming miracle. The Virgin's tears would serve to express her unhappiness at Cubans allowing themselves to live in a divided state for such a long time. Some would interpret this to mean that we had upset the will of God for the entire forty-year reign of Fidel Castro. And now at the millennium it would all come to a head. But what were we supposed to do? Reconcile? There would be even more disagreement, and more than a few people would surely jump to very rash conclusions.

In the back of my mind was another fear. The miracle hadn't been made known to the general public yet, but the Order of the Illumination wasn't exactly hiding it, either—they had already set up a toll-free number, for example. Other people might also know of it. There would be those who would use the miracle to their own advantage, factions who would fight the very concept of a rapprochement between the two Cubas. Not everyone would take the miracle on faith. All sorts of agendas would surface, from believers and skeptics to peace-lovers and the militant. I didn't need a lecture from Alvaro on Cuban politics to come to that conclusion.

I finished my wine. *In vino veritas.* In wine there is truth. If only it were so—and why not throw in some courage for good measure. I was feeling in short supply of both that night.

Tommy nodded to Christian, who cleared my plate away. A moment later I was looking down at a chocolate mousse followed by an espresso. Tommy had the same. We were obviously getting predictable. A few minutes later we sipped Courvoisiers while we waited for Tommy's American Express card to be approved. Neither of us spoke. It was obvious I was going home with Tommy that night; all that talk of heavenly miracles had stoked our earthly desires. And though I hadn't realized it, I needed a respite from my guilt and worry—if only for a couple of hours.

"Tommy?" I whispered into his ear. The green light of the digital clock by the bed read six o'clock. I knew that Tommy always set his alarm for six-thirty. I started kissing his ear, knowing that would get his attention.

"What is it, *querida?*" Tommy moaned.

"You love me a lot, right?" I asked, nibbling his ear. A bit of positive reinforcement never hurt. And if I didn't receive an enthusiastic response after all we had done in bed the night before, then I really was going to join a convent.

"You know I do." His voice was less sleepy. I saw by the dawn sunlight through the windows that his eyes were opening. "What do you want from me now?"

My plan wasn't working as smoothly as I'd hoped. Tommy knew me too well.

"Don't get angry with me," I said. "Please, promise me you won't."

I started to touch him, leaving no doubt of my intentions.

"Oh, hell, Lupe," Tommy sighed, more resigned than mad. "You're going to seduce me and then get me to do a favor, aren't you?"

Tommy looked so dejected; his disappointment was almost more than I could bear. I was about to tell him that the state attorney's office considered him the attorney of record on the Holy Rosary case, but I chickened out. It was wrong of me and I knew it—yet I couldn't risk his reaction, not just then. I flashed back to his reaction when I told him that he was representing Theofilus. I couldn't go through another scene like that one, not yet.

The truth was that my actions this time had been far more serious in terms of how they might affect Tommy. I decided I would tell him soon, but that I would postpone it for just a little while. It would have upset him too much at that moment.

So I took the low road. I wasn't proud of myself. But I had to think fast to explain why I had asked him not to be angry with me. I quickly remembered another sensitive issue—albeit one that wasn't as brazen as the false representation I'd made earlier to Charlie.

I bit his neck. "You know Marisol, right?" I asked.

"Your video vixen queen?" Tommy asked. He groaned audibly. "What? You want me to keep her out of jail, too?"

"Actually, yes," I said. As I spoke I got more serious about making Tommy indebted to me. "She got arrested. She's out on bail. I need you to represent her."

"Marisol arrested?" Tommy could barely get the words out. "What kind of . . . trouble is she in?"

"Marisol violated the occupational license law by selling hot dogs from a cart in Homestead."

Tommy gasped.

"While wearing a bikini," I added.

"What?" Tommy let out a shuddering groan. "Hell. Send her to my office."

I felt badly about what I'd done—or, rather, not done. But I would try to make up for it with passion. I would do anything to make Tommy look at me more favorably, since I couldn't postpone forever the time when I told him I'd dragged him into the case.

At this rate Tommy's office would soon be full of my referrals. I sure as hell knew I couldn't afford his hourly rate of four hundred dollars. I would just have to negotiate a better payment arrangement. As Tommy lay happily spent next to me, I didn't think he would have much objection. And as for me, I always paid my debts.

25

MY heart leapt into my mouth the next morning, when I drove to the office and saw a silver Buick parked in the driveway. I almost crashed into the poinciana tree as I pulled into my parking space at the end of the driveway. My excitement and relief over seeing the car was so great that I dashed out of the Mercedes without stopping to lock it.

Jimmy was waiting on the sofa in my reception area. He was alive and well, and it was all I could do not to fall all over him when I came through the door. I realized then that part of me had given up on ever seeing him again.

Jimmy, a cup of coffee in his hand, looked tired and disheveled. An instant later I knew that he had been informed of his sister's fate.

"I know," I said to him. "I'm sorry."

I took his elbow and guided him into my office, then gestured to one of the chairs facing my desk. I sat down and waited for him to finish his coffee. He shook his head weakly and looked down at the knees of his worn work pants.

"So you heard," he said.

I nodded. There was no trace of accusation in his voice, no hint that he blamed the timing of my appearance in his life for the loss of his sister.

"I tried to reach you," I said.

"I've been staying with a friend," Jimmy said in a monotone. "Couldn't face the empty house, Mary's things. You know."

"I was . . ." I paused. "I was really worried about you, Jimmy."

Jimmy looked at my face for a second, then out the window. "I never thought I'd lose her. I thought I'd be dead and long gone before anything happened to her."

The grief in his voice as he struggled to retain his tough exterior was almost more than I could handle. I pushed a box of tissues across the desk toward him, but he ignored it.

"Sometimes I hated the church," Jimmy announced, as though we were in the middle of some other conversation.

"What do you mean?" I asked.

"The way they took my sisters from me. You have no idea what it was like."

"I don't," I told him. "Would you tell me?"

He looked into my eyes suspiciously, then down at his half-finished coffee. His gaze focused on the middle distance, as though he was drifting into the past—just as he and his sister had done a couple of days before.

"On our seventeenth birthday, right after graduation from Christ the King High School, Rose and Mary entered the convent of the Order of St. Joseph's as postulants."

Jimmy leaned forward, his voice hushed as though in reverence of his own memories. "They had to prepare like they were going to camp," he said. "About a month before they left they got a list of things they had to buy."

"A list?" I asked. "But don't they get issued the clothing they're supposed to wear?" I couldn't recall Lourdes ever receiving such a list from the Order of the Holy Rosary. Mami probably secretly took her to Saks at Bal Harbor and bought her everything she needed—even though silk lingerie likely violated the spirit of the vow of poverty.

Jimmy shook his head. "Some things were given to them, others the family supplied for them," he said. "My sisters bought their own shoes, socks, nylons, things like that. Not all the girls who entered the convent could afford much, so the girls were told to bring a bare minimum. They were supposed to bring enough personal supplies to last them thirty days.

"Mama said it was like packing your hope chest," Jimmy remembered. "They weren't allowed to wear brassieres, only white cotton undershirts. Isn't that something?"

I didn't want to comment on that. I tried to recall how Mary had looked, but I couldn't tell from the shapeless dress she'd worn how much support she might have needed. Things had certainly changed. Lourdes, for instance, had a charge account at Victoria's Secret. I had personally given her lingerie last Christmas from La Perla—bra, panties, garter belt. At least they had all been in white cotton, albeit covered in French lace. Lourdes had liked the gift so much she asked for an identical set in black next Christmas, something to wear under her dark blue habit.

"I remember Mama packed their things in a big black trunk," Jimmy said. "The trunks had to conform to a precise measurement, and we were told where to buy them. Everything had to go smoothly, that was the impression the families got."

This discourse wasn't supplying much to help me with my case, but I knew better than to interrupt. I could tell that Jimmy hadn't talked about these things in years, probably decades. He was trying to put his sister's life into context, to explain a recent trauma to himself. I simply had to hang in there with him.

"I remember that drive to the motherhouse in Pittsburgh like it took place yesterday!" Jimmy said suddenly, almost smiling. "The longest three hours of my life. We knew they were going to be in that convent for the next three to five years.

"Without coming home," he added, apparently remembering the pain he must have felt at being separated from his sisters. "We could visit, sure. On holidays, for three hours at a time in the convent's visiting room. Mary and Rose weren't even allowed to come outside with us."

Jimmy still seemed scarred from these events of nearly a half century past. The more I heard about how the convent controlled all aspects of the postulants' lives, the more it reminded me of a form of brainwashing. First you tell the young woman and her family how special she is, how unique her calling to God. Then you isolate her from her family and from the outside world, making sure that the limited contacts are brief, and extremely structured and supervised. As time passed the other nuns would become the girl's substitute family, while biological bonds to her own family would weaken and finally erode away.

"What about after they became nuns?" I asked. It was hard for me to compare this story with Lourdes's. I couldn't recall ever hearing her talk about her life as a postulant.

"Only a little better," Jimmy replied. "My sisters were allowed home for one week during the summer. But they weren't allowed to sleep in their own home. They could spend the day with us, but at night they had to go back to the convent."

I wished I had a *café con leche*, but I wasn't moving. Not while he was talking like this. Taking notes was out of the question. I could think of no better way to piss off Jimmy than to take out a tape recorder.

"Once they had completed their novitiate they belonged to the church," Jimmy said. I could see in his eyes that he was present in my office in body only; mentally, he was decades in the past.

"My sisters were given wedding rings. They became brides of Christ."

Jimmy looked up, snapping back into reality. He raised an eyebrow, almost daring me to absorb what he was saying.

"Brides of Christ," I repeated, rather stupidly. Lourdes certainly didn't wear a wedding ring on her hand. If she had, knowing Mami, she would have been taken to Tiffany's for an upgraded band of diamond baguettes.

"They wore wedding dresses and everything," Jimmy said, shaking his head. "Just like real brides getting married. The novices walked down the aisle in the chapel convent, then they left halfway through Mass. Everyone waited for them to come back in their black habits, with their new religious names. It was a total . . . a total . . ." Jimmy groped for the right word.

"Transformation?" I offered.

He snapped his fingers. "Right. A transformation. I remember the dresses Rose and Mary wore," he said. "They were donated by a corset shop in downtown Pittsburgh. Every year the shop donated dresses to the convent. The novices shaved their heads, between the time they left in their wedding dresses and came back in their habits. It was a total transformation. Never saw anything like it."

Jimmy shook his head at the memory. His sisters were shaved like army recruits, stripped of their individuality, probably rendered almost unrecognizable to their own families. Today young people shaved their heads as a fashion statement, to rebel. That kind of thing wasn't done years ago. Thank God that custom had changed; otherwise Lourdes would have never entered her convent. I knew God would have had to take a backseat to vanity—Lourdes loved her curly dark brown hair too much to sacrifice it for anything.

Jimmy dropped his head for a moment, then shook it violently from side to side. I tensed, wondering what accounted for this sudden change.

"I apologize for rambling," he said, looking up again. "All that's in the past. My sister is gone, and nothing is going to bring her back."

I folded my arms, then spoke in a gentle tone.

"I want to find who murdered your sister," I said. Jimmy didn't reply, so I ventured on. "If you don't mind, I have a few questions you might be able to help me with."

Jimmy sat up stiffly. "I didn't come to answer questions," he said. "I came to talk to you about my sister. I wanted you to understand what kind of person she was."

I sat still. This didn't sound quite right. Why would Jimmy care what sort of impression I had of Mary? She was gone, I was just someone they'd met once under strange circumstances. Why all this trouble just to share some memories with me?

"Look, Jimmy, maybe you can give me some idea what your sister was involved in." He looked away, but he was listening. "I can help. I've been in this business almost ten years. And I know the homicide detective assigned to the case. I've worked with him before."

Jimmy chewed his lip for almost a minute before speaking.

"You think you can find out who killed her?" he asked, his voice little louder than a whisper.

I nodded. "Probably. If I have some information to get me started."

Jimmy ran his hand over his unshaven cheek, looking at me out of the corner of his eye. I could see that an internal battle was waging inside him. He started to speak, then stopped. I remained silent, knowing that I shouldn't press him.

Finally he got up from his chair. He held out his hand for me to shake.

"I'm sorry, Loopy," he said. "I've taken up too much of your time already."

We shook hands; I was almost too stunned to hold mine out. A moment later he had bolted from the room, leaving me alone. All I could do was stare out the door through which he had left. Leonardo came in a few seconds after I heard the front door chime.

"Wow!" he said. "What was that all about?"

"I'm not really sure," I said with a shrug. Bailing out of conversations the second they became uncomfortable seemed to be an O'Donnell family trait. "I offered to find his sister's killer. That's when he stood up and left."

"A nut," Leonardo observed. "Or else a man with something to hide."

My sentiments exactly. I looked at my cousin, who was wearing lime-green weights strapped to his wrists and ankles. It wasn't exactly reassuring to have him voice opinions that coincided perfectly with my own.

"Leo, do me a favor," I said. "Call up Nestor and have him expedite all the backgrounds. I need them yesterday."

Leonardo left quickly, not even miffed at having received such an imperious command. It was almost enough to frighten me. Even my cousin saw that the case was getting deadly serious.

Rather than let it all get to me, I decided to brew some fresh coffee in the office kitchen; as I listened to the water gurgle in the machine, I heard Leonardo on the phone with Nestor, asking about the expedited background checks.

I poured the fresh coffee, added a dash of milk, and walked slowly back to my office. I decided to review my case notes again, hopefully with a fresh mind.

I had just about finished a second *café con leche* when I noticed a puzzling bit of information in Nestor's reports. I looked over a series of background checks Nestor had compiled on the vehicles that had entered the Order of the Illumination convent during Marisol's initial surveillance. One of the cars was registered in a man's name: Michael Patterson. The state of registration was Massachusetts.

That was something. Mary and Rose's convent was in Massachusetts. I shook my head, wondered how I had missed the connection before. I had been so eager to identify Jimmy O'Donnell's Buick that I had completely overlooked it.

I searched through Nestor's companion file, put the record next to Jimmy's. The car from Massachusetts had entered the convent an hour and fifty-two minutes before Jimmy's. Almost two hours passed between the first car's arrival and the time Jimmy came to pick up his distraught sister. Could this Michael Patterson have had anything to do with the fight Mary had with the sister superior? The timing could have been more than coincidental. Within a three-hour period, two visitors from Massachusetts—three, counting Mary—had been to the convent.

Calm down, I told myself. I picked up the phone and dialed Nestor; after five rings, just as I was about to give up, his voice came on the line.

"Lupe," he said. "Haven't heard from you in a few days. I was wondering what had happened."

"Sorry I haven't been in touch," I replied. I thought I heard in his voice a faint hope that the case would have been concluded by then, that he wouldn't have to get involved any further—although he had to know realistically that he was dreaming.

"What's up?" he asked. "I just got off the phone with Leo—I'm getting on those expedited reports."

"I'm not calling about that," I told him. "I want to follow up on something in one of your reports."

I heard him groan. "OK, what is it?"

"Michael Patterson, from Boston," I read aloud from the sheet of paper. "I want a full background. Social Security, financial, occupational. I want to know what kind of underwear he wears. And I want it expedited, Nestor. ASAP."

"No problem," Nestor sighed. "Of course you want it yesterday. You always do. I dream of the day you tell me to take my time, that there's no hurry. This time it's going to be expensive."

"I know." I blotted out Leonardo's image from my mind. "Just get it as soon as you can. And *gracias*."

When I hung up the phone my mind felt sharper than it had in days. Michael Patterson meant something to the case, I was sure of it. I only had to discover what it was.

26

SISTER Ivana greeted me in the reception hall of the Order of the Illumination of the Sacred Virgin by taking my hands and smiling warmly. I tried to smile back.

"My dear, welcome," she said in accented English. "We are so happy you have come here today."

She was middle-aged, with a wide nose and dark hair that formed a widow's peak on her forehead. I felt a surge of guilt, since I was there to spy on her and her fellow nuns. On a more practical level, I hoped Sister Ivana hadn't noticed that my hands were sweaty from nerves.

"What is your name again?" she asked, handing me a packet of legal-sized papers. I glanced down; it was a questionnaire.

"Magdalena," I replied. "My name is Magdalena."

Sister Ivana beckoned for me to follow her, so I dutifully marched along, trying to take in my surroundings without seeming too obvious.

I already knew a little about the convent. In my office back in the Grove was a file containing Nestor's work on the case. He had found that the Homestead property on which the convent was situated had once been the second home of a Miami banking executive who had liked to spend weekends in the country with his family. The Archdiocese of Miami had bought it a year ago, remodeled it, and converted it into a convent six months later. The Yugoslavian nuns were the first order to live there since the church acquired the property. The main office building, from what I had seen so far, was a rambling warren of small rooms.

As we made our way, I realized that unlike many American nuns who wore civilian clothing, the nuns of the Order of the Illumination were formally dressed in indigo-blue habits with veils that came down to their waists. It gave them an old-world air. I heard the sharp clacking of wooden rosary beads worn low on the sister's hips. It was a sound no Catholic-educated person could ever fail to recognize.

I followed Sister Ivana into the inner sanctum of the order, trying to will my confidence to grow. I had pulled off a lot of undercover jobs in the past, after all. However, part of me still thought that nuns had superpowers—such as smelling an impostor, a sinner posing as a saint.

"Please wait here. Sister Superior will be with you shortly." My guide pointed to the closest of two chairs in the room.

I sat down in a red leather armchair facing a massive wooden desk. The chair was hard and unyielding, and I wiggled in vain to try to get comfortable. I wondered if this was an accident or whether the chair was intended to keep visitors alert and on their toes.

I looked up at Sister Ivana and, for a second, thought I might ask her about the miracle. I decided against it; it wouldn't help for her to think this was my only reason for coming to the order.

Sister Ivana smiled, bowed, and walked out backward so she faced me all the way out the door. I smiled nervously. I had only seen that kind of deferential behavior in the movies.

Alone, I let out a big sigh. I had made it this far. I looked around the room. It was almost a carbon copy of the mother superior's office at the Order of the Holy Rosary. It made me suspect that there was some sort of blueprint for how convent rooms should look—like they were McConvent franchises. I shook my head and willed the thought away. Nuns could read minds, part of me thought from childhood. I had to think pure thoughts.

Almost ten minutes passed in silence; I listened to the sound of my own breathing, trying to stay calm. Finally the door opened and a small, compactly built woman came in. She wore the same indigo-blue habit as Sister Ivana, and radiated a no-nonsense attitude. She moved briskly across the room to her desk, and I barely had time to stand up in respect for her presence.

She sat down with such an air of wordless authority that I knew this was Sister Superior. She looked at me with silent curiosity, taking my measure. I fought not to let my questions about the miracle start leaping from my mouth. And I now wondered: was this smooth-faced, clear-eyed woman responsible for murder? Her gray eyes gave nothing away. She crossed her hands in front of her, and I thought she would probably make a very successful poker player.

"Good morning, my child," she said in a husky voice.

"Good morning," I replied.

Her examination of me felt like a spiritual X ray and MRI combined. I hoped I passed inspection in my knee-length khaki-colored shirtwaist dress, which I had borrowed from Lourdes. I had figured I could pass myself off as a potential nun by dressing in the clothes of a real one. Maybe a little bit of holiness would rub off on me in the process. Unfortunately, the dress had just come back from the dry cleaner's—so the saintliness in the cloth would have to have survived the chemicals that had cleaned it. On my feet I wore sensible, low-heeled black pumps—also borrowed from Lourdes. Her feet were a size bigger than mine, so I had stuffed Kleenex into the toes to keep from making clomping sounds when I walked. Needless to say, the Chanel bag stayed at home this time. Lourdes had provided me with a plain black leather purse that she'd carried for years.

I debated carrying the Beretta in the purse as usual but decided not to do so in case I would have to walk through a metal detector at the front door—these being security-conscious times. I felt naked without the gun, especially after what happened to Mary O'Donnell. I wore no makeup, no perfume, no jewelry. If anyone I knew had seen me that way I would have wanted to slit my wrists.

I must have passed inspection. Sister Superior nodded to herself slightly, as though having made a decision.

"I was told you feel you have a calling," she said. "You would like to explore the possibility of joining us, to see if your calling is a genuine one."

Sister Superior shared Sister Ivana's European accent, though hers wasn't quite as pronounced. She spoke slowly, choosing her words with deliberation.

"Yes, ma'am," I said. To my own ears I sounded completely false. I would have failed a polygraph on the first question—which would have been to state my real name.

"And why do you think you have a calling, Magdalena?" Sister

Superior asked, somehow skeptical and mournful at the same time. "And why does our particular order appeal to you?"

There it was. The $64,000 question. I met her gaze as directly as I could, and tried to remember what Lourdes had coached me to say.

"I know your order is devoted to prayer," I said. "My mother died a slow and painful death, and during her long illness I prayed to the Virgin and received much comfort."

I hated using Mami's memory like that, but I knew in order to be believed I'd have to stay as close to the truth as possible.

"I attended Catholic schools all my life," I added. "I have always felt drawn to the faith, especially Our Lady. Ever since I was a little girl I thought about serving her."

I had rehearsed a much more detailed and elaborate reply with Lourdes, but I found that I couldn't bring myself to brazenly deceive Sister Superior in that way. My Catholic upbringing was too ingrained.

"I am sorry about your mother," Sister Superior said. She made the sign of the cross. "It is admirable that you want to serve Our Lady in your mother's memory, Magdalena. But you know, not everyone is suited for the religious life. It is a lifetime commitment."

"I understand that," I said. "I was told you offer retreats, to see if a person is suited for convent life and has a true calling."

Lourdes said practically every convent runs special retreats for prospective recruits; it was a way of weeding out those young women who had overestimated their religious fervor. There had apparently been a huge exodus of women from religious orders in the 60s and 70s. Now potential entrants to orders were carefully screened—sometimes even to the point of having to undergo psychological testing. I prayed I wouldn't be subjected to that kind of scrutiny, because then I would definitely be found out. I could talk a convincing game, but a test specifically designed to expose unsuitable characters was a different story.

"There are retreats, yes," Sister Superior said. "As well as other tests."

"I see," I said. I must have looked concerned, because Sister Superior laughed gently.

"Don't worry, all these procedures are for your benefit as well as the church's," she said. "You think you have a calling, I understand. Yet it may not be so."

"But—"

Sister Superior held up a hand to quiet me. "You may have a temporary attraction to religion," she said. "Wouldn't you like to explore your calling as deeply as possible? You wouldn't want to feel as though you had wasted years of your life one day."

"Yes, of course." I tried to look convinced. "That makes sense. I'm sure you know better than me."

"You have the questionnaire?" Sister Superior asked.

"Yes, Sister Ivana gave it to me," I replied. "I haven't had a chance to fill it out. I'm sorry, I just looked over it."

"Please, Magdalena, there's no need to apologize," Sister Superior said; she smiled and tilted her head back, laughing without making any sound. She held up her hand and I heard the soft click of wooden beads. "I realize you were just given the form."

"Thank you, ma'am," I answered gratefully. I hoped I hadn't gone too far with the "ma'am's"—presumably a Yugoslavian sister superior wouldn't know that a Cuban girl didn't often use that form of address.

"I would like to tell you about our retreats," Sister Superior said. "We have a program that might interest you. We encourage all young women who come here with an interest in religious life to attend a three-day retreat. It is offered here at the convent four times a year."

Lourdes had said that these retreats were essentially a prerequisite to being accepted as a postulant at a convent.

"The next retreat will be offered on October the first," she said, looking down at her desk calendar.

I blinked, unable to believe my luck.

"I would be very interested in that," I said, trying to control my voice.

"Then you must fill out your papers and return the questionnaire as soon as possible," she said. "At that point you can receive a formal invitation to participate."

"I would like that very much," I gushed. And, I realized with a start, I would, indeed, have found such an experience most interesting. However, I would have to wait to see how the case turned out to actually follow through with going to the retreat.

"You will be assigned a sister whose schedule you will follow during the time you spend here," she continued. "It is the first step in determining whether you have a genuine vocation."

"Wonderful," I said.

I wondered whether the retreat was offered only in English, or whether a Spanish-language retreat was also available. I hoped asking might lead Sister Superior into revealing whether she spoke Spanish. But I decided not to do so. We were conversing freely in English, and I might arouse her suspicion if I started to probe about her language skills.

"It is not an easy life," Sister Superior said. She looked at me with what seemed a sudden feeling of compassion. "You must be totally dedicated to serving the church."

She started to talk about all the sacrifices I would be expected to make, all that would be demanded of me. I couldn't help thinking about Lourdes and whether she had listened to the same speech when she first went to the Order of the Holy Rosary. Although Lourdes's mother superior and the sister superior in front of me shared some traits—both seemed used to being in unquestioned command, with a strong, disciplinarian presence—Lourdes's order seemed more laid-back than this one. Maybe it was the Slavic origins of the Order of the Illumination, in contrast to the overwhelmingly Latino Order of the Holy Rosary.

Sister Superior tapped her desk with her palm as she listed the privations a nun faces—breaking off contact with the secular world, intensive prayers, reflective study. It seemed her order made a Marine boot camp look like a weekend at the Four Seasons. I was exhausted just listening to her, and I wondered what percentage of prospective nuns ran out of the room at this point and were never heard from again.

"Do you have any questions?" she finally asked. Her mouth was tight, though she seemed to have derived satisfaction from trying to scare me about the rigors she had lived with most of her life.

I looked down at my hands. "I have heard stories," I said, hoping I sounded innocent and naive.

"Stories?" Sister Superior asked.

"About a miracle involving the Holy Mother."

"The miracle," Sister Superior repeated, her voice barely more than a whisper. She looked at me with such acuity that I had to fight not to break away.

I nodded. For a second I wanted to ask her why she was surprised—her order had, after all, set up a 1-800 number to advertise their involvement in the miracle.

"What do you know?" she asked.

I took a deep breath. "Our Blessed Mother is going to cry tears to express her sadness over the separation of the Cuban people," I said, my voice breaking from nervousness in mid-sentence.

Sister Superior didn't speak, didn't move; she seemed to have turned into a statue at her desk.

"May I ask a question?" No reply, but I figured she would stop me anytime she wished. "There is something that I fail to understand. I don't mean to question the workings of Our Lady, but why would a miracle involving the Cuban Virgin be announced to a Yugoslavian order of nuns?"

"There are questions in life for which there are no answers, Magdalena," Sister Superior began.

Well, I've heard that one before, I thought.

"If you enter religious life, you will learn to accept and not to question," she added in a pious manner. I felt the hair stand up on the back of my neck, a reminder that I could never stand sanctimony.

Maybe it was a risk, but I had to press on in case I never made it to the retreat. This might be my only opportunity to ask someone in the center of the order about the miracle.

"I certainly don't mean to be disrespectful to the church," I began. "But it seems that this statement by Our Lady will have a very strong impact on Cubans. As a Cuban, I'm very interested in this."

"Let me ask you something, Magdalena." Sister Superior leaned forward in her chair. I heard birds chirping outside. "Do you know anything about the history of the Order of the Illumination?"

"A little," I said, trying to sound uncertain.

"Our order has been involved in other miracles," she said. "It might seem unusual to you that our order is involved in this Cuban miracle, but to us it is plain and obvious. We have always served Our Lady, we have seen other miracles. There will be more in the future. We are the servants of our Blessed Lady. We do her will."

I watched her closely as she uttered these words; while her mouth moved, none of the rest of her body wavered even a centimeter. It was as though her speech was compartmentalized from the rest of her body. She reminded me of a ventriloquist's dummy.

"I can see that," I agreed. "It . . . it must be a very exciting time here, knowing that the order has been chosen by the Virgin to deliver the message of the miracle."

I had started to feel that we had developed a tenuous rapport. I smiled, humble, trying to play on this bond.

"It is a great honor to all of us," Sister Superior said. Then she looked down at her watch. But I wasn't ready to be dismissed quite yet.

"How did you get the message of the miracle?" I asked.

Sister Superior's eyes widened. I hurried on, "How does it happen, I mean. That a miracle becomes known?"

Sister Superior stood up without replying. The interview was over. I cursed my insensitivity, wondered if I could have handled the questioning better. I, too, got up from my chair. Sister Superior walked around her desk and lightly took my arm to lead me out of the office.

"I can see you are very interested in the miracle, and I understand," she said quietly, as though not wanting anyone else to hear. "You believe in Our Lady, and you wish to know why she has chosen this time to send a message to your fellow Cubans."

"Thank you for your empathy," I said. Her hand on my arm wavered for a second.

"I hope that it was not just the miracle that brought you here," she continued. "It would not be enough to sustain you throughout a lifetime of religious devotion."

"No, no," I said. "I came here . . . for the reasons I explained."

Sister Superior pondered this. Her grasp on me tightened.

"The miracle was announced to one of our sisters," she said suddenly. "Our Lady told one of our sisters of her intentions, as well as her reasons."

Wow. I tried to hide my stunned and happy reaction. It had been the answer I was hoping for—if it was indeed the truth.

Of course it was true. Nuns didn't lie, did they?

27

"DON'T say a word!" I held up my hand in warning as soon as I stepped into Solano Investigations. I was still wearing Lourdes's dowdy getup, and I didn't need any comments from my cousin.

Leonardo couldn't resist. It was obviously just too damned good. He picked up the calendar on his desk and pretended to study it.

"Hmmm. Halloween is still about a month away," he said. "Or did they change it while I wasn't paying attention? Maybe you're planning to go trick-or-treating a few weeks in advance?"

"Laugh it up," I snapped. "But fun time is over."

My tone of voice must have convinced Leo that I wasn't in the mood to fool around. I took the pile of pink message slips off the corner of his desk and headed for my office. There was a lot to do, and I tried to keep myself from feeling overwhelmed.

Before I closed the door I heard Leonardo call out, "The backgrounds are on your desk. Nestor dropped them off a few minutes ago—along with the bill."

I sat down at my desk and let my purse fall to the floor, not even bothering to drop it off on the sofa as was my custom. I opened up the file folder and started to read greedily.

Jimmy and Michael Patterson were both born in 1934, and they had both served in the navy at the same time. This gave me an idea. I called Nestor on his cell phone.

"Get me O'Donnell and Patterson's service records—now," I said. "Expedite them."

"What happened to 'hello' and 'how are you'?" Nestor asked, sounding annoyed.

"I'm sorry," I replied. "Thanks for the reports. You did a great job. I didn't mean to be rude, it's just that I think I might be close to a breakthrough."

Nestor digested this in silence. I felt genuinely alarmed that I had been so rude to one of my best investigators—and a real friend.

"No problem," Nestor said. "I'll get on it right away."

"How long do you think it'll take?" I asked, keeping my voice civil and considerate.

"Tomorrow, with luck," Nestor estimated. "Definitely by the day after. It depends."

"As soon as you have anything—" I began.

"I know. I'll call you night or day," Nestor said, chuckling before he hung up.

I went back to the background reports on the two men. An idea was starting to form in my mind as I read. It might have been a long shot, but I sensed a familiar tingle on the back of my neck that meant I was getting close to something important. The only thing I was certain of, though, was that it would be painful to wait up to two days for confirmation. I had to act before then.

"Leonardo?" I called as I came out of my office. I knew where he would be. Whenever his feelings were hurt he would work out his frustrations in the gym. I looked inside; sure enough, he was at the Gauntlet. I must have really upset him, judging from the pool of sweat at the base of the torture contraption. He concentrated intently, his eyes closed to the world.

"I'm so sorry." I kissed his sweaty cheek. "I shouldn't have snapped at you like that. I was wrong. Forgive me? *Por favor?*"

Leonardo opened his eyes, but looked straight ahead instead of at me. "On one condition," he said.

"Anything." I couldn't believe he was letting me off the hook so easily. Sometimes his snits lasted for days. He knew I hated discord, and the older he got the more he was starting to resemble a cranky, oversensitive old lady.

"You take off that ugly outfit right now," Leonardo said. "And you never wear it again. It's upsetting me."

I had to laugh. "Done!" I started unbuttoning the dress.

In spite of his skimpy outfits, Leonardo was a terrible prude at heart. "Not right here!" He started pumping away madly at the Gauntlet, like an electrified puppet about to short-circuit. I expected to see steam coming out of his ears.

"OK, OK." I made a big show of buttoning the dress back up again. His pace slowed, and he started to catch his breath.

I went back into my office and changed into a pair of blue jeans and a T-shirt. I hung up Lourdes's dress carefully in the closet before setting out, telling Leo that I would be back in a few hours. Hopefully by then his bad mood would have blown over. I didn't need any more reminders that this case was making me lose my consideration for those closest to me.

I stepped on the accelerator, driving fast through traffic toward Jimmy O'Donnell's home.

Thoughts ricocheted inside my head. I still hadn't told Tommy that he was the attorney of record on the case—the foundation of my not telling Charlie anything about Mary's family. I was really on dangerous ground. When I stepped back from it, I realized that I had simply told a barefaced lie to an assistant state attorney on a murder investigation.

I had had my chance earlier to confess what I had done to Tommy, but I had let it pass. There was no point worrying about it at that moment, I rationalized. I would take care of everything after I visited Jimmy—in fact, I made a resolution that it would be the first thing I did. I decided to call Tommy and set up a meeting right away to square things with him. In fact, I was going to change in general the way I did things. I would be more sensitive, more considerate. I owed it, especially, to Tommy.

I reached for the car phone as I neared Jimmy's house, but then put it down again. Talking to Tommy would take a while—probably I'd have to grovel and beg his forgiveness—and I needed to see Jimmy as quickly as possible. I was relieved when I saw his silver Buick parked in the driveway. I hadn't made the long trek in vain.

I rubbed the bump on my head as I walked up to the gate, recalling my first visit. Hopefully Jimmy would be more welcoming this time.

The gate was unlocked. I rang the bell, waited. Then I started to worry. I forced myself to count to sixty, slowly. It was a very, very long minute. My heart started to thump. I thumped on the door-knocker for almost another full minute. I tried the knob; it was locked. The curtains were closed, no light inside. God, why was nothing ever easy?

I could leave. I could wait for Jimmy to return. Neither option felt right. He had said he was staying with a friend, but his car was there, after all. I remembered I'd never made it to the back door the first time I was at the house. Maybe it would be unlocked. I took the Beretta out of my purse, stepped off the porch and onto the path that ran alongside the house.

I walked slowly, looking around. No one seemed to be home next door. There was no traffic on the street. As it was fast approaching dusk, I was limited to natural light, and I squinted as my eyes fought to adjust. There was a flashlight in the car, but I thought it would be too conspicuous for me to go back and get it. I called out Jimmy's name, watched for movement in the side windows.

"Jimmy?" I called out repeatedly, walking forward. I switched the safety off the gun. This didn't feel right at all. I kept my eyes wide open, ready to defend myself if I had to.

I needn't have bothered. No one was going to attack me like last time, especially not Jimmy O'Donnell.

He was floating face-down in his swimming pool. His arms were outstretched, like he was being crucified. Just like his sister. He was wearing the same clothes as when I'd visited him in the middle of the night. Though it was hard to discern clearly, I thought I saw marks on his wrists, like rope burns. Like Mary.

I had trouble tearing my eyes away from the bizarre scene in front of me. I reached in my purse for my cellular phone, my hands shaking so much it was hard to dial.

"Tommy," I said when he answered. "I need help."

I started to explain, in a torrent of words. I hung up only when he promised to come right away. Then I punched 911, more slowly this time. There was, after all, really no reason to hurry.

28

"**OH,** Jesus Christ, Lupe!" Tommy's face turned deep purple; I worried about his blood pressure. "How could you fuck up like that?"

I hung my head low like a little girl being chastised for bad behavior. I deserved his anger and contempt. I had been totally unprofessional, and I had involved Tommy in a way that deeply compromised him.

"I'm so sorry, Tommy. I don't know what else I can say."

We were sitting in Tommy's kitchen polishing off a pot of coffee, trying to clear the air between us but not making much headway. It had been a long, grueling night—starting with the police at Jimmy's house and ending up at Tommy's place. I was exhausted in every way—physically, mentally, emotionally. My body cried out for sleep. Tommy and I had spent hours talking with detectives while the police cordoned off the area around the house, securing it for the crime-scene investigators and Detective Anderson's arrival.

There were few questions I was able to answer, other than my own movements since I arrived on the scene and found Jimmy dead in the pool. The police had been reluctant to let me go, since I had known both O'Donnells in the days before their murders. But that was when Tommy had intervened; it had taken until midnight but Anderson had finally let us both go, finally convinced he would get nothing from us.

Now I had to deal with the pair of murders, and wonder whether I might have somehow contributed to their happening. And I had to deal with Tommy's wrath. The more he vented his anger with me, the more I felt as though I was going to crumble.

"Lupe, you know I'd do anything for you," Tommy said in a hurt tone. "But you told the cops I was the attorney on a case I have nothing to do with. It's just insane."

"I know."

"You're willing to get me in a shitload of trouble just to save your own ass!" he shouted. "You know how the cops and prosecutors in this city feel about me! They'll tear me apart if they ever find out the truth about how this went down!"

"I know, I'm sorry," I said. "My back was to the wall. You have to understand. I had no choice."

"You think you can use me any way you want because of our personal relationship," he added. "I said all this to you before. Obviously you weren't listening, because it had no effect whatsoever."

His voice went low. I had never heard him sound so bitter.

"I love you," he said. "I love making love with you. Our personal relationship is terrific. But you're killing me. You use me like I'm on retainer to you, like you're my only client."

"I don't know what I can do to show you how sorry I am," I pleaded. "I could grovel in front of you all day, but I don't see what purpose that would serve."

My words must have struck the right note; Tommy seemed to calm down a bit.

"Look, Lupe," he sighed. "I'm not going to beat you up anymore. It's just going to make us both feel even worse."

He poured himself a fresh cup of coffee and sat down heavily. "I suppose you'd better tell me about the case," he said, "so I can at least know what viper's nest you've dragged me into."

"I've already told you most of it," I said, relieved beyond description. "But now the two murders have made everything more critical."

I took out my notebook and filled him in on the case, as though I hadn't been near tears five minutes before. I ended with the speculation that Mother Superior might be holding out on me, that her motivations might not truly have been as they were presented to me, that I actually suspected that she might have been more deeply involved than she had said. I finished by telling him about Michael Patterson, the fact that he and Jimmy were contemporaries and how Patterson had visited the convent. I told him that I was waiting for both men's service records, and that I had driven out to see Jimmy to ask him in person about his connection to Patterson.

Tommy had listened quietly; now he laughed bitterly and cradled his head in his hands.

"Great!" he said. "You have a dead nun, a dead brother, and a client you now think was lying to you. Not to mention a mystery man you suspect might be involved in the crime who's running around somewhere in Miami."

"Most clients lie, you know that," I retorted, maybe a little too sharply. "I can understand why you're being sarcastic with me, but have a heart. I feel guilty enough that the O'Donnells might have been killed because of my contact with them."

"Sorry, I didn't mean to be so rough," Tommy said.

I thought of the siblings in their crucified poses. Someone had killed them both and left them arranged in that fashion as a message.

Or there was another possibility. The pose might have been set up to lead the police on a false trail—since, naturally, police were focused on Mary's religious affiliation. And both deaths were by drowning—Mary's by holy water, Jimmy's by pool water. Again the water symbolism of the Cuban miracle.

Time of death would be determined at autopsy, which would take a while. Not only did I have to worry about the world learning about the miracle, now I had a mounting death toll. I also might be in danger myself—after all, I had been one of the last people to see either sibling right before their murders—a thought that I pushed out of my mind.

It was starting to get lighter in Tommy's kitchen now that the sun rose outside. I was so tired it was difficult to focus my mind enough to speak.

"Can I take a nap here?" I asked him.

"You know where the bedroom is. I haven't moved it since you were here the last time." Tommy gave me a grim smile. "But before you check out of reality, why don't you call the convent and request a meeting with Mother Superior."

I started to protest that she had told me not to call. But it was too late for that.

"I think I should meet my new client," Tommy added. "Especially since she has no idea I'm on the payroll. I want to check her out for myself. I must say, all this has made me curious."

"I'll take care of it," I said.

"You have a lot of explaining to do," Tommy said, almost playful now. "You'd better get your story straight for Mother Superior."

It was just past daybreak, but I knew from trying to reach Lourdes at odd hours that the convent switchboard would be open. I dialed the number from memory.

"Mother Superior," I said.

"I'm sorry, she's not available."

"Tell her it's Guadalupe Solano," I said. "It's urgent."

"Mother Superior is on an all-day retreat," the operator said. "She won't be available until nightfall. But she said she would be checking her messages."

I wasn't sure whether I was relieved or disappointed. I was just too damned tired.

I was able to sleep for only a fitful hour, so finally I gave up trying; when I got up I found that I had Tommy's apartment to myself. I showered and wrapped myself in one of his oversized, luxurious, fluffy white bath towels, then went to the guest room. There he kept extra changes of clothes for female guests who might unexpectedly stay overnight. I put my dirty pants and shirt in the hamper, knowing Tommy's cleaning lady would launder and iron them without comment. I chose a white cotton T-shirt and found an old denim skirt that I'd given up on as lost. Before I left I wrote Tommy a note, thanking him for his hospitality and apologizing again.

I drove straight to the office. It had rained while I slept, and I enjoyed the just-washed, clean feel of the city. It was too early for Leonardo to have arrived, so I prepared the espresso machine for the day's first *café con leche*.

I checked the answering machine for messages. The first one was from Nestor: he had finished the background checks of everyone who went into the Order of the Illumination during Marisol's surveillance. I was impatient to get the information, but I knew better than to wake up Nestor too early in the morning. I wished for the millionth time that the man believed in the miracles of fax technology.

The second message was from Alvaro Mendoza. He said it had been a pleasure to see me for lunch and was curious to know how

the case was progressing. He had called at six o'clock the night before. I wondered briefly if he was really curious about the case, or whether he had used it as a pretext for calling me. Alvaro seemed very sure of himself, but I knew never to underestimate men's shyness. I felt a tingle in my stomach at the sound of his voice.

I also had to wonder whether Alvaro was interested in the case because of some kind of personal stake. He was thoroughly immersed in Cuban politics, and politics ran through the case like an unbreakable thread. Alvaro might have been interested in me romantically, I knew, but he also might have wanted to keep tabs on the miracle.

I wondered whether I should have told Alvaro so much, then commanded myself to stop being so paranoid. I had come to Alvaro, after all, not vice versa. But then—and this was my investigator's instinct kicking in—would Alvaro have contacted me anyway, if he had learned about the case and the fact that I was working it? Sometimes it was lousy being an investigator. I was compelled to look for ulterior motives everywhere, never to take anything at face value.

The third message was from Charlie. He had heard from Detective Anderson that he had run into me last night at the O'Donnell crime scene. Charlie said he hoped this would be the last dead body I was associated with in the foreseeable future. Then he warned me to watch my ass, that I was treading on thin ice. Great, just what I needed to hear. He had called at midnight.

The fourth call was from Marisol, asking me how Tommy was doing on her hot-dog case. Shit, I had forgotten about that. What exquisite timing. This wasn't the moment to ask Tommy for an update on her case. Marisol also wanted to know if I had any work for her.

The fifth call was a hang-up.

The sixth opened with a soft voice asking, "Detective lady? Are you there?" Theofilus. I moved closer to the machine so I could hear him better. But that was it. He had hung up.

There were a few other calls sprinkled in for variety, all from different members of the Solano clan. Lourdes, Papi, and Fatima had all called to ask when was I coming home, when could they see me again. Apparently Osvaldo hadn't told them about my quick visits home and quicker escapes. I guessed he didn't want to hurt

their feelings by letting them know I'd come to the house without saying hello to anyone. I felt wracked with guilt.

The coffee was ready, so I poured a cup and topped it off with hot milk. I wished I knew how to make *espumita*—the foam poured over coffee that makes it so delectable. Still, after a few sips of what I'd prepared I felt ready to rejoin the human species.

On my way into my office I picked up the pile of phone messages Leonardo had stacked fastidiously on the corner of his desk. I flipped through them. Nothing I had to deal with immediately.

I opened the window and sat at my desk. The parrots were still building. The avocado tree looked like a mini-city, with all kinds of different architecture jutting out from various branches. They were up early, squawking and complaining.

I took out the Holy Rosary file. I had been adding information to it for the past few days but I'd not had the chance to organize the information in it. Now it was September 26, according to my desk calendar—two weeks until the miracle. I had been on the case for eight days. Time wasn't going to reverse itself. I had to make something happen.

I picked up the phone and dialed 1-800-MIRACLE, then the Spanish counterpart 1-800-MILAGRO. No updates, still the same recordings. Part of me had hoped the miracle would be postponed or—I actually dared to think it—canceled. Of course it hadn't been. It was still scheduled for the *Grito de Yara.*

One thing had worked out for me: the press still hadn't picked up on the story. I wondered why. It was a natural to make the papers and television, but no big announcement had been made yet. Perhaps the Order of the Illumination was waiting until the last minute to keep nosy skeptics from debunking the miracle before it could occur.

Or could the archdiocese have been concerned that the miracle might be a fraud, and it was keeping quiet to disassociate itself from it? If that were the case, the archbishop could have put out word that he didn't want press coverage. If various press outlets didn't cooperate, then there would be no more cooperation from the archdiocese on other matters. In a Catholic city like Miami, the church had a lot of power. I wondered if the Yugoslavian order was in conflict with this somehow. I feared I would never know the answer.

The church was secretive, and the miracle's success or failure could be central to its influence among its believers.

I thought that even the Chamber of Commerce would probably get involved, thinking of all the tourists that would descend upon Miami to see the Virgin shedding tears. Miami could finally be portrayed as a place the Virgin was interested in, and not just the devil's playground.

Anyone could call 1-800-MIRACLE and find out about the miracle. But apparently no one in the media had heard about it. Once they did, then my ability to work the case would be crippled.

I looked out at the parrots fluttering around in their edifices. Somehow they encouraged me. Maybe persistence would pay off. I had finished the last of my *café con leche* when the telephone rang.

"Call for you," Leonardo said on the intercom without any greeting. "Line one."

He hung up before I could ask who it was. I recognized this particular behavior pattern on the part of my cousin. Sometimes his thin skin was hard to take. I knew it was going to take a lot of groveling and placating in order to smooth his feathers, even though I thought he had moved on from yesterday's tiff. He would not let me off the hook so easily.

"Lupe Solano," I said.

"Miss Solano," said a female voice. "This is Sister Rose O'Donnell."

I shot straight up in my chair.

"I understand you knew my sister Mary and my brother Jimmy," she continued.

"Sister Rose?" My voice broke for the second time that morning. Calm down, I told myself. "Of course I know who you are. I'm so sorry about what happened to them."

"Thank you," Rose said quietly. "I am here in Miami. I'm calling you from the convent of my order, the Sisters of St. Joseph's."

"You're here in Miami?" I should have anticipated that someone from the O'Donnell family would have to come to claim the bodies as soon as they were released from the medical examiner's office. A terrifying thought hit me. Someone had killed two of the O'Donnell triplets—was Rose also in danger? The killer or killers might have thought Rose had knowledge about whatever was behind Mary and Jimmy's deaths. Rose lived in Massachusetts, but there was no reason to believe that she wasn't in contact with her sister and brother—especially since Mary had left Massachusetts a relatively short time ago.

"The police called and told me what happened to Mary," Rose said, the grief in her voice palpable. "I flew down late last night. And now I just learned about Jimmy."

Sister Rose sounded remarkably calm and composed for a triplet who had just lost her brother and sister to violent murders. Maybe as a nun she was better equipped to deal with cruel blows of fate— or maybe the horror had yet to sink in.

"I'm very sorry about your great loss," I said.

"You might wonder why I'm phoning you," said Sister Rose.

It was a surprise, but then I usually didn't like to discuss sensitive issues over the phone. I decided to keep things vague.

"I'm pleased to hear from you, though I'm sad it's under such tragic circumstances," I offered.

I hadn't really answered her. I did wonder why she had phoned, and I was feeling like my luck was changing. I had considered calling her at the convent in Massachusetts, but had put it off until I could think of the best way to approach her.

"I think we should meet to talk," Rose said.

That meant only one thing: she had information for me. "Of course, Sister," I said, containing my excitement. "I'd be happy to meet you at your convenience."

"I don't have a car here," Rose said. "But I could call a taxi."

So she was willing to come to me. Interesting. "I'd offer to pick you up, but I don't think it would be a good idea," I said.

I didn't explain why I thought this, and she didn't ask for a clarification. Maybe we were thinking along the same lines.

I gave Sister Rose the address and told her what directions to give the taxi driver. Taking a cab in Miami can be a gamble, since few drivers really know their way around the city.

"I'm looking forward to meeting you," I said before hanging up.

Then I prayed Sister Rose would arrive safely at my office. For the O'Donnell triplets, meeting with me had become a deadly proposition.

I was halfway through the latest reports, just getting a feel for what Nestor had found, when Leonardo spoke into the intercom to announce that Sister Rose O'Donnell had arrived.

My heart was thumping hard when I came out and shook her hand. What I saw was shocking, if not unexpected. Sister Rose was a perfect match for her sister; they were almost interchangeable, from what I remembered of Mary. And she also looked startlingly like her brother. Anyone would have seen the almost uncanny resemblance between the three, from her light lashes to her wan smile. She was dressed in normal street clothes, in a dark brown dress that reminded me of the one I'd borrowed from Lourdes.

"Sister Rose," I said formally. "I am Lupe Solano."

Sister Rose held onto my hand for a full thirty seconds. "Lupe," she repeated. "After the Virgin of Guadalupe, I assume."

"My mother named me and my sisters after places where the Virgin made an apparition," I explained.

Rose smiled. "Well, then you are well-named for the events happening in Miami right now, aren't you?"

I hid my surprise that she would be so open with me so quickly. "Please come into my office. Would you like some coffee?"

"No, thank you." Rose chuckled. "I've had enough coffee the last couple of days to last a lifetime."

If she planned to stay in Miami for any length of time, I thought, she'd better get used to it. The city operated on caffeine overload. I ushered Rose to one of the clients' chairs and waited for her to get comfortable. She seemed very composed and at peace, as though her faith was helping her to endure the horrible news of what had happened to her siblings.

"I would again like to express my deep sympathy for the passing of your brother and sister," I began. "It was senseless and brutal."

"Thank you." For a second Rose seemed to lose her equanimity; her eyes watered and she looked away. A moment later, though, she was all business.

"I had the feeling you didn't want to discuss our reason for meeting over the telephone," she said.

"Yes," I agreed.

"And you wanted to meet here, instead of coming to the convent." She gestured, and I caught a faint scent of baby powder. "I was pleased that you are so cautious. I wish Mary and Jimmy had been. They might still be alive today if they had."

"How did you know about me?" I asked.

"My siblings and I are—were—very close," she said. "We stayed

188 | CAROLINA GARCIA-AGUILERA

in regular contact even though Jimmy had moved here to Florida. And Mary, well, I saw her every day—except when she was sent away on a special project. But we talked about everything. There were no secrets between us, not since we were children."

Her light blue eyes stared into mine, not blinking. I was reminded of her sister Mary, who had looked at me in the same manner in Jimmy's house.

"They told you about my visit?" I asked. Again I felt a pang of guilt. Maybe there had been something I should have done differently.

"I received a call from Jimmy and Mary after you left the house that day," Rose began. "They said that you were looking into the upcoming miracle associated with the Order of the Illumination of the Sacred Virgin."

Rose took a breath and looked out the window. It was difficult to shunt aside the feeling that I was conversing with a sort of composite ghost of Jimmy and Mary.

"Jimmy didn't really believe you, at least that's what he said at first." Rose smiled, probably remembering her brother's tough-guy persona. "He thought the nuns might have sent you. But Mary did believe you. She wanted to tell you her story. She thought you might be able to help her."

"What story?" I asked. "And what kind of help did she need?"

Rose looked at me strangely. "You mean you don't know?"

"No, I don't." I tried to keep my voice level and casual, even though I wanted to get up and shake the story out of her. It reminded me that I still had to work on my patience—I was entertaining visions of me flipping a nun upside down right there in my office.

"The miracle," Rose said. I could see her wheels turning, trying to decide if she could trust me. "You see, Mary was the nun through which the announcement of the apparition was made."

OK. That fit—and it also matched Sister Superior's statement that the miracle had been announced through a nun. But why through Mary, a sister from a different order?

"Why Mary? Why should the miracle have been announced through a nun from Massachusetts?"

"You don't know?" she asked, her eyes wide.

Pretty soon Rose was going to start thinking I had a single-digit IQ. I shook my head.

"Mary was the U.S. representative to our order in Cuba." I must have looked blank. "Our convent in Santiago de Cuba. Lupe, do you know anything about the church in Cuba?"

"Well, I once worked a case that dealt with an order of nuns in Cuba, if that helps," I said. Now it was Rose's turn to look perplexed when I didn't elaborate further; I had to admit, it gave me some small satisfaction.

I couldn't go into the particulars of the case, or the fact that it had actually taken me into Cuba, but I did want Sister Rose to understand that this wasn't my first encounter with a group of nuns who didn't play by the book. On that occasion I had dealt with a branch of Lourdes's order, the Order of the Holy Rosary, that had been situated in Sagua la Grande. In that case, I remembered, the mother superior had been the bad guy. I wondered if history was about to repeat itself in Miami.

"Tell me more," I said to Rose.

"The situation in Cuba for those in religious life is very precarious," Rose said. "It was thought that the pope's visit might change things, that there would be an opening up and the church would be permitted to attend more to the needs of its flock. But that has only happened on a very minimal scale."

I nodded, tacitly urging her to go on.

"The church in the U.S. is concerned about this, naturally," Rose said. "So they've sent representatives to various convents for extended stays—to monitor the situation and offer help. It's all done on a voluntary basis."

"How did Mary get sent to Cuba?" I asked.

"Well, there was a rigorous screening process," said Rose, seeming to remember her sister's actions with pride. "And it was a hardship post, really. Life in our convent in Springfield isn't luxurious by any means, yet we're extremely comfortable compared to our counterparts in Cuba. But Mary was determined. She studied Spanish until she was fluent. And when she went, she completely immersed herself in the life of the convent and its parishioners. She felt as though she had been sent on a mission by the Virgin herself."

"How long was Mary in Cuba?" I asked. I wished Mary or Jimmy would have told me this when they were alive. It certainly was relevant to the case.

"Two years," Rose replied. "She came back home six months

ago, but I think her experience in Cuba changed her forever. I suppose it was inevitable. It was a world apart from our everyday life in Springfield."

"Forgive me for making you answer so many questions," I broke in. "I'm still trying to understand what happened."

"Of course," Rose acknowledged. "Ask me anything you want."

"I'm still confused," I said. "I don't understand the connection between Mary and the Order of the Illumination of the Sacred Virgin."

Rose took a deep breath that turned into a sigh.

"When she was in Cuba, Mary became interested in the Virgin of the *Caridad del Cobre*—am I pronouncing that properly?"

"Yes," I said. Actually, Rose's pronunciation was close to perfect.

"She often went to the Virgin's shrine to pray," Rose said. "She was moved by the Cuban people's devotion to the Virgin, their patron saint. They never lost faith in her, no matter how many hardships they suffered. Mary admired that greatly."

My mind raced for connections. It seemed unlikely that a nun born in Altoona, who lived in a convent in Springfield, Massachusetts, would be captivated by a little mulatto Virgin in Cuba. But the power of that Virgin was known and respected.

"I don't want to upset you, Rose," I said, speaking slowly. "But do you have any idea who would want to kill Mary and Jimmy?"

Rose flinched as though I had physically struck her. I wondered how much longer she could hold out until the weight of her loss was too much. I could see from her reaction that I had to soften my tone, but there were questions that needed to be asked.

"Who were they frightened of?" I asked.

"I'm sorry, I can't help you," Rose said quickly. "Mary didn't go into the details of the miracle with me. She knew I didn't like her getting involved with all of that."

"What do you mean, 'all of that'?" I felt like a grand inquisitor browbeating a nun. But I had to keep going.

"A few days after she got back from Cuba, Mary said she was coming here." Rose frowned at the memory. "She said she had a special assignment, but that she couldn't tell me more. Can you imagine—she didn't feel she could trust her own sister."

"It must have been upsetting."

Rose wagged her finger in the air. At least it was better than seeing her melancholy.

"I tell you, I didn't like it one bit," she said. "This secrecy! Mary and Jimmy and I never kept anything from each other!"

"So it became known that Mary was moved by this Virgin?" I asked.

"Not just moved. Mary became an expert on the Virgin," Rose said. "As a matter of fact, she wrote a short monogram about her. Our mother superior was so proud of Mary's work that she had a number of copies printed that were distributed to other religious orders."

"And that's how the Order of the Illumination of the Sacred Virgin heard about Mary and the Cuban Virgin," I offered.

"Could be," Rose replied. "I know it was talked about quite a bit for a while. It was a wonderful piece. Mary was very talented, and she said the Virgin herself had directed her writing."

A faraway look came over Rose's face. "Mary was so passionate about anything to do with Cuba," she said. "She used to write and tell me that she finally understood the reason for her calling, that she had been sent to Cuba to carry out the Virgin's wishes for the Cuban people—and that the Virgin would make these wishes known at the appropriate time."

Listening to Rose speak about her sister, I was almost convinced that the Virgin had channeled her intentions through Mary, that Mary had been chosen to transmit the Virgin's desires for Cuba to the world. But had Mary really heard the Virgin, or had she projected her own desires onto a vision of the Virgin? From what I could imagine, it was probably hard to tell the difference. Mary felt she was the Virgin's messenger, that she had a duty to share the Virgin's wishes to the world. But what was reality, and what was duty, where religious visions were concerned?

I wondered if Lourdes's mother superior at the Order of the Holy Rosary knew about Mary's monogram. She must have, since it dealt with the Cuban Virgin. And that meant she had been keeping information from me that was vital to investigating the case.

A picture was emerging in my mind: this miracle had started like a courtship. Mary was an authority on the *Virgen de la Caridad del Cobre*. Whatever she said about the Virgin would carry a lot of weight in church circles. The Order of the Illumination of the Sacred Virgin was known for producing miracles back home in Eastern Europe. So they would also be taken seriously.

Mary had returned home from Cuba six months before. The Order of the Illumination had set up their local order at the same time. The timing couldn't be coincidental. The question now was: who put together the deal? And to what end? And of course there was still the question of who killed Jimmy and Mary, and why. But I thought answering the first set of questions would go a long way toward solving the second.

"Do you think Mary told Jimmy something—whatever it was— and that's why he was killed at the same time as her?" It was the only thing that made sense to me.

"I suppose," Rose said sadly. "That day you went to the house, when Jimmy and Mary called me, Jimmy stayed on the phone after Mary went to bed to take a nap. He told me he'd spoken with Mary about something she was involved with, but that she didn't want him to tell me about it because I would worry too much. Jimmy told me he would call me later, when he had the house to himself. But he never did."

"Do you have any idea what it was?" I asked. I felt my frustration rising. Every time I learned something, it only served to demonstrate to me how far I still was from the truth.

Rose shook her head. "I suspected it had to do with something that happened in Cuba, something with the Virgin," she said. "My sister's experience changed her. She wasn't the same person who left St. Joseph's in Springfield. She underwent a kind of conversion, developing a closeness to the Virgin that she had never described before."

"What about your convent?" I pressed. "Have there been any rumors, any talk?"

Rose smiled sadly, a sight that nearly broke my heart.

"I came here because I wanted you to find the person who killed my sister and my brother," she said. "But I haven't been much help to you, have I?"

"You've helped a great deal," I said, trying to reassure her. And she had, by telling me about Mary's connection to Cuba. "Investigations are always like this," I added. "Answers rarely come quickly. You just have to keep trying."

"It's not like television, is it?" Rose said.

"Not at all." We shared a small smile. I sensed that Rose would come through her tragedy, that she would just need time to grieve.

"I spoke to Detective Anderson," she added. "He said he didn't know much, either. But he said the investigation was just beginning."

Rose dug around in her plain black leather purse, pulled out Anderson's business card, which she showed to me. She then looked at it herself, frowned, and put it away.

"I wasn't much help to him, either," she said.

"I know Detective Anderson," I told her. "He's very professional and diligent. The case is in good hands."

"Thank you for telling me that," said Rose.

We sat in momentary silence. I feared Rose was castigating herself for not doing things differently, for not somehow forcing Mary to tell the truth about her time in Miami. As for me, I didn't know what role I might have played in their deaths, and this was something with which I had to live.

Rose looked out the window at the parrots, a smile forming on her lips. Her skin was spectral white.

"Have they lived out there in that tree for a long time?" she asked.

I nodded. "For as long as our office has been in this cottage."

"Are they always this industrious?"

"Yes." For some strange reason, I didn't like talking about the parrots. I felt proprietary about them.

"Good for them," said Rose. She gathered her purse and stood up. "I'll say a prayer for them and their nests. I think I'll be going now."

I stood up quickly, came around the desk.

"Can I call for a taxi?" she asked. "I'll be returning to the convent."

For a second I didn't know which one she meant; there were so many involved in the case. But of course she was referring to her own order, St. Joseph's, and their Miami convent.

"There's no need for that," I said. "Leonardo will drive you back." I escorted Rose out to the reception area and called out Leo's name.

He came running in from the kitchen. "Leonardo, would you mind driving Sister Rose back to her convent?" I didn't wait for an answer.

"This is the address," Rose said, handing Leonardo a slip of paper.

"*Gracias*, Leo," I said, smiling sweetly.

He shot me a petulant look. Chauffeuring nuns all over Miami wasn't in his job description, but too bad. Maybe he was worried that someone would see him driving a nun through Miami, thus destroying his reputation as a New Age bon vivant. Leonardo and I hadn't coexisted for years of relative peace without me understanding the workings of his mind. When he got back, I thought, I would placate him by reminding him of all the Catholic brownie points he'd earned from his good deed.

"These calls came in while you were talking with the sister," he said, shoving a wad of pink slips in my hand.

"How much longer will you be in Miami?" I asked Rose as I escorted her to the door.

"As long as I'm needed," she said. "It's not really up to me."

On impulse, I reached out and kissed her cheek, hugged her briefly. Leonardo looked on in amazement. He knew I didn't like physical contact with other women. I normally behaved as though they had a contagious disease.

"Thank you very much for calling me," I said, recovering myself.

"You're welcome," she said. "Thank you for trying to help."

I stood in the doorway and watched them walk out to Leonardo's black Jeep. I was pleased to see that my cousin minded his manners and held open the car door for Sister Rose.

Just before she got in, I heard her ask, "Could we make just one stop on the way to the convent?"

I strained to listen. Leonardo nodded.

"I hope the shrine to the Virgin of the *Caridad del Cobre* will not be too far out of the way," said Rose.

Actually the two places were on completely different ends of Miami. I hoped Leonardo had gassed up his car recently. He was in for a little detour.

29

WHEN I went back into my office, still picturing Leonardo's new job as a nun's chauffeur, I looked through the crumpled message slips that my cousin had stuffed into my hand. Some people had called me twice, including Tommy. I didn't really know who to call first, so I picked one out of the pile and dialed my desk phone. Maybe, I thought, I'd return the calls alphabetically.

Detective Anderson picked up on the second ring. "This is Lupe Solano returning your call, Detective."

"Oh, good, I was hoping I'd hear from you," he said in a voice drained of emotion. "Can we meet? In person? Soon?"

I had forgotten how much Anderson preferred the interrogatory mode of conversation. It was almost as though all his time spent questioning suspects had spilled over into other parts of his life.

"Sure. When? Where?" I cringed as I heard myself. Anderson's speech was contagious.

We set up an appointment for six that night. Anderson must have been in a conciliatory mood, because he suggested meeting at my office—an almost unheard-of courtesy for a homicide detective.

Next I returned Alvaro's call. The receptionist put me through immediately as soon as I identified myself—as if, I suspected, she had been put on notice to do so.

"Lupe! Great to hear your voice!" Alvaro's tone gave me a shiver; I felt vaguely ashamed that not even the O'Donnells' drownings could dampen my sexual attraction for Alvaro, even temporarily. "How's the case going?"

"The more I find out, the more questions I seem to uncover," I said, pleased that he had asked. We could at least maintain the facade that ours was a purely professional relationship.

"Do you need to talk Cuban politics or religion again?" he asked. "We could talk over dinner tonight. If you're free, of course."

"That would be great," I said, looking down at my calendar. "There's a complication, though. I'm meeting a detective about the case at six. It would have to be after that."

"No problem," Alvaro said quickly. "I work late, anyway. Just call me here at the office when you're done. Let me give you the number for my direct line. The switchboard here closes at six."

I wrote the number down. I knew I had cleared a big hurdle with Alvaro; his direct office number wasn't something he would be prone to handing out casually.

After I hung up I punched Tommy's number on the speed dial. I had already lost track of making the calls alphabetically. That stupid ABC song had always tripped me up.

"Tommy?" I said.

"Where the hell have you been?"

"I was at a convent," I said. "I was seeing if I had the right kind of personality for becoming a nun."

"You? A nun?" I had to hold the phone at arm's length or be deafened by Tommy's howls of laughter. It was a little insulting. OK, I was no candidate for sainthood but, really, this was uncalled for. Besides, he had often been the happy recipient of my waywardness.

Finally his guffaws died down into chuckles. "I know I yelled at you for screwing up the case," he said. "But you don't have to go overboard trying to repent. I mean, I know you've always been a creature of excess, *querida*, but you don't have to banish yourself to a nunnery!"

"I'm not really enlisting for the religious life," I said, trying to be patient with his stab at humor. "I was working undercover."

"So, what's the deal?" Tommy asked, loving this opportunity to enjoy himself at my expense. "Do you really have the right kind of personality for joining up?"

"I haven't been told yet. It was a getting-to-know-you kind of thing," I replied. "Look, Tommy, I'm under the gun for time here. Detective Anderson's coming here to meet me at six, and I have to prepare."

"Meet with him, and then we'll have dinner to discuss it," Tommy said. "You can bring me up to date on what's happening. Just call me as soon as the meeting is over."

Tommy was about to hang up, assuming that I agreed to his plan.

"Actually, I can't have dinner with you tonight," I said. I knew how much Tommy hated to be rebuffed, so I added, "I'm interviewing someone about the case after Anderson and I are finished."

"No problem. Then we'll have a late dinner," Tommy said, again seeming to think our conversation was finished. "I'll stay late here at the office. Just call when you're done with the interview."

"I'm sorry, I think it would be too late," I said. "Besides, I'm probably going to have dinner with this person."

I chose my words carefully. Although Tommy and I weren't really a couple, we did have a sort of understanding. Being Cuban, that meant to me that whatever Tommy didn't know about was all right for me to do. Although he was American, I assumed he felt the parameters were the same. We never flaunted our other relationships in each other's faces.

"You're having dinner with a witness in a case you're working?" From his tone it was obvious that Tommy felt this was a lapse in judgment—or else he was jealous and didn't want to admit it.

"Not really a witness." Now I was splitting hairs. "Just someone who can provide background."

"You're never going to be invited to become a nun if you keep acting this way," Tommy sighed. Thankfully, he decided to let it go. I wondered if he would have been so charitable if he had known about the private tutoring I was about to receive on Cuban politics.

"Oh, I almost forgot," Tommy said. "Sonia went ahead and set up an appointment for ten tomorrow morning with the mother superior at the Order of the Holy Rosary—my new client."

I didn't miss the sarcasm in his voice. "I'll come by your office at nine," he said. "You can bring me up to date, and we'll drive over to the Holy Rosary together."

This time he hung up without asking me whether I agreed with his plan. It was his way, I knew, of letting me know he wasn't pleased with developments.

Lourdes was next on the list. I called her cell phone. "I'm sorry I haven't been in touch with you," I said to her. "It's been crazy working the case for Mother Superior."

"No problem," Lourdes said, calm as always in the face of my barely contained frenzy. "I was just checking to see if you're OK. The family's been complaining that you're never home, that we never get to see you anymore."

I didn't reply. Lourdes had the power to make me feel bottomless guilt with a few well-chosen words.

"Please, Lupe, just show up once in a while," she continued. "They've been on my ass about it. They figure I'm the only one you listen to."

"I'll come home soon, I promise," I said. I felt badly, and I missed them. "I know I've been neglecting everyone, it's just that this case has kept me busy."

I tried not to whine, but it wasn't easy. "Believe me, Lourdes," I said. "One of these days I'll tell you everything. You'll be amazed."

"So are you making any progress?" she asked. "Mother Superior asks me about you every time I see her at the convent."

"I'm meeting her tomorrow," I said.

"You know, I'm not telling you how to work your cases, but a call to her once in a while would be helpful," said Lourdes. "And it would get her off my case."

I started to protest, to say that Mother Superior had expressly told me not to call her. But there was no use. I was annoyed with Mother Superior's duplicity, intimating to my sister that I wasn't keeping her informed on the case. I accepted Lourdes's friendly warning in the spirit with which it was delivered; after all, it would reflect badly on her if I screwed up.

"Well, we'll be caught up tomorrow morning," I said. "Tommy and I are coming over to the order at ten."

"Why is Tommy involved?" Lourdes asked quickly. "Why do you need a lawyer?"

I didn't like to brush off my sister, but this wasn't the time to start divulging details about the case.

"It's a long story. I'll tell you about it later." I said good-bye to Lourdes and hung up just as she started to ask another question.

Charlie Miliken had phoned, wondering why I wasn't returning his calls. Leonardo had written "Bad girl" in the margin. Now what had my cousin picked up with his touchy-feely radar? I didn't want to have to deal with Charlie, not just yet. I wanted to keep him at arm's length so he wouldn't question me about the investigation; I hated to be forced to brush him off, or to give him evasive answers.

There was another call from Theofilus, again with no number for me to return it. I wondered how on Earth he ever got gardening jobs if he didn't have a phone or at least a beeper. Maybe his cushy contract with the archdiocese was all he needed. On the message he said that he would keep calling until he reached me. I made a note to tell Leonardo to give him my cell phone and beeper numbers. It had been a mistake not to pass them on to Theofilus the last time we spoke.

I looked at my watch. Four hours until Detective Anderson was arriving. I set about reviewing and updating the case file, knowing that I would need to have my head together to deal with him. I was very conscious of the fact that I wasn't obligated to reveal much of anything to him, but with the police cooperation was always better than confrontation. It was a matter of revealing some things and keeping others hidden. Bees were caught with honey a lot easier than vinegar.

Detective Anderson was prompt, just as I knew he would be. Leonardo had gone home for the day, so when I heard the doorbell ring I sprang up from the sofa in my office. I had been lying down, reading over the case file—I always did my best thinking lying on the sofa, looking out the window at my feathered friends. I tucked my T-shirt into my blue jeans and walked through the reception area—it wasn't exactly professional attire, but it would have to do. I greeted him through the door, unlocked it, and let him in.

Detective Anderson was an anomaly in Miami. He was a native-born American, what the census-takers called a non-Hispanic white. He also could have been sent over by a request to Central Casting for a TV detective: tall, close-cropped sandy-colored hair, washed-out blue-gray eyes, always expressionless and soft-spoken. His hands were pale white, dusted with hair the same color as that on his head.

Every time I had seen him he wore the same thing: a khaki-colored rumpled suit, a white shirt, and a tie that seemed about to strangle him. If the wind blew right, he gave off a faint scent of formaldehyde. I tried not to imagine him undressed. If I had, I would have been either attracted or repulsed. There would be no middle ground. And, now that I thought about it, I had never heard mention of a Mrs. Anderson, and there was no ring on his finger. From time to time I was intrigued by the concept of his personal life, but it was only curiosity—I always wanted more details about everything, a by-product of being an investigator.

Detective Anderson and I enjoyed a good working relationship. We shared a mix of mutual trust and distrust that was about right. I had bumped into him the year before on another case I worked, and found him to be what cops liked to call a "stand-up guy." Which was pretty good in Miami, where stand-up guys tended to be those who didn't stab you in the back after buying you a *mojito*. I would have liked to have considered him a friend, but I didn't know if it was possible considering that we were usually on different sides of the cases we worked. Still, we were at least friendly, and I enjoyed that.

"I heard Tommy McDonald is the attorney of record on the case you're working," Anderson said as soon as he came in the door.

"Right. Sorry about that one," I said as I locked the door behind him. Cops would rather deal with a case of *E. coli* bacteria than deal with Tommy. "Come on in, my office is in the back. Can I get you anything to drink?"

"No, no, I'm fine," Detective Anderson barked as he led the way to my office. He sat down in one of the armchairs facing my desk. I took my time sitting down, letting him check out the surroundings.

Detective Anderson was the kind of straightlaced person whose presence made me look at myself in a new light. I glanced around the office, trying to see it through his eyes. There were Mami's expensive Louis-the-someone antique chairs upholstered in gold brocade, the worn, patched brown suede Crate and Barrel sofa, the industrial-gray filing cabinets bought on closeout from an office-supply chain that had lost its lease. There were the oil paintings covering most of the wall space, each depicting Cuban palm trees, given to me by various clients who hadn't been able to pay my fee.

Anderson checked his surroundings with an air of quiet amusement. I don't know what he had expected, but I guessed the Anderson office and homestead didn't look much like this.

"I know you have confidentiality concerns," he said, looking down as he flipped through a worn imitation leather notebook full of papers. "But I'd appreciate whatever you can give me. We could, you know, swap a little 411."

I refrained from laughing at hearing Anderson try to use slang. Then I pretended to carefully consider his suggestion. I had, of course, planned to exchange some information—but I wanted to give him the impression that I was doing him a favor in the process.

"All right," I said.

"We think the two murders are linked—it's the only thing that makes any sense," Anderson said, still looking down at his notes. "Brother and sister, killed the same way. Placed in the same physical position and within hours of each other. We don't have the complete report back from the ME, but this is the assumption at this point."

"I saw them both earlier the day of Mary's murder," I replied. I was relieved he was not interrogating me. There was no reason to be coy with Anderson. He was sharp, and could spot bullshit. "I interviewed them at Jimmy O'Donnell's house about the case I'm working."

"I see," Anderson said, looking as though he barely had a pulse. I could almost see his brain working.

"Obviously I can't give you any details about the case," I pointed out. "But I can tell you that they were both frightened. So frightened, in fact, that the first time I met Jimmy he hit me on the head and knocked me out."

Anderson's bleached-out eyes perked up. "Did they give any indication what they were scared of?"

"Not really. They suspected that I had been sent by the people they were scared of—which I wasn't."

I noticed that Anderson didn't much care that I had been knocked out earlier in the week. Oh, well. So much for chivalry.

"Their fear was real," I added. I told him about Jimmy's late-night call after Mary had disappeared, that he couldn't tell me what was happening because Mary had sworn him to secrecy.

"So the sister was the one in trouble," Anderson said slowly, thinking out loud. "And the brother knew the reason, but he wasn't talking."

"Exactly."

"Too bad he made that promise to her," Anderson said. "They might both be alive today if he'd spilled his guts to you."

"Maybe so," I said, noncommittal. I wasn't about to volunteer my misgivings about Jimmy's behavior, or the fact that he'd recently sat in the same chair that Anderson now occupied. Nor was I about to hand Michael Patterson to Anderson. I didn't want to look as though I was on a wild-goose chase. Better to keep my cards close to my chest—and I knew that Anderson was doing the same.

Suddenly Anderson changed gears, catching me by surprise. "You ever worked any cases that involved drowning?" he asked.

I hadn't. This was in particular my first case involving a nun being drowned in holy water. I certainly would have remembered if that had happened before.

"The correct classification for a death by drowning is suffocation—and that applies only after all other types of death have been ruled out," Anderson said, his voice flat but louder, as though he were teaching a class full of new recruits. "It takes a great deal of force, typically, to drown someone. The victim will fight ferociously. I'm waiting for the pathology report to let me know exactly how the O'Donnells died. It's hard to drown someone, in other words, and I'm reserving judgment as to whether that was the single cause of death in this case."

Anderson's professorial attitude was starting to alienate me; fortunately he dropped his tone of voice to a more natural level.

"I think we can safely eliminate accidental drowning," he added. "And we can also probably dismiss alcohol or drugs—which usually are involved in most drownings. There wasn't even a bottle of beer in Jimmy O'Donnell's house. A neighborhood canvass turned up nothing. No one saw or heard anything. And I don't think we even need to consider suicide, not with these two."

"Seems logical," I replied. "So the autopsy is even more crucial than usual."

Anderson smiled, his thin lips curling at the corners. "I'm very interested in the autopsy," he said. "The circumstances surrounding these deaths are uncommon."

Anderson was, as always, the master of understatement.

"And you'll share the report with me when it comes in?" I asked. I wanted the terms of our cooperation to be clear.

"Of course," Anderson said, apparently surprised that I had felt the need to ask. He turned his head at a commotion outside the window, seemed startled for an instant when he saw a big parrot looking inside, staring at him. An instant later we heard the sound of a phone ringing.

"Must be yours," I said; the ringing was different from my desk phone and my cell phone. I knew their distinctive sounds in the way that a mother could identify the cries of her children.

Anderson took his cellular phone out of his jacket pocket. He read the number printed on the screen with narrowed eyes.

"The medical examiner's office," he said.

I sat back and took deep breaths and tried to listen in to Anderson's conversation. But he said almost nothing, instead scratching notes on his pad. His face betrayed nothing. Almost a full five minutes later he thanked the person on the other end of the line and clicked the phone shut.

"Well, that's a surprise," he said, looking up at me with a puzzled expression. "We have both reports at the same time. The official cause of death for both Jimmy and Mary was suffocation."

"But you said—"

"They were unconscious before they hit the water," Anderson interrupted.

"What does—"

Detective Anderson quieted me with a look.

"That's not all," he added. "There was water found in their lungs, as you would expect. But it was seawater. Gallons of seawater."

Seawater.

"Not holy water," I said.

Anderson nodded. "Or pool water," he replied.

30

I watched Detective Anderson's nondescript brown American sedan back out of the driveway before returning to my office. Seawater, I thought. It meant they were drowned in the ocean somewhere, then taken to the places where their bodies were discovered. Or were their heads somehow immersed in seawater someplace else?

Either way, the murderer—or murderers—would have to know that an autopsy would eventually reveal the seawater. A message had been sent, I thought, but what message? The Virgin's tears, the Florida Straits, the contents of the O'Donnells' lungs. Seawater was everywhere.

I found the number for Alvaro's private line. He answered before the first ring was completed.

"This is Lupe," I said.

"I knew it would be you." Alvaro spoke in an intimate voice that sent a shiver down my back. I tried to remember what underwear I was wearing, hoping it was a sexy pair—the ones Aida disapproved of so much that she tried to shrink them by washing them in the hottest possible water.

Alvaro and I tried to figure out where to meet for dinner. We had to think of a place where he wouldn't be shot on sight, and where I could dine in a T-shirt. We settled on Joe Allen's, a laid-back restaurant on Miami Beach right by the Venetian Causeway. We agreed to meet at eight. I looked at my watch; I would have to hurry to get there on time, although we were both Cuban and there was at least a fifteen-to-twenty-minute window of no-explanations-necessary tardiness for each of us.

I jotted down a short list of questions I wanted to ask Alvaro over dinner—this was supposed to be a business meeting—and began closing down the office for the night.

I was setting the alarm by the front door when the phone rang. I debated whether to leave anyway, but then I heard a familiar soft Jamaican accent from the answering machine. I sprinted over to Leonardo's desk and picked up the receiver.

"Theofilus, it's me, Lupe," I said breathlessly into the phone.

"Thank goodness," Theofilus sighed. "I've been calling and calling, detective lady. I need to show you something."

"What is it?"

"It's at the shrine," he said. "That shrine for the Cuban Virgin."

Something clicked in my brain. "Theofilus, do you take care of the grounds at the *Ermita de la Caridad?*"

"Fridays," Theofilus explained. "That's my Friday job for the archdiocese. I saw something there last week that I want to show you."

"When?" I asked.

"Now, as soon as possible." A hint of impatience poked through Theofilus's mellowness. "I think this is very important, lady. I've been calling to tell you about it."

"I'm sorry, but you're not easy to get hold of either," I said. I thought for a moment. "Do you want to get together tonight?"

"Yeah, I'll be there in a few minutes."

"Wait! Wait! Not right this second." I couldn't bring myself to pass up dinner with Alvaro. "I'm on my way to a meeting right now. How about in two hours, at ten?"

"OK, ten o'clock," Theofilus agreed. "At the shrine, in the back."

"Theofilus, let me give you my cell phone number—"

"No, I don't have a pen," Theofilus said. "I'm at a pay phone."

I sighed. I supposed the Jamaican gold didn't help his ability to memorize phone numbers.

"Hey, if you're going to meet Mr. McDonald, you tell him how much I am helping you," Theofilus added.

"I'll tell him. See you at ten."

Theofilus's last comment made me feel guilty for not being with Tommy that night, but I reminded myself that I was seeing him in the morning. It was just a minor postponement.

I hung up, set the alarm, and hurried out. I felt a sense of unease after speaking with the gardener. I couldn't imagine what was happening at the *Ermita* that I had to see that very night. But Theofilus, despite his pot haze, was smart enough to know when something was important. I just hoped his track record would continue unblemished.

All the way to Miami Beach I could think only of how fast the case had started to move, and how it was widening. At first the miracle had simply been cause for Mother Superior's consternation at losing potential new recruits to her order. Now there were five convents involved somehow: the Holy Rosary in Miami, St. Joseph's in both Springfield and Miami, the convent in Santiago de Cuba where Mary had lived for two years, and, of course, the Illumination of the Sacred Virgin. There were two dead bodies. And there was the miracle itself, looming in the near future as a moment that could change the life of my country and its people forever.

Night had closed in, and it was possible to clearly see the lights of Miami Beach beyond the causeway. I drove east, first past Hibiscus and Palm Island on my left, then I stopped at the red light guarding the entrance to Star Island. Then I headed north, passing Lincoln Road before making a left onto Seventeenth Street.

I drove west, past a Russian delicatessen that had always intrigued me. I resolved, as I always did when I drove by, that I would stop inside one day and see what they sold. I visualized myself walking out with an armload of Beluga caviar, then remembered that that wasn't going to happen—not with the fee I was charging on this case. I hadn't even thought to ask Leonardo whether we'd run through the cash retainer yet, not wanting to hear the answer.

I drove over the first little bridge and turned onto Purdy Avenue, where Joe Allen's was located. I looked at the cars outside, wondered if one of them was Alvaro's.

Alvaro was at the bar nursing a scotch. When he saw me, he jumped up as though he had springs in his feet.

He said my name and put his hands on my shoulders, drew me close, and kissed me. I smelled his cologne, the same as he'd worn at lunch. I returned the kiss, cursing the fact that I'd set up a meeting with Theofilus in less than two hours.

"You're more beautiful than ever," Alvaro said, his big brown eyes on mine. He was dressed casually again, in an open-necked blue-striped shirt, chinos, and boat shoes. No belt, no tie, no socks.

He was either a minimalist dresser, or else he planned to get undressed later in a hurry.

Alvaro kept his hands on my shoulders. His grip was strong, and
felt good. Oh, God, I was getting soft. I was considering what Mami
and Papi had begged me to do for years—get involved with a nice
Cuban man. I wondered whether Papi could overcome his political
convictions and accept Alvaro with his liberal beliefs. It might have
helped Mami and Papi that Alvaro was from an acceptable Cuban
family, one on the same social level as ours—but would this be
enough to make Papi overlook the fact that Alvaro supported dialogue with the Cuban government rather than the embargo? It was
a tough one. I couldn't see Aida happily cooking for Alvaro, not
after what she had said about him the week before. And, come to
think of it, Papi's cronies were from the same crowd that had threatened to shoot Alvaro dead. It was hard to imagine them on the
terrace having cigars together.

"*Gracias.*" I replied. I pulled away from him a little, feeling that
people were looking at us. "I hope I didn't keep you waiting long."

"No, no." Alvaro waved his hand. "I was a bit early, in case you
showed up on time. I didn't want you to have to wait alone."

I smiled. Now I was definitely melting, although it was a little
amusing to have a man worrying about me sitting alone in a public
place. As an investigator, I'd waited alone for hours on surveillance
in bars, restaurants, hotel lobbies, every kind of place imaginable.

"Come." Alvaro put his hand under my arm to guide me toward
the main dining room. "I spoke to the hostess and picked out a
table."

We walked together to the corner of the room, where Alvaro held
out a chair for me. I noticed we were to sit side-by-side, with both
our backs to the wall.

"Is this all right?" he asked.

"Perfect." I sat down before my knees buckled; chivalry always
worked on me. His manners were impeccable. Mami would have
approved. For her, a person could practically be a serial killer as
long as his behavior was up to Emily Post standards. Papi wasn't
such a pushover. Manners wouldn't trump politics in his case.

"I remembered you like wine, so I ordered ahead of time." Alvaro
looked over the room and, with a slight, almost unnoticeable inclina-

tion of his chin, motioned for the waiter to come over. When he arrived, Alvaro said, "I believe we are ready for the wine now."

I watched all of this unfolding in front of me. I was used to suave men, but the smoothness with which Alvaro controlled the situation made most of them look like fumbling little boys in comparison. I was a liberated, gun-toting woman, but Alvaro made it feel nice to be protected. I knew I was setting the women's movement back about a hundred years, but it was impossible to resist. I couldn't help wondering whether he was as skilled in more intimate settings.

We toasted our renewed friendship with red wine and ordered dinner. Joe Allen's was considered by many to be a sort of neighborhood restaurant—it served relatively simple food at reasonable prices, and catered to a varied clientele. I felt comfortable there, with its pale green walls and small statues of surfers that lent an ocean motif. Silver boat propellers were hung on the walls, spinning slightly when the air stirred.

I started the evening by informing Alvaro of our time constraints. He took it well.

"It's a shame, but work is work," he said. "It sounds like this man has important information for you. It can't be helped."

"Thanks for understanding."

"Besides, it's not all bad news," he added with a twinkle. "It means we'll have to meet again. We can't possibly conclude all our business in such a short period of time."

I smiled and wondered what "our business" might turn out to be. Was it me, or was it that he wanted to find out more about the miracle and the progress of the case? I told myself to stop being so suspicious. He was simply behaving like a gentleman of the old school, making me feel interesting and desirable.

"OK, let's start," Alvaro said, refilling our glasses.

"The last time we spoke it was about what the miracle might mean to liberals in the exile community," I began. I dispensed with the questions I'd prepared, not wanting to create too formal a setting.

"I've given it a lot of thought," Alvaro replied. "And I don't think there's any one way of looking at it. On the one hand, there's no place for religion in Communism. If freedom of worship is permitted in a strictly Communist nation, then automatically worshipers have split their previously undivided loyalty to the government. As for the

Catholic Church, it also requires allegiance. 'Render unto Caesar' is all well and good, but the church doesn't permit its faithful to engage in antireligious activities—such as being a Communist."

"But Castro invited the pope to visit Cuba last year," I said. "Isn't there a contradiction in that?"

Alvaro chuckled as he buttered a piece of bread. "Fidel Castro hasn't outlasted and outwitted eight American presidents by being stupid. He used the pope's visit to further his own agenda. Any visit by the pontiff confers stature to the leaders of the country he's visiting. The pope's visit to Cuba granted Castro a front seat on the world's stage. Castro showed deference to the pope, almost behaving like the altar boy he once was. People thought relations with Cuba would subsequently improve, but none of that happened."

I sipped my wine, listening intently. Everything he was saying made sense.

"But Fidel had some bad luck," Alvaro continued. "The Monica Lewinsky scandal broke at the same time as the pope was in Cuba. All the TV anchors left Cuba to cover the story. The biggest Catholic event of the decade was blown off the map by an adulterous affair with an intern."

I laughed along with Alvaro. "So this was one time Castro couldn't be in control," I offered.

"One of the few times," Alvaro agreed.

"But what about the miracle and the liberals?" I asked, bringing the conversation around. "I know what the right-wing thinks, after listening to my father all these years."

"The liberals? You mean all three of us?" Alvaro held up three fingers with a grin. "Well, look. This is only my opinion. But I think the miracle you've described would be a good thing. Cubans need to at least admit it would be positive for all of us to come together. We all want it in our hearts, no matter what our political thinking might be on the surface."

"I agree," I said.

"The problem is: what sort of post-reunification government are we talking about?" Alvaro shrugged. "Look at Germany. West Germany is having to deal with all the problems of Communist mismanagement in the former East. It should have been easy, but it wasn't. They're one people again, but it'll take years before they've recovered."

"But in the long run," I said, "bringing together the two Cubas is a positive thing."

"Yes, I think so," Alvaro said. "If you want my opinion as a liberal member of the Cuban diaspora, yes, it would be a positive thing for all Cubans to be reunited in our home country. If the Virgin helps this come to pass, then all the better."

He reached over and put his hand on mine. "Is that the answer you were looking for?" he asked.

I didn't pull my hand away. "I don't know what I was looking for," I said, looking into his eyes. "I've had a lot of difficult cases in my career, but I feel like this one has troubled me the most. I've had to think about topics I've always avoided, come to terms with ideas that go right to the center of who I am."

"If you want another opinion, I think this is also a good thing." His gaze at me made me feel as though my soul was exposed.

"I guess I'm just starting to recognize that I had only looked at my own beliefs superficially," I went on. "And the problem is, now I'm not even sure what I believe in. After all this time and work, I still don't know whether I want the miracle to be investigated, to be proven or disproven. Sometimes I think I should just step back and leave it all alone."

If the miracle was going to take place, and be considered real, then perhaps, I realized, I might have to believe in all the dictums of the church. I would have to rethink the things I did, the way I lived. If the miracle turned out to be a sham—something contrived to manipulate the faithful for the ends of a hidden agenda—then my belief in Catholicism would be rocked. And if it were made public, then the beliefs of millions could be shaken.

October 10th was looming closer. I wondered whether I was going to be able to remain objective and complete the investigation. I had to detach myself, but it was becoming more and more difficult.

I sneaked a look at my watch just as the waiter was putting the main course in front of us. Time was whizzing by. At this rate, dessert and coffee would be out of the question if I wanted to be on time for my meeting with Theofilus.

Alvaro must have seen my anxiety. "Don't worry," he said. "I'll make sure you get to your appointment, so stop looking at your watch."

At my suggestion, we didn't discuss the case for the rest of the meal. I didn't want to volunteer much more information to him. He had come back into my life just a few days ago, at the start of the investigation. I wanted to get to know him better, but I also wanted to keep my professional and personal lives as separate as I could, although the waters were already very muddy.

Besides, in the time we had remaining that night I wanted to find out as much as possible about Alvaro's personal life—most of all, if there was a woman I should know about, and whether his attentions toward me were perfectly normal and routine for him. With Cuban guys, one never knew. My sisters have always told me that Cuban men are the original bullshit artists. But when I looked into those brown eyes I decided to give my countryman a chance. After all, both Papi and Mami couldn't be wrong.

In spite of Alvaro's best efforts, and my breaking numerous speed and traffic laws, I arrived fifteen minutes late for my meeting with Theofilus. I drove twice around the driveway that encircled the shrine but saw no vehicles parked anywhere. It was strange, since he had been so eager and enthusiastic about showing me what he had found. The smell of the sea was strong in my face as I drove with the window down so I could hear Theofilus in case he called out to me.

The place was deserted under the stark light of the full moon. I heard waves crashing against the seawall. In the distance I could see the lights of the shrimp boats in the bay, outlined against the night sky. There was no movement of any kind in or around the building. I didn't scare easily, but the scene was giving me the creeps. Only dim lights revealed the inside of the shrine itself, and everywhere around my car were shadows that danced in my headlights. The wind off the water blew through the Australian pines along the north end of the property, casting undulating shadows across the parking lot. The shrine at that time of night was far from reassuring and welcoming. I tried to take comfort by thinking of the Virgin inside, hoping that she would protect me.

I stopped the car and debated with myself. The most prudent thing to do would be to leave and wait for Theofilus to contact me again. But being prudent wasn't part of my makeup. I opened the glove compartment and took out my flashlight, then pulled the Beretta out of my purse and checked to make sure it was loaded. I suppressed an urge to run my finger along the perfect circle that had been repaired on the side of my purse. Doing so, I thought, could only bring bad luck.

I would give Theofilus twenty minutes before I got out of the car. I switched off the engine and looked around. Nothing. I hoped Theofilus hadn't hit the Jamaican gold that evening, that he wasn't asleep somewhere with Bob Marley and the Wailers playing in the background. Although at that point, I could have used a hit or two myself.

Gusts from the bay whipped around the Mercedes, howling, buffeting the car. Clouds were drifting overhead in the night sky, casting the parking lot into deeper darkness then lifting again. There was no one around, though I had to make myself stop staring into the shadows—my eyes started to play tricks, seeing forms and movement in the darkness.

It was at this point that I began considering whether I should have followed Mami's advice and pursued a career as a buyer for Bloomingdale's. At that very moment, I would probably have been sipping Chardonnay and nibbling brie at some relentlessly trendy bar, listening to some bond trader from Goldman Sachs telling me about buying the latest-model Porsche with his bonus check. Come to think of it, I said to myself, gripping my gun and imagining that nightmare scenario, I had probably made the right decision.

I looked down at my watch. Almost twenty-five minutes had gone by. I slipped the cellular phone into the pocket of my jeans, opened the car door, and stepped quickly out into the night. My heart pounded so loudly I was sure anyone within a hundred feet could hear it; if that didn't notify them of my presence, my smell of fear certainly would.

I locked the car door behind me and squared my shoulders. I heard waves crashing on the seawall behind me. I took a step carefully, a feeling in my gut alerting me that something bad was about to happen. I knew better than to ignore the sensation. I focused the flashlight beam a few yards ahead of me, the gun tight in my other hand.

As I walked toward the seawall, I called out Theofilus's name without much conviction. There was no reason for him to have hidden from me. And his truck was so conspicuous there was no way I could have missed it if it had been there.

I stood close to the seawall and felt cool water spray my face. For an instant I closed my eyes. I was reminded of a night not long ago, when I pushed a man into these waters. There in the darkness, I surprised myself. Tears fell down my cheek and mixed with the seawater. I felt a melancholy that I couldn't have explained just then, even if I had wanted to.

I was brought back to reality by the sound of a thud in the waters below me. It was a subtle noise, barely enough to break the quiet. For a second I thought I had imagined it.

The moon broke through the clouds. I put my hand on the seawall and shone the flashlight down.

I could identify the black, yellow, and green of the Jamaican flag in Theolifus's overalls. He was in the water, his arms outstretched, his dreadlocks floating around his head like a halo. The current pushed him against the wall, and I realized that this was the sound that I had heard.

I punched in some numbers in my cellular phone and stared at Theofilus floating in the water. As I listened to the phone ring, I figured out why Theofilus had remained close to the seawall. One foot, shod in the red high-top canvas sneaker he'd been wearing the first time I met him, had caught in the rocks barely visible a few feet underwater. If that hadn't happened, the tide certainly would have carried him out to sea.

I sat down on the seawall and waited for an answer on the phone. This was the third recent death with which I'd been involved. It was becoming life-threatening to be associated with me.

The water caressed the seawall. It seemed calm, as though placated now that it had claimed another victim. I kept the Beretta pointed at the darkness, unwilling to become the next.

31

THE shrine was quiet. Theofilus's body was still stuck in the water, not going anywhere. The first number I called was Detective Anderson's cell phone. If he was taken aback by the news that I'd found another body, he didn't show it. He was too much of a pro.

"Wait there," he said, deadpan. I notice he didn't ask if I was carrying a gun to protect myself until he arrived. For all we both knew, there was a killer somewhere in the vicinty, and I was alone at the shrine. My first instinct was to be hurt, until I realized Anderson was merely treating me as an equal, someone who could take care of herself.

I reached Tommy at his apartment. He wasn't quite as calm and measured as Detective Anderson, instead letting off a string of expletives—several involving lewd and vivid descriptions of sexual practices—the likes of which I hadn't heard since my last visit to the Dade County correctional facility for men. Ultimately, I discerned through the cursing, Tommy was unhappy to have been turned down by me for a date, then called with the information that one of his clients had been found floating face-down in Biscayne Bay.

Detective Anderson was on his way. I didn't have long. I knew what I wanted to do, and also that it was illegal. But the temptation was too strong. I thought of the quote, which I'd submitted myself, placed next to my picture in the high-school yearbook: "Lead me not into temptation for I shall find the way myself." So I decided to have a look around, even though it was against the law for me to disturb a crime scene in any way.

I left the seawall and walked around behind the shrine. This would be my last chance; once the police arrived, I'd be denied access to the scene. I shone the flashlight ahead, trying to quiet my breathing so I could hear, although the wind gusted and filled my ears. I peered into the shadows ahead, moving slow, ready to defend myself if someone was waiting in the shadows. Fortunately, I thought, it was unlikely that whoever had killed Theofilus was still hanging around—at least that was what I planned to tell myself as long as I was still alone at the shrine.

Clouds passed overhead. I could see less than before. I walked slowly through the parking lot, edging close to the shrine itself. If the police found signs of my actions, I would tell them that I'd walked around *before* discovering Theofilus's body. There would be no witnesses to disprove my version of the truth.

I replayed the last conversation I'd had with the gardener, searching in my memory for some clue or hint as to what he wanted me to see. Theofilus had said almost nothing. Only that it was important that we meet. I knelt down, flashed the light across the ground. Now Theofilus was gone.

I heard sirens approaching and switched off the flashlight. I switched on the Beretta's safety, put it in my pocket, and retraced my steps back to the seawall. I arrived there just as a line of Miami police squad cars pulled into the parking lot. I raised my hand in greeting.

Detective Anderson's brown sedan parked at the front of the pack. He got out and winced at the lights, dressed in the same outfit he'd worn earlier that evening. He saw me, nodded, and set about his work. He quickly took over the crime scene, ordering it cordoned off with yellow plastic tape. The uniformed officers obeyed his orders, though perhaps without too much urgency. At that time of night, no one was going to come around to contaminate the crime scene.

Anderson approached me with what, for him, was affectionate recognition: a thin, pained grimace that verged on a smile.

"We need to talk," he said.

I looked over Anderson's shoulder and saw Tommy screech to a halt in the driveway. More than a few of the cops recognized him and pointed to where Anderson and I stood. One look at Tommy walking through the lights, and I could see that his mood hadn't improved since we spoke earlier. He was perfectly attired in a three-piece suit, not a hair out of place. Obviously I had interrupted his evening.

"You should have had dinner with me," Tommy hissed as he walked past me to Detective Anderson. "Then we wouldn't be here. We'd be doing something a lot more pleasant."

And that was it, all Tommy had to say to me. Short and to the point. It felt as though each time I saw him he was more angry with me. I was beyond fear and guilt; now I was shocked and numb.

We all watched as Theofilus's body was brought out of the water. It was a lonely sight. I wondered about his family in Jamaica, whether he was supporting them as so many immigrants did who came to America from impoverished countries. Sometimes people like Theofilus, through their collective effort to send money home, kept the economies of their countries afloat. I knew that somewhere in Jamaica, people were going to suffer hardship and sadness at the passing of the Jamaican gardener.

Detective Anderson finally came back to me. I didn't have much to tell him, just the vague circumstances of the meeting Theofilus had requested.

"I see," Anderson said, snapping shut his notebook. "Look, if it's not too much trouble, I want you to stick around."

I looked over at Tommy and, before he could begin to argue, nodded my agreement.

"Maybe he wants to keep me nearby in case something occurs to him," I said to Tommy as Anderson went to join the just-arrived medical examiner. "You know, so I'll be here in case he has more questions."

Tommy sighed and sat down on the hood of his car. "Maybe he's sending you a message," he said in a cold voice. "About how much extra work you're creating for the Miami police."

I didn't reply. I didn't think Detective Anderson would be so petty, but then I couldn't be sure. Maybe, I thought, he wanted me to stay on the scene as a deterrent to my making any more dead bodies appear in Dade County. As long as I was in his sight, then no one else was going to die. It wasn't a very uplifting thought.

I joined Tommy on the car, neither of us saying anything. I watched Detective Anderson taking notes, talking with other officers. He looked irritated in a bland sort of way, although I couldn't really claim to be able to read his emotional state. I supposed I had ruined his plans for the evening as well, though I couldn't imagine he had a personal life. He looked as though he slept in his clothes rather than out of them.

Tommy waited for less than an hour. Finally he got up from the car without saying anything to me and motioned for Detective Anderson. Anderson loped over slowly, as if taking some small measure of revenge by making us wait a few extra seconds.

"It looks like you're done with Lupe," Tommy said.

"Just about," Anderson replied. "Although she's indicated her willingness to stay until we're finished."

Both men looked at me. "I'll stay," I said.

Tommy chewed his lip. "All right," he said to Anderson. "Just as long as you understand she's staying voluntarily."

"All righty," Anderson said, as though he couldn't have cared less. He turned his back and walked toward the crime scene. Tommy watched him with a look that I recognized as slow-boil, long-fuse anger.

"That's that," Tommy said, jingling his keys. "I'll see you in the morning."

"What?" I asked, disoriented.

"Don't you remember?" he said. "Our meeting with Mother Superior."

Tommy looked uncharacteristically uncomfortable sitting in the red velvet chair in the convent's waiting room. I felt pretty much at ease; it seemed that lately I had spent quite a bit of time waiting in various mother superiors' waiting rooms.

Maybe I was so comfortable sitting down because I was so exhausted. I had gotten home at dawn, only a few hours before, and had showered and dressed without bothering to try to sleep. I had arrived so early at my office that even the parrots in the avocado tree had yet to rise. The only positive element from the previous night was that I had been up early enough to have breakfast with Fatima and the twins, though it had been hard to block the thoughts of the recent murders from my mind as we talked about the twins' school play premiering in a week.

Tommy squirmed next to me. In my mind I kept replaying the scene from the night before. Theofilus's corpse floating in the bay.

The bright lights of the crime scene. Detective Anderson's bland, businesslike manner. It came back to me like a vivid nightmare.

I glanced over at Tommy, who, I knew, was thinking about the same thing. No lawyer likes losing a client, even one that was forced on him against his will. And no lawyer would like to think his or her investigator might have contributed to the client's death. Tommy would never have said as much, but I knew there was a cloud of suspicion in his mind.

Tommy seemed to have molded his body into the chair's sharp angles, looking like some kind of disjointed doll or a puppet whose owner had failed to straighten out his strings before laying him down.

I looked up at the clock: exactly ten. The nun behind the reception desk got up, gestured toward Mother Superior's office. I went first, Tommy followed behind.

Mother Superior sat behind her desk, almost as though she hadn't moved since I left her there weeks before. Her blue eyes were like shards of ice, her expression firm and unwelcoming. Before Tommy and I had left the office that morning, Leonardo had taken me aside and issued an uncharacteristically firm order: tell Mother Superior that her cash retainer was long gone, present her with a written bill that Leonardo produced from his word processor. I could already sense this task was going to be difficult to accomplish.

"Mother Superior," I said. Although she was Cuban, I knew leaning over and kissing her on the cheek was out of the question. Even if I were to act so familiar I probably would have gotten frostbite. "This is Thomas McDonald."

If Tommy was put off by Mother Superior's demeanor, he didn't show it. He stepped up to her desk and shook her hand very formally. Then he took a step back, waiting to be invited to sit. I knew he wasn't used to this kind of reception; usually his clients were so grateful to be in his presence that they fell all over themselves to show it.

"Pleased to meet you, Mother Superior," Tommy said with his ice-breaking smile.

"I don't understand why you are here," Mother Superior said flatly. "There is no need for an attorney to be involved in the matter I've hired Lupe to address."

I flinched, embarrassed by her hostility. I tried unsuccessfully to read her expression, looking for anger, or guilt.

"There have been several developments in your case which require the services of an attorney," Tommy said courteously. "Ms. Solano brought me into the case to lend her the legal protection of attorney-client privilege."

"Mother Superior," I interjected, "when I agreed to investigate the Order of the Illumination, I thought my job would merely involve checking out the order to see what was behind the miracle they were claiming was going to take place."

"Sit," she said, pointing at the chairs in front of her desk. As we did, she watched us, immobile and cold. I wondered whether hers were the eyes of a woman capable of murder.

"Several serious events have taken place in the course of my investigation," I went on. I chose my words carefully, wishing to ease into the fact that three people had died.

Tommy interrupted, starting to explain attorney-client privilege, how it helped me avoid being questioned by the police, how it protected me professionally. As he spoke, Mother Superior sat completely still, almost as if she wasn't listening.

I felt like half of a tag team. When Tommy paused for breath, I opened my notebook and started reading from my case notes. I told her about Marisol's surveillance, about Jimmy and Mary O'Donnell. Then I told her about their deaths. She didn't show any expression. I watched carefully her reaction to the names, especially Mary's, but Mother Superior retained her equanimity.

She looked at Tommy. "Is all of this true, Mr. McDonald?"

My mouth dropped; I was so angry I could have kicked her. She had the nerve to ask Tommy to verify the veracity of my case report. It might have been because he was a lawyer, or because he was a man.

"Everything Lupe told you is the truth," Tommy said. I could see his neck turning red; he was getting pissed off as well. "And last night there was another death connected with the case. Theofilus, your gardener. He wanted to show Lupe something at the *Ermita de la Caridad*. His body was found in the bay before we could learn what he had discovered."

Mother Superior crossed herself. At least she had finally showed some emotion, perhaps because she knew Theofilus.

"The poor man," she whispered. "This is terrible."

Mother Superior's tight lips began to move silently; I realized she was saying a prayer for the dead.

Then she looked up at us. "Who has committed these crimes?" she asked.

Did she really want to know, or was she pumping us to see how much information I'd uncovered during the investigation? I still couldn't read her thoughts or intentions from her glacial demeanor.

"We don't know," I replied. "If I did, don't you think I would have told the police?"

Tommy ignored my flaring temper. "Do you have any information that might shed some light on these matters?" he asked Mother Superior.

Tommy never asked a client a direct question. He always phrased his interrogatives to allow the client to keep from admitting guilt.

Mother Superior's eyes remained fixed on Tommy's. They stared at each other for a full thirty seconds.

"I gave Lupe all my information during our first meeting," she finally said. "I know nothing about these murders. I did not know the nun or her brother."

"So the name Mary O'Donnell means nothing to you?" I asked.

"It does not," she said.

"How about Sister Rose O'Donnell?" I asked.

Her eyes turned even colder. "No," she said.

"Mother Superior," I began, as innocently as I could. "Does the archbishop of Miami know that you retained me to conduct this investigation?"

If it was possible, her eyes turned more frozen and unreachable. "What business is it of yours?"

"I just wondered. This case involves different church factions." I ignored her withering look. "Different orders, dead nuns, the desecration of a church."

Mother Superior raised her finger at me. "You were expressly requested not to contact me until this investigation was completed," she said.

"That's no longer possible," I shot back. "Too much—"

Mother Superior stood up, eyes flashing. "I am terminating your investigation," she said imperiously.

"What?" I said.

Mother Superior turned to Tommy. "I'm sorry you wasted your time this morning, Mr. McDonald," she said. "There is nothing further for us to discuss."

She stepped out from behind her desk, moved toward the door. "I believe there is still money remaining from the retainer fee I paid you," she said, her hand on the doorknob. "See that Mr. McDonald is compensated for his services."

I nodded. I guessed I shouldn't have been so surprised. I thought of the bill in my purse. I didn't know how I was going to face Leonardo.

Mother Superior leaned toward me. "I trust our relationship will remain confidential," she said.

"We're both bound by law not to discuss any aspect of the case," Tommy said, holding out his hand to shake. "No one will know about any of this."

Mother Superior gave him a limp tap on his hand and opened the door to the reception room. She ignored me completely. It felt as though I had come asking for a job; forgotten was the fact that she had contacted Lourdes to get my help. I couldn't help feeling that I had touched a nerve, come close to whatever she was hiding. Now that I was fired, I felt truly free to indulge my suspicions of her.

Tommy and I walked out to the parking lot in silence. He opened the passenger door of his Rolls and waited for me to get in before closing the door gently. When he got in the driver's side he let out a deep sigh and handed me his case of CDs.

"Pick something out," he said. "Something to fit the mood."

I flipped through the dozen or so disks, put one in, pressed play. A few moments later the melancholy trumpet of Miles Davis filled the car.

"When was the last time you got fired from a job?" Tommy asked as he started the engine.

"Never." I settled back in the plush leather seat. "I guess there's always a first time. But I never thought I'd get canned by a nun."

"Especially a mother superior," Tommy added, pulling out of the lot. "It's ironic, both of us being Catholic and all that."

"We probably only took her shit as long as we did because we both went to Catholic school," I said.

Tommy nodded sagely. He drove for a while.

"I mean, I've never had my professional integrity questioned like that before," I went on. "She hired me, then she sits there and has the gall to treat me like I'm the one asking for something."

Tommy stared at the road ahead. He looked very tired.

"The hell with it," he said. "Let's go get a drink."

32

I sat in the plush embrace of a dark leather armchair at the bar of the Grand Bay Hotel. Tommy and I were waiting for our second round of *mojitos* to arrive.

I really didn't care if Mother Superior fired me. It was almost immaterial. I was interested in the reason I was fired, though, which was part of why I was going to keep working the case. But I had to reconcile this with the fact that Solano Investigations was going deeply into the red. Not only would we not recoup what was owed us by the Order of the Rosary, but no money would be coming from the order in the future.

And I was responsible for bringing Tommy into the case. I had retained him without consulting Mother Superior, and all to cover up my own mistakes. Tommy hadn't done a thing, and now he was enmeshed with Marisol, as well as the late Theofilus. I knew he wouldn't accept any kind of financial restitution for the time and money he would expend on the case—a fact that deepened my already bottomless guilt. Tommy had a reputation as a sleazeball ambulance chaser, but deep down he was as good a man as anyone could find. He would chalk up his involvement on the case to experience, and shrug off all the empty billable hours. It wasn't all sheer altruism, though. He would be able to write off the hours as a tax loss, and he would also have me in his debt. As always, he would come out ahead.

"What do you think?" he asked, looking up from his cocktail napkin. "We've had some time to absorb Mother Superior's little performance back there at the convent."

"The first thing is facing Leonardo," I said. The drinks arrived and, as I took my first sip, I noticed that my knuckles were white against the glass. I was almost more afraid of dealing with Leonardo than the killer.

"You know how to handle your cousin," Tommy said. "Buy him some piece of exercise equipment, put it on your American Express card. That'll get him off your back for a while."

Ah, the American way. Charge your troubles away.

"Seriously, Tommy, I'm taking a financial bloodbath on this case," I moaned. "But I'll find some way to set it right. I have to."

Both of us knew that if Solano Investigations ever really teetered on the brink of total ruin, I could ask Papi for a temporary bailout. But things had been tight in the past, and we had always gotten through the crunch on our own. Leonardo would line up domestic cases back-to-back, and we would move on. The prospect of working domestics for the next few months was enough to make me shudder.

"Put the money issues aside for now," Tommy said. "What are you going to do? You're not going to walk away, not with this miracle involved. I know you too well."

I took a sip of my drink and smiled. He was right.

"Watch yourself," he warned, serious now. "The body count is too high as it is. It's getting a little scary."

Then Tommy leaned over and kissed me lightly on the lips. I blinked with shock. Tommy wasn't much for public displays of affection—probably because of his Anglo-Saxon blood, also because we were well known in Miami as professional allies. This was, as far as I could remember, the first time he had kissed me in public. It was almost alarming.

Stop analyzing everything, I told myself. I needed to stop being an investigator, if only for a few minutes a day. Sometimes I needed to accept words and deeds at face value and accept them.

I took his hand under the table. "That was nice," I said. In spite of our quarrels, there was a bond between us that nothing could break.

Tommy muttered something, flustered. He waved for the check. At least something good had happened that day. I had actually broken through Tommy's wall of cool.

It was a two-block drive back to my office. Mercifully, Leonardo wasn't there when I came in, so I was able to delay telling him the grim news about our finances. I had only bought a couple of hours,

I knew, so I fixed myself an extra-large *café con leche* and drank it fast. I felt myself coming back to life. Drinking before noon wasn't a habit that I wanted to cultivate, but it had been an exceptionally frustrating morning.

I picked up the phone and punched in the number for the St. Joseph's convent in Miami. A pleasant female voice answered, and I asked to speak to Sister Rose O'Donnell. The woman said Rose was in chapel, but that I could leave my name and number. I decided not to—I feared somehow it would get back to Mother Superior at Lourdes's order—and said I would try back later. Mother Superior had claimed no knowledge of the O'Donnell triplets, but I wasn't sure I believed her.

I flipped through reports, rubbed my eyes. I tried not to think about the fact that I was working for free. The O'Donnells, Theofilus, Tommy's ruined schedule, Marisol's arrest, Leonardo's Cuban ass—I felt responsible for all of it.

After about twenty minutes the phone rang on my desk. I identified myself.

"Lupe?" a familiar voice asked. "This is Sister Rose O'Donnell."

"Yes," I said, sounding calm.

"I hope I'm not disturbing you."

"Not at all," I replied.

"I wondered if it would be possible for me to stop by your office again," she said. "If it's not too much trouble."

Someone was rewarding me for my patience. I could feel it. I had planned to get Rose into my office under some pretense I had yet to devise, and now here she was calling me.

"Of course," I said. "Would you mind taking a taxi again? I don't think it would be a good idea for me to fetch you."

"I understand," Rose said. Her voice sounded tired and reedy. "I'll be over as quickly as I can. If it's all right with you."

"It's not a bother, really," I replied. "I'm very glad you called. I'd like to speak with you as well."

While I waited for Sister Rose I updated my own notes on the case and organized my thoughts for the interview. It felt a little strange, since there was no longer a paying client to whom I could give my eventual final report. But in a way it was liberating. It seemed I was now working a case that no one wanted solved—not

Lourdes's mother superior, not the archdiocese, certainly not the Order of the Illumination.

Leonardo still hadn't returned to the office by the time Sister Rose arrived. I let her into the building and escorted her to my office. She was dressed in the same dowdy dress she'd worn during our last meeting.

"Here, please sit down," I said, motioning toward a chair. "Can I get you something to drink? Coffee? Juice?"

Sister Rose shook her head. "No, thank you," she said. She sat down and folded her hands in her lap.

I stacked up my files and pushed them to the edge of the desk. Sister Rose watched me in silence, apparently uninterested in the piles of documents I'd amassed on the case.

"Thank you for meeting with me on such short notice," she said.

"It's my pleasure," I replied. I looked at the nun to see if I could discern exactly why she had requested meeting with me. "I know how difficult this has been for you. Have the police contacted you again?"

"Not since the last time," she said. Her pale skin shone in the early-afternoon light. "I assumed there was no news. That's . . . that's why I wanted to see you. I felt we had a rapport. I wondered if there was anything you've learned about my brother and sister."

"Perhaps indirectly," I said, pausing to calculate how much to tell her. My instincts—and training—told me to selectively choose what to reveal. However, I decided I owed it to her siblings to be direct. "There's been another death."

Sister Rose gasped and crossed herself. "Another," she whispered. "Who was it?"

"The gardener at the convent," I replied. "Apparently he also took care of the grounds at several of the archdiocese's properties."

It felt very strange to be talking about Theofilus like this. I had, after all, spoken with him on the phone less than twenty-four hours before. But now he was gone. All I could do for him was to help find out who had killed him.

"May God bless him and care for his soul," Rose said, crossing herself again, her hands shaking. "When will this end? How many more will it take?"

Rose surprised me with the depths of her sudden anguish. It

seemed strange to me that she was reacting more strongly to Theofilus's death than she had to that of her siblings, but maybe I was mistaken. People react in their own way to tragedy, I reminded myself, and it wasn't my place to judge Rose.

I heard the chime of the office's front door and felt a sinking sensation in my stomach. Leonardo was back. I could no longer put off telling him that I'd been fired, that our bill would be unpaid. We had never kept secrets from each other, and now wasn't the time to start. I steeled myself for the conversation that would begin as soon as Sister Rose had left.

I heard a soft knock at the door, then the knob turning. I closed my eyes and hoped he wouldn't be dressed too inappropriately that day. Rose was in delicate shape; seeing Leo half-naked surely wouldn't help.

Thankfully he had gone for a sedate look: fairly tasteful bicycle pants and a normal green workout top. I felt a wave of relief. When he came into the office I saw that he was wearing his heart monitor strapped across his chest—he would never allow himself to become too agitated while the device was hooked up, and this increased the chances that our looming talk would be less traumatic.

Leonardo apologized for interrupting when he saw Sister Rose sitting in front of my desk. A slight frown crossed his face when he took in the fact that Rose didn't have a beverage anywhere nearby. His sense of hospitality was obviously affronted.

He addressed me in Spanish, asking whether I had offered the sister something to drink.

She looked up at him and said, "No, gracias." Then she added in English, "Oh, no, thank you. You're very kind, but Lupe already offered."

"OK," Leonardo said. "Sorry to burst in." He backed out of the room and closed the door behind him.

"We might not get to talk again, Sister Rose," I said when we were alone. "Can you think of any information that would help me?"

"No, Ms. Solano, I'm sorry." Rose smiled sadly. "I've thought about nothing else since we spoke. I'm afraid I have no answers for you."

"Well, the gardener's body was found in Biscayne Bay last night," I said, "behind the shrine of the Cuban Virgin."

"Another drowning?" Rose asked, her eyes wide. "And you think this death is connected to Jimmy and Mary?"

I couldn't say why, but something in her attitude toward Theofilus's death sparked suspicion in my mind.

"There's a high probability," I told her. "We'll have to wait for the police to make their determination."

"I appreciate your speaking with me today," Sister Rose said. "I feel foolish, calling you up out of the blue."

"It's nothing," I said. "I wish I had answers as much as you do."

"I should go." Sister Rose stood up and collected her purse. "The police should release the bodies of Jimmy and Mary to me soon. Then I'll be going back home. It was very nice to meet you. Godspeed and good luck to you, my dear."

I opened up my purse and fished around for a bill. "Let me pay for your taxi expenses," I said.

Rose started to refuse, then probably remembered how little money she had.

"Well, thank you," she said apologetically. "I wouldn't, but since your own sister is a nun . . ."

I walked Rose to the outer office, wondering how she knew that Lourdes was a nun. I couldn't remember telling her that. But I also checked myself before my suspicions got the best of me. If I wasn't careful, I was going to start accosting nuns on the street and questioning them.

I considered having Leonardo drive Rose back to the order again, but I recalled how much he'd had to go out of his way the last time. Anyway, we needed to speak, and I couldn't bear to delay any longer.

"Leo, could you call a taxi for Sister Rose?" I asked.

I watched a surge of relief cross his features; he bowed his head so it wouldn't be too obvious. I knew he had no ill will toward the sister, but she had no idea how difficult driving in Miami could be; this time, she might have requested a trip to Key Biscayne or some more treacherous crosstown expedition.

"Sure, no problem." He reached for the phone, dialed, spoke for a moment. "Five minutes. The dispatcher said there's a car in the vicinity."

I put my hand on Rose's shoulder and escorted her through the reception area. She smiled at Leonardo and said good-bye, then glanced in the open doorway of the gym. She paused with her purse held in both hands, obviously unable to process what she was seeing. She probably suspected we were running some kind of exotic S and M ring after-hours.

A moment later we heard a car horn honking outside. Sister Rose moved fast for the door. I guess I shouldn't have been surprised. Her life had turned into a nightmare. She was probably eager to get away from Miami and everyone in it.

I had had plenty of experience with Miami's taxi drivers, so I escorted Rose to the cab and gave the driver the address for the convent. It was a good thing I had, because he couldn't speak a word of English and I didn't think Rose would be able to communicate with him. I gave directions in Spanish as I waved good-bye to Rose, hoping the driver could hear me through the loud barrage of Spanish-language radio coming from the taxi's sound system.

When I got back inside the office my stomach was grumbling. "You want to go out to lunch?" I asked my cousin.

"Lunch or brunch?" Leonardo asked with mischief. "Don't tell me you're starting to keep American hours, Lupe."

We opened the door and stepped out, locking the place behind us. When we had taken a few steps I had a thought. Something about the taxi driver a few minutes ago had stimulated an idea.

"Leo, remember when you came into the office a little while ago?"

Leonardo was fiddling with his heart monitor. "Huh?" he asked.

"When Sister Rose and I were talking, you came in and asked me if I'd offered her anything to drink."

"Well, Lupe, it's only a matter of good manners," Leonardo replied. "I mean, our clients are our guests, and—"

"No, no, listen," I interrupted. "You asked me in Spanish, didn't you?"

"What do you mean?" Leonardo frowned.

I could have shaken him. "Just tell me. You asked me in Spanish. Am I right?"

"*Sí*, what's the big deal?" he asked. "Sometimes we speak English, sometimes Spanish. It's always been that way. You're not thinking of turning our office into one of those asinine 'English-only' environments, are you? Because if you are—"

"No, no." I spoke slowly. "The point is, Leo, she understood what you were saying to me. And now that I think about it, when I was speaking Spanish to her taxi driver, she looked like she knew what we were talking about. I'm almost sure that Sister Rose speaks Spanish."

Leonardo shrugged. "So what?" he asked. "She wasn't thirsty in the office, that's all. And you were dealing with the taxi driver for her, so she didn't have to get involved."

I could tell Leonardo wasn't overly impressed with this piece of crack deduction on my part.

"It's weird in Miami not to speak Spanish," he continued. "Everyone here does, if only a little bit."

"My point exactly," I said, triumphant now. "Sister Rose isn't from Miami. She's from Massachusetts by way of Pennsylvania."

And, I thought, she knew about Lourdes. All of this was pointing me in a new direction.

Leonardo shook his head as we walked, not recognizing the enormity of what I'd found out during an innocent meeting. I raced back to the office to put in a quick call before lunch, leaving Leonardo flummoxed on the sidewalk. It didn't matter. I was on the scent again.

33

WE ordered two pita sandwiches—tuna for me, hummus for Leonardo—at the Last Carrot. Leonardo and I often ordered takeout from there, but that day we decided to have a sit-down lunch. The Last Carrot was a relaxed, informal vegetarian restaurant that mostly served regulars who lived and worked in the Grove. It consisted of a long lunch counter and served perhaps twenty diners at a time. There was a mountain of fresh carrots behind the counter, waiting to be ground to a pulp.

Just as our sandwiches were put on wax-paper placemats in front of me and my cousin, my cell phone rang.

"Lupe?" Nestor's voice growled over the line. "I got the background on that guy from Massachusetts. It just came in."

"Oh, great, that was quick." I pulled a pen out of my purse. "Give it to me, but slowly, please. Leonardo and I are at the Last Carrot having lunch."

"Sorry to interrupt, but you asked me to expedite." Nestor paused. "OK, the name's Michael Stephen Patterson. DOB 3/12/34. You want the other details, Social Security number and all that other *mierda*, or just the interesting stuff? I'll courier the hard copy to your office after we hang up. It'll be there soon."

"Just give me the good stuff now." I had a prickly sensation on the back of my neck. I pushed aside my sandwich and carrot juice.

"Mr. Patterson is a registered Republican and a practicing Protestant." Nestor chuckled; he was obviously enjoying himself. I hated to think what each tidbit of information was going to cost me. "He was in the service. He was sent to Korea, where he received a Purple Heart."

As I listened I tried to think of connections between Patterson and the order of Yugoslavian nuns in Miami. It seemed statistically unlikely that he had a female relative in the convent, or that he was canvassing for Republican votes.

"Do you have any idea why he's in Miami?" I asked. I took a sip of carrot juice, thinking the Vitamin A might help improve my vision in case I had to go out on a surveillance.

"No," Nestor said. "But let's skip down to Señor Patterson's academic credentials and present occupation."

"That would be good," I said. Leonardo sat next to me, chewing away.

"Our man is an MIT graduate," Nestor said. "He has a master's degree in chemical engineering, a career that he currently pursues with a self-employed status."

"OK," I said, my mind racing. "And thanks, Nestor. I know you had to work hard to get this information so fast."

"I'm messengering the report now," Nestor said. "Along with my bill for fees and expenses. I'm warning you, Lupe, this one wasn't cheap."

As if I needed reminding that my finances were going down the toilet. Leonardo had finished his sandwich and was now eyeing the brownie display with a salacious expression.

"Go ahead, have one," I said as I put the phone away. "They're made with carob syrup instead of sugar. And I need time to finish my sandwich."

Leonardo bought a brownie and returned. He took a bite and a positively beatific look came into his glazed eyes.

"That was Nestor, right?" he asked between bites. "Any news on the case?"

I hated to do it, but there was no way out.

"There's something I have to tell you, Leonardo."

My cousin finished the brownie and delicately daubed his mouth with a paper napkin. "That was delicious," he said. "Thank you for forcing me to eat it."

"Leo." I took out the envelope he'd prepared which contained the invoice for Mother Superior. "I didn't submit this this morning."

"Oh, that's OK," Leonardo replied. "I knew you wouldn't. I didn't really expect you to."

One eye on the brownie basket again, he took the envelope and stuffed it in his fanny pack. "We'll mail it to her," he said. "I'll send it out when we get back to the office, along with a nice, polite cover letter."

I put my hand on his arm. "No, don't do that, please."

Leonardo nodded warily. "You're right," he said. "The mail takes too long. No problem. We'll courier it over to the convent. I'll call Speedy as soon as we get back."

There was no elegant, painless way to inform Leonardo that there would be no point mailing, couriering, e-mailing, or faxing the invoice to Mother Superior. Being paid simply wasn't in our future.

"Leonardo, listen." I tapped his arm gently. "We're off the case. Fired. Terminated."

Leonardo shook his head from side to side, as though trying to clear out his ears.

"But I just heard you talking to Nestor about it." His eyes narrowed suspiciously; for all his eccentricities, he was no fool. "Tell me, Guadalupe, please tell me we're not going to get stiffed for services rendered. And that you aren't working this case for free. Lupe, please, tell me I'm wrong!"

Leonardo's dramatic display was attracting the attention of the Last Carrot's staff and patrons—no easy feat, considering the world-weary characters who frequented the place.

"Leo, get hold of yourself." I stroked his arm. "I'll make up the lost income. I promise you."

"Domestics! You'll work domestics!" Leonardo's mood shifted in an instant, his anguish gone. I knew he saw pieces of gym equipment dancing in front of his eyes.

"I'll work domestics," I said, defeated. "You can line them up as soon as this case is completed."

Shit. I couldn't reconcile moving from miracles to investigating domestic crises. But that was exactly what was going to happen. It was just another day in Miami.

As soon as we were back at the office I saw the messenger pulling into the driveway. Nestor was true to his word, and he had sent me his report on Michael Stephen Patterson. I grabbed the half dozen pages and raced back to my office. I heard the sound of Leonardo checking the messages on the answering machine on his desk.

Nothing in Nestor's report jumped out at me immediately. I jotted notes on a legal pad. Patterson was born in 1934. That made him sixty-four—almost the same age as the O'Donnell triplets. I picked up the phone and dialed Nestor.

"Thanks for getting this done so fast," I said to him. "You're the best."

There was no harm in stroking him sometimes; people tended to forget that Nestor was human, rather than an investigating machine.

"Thanks," he said, his voice warm. "Now what's the catch?"

"Well, I have another request. Do you still have the file on James O'Donnell?"

"Sure, right here," he replied. I knew he would. Nestor was too much of a professional to place the file where he couldn't access it in an instant.

"I need O'Donnell's service record," I said. "He told me he was in the navy. Find out all you can—where he was stationed, when, how long. And do it fast."

I hung up and called Marisol. She picked up the phone on the first ring. "I know what I need out of your surveillance," I said. I explained to her the plan that had begun to solidify in my mind. I thought I detected a little annoyance in her voice, but I assured her that this time I wouldn't land her in jail.

Leonardo poked his head in the doorway. "You want your messages?" he asked.

I groaned. More things to deal with. "Sure, *gracias*," I said, holding out my hand for the message slips. There were four. How could so many people have called me while I was wolfing down a sandwich? I flipped through them. Well, at least they were all from men. I shuffled them and picked one at random to see who I would call first. Charlie Miliken was the lucky victim.

"Charlie, this is Lupe." I tried to sound sweet. I suspected this wasn't going to be pleasant.

"I heard you found another body—a floater," Charlie shouted, not bothering even to say hello. "What the hell's going on with you, anyway?"

Miss Manners wouldn't have approved of Charlie's tone.

"I had nothing to do with the murder," I said, trying to think of a tactic that would get him off my back. "I went to meet Theofilus because he asked me to, and that's when I found him. Anyone could have stumbled onto him, it just happened to be me."

"I doubt it, not with your track record," Charlie said cryptically.

"Well, anyway, how are you?" I asked, halfheartedly trying to change the subject.

"Busy," Charlie barked. "Every time you find a body, I get assigned the file."

"Any suspects?" I asked. "Do you think the same person was responsible for all three deaths?"

"No, I don't have any suspects," Charlie said. "But it does seem strange that all three of the deceased had contact with you just prior to their murders."

I looked for a playful, teasing tone in his voice, but it wasn't there. "Come on!" I said. "You don't suspect me!"

"I don't know. Three bodies. It's too much." Charlie's voice was hard. "You're lucky you have Tommy McDonald protecting you. Otherwise who knows what might be happening."

I couldn't believe this was the same man I'd been with just a few days before, meeting in his office in a friendly fashion. Maybe he was on the wagon, or had stopped smoking again.

"Give me a break," I said. "Charlie, you can't be serious."

"I'm not sure you realize how much I protect you around here," Charlie replied. "If you were up for a popularity contest, there are some people here who would do anything to make sure you lost."

We both knew Charlie was referring to Aurora Santangelo, my nemesis at the state attorney's office who had been trying to nail my ass for years. She had been sent into exile to Hialeah's traffic court for six months over a matter that related to me, and since her return I knew she hated me more than ever. She would have had me once, but Tommy had saved me. I might not be so lucky next time.

"One thing," I asked him. "Were there rope burns on Theofilus's wrists, like there were with the O'Donnells?"

Charlie paused. "Yes," he said. "Why? Are you getting your story straight?"

"That's a cheap shot, Charlie."

"Look, I'm sorry, Lupe," Charlie said. "I don't mean to come down so hard on you. It's just that this situation is getting worse and worse."

"It's OK," I said, grateful for his conciliatory attitude. "I know you're under a lot of pressure. We both are."

"Want to have dinner?" Charlie asked.

"Yes," I said. Apparently he hadn't given up on drinks and cigarettes altogether. It would be nice to see him away from the office setting; I liked him and always enjoyed his company. Plus, I might get the inside scoop on the case. Maybe the thought was a little mercenary, but I knew better than to turn down a good opportunity.

"I have a trial tonight," Charlie said. "I don't know how late I'm going to have to be here. But I'll call you the minute I have free time. Would that be all right?"

I grinned. Charlie sounded like a teenage boy asking a girl out for his first date. It was out of character, and strangely touching.

"Call when you can," I said, as I tried not to laugh. "In the meantime, I'll try not to discover any more dead bodies."

I hung up before Charlie could say anything. It was too hard to resist poking fun at him.

I picked out the next slip at random. Detective Anderson. He was out of his office, so I called his cellular phone.

"Thanks for calling back so quickly," Detective Anderson said. "I just wanted to inform you that the preliminary autopsy report on last night's deceased is the same as the O'Donnells'—seawater in the lungs."

"Must be the same perp for all three," I said.

"It's the only logical conclusion I can draw at this point," Anderson replied.

"Any suspects?" I knew the answer before he told me.

"Not right now," he said. "Got any names for me?"

I couldn't tell whether Detective Anderson was joking. He was so serious, I decided to take him at his word. I was never comfortable joking with law-enforcement officers unless I happened to be sleeping with them—and that stipulation certainly didn't apply to Detective Anderson, nor was it ever going to.

"Anything else interesting?" I asked. We both knew that I hadn't answered his question. "Find anything at the crime scene?"

"Not really," Anderson said. "Just thought you might like to know about the ME's findings. Seeing as how we're exchanging information and cooperating on the case."

"Thanks."

"Anyway, you were the one who found two of the bodies," Anderson continued. "So I figured you have a personal interest in the case, as well as professional."

I wasn't sure if I was being warned that I might be in danger from the murderer, or from the police. I suggested to Anderson that we stay in touch, keep each other informed. He agreed in his flat voice and hung up.

Next I called Tommy. He laughed as soon as I got on the line, making me feel relieved that his heavy mood was lifted.

"How did it go with Leonardo?" he asked.

"OK," I said. "I guess he'll be able to afford the Cuban-ass machine, after all the domestics I'll be working."

We talked a few minutes more. I felt reassured that our relationship was back on solid ground. I knew that relationships weren't always balanced, that control and power passed from one person to the other all the time. For now, I was in Tommy's debt.

Finally I punched in the number for Alvaro's private line. He answered right away and sounded delighted.

"I wanted to know how your meeting went last night," he said. "I was worried that you might have arrived too late."

I thought before replying. What should I tell him? That I *was* late? That the person I was supposed to meet was carried off in a body bag? That I might be next, whether the cops or the murderer found me first? I decided not to say much. Theofilus's murder might make the papers soon, but Alvaro didn't know specifically where I had gone last night.

"Everything went fine," I said. "Thanks again for dinner. I had a very nice time."

"We could do it again if you're free tonight," Alvaro suggested.

"I'd love to," I said. I knew from past experience that my late date with Charlie would never take place. It was always that way when he was in trial mode. No doubt about it, his voice made me feel as though we had some unfinished business.

Alvaro put me on hold for a few seconds; when he came back,

he said an attorney he'd been playing phone tag with for a week was waiting on the other line. We agreed to talk later. It made me glad that Charlie had been occupied with his trial. I realized, after thinking for an instant, that I would much rather see Alvaro.

I knew that I should probably go home and take a nap before meeting with Alvaro that night, but instead of going to Cocoplum after I left the office for the day I headed north toward the *Ermita de la Caridad*. I had gotten by with almost no sleep the night before, but I wanted to look around behind the shrine while there was still daylight remaining. The police had combed the area, under Detective Anderson's direction, but I wanted to see the place myself.

It wasn't that I didn't trust the crime-scene investigators, but I felt I owed Theofilus at least the courtesy of a personal search. After all, whatever he had wanted to show me had cost him his life. And there was always the chance that Anderson was holding out on me, that he had found something he didn't want to disclose.

I turned east off South Miami Avenue onto the road leading to the shrine. It felt like I had been there weeks ago, instead of just twelve hours. I drove straight through to the end of the road, passed through the wrought-iron gates. I turned to the right, circled the building, and parked in the same spot as the night before.

I turned off the motor and sat in the car for a few minutes, trying to control the weird disjointed feeling that had come over me. I looked around. There was no trace of the horror that had happened there the night before. Whoever had cleaned up the crime scene had done an outstanding job.

After I said a little prayer for Theofilus I stepped out of the car. There were about a dozen other vehicles parked in the circular driveway, most adorned with religious symbols—rosary beads wrapped around rear-view mirrors, plastic statuettes of the Virgin on dashboards. Most cars had bumper stickers reflecting the church's stand on abortion.

I was alone in the parking lot. No one was walking around, no one was sitting in any of the cars. I reached inside my purse and felt the cool metal of my Beretta, hoping I wouldn't need it.

The wind blew hard off the bay, whipping my hair into my face. I twisted it back into a ponytail to get it out of my eyes. I stood at the edge of the bay, taking in the sense of serenity. Birds swam down in great arcs to eat fish swimming close to the surface. Boats headed out on channels taking them to sea. Some hardy souls were out there on sailboats, braving the strong wind and tides. I looked every place but down to the spot where I had found Theofilus.

I began my search at the wall on the far side of the property, slowly moving across. I had no idea what I was looking for. I spent more than half an hour looking around, finding nothing. I sat down on the seawall and looked across the bay toward Key Biscayne. Whatever Theofilus had wanted to show me was gone, I thought.

But how had he arrived at the shrine? As far as I knew, his truck full of gardening implements hadn't been found at the shrine. The night before I hadn't seen a car, a motorcycle, not even a bicycle. Surely Theofilus hadn't walked. No one walked in Miami. It was practically against the law.

I looked around again. Maybe he had come on a bike and stashed it somewhere, wanting to remain hidden until I arrived. Theofilus took care of the *Ermita*'s grounds, so there must have been a shed on the grounds where he could keep extra groundskeeping equipment that didn't fit into his truck. I walked through the grounds again, past a copse of trees. From where I stood, I could barely see the shrine and the seawall was completely obscured. And there it was, covered in vines—a dilapidated shed, painted green to blend in with its surroundings, hidden from sight by Australian pines.

The shed was nothing more than a glorified lean-to, but I was surprised to see a brand-new lock on the rusted double door. I wasn't sure what this meant, so I walked around it.

There were more than a few sets of footprints on the ground, crushed into lush piles of fallen pine needles. I knelt down. These were big prints, made by a heavy person wearing thick-soled shoes. Not Theofilus's sneakers. My heart beat a little faster.

The afternoon light was starting to fade. I walked around to the double door again, knowing that I should walk away, call Detective Anderson, tell him what I'd found. I had been at the crime scene all night, I knew no one had noticed the shed as they concentrated their search close to the seawall and the *Ermita* itself. Anderson could get access to the shed right away, since he was the detective in charge of an ongoing investigation.

Walk away, I thought. But I didn't want to. The hell with it.

I reached into my bag and unzipped the bottom compartment. Inside was a small leather sack which contained my emergency supplies—an extra pair of tweezers, cuticle scissors, and lock-picking tools. If the folks at Chanel knew what I put in their bag, they might start enclosing a disclaimer along with the certificate of authenticity they include with each item they make.

It wasn't against the law to own a lifter pick and a tension wrench, but it was a felony to use them. I had learned this from Slick Mick, a former client who was currently serving three to five at taxpayers' expense at Raiford. He had given me his tools as a Christmas present before he went away. He had said he held me in the highest esteem, and so he had given me his best set of tools—as well as a lesson in how to use them. In case I ever got locked out of my home or office, he had said, winking at me.

I held the pick and wrench in my right hand, reluctant to use them but burning with curiosity. I glanced over my shoulder. No one was watching. I took out the Beretta and tucked it in the waistband of my skirt.

Slick Mick had trained me well. It took me about fifteen seconds before I felt the lock turn in my hand. I quickly replaced the lifter pick and tension wrench in the bottom of my purse. The last thing I needed was to get caught with burglary tools at a shrine, especially after discovering a body there the night before. Aurora Santangelo would have hit a home run on that one—without even breaking a sweat.

I opened up the door and stepped inside. It was pitch black, and I hadn't brought my flashlight. I waited for my eyes to adjust, deciding not to risk going back to the car.

Shapes emerged. I took another step into the gloom. It took a moment to realize what Theofilus had wanted to show me, but then it started to make sense.

This was where Jimmy and Mary had spent the last hours of their lives—and probably Theofilus as well.

The shed looked like it hadn't been used for gardening in years. There was a rusted rake, a shovel. Theofilus had probably gotten into it because he wanted to store something of his, or maybe because he was looking for information to give me.

The rusted shed had become a jail. There were dirty blankets in a pile in the corner, strips of cloth littering the floor. In the middle of the shed was an inflatable raft filled with dirty water a few feet deep.

I stuck my finger in the water, first smelled, then tasted a drop. Seawater.

There were coils of rope on the floor, no doubt the same rope that had burned all three victims' wrists. I put my hands on my thighs and dropped my head, fought off the urge to vomit.

I turned away and reached in my purse for the cellular phone. By then, I didn't have to look up Detective Anderson's number. I knew it by heart.

34

DETECTIVE Anderson approached me at the seawall behind the shrine. In spite of the darkness I could see the grim look on his face.

"I'm not going to ask you how you got the shed's lock open," he said. "I'm going to let it pass. At least there was no body this time when you called me."

It wasn't much of a greeting, but at least he wasn't going to charge me with breaking and entering. We both knew how the lock had been opened; well, I knew, and Detective Anderson could guess.

"So do you agree with me," I said, "that the shed was probably where the three victims were taken to be killed?"

"The forensic techs are in there dusting for prints." Detective Anderson coughed. "But yes, I agree with your conclusion. That was a good piece of investigative work, Lupe."

"*Gracias,*" I said. I knew how much this praise cost him, since his people had been there for hours the night before without taking notice of the little shed. I only wished that Anderson could break himself of the habit of coming off like a Joe Friday caricature.

Anderson sat down on the seawall next to me. I almost fell over. I don't think I had ever been in such close physical proximity to the homicide cop before. Maybe he was really serious about cooperating with me, and had started to feel relaxed with me.

"Any theories?" he asked, looking out over the water.

"Not really." Actually, that wasn't technically the truth. But in spite of our growing closeness, I didn't feel ready to confide in Detective Anderson. I hadn't developed my thoughts fully, and I didn't want to share them with someone who might run with them. "How about you?" I asked.

Detective Anderson shook his head. I had the feeling we were both lying through our teeth, but there was no problem with that. Secrecy was at the core of both our professions, and we were merely following the unwritten rules.

"Do you need me to stay?" I asked. I looked down at my watch. There was time for a quick shower before I had to meet Alvaro. It would have been more proper for Alvaro to pick me up at my house, but my family's politics weren't necessarily conducive to a warm welcome. Aida probably wouldn't offer him conch fritters, and who knew what Osvaldo might put in the *mojitos*.

In a household such as ours, Alvaro would be considered a Communist and a traitor. In any place other than Miami, he would be thought of as a centrist. I knew that if we happened to become involved, I was going to have to deal with my family's hostility toward those who shared his politics. But for now, I had enough to worry about with dead bodies showing up at a regular rate.

"You can go whenever you want," Anderson replied. "I have your statement."

Detective Anderson patted his jacket pocket—the same jacket I could have sworn he wore every time I saw him. I briefly considered putting a little pen mark on it, to see if he just wore similar suits or if he never changed clothes. I knew that public servants weren't paid much, and it was obvious that Anderson didn't set aside a large portion of his disposable income toward clothing.

I walked away, leaving him sitting forlorn on the seawall, watching the pelicans swooping down for their dinner. I wondered if I would have gotten off so easily if he'd known I no longer worked for a client, that I was pursuing the case on my own.

"I'm on my way, Alvaro," I said into my cellular phone. "I'm sorry, I'm running a few minutes late."

I turned north on LeJeune Avenue until I reached Giralda, the street where the restaurant was located. I had been mildly surprised that Alvaro had chosen a place in Coral Gables, knowing that he avoided places in Miami frequented by Cubans. As soon as I entered the place, though, I understood his reasons. The restaurant was pitch dark inside; I almost stumbled in the foyer as I made my way through the bar into the dining room.

Not much had changed since I had been there years before. La

Bussola had been Mami's favorite Italian restaurant. I had always liked it, though when I was younger I fidgeted uncontrollably waiting for the food to be served. I knew as an adult that it was done on purpose, so the diners could have a leisurely meal, but for a child it was torture.

One look at Alvaro waiting for me and I knew this evening would be anything but tortuous. If I ordered fish, it was fine with me if the chef went out on a dinghy into the Atlantic to catch it. For an omelet, I would wait until dawn for the hen to lay her eggs.

"Lupe." Alvaro kissed me on the cheek, so close to my mouth that our lips brushed lightly. "You look beautiful."

"Thank you," I said, knowing that I was beaming.

Alvaro held out the chair for me to sit, an old-fashioned gesture but one that he performed with total grace.

"I want to hear about your day," Alvaro began, "but first, we should order wine and toast to our being together."

Alvaro made eye contact with the sommelier; he moved his chin a millimeter, and a wine list appeared in his hands. He skimmed the list a few minutes and ordered a Barolo. I blinked, and two glasses materialized. I could get used to this treatment.

"How is your case progressing?" he asked after we toasted.

Oh, God, and I had been having such a nice time. I had wanted to get away from the case, just for a couple of hours, and now the mood had dissipated in an instant.

"Alvaro, it's not going well at all," I said, taking a sip of wine. "The last witness I went to meet was dead. Drowned."

Alvaro's eyes widened. "What do you mean?"

"Dead. No longer living." I was afraid he would take offense at my tone, but instead he inched toward me, curious.

"How did he die?" Alvaro asked. "I mean, was it in a swimming pool? Did he fall out of a boat?"

It was almost endearing, to see this naive side of Alvaro.

"None of the above," I replied. "He was killed. His hands were tied behind his back. His head was forced into a couple feet of water in an inflatable raft in a garden shed. Then his body was dumped into the water behind the *Ermita de la Caridad*. I found him wedged in some rocks there. It was low tide, or else he would have been a snack for the crabs there."

Alvaro looked into his wineglass. "Doesn't it ever get to you,

Lupe?" he asked quietly. "All the inhumanity that people inflict on each other. It wears you down sometimes, doesn't it?"

Alvaro was hated, ridiculed, insulted, scorned, and threatened in Miami. I wished his enemies could see this compassionate, gentle side of the man. I felt my defenses lowering. It was a new sensation for a woman whose nickname in college had been "Porcupine" because I never let men get close to me.

"Let's talk about Cuba," I said and laughed inwardly. I had American girlfriends who talked to prospective mates about children; for me, the primary topic was Cuba. I supposed this explained why I was still working the case without pay—because it was my duty.

"Have you ever gone back there, Lupe?" Alvaro asked.

I shook my head, not wanting to discuss my one visit to the island. Cubans always asked each other if they had "gone back," speaking about returning to a place they had never visited.

"I've been there." Alvaro held up three fingers. "Three times."

I tried to quell a burst of suspicion. It was neither easy nor common to have traveled to Cuba so many times. The U.S. government granted visas for Americans to travel there only for specific reasons. As for the Cuban government, it tended to welcome all visitors— Cuban exiles as well as others—because of the cash they brought with them. Alvaro was the only person I knew who had been to Cuba as many as three times during Castro's reign. I resisted my investigator's impulse to press for more information.

He sipped a fresh glass of wine, a dreamy look in his eyes. "It's not the Cuba our parents left," he continued. "It's a new place that they would not recognize. I don't know if the exiles and the Cubans on the island can ever become one people again. Too much has happened, too much time has passed."

"The time for the miracle is coming closer," I said.

"I know," Alvaro said. "And I really can't predict what will happen."

I sighed. The events of the past couple of days were catching up with me. I suddenly remembered that I had gone virtually sleepless the night before. My eyes felt heavy, and I longed to close them. I hoped dinner would come soon.

"All you all right, Lupe?" Alvaro asked, concerned. "You look exhausted."

"I'll be fine once I eat something," I said. I had plans for the evening, and I didn't want to spoil things.

Our waiter arrived with our meal. I had ordered the veal chop, Mami's favorite dish there. She would have been proud of me: eating in one of her favorite restaurants, dressed properly, on a date with a Cuban—even if it was someone whose politics ran counter to our family's. The only problem was that I was falling asleep at the table, and there was apparently nothing I could do about it.

"One more thing about Cuba," Alvaro said, lifting his glass in a toast. "After Fidel is gone, I am going back there. Permanently."

Thank God. Politics be damned. The man had passed his Cuba test with flying colors.

35

I woke at about ten the next morning in my own bed in Cocoplum, fresh and rested but a little chagrined that my evening with Alvaro had ended with only a kiss on the lips. However, it did seem appropriate for it to be so chaste, seeing as how I was working a case involving the Virgin.

I showered and dressed, gulped a *café con leche* and wolfed down a couple of tostadas standing up in the kitchen. Aida almost had a stroke watching me eat standing up. I had obviously started down the slippery slope to complete vulgarity. As I left I glanced back in the hall mirror and saw her crossing herself, no doubt apologizing to Mami in Heaven for my bad manners. Traffic was light on Main Highway, and I arrived in the Grove in half the time it usually took. I decided to view this as a positive omen.

Leonardo wasn't at his desk, so I knew he was in the throes of his post-breakfast workout. It was one of his favorites; he claimed it got his insides working properly. I had avoided asking for more information, since I had already involuntarily absorbed more about the inner workings of my cousin's anatomy than I had ever been taught in high-school biology.

I was about to call Detective Anderson when I heard the chime indicating that someone had come into our outer office. A few seconds later Nestor poked his head into my office. He looked terrible, the dark circles under his eyes blending with his black T-shirt. He waved a manila folder in the air while he headed, as usual, for the sofa.

"Those are the service records for James J. O'Donnell and Michael Stephen Patterson," I said. "Please, Nestor. Tell me it's true."

"It's going to cost you, Lupe!" Nestor placed the envelope under his head on the sofa. He was obviously sleep-deprived and delirious. "I hope Mother Superior forked over a lot of cash. My expenses are mounting very, very fast."

Nestor was obviously under the impression that we were still working for the Holy Rosary. I hoped he wasn't putting together his bill under the assumption that the pope would pay for it out of the Vatican's riches. I decided to deal with that tomorrow, not just then.

"You're worth every penny," I said. I moved around the desk and made a move for his head, trying to grab the envelope.

"Here, here." He handed it over without a struggle, then closed his eyes. Within a half minute he had started to snore.

I opened the files at my desk and read greedily. My hunch had been right. Both men had served together in the late fifties—at Guantánamo Naval Base. In Cuba.

I looked through Michael Patterson's record carefully. Guantánamo was a naval base; it was somewhat unusual for someone in the army to be stationed there. I saw that Patterson hadn't just been in the army. He had been a member of the Army Corps of Engineers; his record indicated that he had worked on a water-desalinization plant on the base. I supposed his chemical-engineering background qualified him for the job.

Both men had been in Cuba at the same time. I was sure it wasn't a coincidence. And I was positive that their presence at the Order of the Illumination of the Sacred Virgin, within an hour of each other, wasn't either. I thought about brainstorming with Nestor, but he was snoring sweetly on the couch and I didn't have the heart to wake him. Besides, I needed to know specifically what further information I might need from him, and I wasn't sure what approach I was taking.

I picked up the telephone and called Detective Anderson. I had a couple of questions for him. I tried to reach his cell phone first, but it seemed to be turned off. Next I left a message on his voice mail, to call me back as soon as he could. Then I tried his office and was disappointed to learn that the detective would be in court most of the day.

It was frustrating to realize I would have to wait to speak with

Anderson. I was just contemplating waking up Nestor when Marisol called me.

"Lupe?" I could barely make out her voice through the static on the line. "I'm at the Holiday Inn on U.S. 1—across from the university. I followed the mark's taxi here, watched her go inside."

"What happened when she went inside?" I asked. "Could you see who she went to visit?"

"No," Marisol said. Her voice started to break up. "I thought . . . call . . . before I did anything."

"Wait there," I ordered her. "I'm on my way. Where are you?"

"The northeast corner . . . parking lot," Marisol said. At least that's what I thought she said.

I stopped off in the gym, where Leonardo was straining away on his chest machine. I told him I was going to meet Marisol on a surveillance, but he barely seemed to hear me. I supposed his endorphins had kicked in already.

I drove to the Holiday Inn even faster than my usual self-imposed twenty miles per hour over the limit. I wasn't sure how long I could count on our mark remaining in the hotel, and my heart raced when I thought I might miss her. I made a turn into the parking lot so fast that I almost performed a wheelie—not exactly the best way for a twenty-eight-year-old woman in a Mercedes to remain anonymous.

Marisol's dark blue sedan was parked by the back fence, a good position that gave her a view of the parking lot while minimizing her visibility. I slid my car in next to hers, got out, looked around, and got into her car.

"Anything going on?" I asked.

Marisol shook her head, still staring straight ahead. "Nothing since she went in. Here's the log."

I opened Marisol's surveillance log for Sister Rose O'Donnell. She hadn't left the convent all day until she came to this Holiday Inn. I looked around the parking lot. There were more than a few cars parked there, not surprising since the hotel was across the street from the University of Miami. It was my alma mater, an institution that attracted faculty and students from all over the world.

"You look tired," I said to Marisol. "I'll watch the hotel for a while."

Marisol thanked me, closed her eyes, and, within seconds, was breathing deep and regular. I could have laughed. Both my best contract investigators were napping at the same moment—Nestor in my office, Marisol in the car.

On TV and in movies, investigators on surveillance regularly read books and flip through magazines while on a stake-out. A good investigator never did that. She kept her eyes focused on the target—in this case, the Holiday Inn's front door—without letting her concentration waver. Focus was very hard to regain once it was gone. I was blessed with excellent peripheral vision, so I could take in a lot of area without losing sight of my main area of interest.

I started to look around at the license plates of the other cars. There were quite a few from other states—probably parents visiting their children at the university. But then a maroon car from Massachusetts caught my attention. I found the case file in my bag and flipped to the background information on Michael Patterson.

I compared his vehicle registration to the tag on the car parked less than twenty feet away from me. They were the same. Finally, I thought, I had caught a break.

Rose would eventually lead me to Patterson, I had thought. But now she had certainly made my job a lot easier. I wondered whether Patterson was staying at the hotel, or whether they were just meeting there. I didn't need to get to Patterson at that moment, but now I had a trail that Marisol could trace for me.

I was savoring my luck when my cellular phone rang. Marisol was so deeply asleep that she didn't stir. It was Detective Anderson.

"Lupe, I got your messages." He sounded rushed and worried, not his usual laconic self. "Can't talk for long. I'm outside the courtroom on a five-minute break."

"I have a couple quick questions," I said. "Did you identify Mary O'Donnell by her prints, or just by ID from the next of kin?"

Anderson thought for a few seconds. "No, we didn't print her," he said. "There didn't seem to be any need. She was ID'd by her brother." A moment of silence. "Why are you asking me this, Lupe? Are you on to something?"

I didn't reply. "When are you releasing the body?"

"As far as I know, it's already been released, along with the brother's," Anderson replied. "We're done with them. I think the bodies were released to a funeral home. The other sister is taking them back up north for burial."

I could almost hear the wheels turning in Detective Anderson's mind. By his standards, he sounded positively agitated.

"Which funeral home?" I asked.

He paused. "Johnson's, on Bird Avenue," he finally said. "They have a contract with the county, for whenever there's out-of-town work to be done."

"Thanks," I said sweetly. "I'll keep you posted."

"Lupe, what is this all about?" Anderson barked. It was comfortable to see that he was indeed human.

"Thanks," I repeated, and hung up.

Now what was I going to do with this newfound knowledge? I didn't want to take a false step. After all that had happened, I didn't want to upset a miracle.

36

I woke up Marisol, told her where I was going and what I was going to do. I left her there at the Holiday Inn with the intention of returning to my office. Instead, on a whim, I thought I would pay a visit to the shrine of the Cuban Virgin. This whole case had been about her, and I had yet to stand in her presence since hearing about the miracle.

Instead of lurking around the back of the shrine, this time I parked right next to the front door. A stiff breeze blew off the bay, carrying the salty smell of the sea.

The door to the cone-shaped chapel was unlocked, so I walked in. Save for one old lady tending the altar flowers and a family settled together in the back of the place, I was alone in the building. I walked to the front pew and crossed myself as I sat. It had been a while, but the familiar moves came back to me automatically.

I knelt down and prayed for Mami, then for the rest of my family. I prayed for an end to suffering in the world, for an end to cruelty. Once I was done, I sat back again and looked up at the statue of the Virgin perched high above the altar.

Most people are surprised to see how small she is, particularly sitting underneath the huge image of her likeness painted on the wall behind her. I fixed my eyes on her face, her radiance. She gave me a feeling of peace and serenity although, when I looked for a message in her gaze, I found none.

Would I have taken this case if I'd known everything that was going to happen? I couldn't say. All I knew was that I was tired, I was worn out from fear and anxiety. I had had to examine my assumptions and beliefs, instead of working in an automatic mode as I normally did.

I wanted it to be over. And, I realized, I wanted the miracle to happen.

But what if my suspicions were founded—what if I exposed a fraud? Then there might never be a reunion of the Cuban people. But how could I let people live a lie? Where was the line between symbolism and truth? And why was it up to me to draw it?

I walked up to the altar, not even thinking about what I was doing. I was close enough to touch the Virgin.

"Tell me what to do," I whispered. She looked back at me impassively. I had to do what I thought was right.

I slowly walked back up the aisle and then outside. I resisted the impulse to look around the grounds, revisit the place where three people had died. It would serve no purpose, other than making me feel more melancholy and guilty.

When I got back to the office, I saw that Nestor's car was gone. I hoped he had gotten some well-deserved rest on the sofa. Leonardo sat at his desk, busily organizing what looked suspiciously like a stack of new files.

"Don't tell me," I said. I held up my hand. "Please, Leo, don't!"

"That's right, Lupe!" He grinned, a positively demonic look in his eyes. "Domestics! A dozen open files so far, and lots more where these came from."

I knew he was visualizing his ass shrinking with all the new equipment he was going to buy. The whole thing was too depressing for me to consider.

"I know you're teaching me a lesson about letting clients get by without paying," I said. "But have a heart."

Leonardo pursed his lips, maybe considering what I had said. "By the way, Detective Anderson phoned," he called out to me as I went into my office. "He said to page him the minute you come in."

I groaned, knowing that Anderson was going to grill me now that he had a few minutes of free time. I had no choice but to call him: a deal was a deal. And I knew this wouldn't be the last case we worked simultaneously in Dade County. I couldn't afford to alienate him.

The phone rang as I was looking up Detective Anderson's beeper number. It was Marisol. I pressed the phone close to my ear.

"The mark left the Holiday Inn in a taxi," she said, breathless. "She's heading south on LeJeune. I'm staying with her."

Her voice broke up. I was going to have to get her a new cellular phone as a Christmas present.

"Is she alone?" I asked.

"Yeah, she's alone," Marisol replied. "Oh . . . taxi just . . . west on Bird Avenue."

"Stay on her. Call me when she gets to where she's going," I said, though I knew Rose's destination. She had already gone on her scenic tour of Miami and wasn't starting another.

Less than a minute later Marisol called again.

"She got out at Johnson's Funeral Home," Marisol said. "I'm parking . . . Burger King . . . street. I can see the front entrance but not the back. I don't know . . ."

Her voice dissolved. "Don't worry about that," I said.

It was show time. I beeped Detective Anderson, punched in the 911 emergency code after giving my office number.

The phone rang in thirty seconds.

"Lupe, what's up?" Detective Anderson asked. "What's the big emergency?"

Without going into details, I gave Anderson a *Reader's Digest* abridged version of what I thought was going on. I had to give him credit—he listened without interrupting once.

"We have to act on this right away," he said when I was done. "You want to meet me at Johnson's?"

"I'm on my way," I said. "We'll meet in the parking lot of the Burger King across the street."

As I ran out the door I called out to Leonardo, who looked placid and content at his desk.

"This might be it," I yelled. "Get out the champagne."

Or, maybe more appropriately, the holy water.

37

I arrived at Johnson's Funeral Home before Detective Anderson, so I circled the block once and pulled into the Burger King lot across the street. I parked next to Marisol and lowered my window.

"We have to stop meeting this way," she called out from her car to mine. I could see the tension in her face—she hadn't liked the idea of tailing a nun, and now she knew enough to understand that we were involved in serious trouble.

I twisted my neck straining to look up Bird Avenue, wishing Anderson would hurry and show up. I wanted to get this over with as soon as possible. I looked over at Marisol, who had started to bite her nicely colored nails.

"Stop that," I said. "You're ruining your manicure."

An instant later I saw a nondescript four-door dark brown car—so ugly it could only be an unmarked cop car—turn into the Burger King toward where I was waiting. There were two other men in suits in the car besides Anderson, though I didn't recognize either of them.

"She still in there?" Detective Anderson asked me, poking his head out the driver's-side window.

"We think so," I said. I motioned to Marisol. "We haven't seen her coming out the front door."

I got out of my car. Anderson nodded to the men with him, and they got out as well. Marisol shook her head at me, rolled up her window, and drove away. I couldn't say I blamed her.

We crossed the street against traffic; Detective Anderson pushed open the tinted-glass front door of the funeral home. The first thing I noticed was how cold it was inside. I supposed this was to protect the bodies. The heat in Miami would surely make flesh decompose faster.

Detective Anderson flashed his badge at the middle-aged woman sitting at the reception desk, who half-stood with a startled expression.

"I'm looking for the O'Donnell bodies," he barked.

The receptionist, dressed from head to toe in black, put her hand to her mouth.

"Yes, sir," she said. "The O'Donnells. Their sister is here right now, claiming the remains. The last I saw, the caskets were being loaded into the hearse for the trip to the airport. They might have left by now."

"Let's go!" Anderson said to his men, already sprinting down the corridor toward where the receptionist had pointed. I followed as Anderson burst through an unlocked double door; a moment later we were standing in a shaded concrete driveway. There was a pair of hearses, an attendant standing behind one. I peered inside. It contained two caskets.

The hearse's passenger door opened up and Sister O'Donnell stepped out.

"What's the problem?" she asked. "We're going to be late."

Then she saw us. Anderson approached her, his badge held in front of him like a talisman.

"You're not leaving here, Sister," he said.

"Detective!" The nun's face drained of color. "Lupe Solano! What are you doing here?"

"We came to—" Anderson began.

"Oh, I understand," she interrupted, rapidly regaining her composure. "You've come to see me off. That's so thoughtful!"

"We came to make sure you don't leave Miami," Anderson said, fixing her with an openly skeptical gaze.

Sister O'Donnell approached us, smiling, holding her hands together in a contemplative gesture.

"I don't understand," she said. "I don't want to miss my flight. It was very difficult to arrange for my sister and brother's return home. There was so much paperwork."

"I don't think you understand me," Anderson said. "We're going to my office. There are some questions you need to answer."

"Questions?" The sister laughed, as though Detective Anderson was being silly. "Can't we do this over the phone, after I go home? I really can't miss my flight."

She was very convincing. Anderson's two men, who stood behind him, actually looked down at their feet with uncertainty. The funeral-home attendant stood by with an embarrassed expression.

"Mary," I said.

Sister O'Donnell turned at the sound of my voice.

"It's over, Mary," I said.

"Why are you calling me by my sister's name?" she asked. She looked at Detective Anderson for support. "You know who I am, Detective. This is ridiculous."

Mary had started to breathe in jagged gasps; her hands trembled, though she struggled to keep them still. She suddenly seemed to have trouble focusing her eyes. Her physical symptoms reminded me of my grandfather Solano when he had his stroke right after a Sunday lunch at our house. Abuelo Solano had died on the way to the hospital; I wondered whether Mary was going to share his fate.

"It will be easy to prove who you are," Detective Anderson said, seeming not to notice. "I'm sure your fingerprints will be on file from your application to go to Cuba."

With that, Mary dropped to her knees so fast that the attendant next to her had no time to keep her from hitting the hard cement. We circled around her, watched her gasp for breath. I had a painful vision of my grandfather's waning moments of life.

"Call an ambulance!" Anderson ordered.

One of the cops stepped away from the group, flipping open his cell phone. Mary looked up at us, her expression confused until she saw my face. I knelt over her, and she grabbed my lapel to pull me close.

"It was wrong," she whispered. "I know it was wrong. But we couldn't stop him. Please stop him."

"Are you talking about Michael Patterson?" I asked.

She nodded slowly. Her lips trembled. Half of her mouth seemed almost frozen, as though immobility was setting in. Her grip on me was death-tight.

"Why Cuba?" I asked, crouching closer. The world had telescoped down to just the two of us. "What was so important about Cuba?"

Mary's eyes turned dreamy, unfocused. "You should understand," she said, her voice a trebly croak. "It was the last Catholic country where freedom of religion wasn't allowed."

"I don't understand," I told her.

"I was there, in Santiago," she said. "I made a difference in those people's lives. They took religion and faith into their hearts because of me. I knew I could bring the church back to Cuba. And the Cuban Virgin would be the way I could make it happen. The Virgin chose me to be her messenger."

"The *Virgen de la Caridad del Cobre*," I whispered back to her. Her grip on me had started to loosen. "You knew the effect she would have on Cubans."

Mary closed her eyes, her head shaking. A line of saliva fell from her mouth to the ground. "How did you know I wasn't Rose?" she gasped.

"Because you spoke Spanish in my office," I said. "I guessed the real Rose wouldn't speak Spanish, not with her background."

"I didn't have anything to do with Rose or Jimmy dying, or that poor young man," she said. She looked impossibly small and frail on the ground.

It might have been cruel to press her, but I needed answers and I felt her slipping away from me.

"Michael and Jimmy met in Cuba, right?" I asked. "At Guantánamo?"

She moved her head up and down slightly. I glanced up at Anderson, who compelled me to continue with a hurry-up gesture.

"Michael killed Jimmy and Rose because they got scared," I said to her. "He got to them one at a time, asked them to meet him at the shrine. He knew the shed there was unused because he'd been there in preparation for the miracle."

"Don't let him do it," Mary whispered.

I heard the sound of sirens approaching.

"Why did he drown them?" I asked. "Why not shoot them, or—"

"Water," Mary whispered.

"Because he worked with water, or because of the Virgin's tears?" I asked. "Why did he—"

"Water," she said, even quieter this time. "Michael knew water. He worked with water. He was fascinated with it."

The ambulance was less than a block away. I knelt down closer.

"Tell me one more thing," I begged. "Why did you switch places with Rose?"

"Jimmy told her what we were planning to do," she said, opening her eyes. She was in pain, either from the recollection or from what was happening to her body. "She was going to tell the police. She'd never been to Cuba, she didn't understand."

Brakes screeched behind us. Mary inclined her head toward mine.

"We loved Cuba, Jimmy and me. And Michael, too, I suppose, in his way," she said. She seemed to gather strength. "Rose didn't. But we never meant for her to die. We thought we could keep Rose quiet until the miracle. But look what Michael did. He was more interested in affecting history than with the goals of the Virgin. Michael was patriotic. He hated Communism. He knew the world wouldn't know that he had helped to fight Castro, but it would be enough that he had. We all . . . we had good reasons . . ."

Mary closed her eyes. The emergency technicians reached us with a stretcher, pushing me aside. They took her pulse, gently lifted her up onto the stretcher. They took no notice of me or Anderson, apparently having received the circumstances of Mary's collapse when one of Anderson's men called.

I walked across the street to the Burger King with Detective Anderson. His two men were inside, buying hamburgers. Cops, I thought. They could eat through anything.

"I'll keep you posted, Lupe," Anderson said, standing by his car. "By the way. You did good work."

I started the Mercedes and pulled out into traffic. At the first red light I looked at the car in front of me. Its bumper sticker read: THE LAST TIME WE MIXED POLITICS AND RELIGION, PEOPLE GOT BURNED AT THE STAKE.

I couldn't have said it better myself.

38

I decided to take two days off work, staying at home and spending time with my family. They knew better than to ask why I'd been gone so much lately, simply accepting my presence on the patio and in the pool as though it had always been that way. I didn't make any calls about the Holy Rosary case, other than to call Leonardo and tell him to save all my messages until I came in in person.

The third day, without really planning it, I woke up in the morning, got dressed, and left for work. It just felt right. Leonardo was a paragon of discretion; he made no comment about my disappearance when I came in the door and found him at his desk.

"*Buenos días,* Lupe," he said brightly. "Would you like some *café con leche?* I just brewed some.*"

I said thanks and went into my office and sat behind my desk. It felt familiar and strange at the same time. It felt as though I'd been away for months rather than a couple of days.

Leonardo came into my office with my favorite mug, the one with the Cuban flag on the side. I looked out the window to see what the parrots had been up to. They must have been feeling European lately: the Eiffel Tower completed, they had moved on to a facsimile of the Tower of London.

It took me about half an hour to summon up the nerve to call Detective Anderson. He had probably called me more than a few times, but Leonardo had been kind enough not to give me any messages yet.

I had my hand on the phone when Leo came in, without a word, and handed me a batch of pink slips. It had been good while it lasted. Leonardo retreated to the safety of his gym before I could say anything to him.

I flipped through the papers and saw that most of the calls related to cases, but among them were calls from Alvaro and Tommy. I set those aside, as I was in no mood to deal with the effort it would take to sort out my complicated relationship with those two men.

My first call was to Detective Anderson. The biggest surprise was how chipper he sounded.

"Lupe, how are you?" he asked. "Your secretary said you were feeling under the weather."

Under the weather. Unlike his fellow patriots, Leonardo was a master of understatement. After the funeral home I had felt as though a force-five hurricane had hit me. I was grateful to Leonardo, though, for doing me a small favor. It wouldn't do to have Miami law-enforcement officials seeing my vulnerable side. The next thing, they'd probably be asking me about my "female troubles."

"Thanks for asking," I said, very cool. "Just a bit of a cold."

"I thought you might be interested in knowing the details of Mary O'Donnell's statement," he said.

Detective Anderson and I were being so polite and proper, pretty soon we would be inviting each other over for tea.

"It's a good thing I got a statement," he added. "Because I don't think we're going to have another chance."

"What?" I asked, stunned.

"She had a serious stroke," Anderson said. "She's in a vegetative coma. Doctors don't expect her to regain consciousness."

I crossed myself, thinking that, in a sense, it was just as well. Mary's torment over her siblings' deaths would probably be too much for her to bear—not to mention the fact that she was facing criminal charges as an accessory to murder.

"So that's what happened," I said. Her collapse had been almost the same as my grandfather's, though I hadn't wanted to jump to any conclusions until a doctor saw her.

"She only lasted about ten hours after they brought her in," Anderson said, a little indelicately. "I was allowed to talk to her when they had her stabilized and they thought she was improving. A couple hours later, though, she was out."

"I guess she filled in the blanks from what she told me at the funeral home," I suggested.

Silence on the line. "Listen, Lupe, do you want to meet for a few minutes?" he asked. "You know, talk in person?"

I was momentarily stunned. Was Detective Anderson going to confide some secret information to me? No, it couldn't be. I was getting out of the miracle business, anyway.

"Sure," I said. "That'd be fine."

We agreed to meet—where else—at the seawall behind the *Ermita*. It seemed the perfect place for some closure. I told Leonardo that I'd be gone for the rest of the morning, then left for the shrine of the Cuban Virgin—for what I hoped was the last time, for a while at least.

I turned down the driveway into the shrine and slowed down when I neared the chapel itself. I circled slowly and parked at the end of the lot, near the spot where I'd found Theofilus.

I wanted to feel the breeze and the sun, so I walked over to the seawall. I closed my eyes and listened to the birds squawking, the only noise to break the perfect peace of the moment.

It wasn't long before Detective Anderson parked his unmarked police car next to mine. I could have fainted when he got out; instead of his standard suit, he was wearing blue jeans, a work shirt, and boat shoes. He looked almost mortal. I wished I had a camera so I could record the image for posterity.

"Lupe, hello," Anderson said as he sat down next to me on the seawall. His eyes were hidden by reflective sunglasses.

"Thanks for meeting with me," I said. We didn't shake hands, didn't touch. "I have a lot of questions still. Things have happened that I don't understand."

"Well, if it makes you feel any better, I feel the same way," Detective Anderson said, looking out over the water. The man really wasn't bad-looking, now that I saw him as more human than robot. "I have a sister who's a nun, you know. The Order of the Sacred Heart."

I must have looked completely stunned, because Anderson hastily added, "Well, you know, I understand you have a sister who's a nun as well. I figured we understood each other on this one."

Detective Anderson was getting positively touchy-feely. I considered getting him together with Leonardo for an emotional-encounter session. But Anderson seemed to catch himself: he straightened up, ran his hand through his hair, and coughed uncomfortably.

"I suppose we should be talking about Mary O'Donnell," he said.

"Please," I said. "Anything you can tell me—"

"The woman was delusional, if you ask me," Anderson said, shaking his head. "When she got back from Cuba, she was under that kind of spell that missionaries get. She thought she'd been sent into the world by the Virgin to make things better. She was convinced she had a mission, that she had the power to accomplish something no one else could. She took it too far, lost touch with reality."

"So that's how it started," I said. "Did anyone else notice?"

"I checked out her story after she told it to me." Anderson's face was impassive, his glasses reflecting the water and clouds. "No one at her order wanted to admit that one of their own had gone basically nuts, but I coaxed the truth out of them. Mary's own mother superior was actually relieved she came down here so she wouldn't have to deal with her anymore."

"Kind of like passing the buck," I observed.

"Well, the order didn't want to admit that one of their own had gone crazy on a missionary tour of duty," Anderson said. "What kind of precedent would that set? They sent a normal, idealistic nun to Cuba and got back someone who thought she was anointed by the Virgin to complete a sacred mission. The church might allow that miracles can be announced through humans, but even Mary's mother superior had to admit that Mary wasn't all there. It was a lot easier to see Mary run off to Miami than to confront her delusion."

"How did Jimmy get involved?" I asked. I felt it was not the right time to point out that Mary had indeed confronted the issue of the miracle, by fighting it out with the sister superior, and what that had cost.

"The first thing Jimmy did after his duty station in Cuba was to go back to see his sisters in Massachusetts," Anderson said. "Turns out he also was visiting his friend Michael Patterson, who he met in Cuba and who's a Massachusetts native."

"The killer," I said. It had to be Patterson. There was no one else.

Detective Anderson looked up at the pelicans flying low over the water. I had the feeling he wouldn't have minded being one of them, free to do as he wished.

"Yeah," he said. "We don't know where he is. He skipped out after Mary went to see him at the Holiday Inn. Turns out she went there to tell him to leave her alone, that she was going to take her brother and sister home to bury them. I guess she was scared that she'd be the next victim."

"For good reason," I said.

"Triple murder," Anderson muttered, those four syllables carrying an incalculable weight. "We've got an all-points bulletin out on him. We'll get him eventually."

I hoped they got him before October 10. I remembered what Mary kept saying outside the funeral home: *Don't let him do it.* She knew Patterson would try to see through the plan that had cost Mary her brother and sister. In a moment of clarity, she had begged me to stop it.

"So let me guess what came next," I said. "Mary had the initial idea, and Jimmy and Patterson came into it next."

Once the ball was rolling, there would have been no stopping it. The players had been a nun convinced she was carrying out God's will in a special, secret fashion, along with two retired servicemen with special skills and probably a fondness for a country in which they'd once been stationed—and whose Communist leadership probably rankled them, if they were typical products of the Cold War years in which they grew up and served in the military.

"Mary really got talking," Anderson said with a grim smile. "It turned out to be basically a deathbed confession. Anyway, she said it was Jimmy and Michael Patterson who planned all the details."

"Mary knew the ropes of the Catholic Church," I added. "She would have realized that being seconded to an order of nuns associated with miracles would add to the authenticity of her miracle. And that order—the Order of the Illumination—must have been sold on the miracle completely, since they opened a convent in South Florida as a result. I found out from my reasearch that the order hasn't had a miracle in a hundred years. They needed something to keep the order alive, to keep young women joining. A fresh miracle, one with a profound political dimension and such spectacular possibilities, was just what they had to be looking for."

"I'll have to take your word for it," Anderson said with a shrug. "We didn't go into it that deeply. And frankly, I didn't care. It was enough that she was giving me information about the murders."

I also thought that it didn't reflect very well on the Order of the Illumination of the Sacred Virgin that they didn't search deeper into the origins of the miracle that had been dropped on their doorstep.

They must have wanted to be associated with the miracle so badly that they accepted it at face value. It also must have been exciting to be expanding into the New World, after being an exclusively European order for so long. They must have thought that, shortly after October 10, they would be installed in Cuba as a leading spiritual force in Latin America.

As for Lourdes's mother superior, her motivations must have been pretty much as I had read them the first day I met her—jealousy, resentment, and ambition. This was a Cuban miracle, and she was the only Cuban mother superior in the Catholic hierarchy, a position that surely hadn't been easy to attain. If the miracle—real or fake—took place, then the Order of the Illumination would be assured a place in Cuba. A Yugoslavian order, rather than a Cuban one, would gain a reputation for miraculous works and the reconciliation of the Cuban people. I could only assume that she fired me because the idea of my delving deeper into the investigation—not to mention the dead bodies that were starting to appear with alarming regularity—frightened her and filled her with uncertainty. If the truth about her hiring me were to become known, her reputation would have been damaged, her career potentially destroyed.

Maybe I didn't know the entire story. Perhaps I never would. But little of what I knew reflected well on religious orders. As a Catholic, I wasn't happy to have gotten such an unflattering view of nuns. I wanted to believe in their selflessness and dedication to helping humanity. Exposing some of them as grasping and ambitious had brought me no pleasure, and I clung to the certainty that there were many more out there who were pure of heart.

Detective Anderson had grown pensive, so I ran him through the story on my end, filling in the gaps that he didn't know. It was kind of a relief, and I felt a weight being lifted from my shoulders. Detective Anderson was a good listener, and he offered little in the way of comment, save for saying a sympathetic "Ouch" when I described in more detail Jimmy's knocking me out beside the O'Donnell house.

We had a good rapport going, but I did omit one crucial fact—who had hired me on the case in the first place. And now that I had met my end of our deal to share information, there were a few more things I needed to know.

"What about Theofilus?" I asked. "Why was it necessary to kill him? He was harmless."

We stared out over the water; it was apparent that neither of us wanted to look down to where the gardener had been floating several days ago.

"Theofilus's death is what woke Mary up," Detective Anderson said. "She had known she would have to live with Patterson killing her brother and sister to shut them up, but Theofilus was an innocent stranger. She couldn't deal with it. When she went to your office and you told her about Theofilus, that's when she decided it had to stop."

"But she was leaving town," I said.

"She was scared." Detective Anderson pulled out a toothpick and stuck it in his mouth. An ex-smoker, I realized. "She was scared, and she wanted to get away. She said she was going to call the police when she got back home, after her brother and sister were buried. For what it's worth, I believe her."

"I can't believe she got away with posing as her sister," I said.

"Imagine what they must have been like as girls," Anderson said. "They looked so much alike, it must have driven everyone crazy."

"So Michael Patterson murdered Theofilus because of the shed," I added. "That has to be it."

Anderson nodded. "Patterson had been casing the shrine for a while; he knew Theofilus wasn't due to work at the shrine for four more days. But for some reason, Theofilus came to the shed early. Patterson saw him there and followed him around for almost a full day. From what you tell me, he was going to show you the ropes and all the other fun stuff instead of just calling the police."

"Theofilus had some problems with law enforcement," I said.

"A pot bust, big deal," Detective Anderson said. "If he'd called us he might still be alive. Patterson followed Theofilus until he was alone in the parking lot outside the shrine the night you found him. Patterson knocked him on the head from behind, then pulled him back to the shed and drowned him in the raft. If nothing else, he was consistent in finishing off his victims with water."

"*Dios mio*," I whispered. Guilt washed over me as I considered the fact that Theofilus had been waiting for me when he was killed. "You know, Theofilus wasn't a big man, but he was wiry. How could—"

"Take a look at this," Anderson said. He pulled a folded envelope from his shirt pocket and handed it to me.

It contained a photograph of a man in late middle age sporting a military crew cut. His dark eyes were fixed on the camera like pinpoints. His expression was vacant, his mouth a tight line. Though the picture was from the chest up, I could see through his T-shirt that he was bulging with muscles probably acquired during military service and maintained through decades of heavy weight lifting.

"Michael Patterson," I said.

"You got it." Detective Anderson took back the picture, glanced at it for a moment. He shook his head. "In their own way, Mary and Jimmy had wanted to do something good. They were misguided, but you could argue that their hearts were in the right place. Unfortunately, their old friend turned out to be a nutcase. Mary telling him about the miracle set off his political obsession. Mary said he considered himself a patriot—and he saw the miracle as a way to help bring down one of the last Communist dictators. Mary said Patterson was living in the Cold War. He'd been in the service all his life, and he still thought about Communism like it was still a major threat to the American way of life."

Anderson squinted out over the water, as though he could see the island of Cuba off in the distance. "Patterson thought that if the two Cubas were united, as Mary said the Virgin wanted, then Castro would be finished. And with Castro out of the picture, Patterson thought that somehow America would return to its lost glories. He thought he was saving the world, in his crazy way. I guess it's no surprise he was willing to kill to see his dream come true. He'd probably been waiting his whole life for an excuse to go off like this."

Suddenly we had nothing more to say to each other. We sat in silence, taking in the scenery. Somehow in the moment we shared was the understanding that the very horrific things with which we dealt also gave us the ability to appreciate the quiet beauty of a Miami afternoon. We were both glad to be alive.

We walked together to the parking lot.

"Keep me posted?" Detective Anderson asked.

"Definitely," I replied. "And you'll let me know when you get Patterson?"

"No doubt," Anderson said. "Don't worry, Lupe. We'll get him."

I smiled as Anderson got in his car. *You'd better,* I wanted to say. Because something told me that Michael Patterson wasn't going to allow himself to be stopped easily. Not after all the distance he had traveled.

39

AFTER a week of working domestics, I swore to myself that I would never, ever get married. But as a result of all the cases Leonardo had lined up, Solano Investigations was soon back on an even keel after the financial hit we'd taken on the Holy Rosary case. Our bills were paid, our investigators had been reimbursed for their time and expenses—and there was actually a little left over for a down payment on Leonardo's ass-reduction machine. After all he had gone through on the case, I decided to let him buy it on the installment plan.

There was nothing left for me on the Holy Rosary case, but it was difficult to let it go. I was pleased to discover that the Order of the Illumination of the Sacred Virgin had disconnected their 1-800-MIRACLE phone line. I guessed that they had gone into isolation following Mary's death, which occurred the day after I last met with Detective Anderson on the seawall behind the *Ermita*. I wondered if the order would still find a way to announce the miracle—if it was still happening—but I didn't have the time to find out. No official proclamation had yet been made, so I simply had to wait.

I had sat with Lourdes by the pool at the house in Cocoplum a couple of evenings past, filling her in on everything that had happened. She had been shocked, and a little guilty because she had brought me into the case in the first place. Perhaps to assuage her guilt, she had asked around in the local religious community to find out information that I couldn't access.

"The church screwed up when they let the Order of the Illumination go ahead with the planned miracle," Lourdes said, sipping a glass of mango juice in her one-piece bathing suit. "But what's done is done. They're not going to back it, and they're not going to deny it."

"They're playing both ends against the middle," I said.

Lourdes looked up, closed her eyes to the sun.

"You said it, not me," she replied cryptically. "Basically the church isn't going to get involved in something so politically loaded."

October 10 loomed closer. Papi was planning a big meal at the house with some of his old cronies. I telephoned Detective Anderson to see if he had any news about Michael Patterson.

"Nothing," Anderson said. He sounded chagrined.

I got the same reply the next time I called, then the time after that. Anderson hated to admit it, but Patterson was a lot harder to catch than he had thought. The fact that the old soldier was still free ate away at the pit of my stomach. I sat on the patio, watching Papi on the phone preparing for his dinner; inside, I felt a foreboding.

On the ninth I called Anderson again.

"I know you think I'm fixated on this guy, and I hate to keep calling all the time," I told him. "But I really have a feeling that Patterson's going to try something at the *Ermita* tomorrow."

"Lupe—"

"Mary thought so, too," I interrupted. "She said he had to be stopped. What else could she have been talking about?"

"There's an all-points bulletin out on him," Anderson said. "His picture was on TV. He knows we're looking for him, and he's not going to be stupid enough to try anything."

I could hear in his voice that Detective Anderson was humoring me. As far as he was concerned, it was just a matter of time until he caught his man.

"Look, I hope he *does* try something," Anderson added. "It'll make it a lot easier to catch him."

"Is the shrine going to be under surveillance tomorrow night?" I asked.

"Of course it will be," Anderson said. "Not just because of Patterson. We're putting men there because of the political significance of the date. We don't want anyone playing hero, or martyr."

I was a bit mollified by Anderson's response, but I wouldn't breathe easily again until the tenth had come and gone. I told Leonardo to cancel all my appointments for the following day; he was so pleased by the fact that his exercise machine was coming in the morning that he gave me no trouble at all.

That night, after a rare dinner with everyone at the table at the same time, I took Papi aside as he strolled out for some night air. We looked out over the water in silence for a few minutes.

"What did you want to talk to me about?" Papi finally asked, breaking the spell. The sky was calm and clear, with no dark clouds to symbolize the storm I sensed was brewing.

"I just had a question," I began. "You work with other engineers on your building projects, right?"

Papi nodded. "Sometimes."

"What is a chemical engineer?" I asked. "What do they do for a living?"

"Well, Lupe, I'm a structural engineer." Papi looked at me strangely. I couldn't blame him; as far as he was concerned, I had asked quite an off-the-wall question. "That's my background, that's what I studied in school and got my degree in. But not all engineers are alike, you know."

I took Papi's arm as we walked along the terrace. The full moon shone down on the bay and illuminated the calm waters like a sheet of glass. We leaned over the railing of the dock.

"I didn't mean to imply that all you plastic-pocket-protector kind of guys were the same," I teased him. I was pleased to see a smile come over his features.

"All right then," he said. "Basically a chemical engineer applies knowledge of chemistry to industrial needs. Devising solvents, for instance. Or studying the way different chemicals react in different real-world, outside-the-laboratory settings. I hired a chemical engineer as a consultant just a couple of months ago, in fact. I needed him to help me figure out how well I was going to be able to depend on certain industrial adhesives I use in my business. I actually found out that one of them didn't perform as well as the manufacturer claimed it did."

I could see that Papi was pleased to be asked a professional question that played into his expertise. He didn't often have the chance to talk about his work around the house.

We stood out there for a while longer, not speaking. Papi didn't press me for why I had asked him such an obscure question, for which I was grateful. I didn't want to have to tell him about Michael Patterson, and how I feared that tomorrow the world might find out how skilled he was as a chemical engineer.

The next morning I woke up to the news that an unnamed caller had alerted the media to the miracle. I flipped through the local stations, as well as the national cable news.

"—Cuban Virgin in Miami—"

"—crying real tears this dawn—"

"—other miracles in the past, there has been a great deal of skepticism—"

"—in the category of millennial anxiety—"

"—what this will mean to the Cuban people—"

I flipped off the TV in my bedroom and slipped out of the house. I could hear Papi, Aida, Osvaldo, and Fatima talking in animated voices in the kitchen. Lourdes was gone already, probably at her order dealing with the ramifications of the miracle.

I got in the Mercedes and started driving. I didn't turn on the radio, because I didn't want to hear anything more about the miracle. It had happened. It was public. There was no going back.

I stopped by the office and read the newspaper. The paper had mercifully been printed before the miracle's announcement. Apparently whoever had called the local media hadn't been savvy enough to know what time the *Herald* went to press.

"This is really weird," Leonardo said, poking his head in my office. "Everyone's talking about it."

"I knew it would be like this," I said. I caught myself chewing a nail, forced myself to put my hands on my desk.

"What does it mean?" Leonardo asked. "I mean, we know it's not real. Should we tell anyone?"

"No," I said.

Leonardo looked troubled. "Why not?" he asked. "This is a hoax, right? People are going to believe in it."

"People will believe what they're going to believe," I said. "Anyway, the miracle isn't going to happen."

"That's a cop-out," Leonardo replied.

"Is it?" I asked. "What if people's belief in this miracle turns out to be positive? Have you considered that?"

"No," Leonardo said, leaning on the doorway.

I sighed. "Look, I don't like this any more than you do. In fact, I agree with you. It's just that this is a complex situation."

Leonardo adjusted his wristband, looking miffed.

"Come on, don't get that way," I said. "Michael Patterson is the only one left to pull off the hoax. I don't know how he means to do it—it's probably tied into his chemical-engineering background. But if he sets foot at the *Ermita*, then the police will arrest him."

"So we don't have to worry about it," Leonardo said. "Because it's not really going to happen."

"Precisely."

This seemed to cheer him up and, a moment later, the sound of our front door opening made him spring into action. Sure enough, it was the delivery guy from the sporting-goods shop. Leonardo forgot about the Virgin's miracle, now on a quest to make his own come true—the miracle of the diminished Cuban ass.

In the late afternoon I left for the *Ermita de la Caridad*. As I drove I thought about the three people who had lost their lives for this phony miracle, all the damage that could never be undone. In spite of my reassurances to Leonardo, I felt a tight knot of tension that wouldn't go away until I saw the day come and go without the Virgin shedding tears.

Hundreds of cars had beaten me to the shrine. I saw a half dozen news trucks parked close to the chapel, their satellite dishes poking up above a throng of people. I wasn't even able to park inside the gates; I had to leave my car by La Salle High School and walk over.

Outside the shrine news reporters were taping segments. People were milling around carrying placards. I saw a small group of uniformed officers, who looked surprised and overwhelmed. I hoped they had the presence of mind to call for reinforcements. I looked around but couldn't see Detective Anderson anywhere.

The chapel was packed with the faithful and, of course, the skeptics. Every seat in the pews was taken when I walked inside. The place was abuzz with conversation, people praying, subdued arguments breaking out. There were still hours until the miracle was scheduled to take place, and I stayed at the periphery of the crowd. More and more people continued to arrive.

I scanned the crowd for Michael Patterson. He would be easy to spot, with his muscular build and crew cut. But I didn't see him anywhere. I closed my eyes and leaned back against the wall, saying prayers.

Time passed. I ran out of prayers. The crowd in the *Ermita* started to grow quiet, alert, expectant. I found myself getting caught up in it, although I knew better. I skirted along the edge of the crowd, scanning the faces. They looked eager, reverent, a few looked openly doubtful. Still I didn't see Michael Patterson.

I had been sitting against the back wall for almost half an hour when the growing stillness was shattered by the harsh sound of a bullhorn just outside the open front door.

"This is the Miami Police Department!" shouted an officer. "Everyone out now! File out in an orderly manner!"

Shrieks and groans erupted throughout the chapel. People were protesting that they didn't want to leave, that they couldn't. Voices shouted in a pandemonium of mixed English and Spanish. A wedge of police officers entered the chapel.

I ran outside. I wasn't sure what was happening, but I feared that an ugly scene was going to start any second. All the elements were in place. I headed for the seawall and, not looking, ran into and almost knocked down Detective Anderson.

"Lupe—" he began.

"What the hell is going on?" I yelled. I grabbed his jacket lapel and pulled at him.

"Bomb scare," Anderson said, raising his voice to be heard over the din of voices and the bullhorn giving orders to vacate the building. "Someone called in and said a bomb's been planted inside the chapel to go off at the exact moment the Virgin is supposed to cry."

"And you believed it?" I screamed. "You know there's no bomb in there! Patterson called in the threat to clear out the building! He wants the building all to himself while he does what he has to do!"

We heard wailing sirens, saw the flashing lights of fire trucks and emergency vehicles moving slowly down the crowded driveway. Detective Anderson hurried away, helping to clear out the building. I saw his head above the crowd as he stood on his toes, scanning, probably looking for Patterson. I watched helpless as people were herded out of the chapel and into their cars. Within fifteen minutes the driveway was a solid line of red taillights. The bomb squad arrived next. They jumped out of their trucks and assembled outside the building, looking at their watches.

I knew I should leave. I took a couple of steps toward my car. But then I turned. I saw Detective Anderson conferring with a couple of uniformed officers.

"Come with me," I said, taking his arm.

I led him toward the *Ermita*.

"We can't go in there," Anderson said, struggling with me. "The bomb squad's about to enter."

"We're going in with them," I said. "You're the lead officer on a murder investigation. It's the only way I can get inside."

Anderson stopped, pulled his arm away. He looked into my eyes, at the *Ermita*, then back at me again.

"No," he said.

"We have to," I said. "You know we do."

Anderson rubbed his cheek, looked around. The bomb-squad techs had opened the front door and gone inside.

"Shit," Anderson hissed. He grabbed my arm and led me to the door, waving his hand to silence the officers who shouted in protest.

The bomb techs were searching the periphery of the room. There was no one at the shrine itself, so I walked up to it, crossed myself in front of the Virgin, and knelt in front of her. I said a couple of Hail Marys before I realized that I was kneeling in a puddle.

"What is it?" Anderson whispered from behind me. His voice broke the silence.

My heart beat loud in my ears, I didn't dare raise my eyes to look up at the Virgin's face.

"Oh, fuck," Anderson said. He frowned an instant later, apparently realizing how inappropriate such language was for such a sacred place.

I raised my eyes to the Virgin's white cape. It was glistening with moisture.

I looked down again. I couldn't raise my eyes to look up at the Virgin's face. I simply couldn't. I sat that way for what was probably only seconds, but felt like an hour.

Then I reached out to the Virgin's feet, touched them, brought my fingers to my lips to taste.

It was seawater. The Virgin was soaked with saltwater. Had Mary's miracle happened, or had Patterson engineered it? My breath was coming in short, sharp gasps at the enormity of what had just transpired.

Ten minutes later I wandered outside the shrine, dazed by what I had just seen. Maybe I would have to wait to find out what had really happened there in the shrine by reading about it in the press analysis. But then my steps quickened; my body seemed possessed with a will of its own.

"Lupe, where are you going?" Detective Anderson called out, jogging to keep up with me.

I didn't answer him, instead picking up my pace. I stumbled over a fallen branch but reached the shed on the corner of the property within seconds. I felt a warm buzzing in my ears when I saw that the shed door was slightly ajar.

Detective Anderson caught up with me. I pushed open the door and stepped inside. It was pitch dark in the windowless space, and I waited for my eyes to adjust. I felt Anderson brush past me as my eyes refocused.

I had a sense of déjà vu when I saw a shape huddled over in the corner. I heard Anderson punching numbers into his cell phone, then calling in a soft voice for backup.

I walked over to the body in the corner and stood over it, shaking off Detective Anderson's attempt to hold me back. I was beyond caring that I might be contaminating a crime scene. Anderson would have had to arrest me to prevent me from looking into the eyes that had caused so much suffering, death, and, perhaps, illusion. It was too soon to understand what had happened inside the shrine, but I knew that Michael Patterson had been at the center of it.

Patterson lay with his eyes open, his face slack. For him, at least, the miracle was over. He had seen to that himself.

I dipped my fingers in the bucket of water next to his body and brought them to my nose. It was a strange, chemical aroma mixed with the familiar scent of seawater. Patterson had poisoned himself, I thought, using his expertise to mix some toxic chemical into the same seawater he'd used to drown his victims. I looked closer and saw that his chin was tainted a light green, where the poison he'd ingested had spilled from his lips.

Water had run down to the ground, soaking his pants. I wondered whether the water in this very bucket had found its way to the Virgin's face. Whatever had happened, Patterson would hurt no one else.

He was the Virgin's to deal with now.